THE SOURCE

Michael Cordy

D1644003

CORGI BOOKS

TRANSWORLD PUBLISHERS
61–63 Uxbridge Road, London W5 5SA
A Random House Group Company
www.rbooks.co.uk

THE SOURCE
A CORGI BOOK: 9780552156981

First published in Great Britain
in 2008 by Bantam Press
an imprint of Transworld Publishers
Corgi edition published 2009

Addresses for Random House Group Ltd companies outside the UK
can be found at: www.randomhouse.co.uk
The Random House Group Ltd Reg. No. 954009

The Random House Group Limited supports The Forest Stewardship
Council (FSC), the leading international forest certification organisation.
All our titles that are printed on Greenpeace approved FSC certified
paper carry the FSC logo. Our paper procurement policy can be found
at www.rbooks.co.uk/environment

Typeset in 11.5/13pt Garamond by
Falcon Oast Graphic Art Ltd.
Printed in the UK by CPI Cox & Wyman, Reading, RG1 8EX.

2 4 6 8 10 9 7 5 3 1

For Phoebe

Author's Note

The Voynich Cipher Manuscript featured in this novel exists. Every detail of its appearance, unique text, bizarre illustrations and known history is accurately described. The reproduced pages are from the original, which resides in Yale University's Beinecke Rare Book and Manuscript Library. Despite the best attempts of leading scholars and experts, including the cryptographers of America's vaunted National Security Agency, it has never been deciphered. To this day the Voynich Cipher remains the most mysterious manuscript in the world.

Michael Cordy
London, 2008

Prologue

Rome, 1561

When his eyes scan the small crowd she forces herself not to look away. If he is strong enough to endure this, then she is strong enough to watch.

He hobbles on bandaged feet, charred and broken by the Inquisition's torturers, as the executioner makes him a final offer: recant and be garrotted mercifully before being tied to the stake, or refuse and be burnt alive. His eyes find hers and, defiantly, he shakes his head. She wants to signal her support and her love, but she cannot move. She is mesmerized by what is happening, and in shock from what he has asked her to do.

What she has vowed to do.

The *auto de fe* is being held at night, in the torch-lit courtyard of an anonymous church in the outskirts of Rome. A small group, less than twenty, has gathered round the lone stake. The Holy Mother Church has no desire to publicize this heretic's death – or his heresy. She catches a flash of red in her peripheral vision, but doesn't divert her gaze when the Grand Inquisitor, Cardinal

Prefect Michele Ghislieri, steps forward in his scarlet robes. The Grand Inquisitor has 'relaxed' the heretic to the secular authorities to perform the execution so the Holy Mother Church can abide by its maxim: *ecclesia abhorret a sanguine*, the Church shrinks from blood. But this is still his show. And with fire there will be no blood.

'Burn his book with him,' the Grand Inquisitor orders. 'Burn the Devil's book with the heretic.' There is a moment of consternation as the executioner and the clerics search him and find nothing. 'Where is it?'

A jolt of fear surges through her but the condemned man stays silent.

'Heretic, surrender the book or face the consequences.'

A bitter laugh. 'What more can you do to me?'

'Burn him,' orders the Inquisitor.

The men drag him to the platform and rope him to the stake. They pile the final bundles of wood around the base, then apply torches. As the fire catches, she prays he will suffocate before the flames reach his flesh. Clutching the crucifix he gave her, she holds his gaze until the acrid smoke obscures his face. Only then does she allow the tears to come. As the smoke rises into the night sky and his flesh starts to burn – to cook – the sweet, disconcertingly familiar smell sickens her. His screams are mercifully short, but she takes little comfort from that.

When the flames are at their height the Grand Inquisitor and his retinue leave. Then the others dissolve gradually into the night. Alone, she waits until only bone, ash and glowing embers are left. Then she approaches the pyre and collects what she can of his remains. As she bends she feels the manuscript concealed in her robes and hopes this 'Devil's book' is worth his torture and agonizing death. And she prays that it justifies the terrifying vow she made to him before he died.

'In time all will be revealed,' she whispers, as she walks off into the dark night. 'Time reveals all.'

PART ONE

The Devil's Book

1

Switzerland, four and a half centuries later

He felt no fear at first, only sadness that it should end like this. He had made a fortune, amassed a portfolio of properties around the world, learnt several languages and bedded more beautiful women than he could remember, yet it seemed meaningless now. He had lived alone and would die alone, unremarked and unremembered, his body fed to animals or buried under concrete in a building site. It would be as if he had never lived, never existed.

'Kneel in the middle of the plastic sheet.'

As he knelt, hands clasped as if in prayer, he noted the surgical saw, Ziploc plastic bag and roll of duct tape by the killer's right foot. He didn't need to look up at the Glock 19 semi-automatic pistol in the assassin's left hand to know what was coming. He knew the procedure better than anyone: he had invented it. First there would be two bullets to the head. His left hand would be severed and placed in the Ziploc bag, then his body wrapped in the black plastic sheet and sealed with the duct tape. Finally, a vulture squad would be called to dispose of his corpse, and the killer would deliver his severed left hand to the client as proof of death.

'You know who I am?' the killer asked.

He nodded. '*La mano sinistra del diavolo*, the left hand of the Devil. The most feared assassin in the world.'

'My real name. Do you know my *real* identity? Look at me. Look at my face.'

It was now that the fear came – paralysing fear. He couldn't look up. He was too frightened of what he would see.

'Look at me,' the killer ordered. 'Look into the eyes of the man who destroyed your life and damned you to Hell for ever.'

He looked up slowly. His heart seemed to stop in his chest. The killer's face was his own. As he trembled in terror, the din of fierce barking pierced his nightmare and dragged him to consciousness.

Marco Bazin emerged slowly from his medicated sleep and opened his eyes, but the guard dogs outside his house still sounded like the hounds of Hell baying for his soul. Panicked and disoriented, he stared into the gloom. At first he didn't recognize his own bedroom: the clinic had filled it with so much equipment it was more like a hospital room. He wiped sweat from his forehead and scalp. His hair, thick for a man in his late forties, had been his one vanity. The surgeons had said it would grow back but had been less optimistic about purging the disease.

He slowed his breathing and calmed himself. He despised fear. A few short months ago, before he had admitted himself to the exclusive Swiss clinic near his alpine retreat above Davos, he had been the source of fear: *la mano sinistra del diavolo*. He was renowned for the ruthless efficiency of his kills, and it was said that once a client gave him a name its owner was already dead.

Now *he* was about to die.

Bazin's hand brushed the crotch of his cotton pyjamas, as if reaching for what they had taken from him. The surgeons wished he had come to them earlier, before the aggressive non-seminoma could spread. They'd told him to watch for several symptoms when this last course of chemotherapy was over. But the cancer was only one of his problems.

As he stared into the dark, listening to the instruments and his breathing, he took stock. He had told no one of his illness and the staff at the clinic had assured him of their total discretion. Yet he knew the whispering must have started. He had turned down three major jobs before he'd entered the clinic, and many other clients had tried to contact him while he had been incommunicado during surgery and chemotherapy. Soon the rumours would harden into conclusions, then actions. Clients would wonder why their calls had gone unanswered; some would suspect he was working for rivals. Enemies would scent blood and seek the opportunity to settle old scores. He may have been a lion once, a king of the jungle, but he was wounded now and the emboldened jackals were circling. If the cancer didn't get him, a bullet would. Either way he was dead.

The dogs barked again and panic surged.

For the first time since his childhood Bazin felt fear. Not of dying – the novelty of that had long worn off – but of what lay beyond death. Since diagnosis and surgery he had been forced to reflect on his life and concluded that, in exchange for losing his soul, killing for a living had yielded nothing of real value – only money and its hollow trappings. A chill ran through him. He reached for the string of wooden rosary beads on the side table – a childhood gift, kept more out of sentiment than faith. He focused on the expensive curtains drawn across the window and imagined the looming mountains beyond. Usually their beauty calmed him but now it intensified his loneliness.

Why were the dogs still barking?

He shook his head, trying to focus his mind, and checked the clock beside his bed. Three sixteen a.m. He heard the night nurse murmuring on the landing outside his room, then another, deeper, voice.

Bazin sat up, dizzy and breathless.

A man – at least one – was here. In his home. In the middle of the night.

It was no surprise that his enemies would come for him when he was weak and defenceless. But

18

how had they found him? No one at the clinic was aware of his profession, and hardly anyone knew the location of this house. But that meant nothing, he realized. Everyone had a price. He considered the people who had tried to hide from him in the past. He had found them. And killed them.

Fear galvanized him. He had to live. He searched the gloom for something with which to defend himself, but the nurses had cleared everything away, except the equipment and medicines to keep him alive. There was nothing here with which to take a life.

He listened as the footsteps approached the closed door, something oddly familiar in their irregularity. Ignoring the pain and fighting the nausea that threatened to overwhelm him, he climbed out of bed. More sweat dripped from his forehead. They dared come for him only because they thought he was weak, half the man he had once been. But he'd show them. He tested the thin string of rosary beads. It snapped. He dropped the beads on the bed, yanked one end of the intra-venous tube from the cannula in his wrist, the other from the drip stand, then pulled the tube tight in his hands. He steadied himself, then moved across the room and positioned himself behind the closed door.

It opened slowly and a dagger of light cut across the rug. He no longer felt sick or weak as he focused on eradicating the threat to his life. The intruder stopped in the doorway, as if considering whether to enter. As soon as the man's head appeared Bazin pulled the garrotte round his neck and twisted it.

With cheese-wire Bazin could garrotte a victim in seconds, rupturing the jugular and crushing the windpipe. However, the plastic tubing stretched, and as Bazin struggled to tighten it he noticed the man's clothing – and that he was unarmed. Then he remembered the man's gait – his limp. He yanked the intruder round so they faced each other. As he stared into the man's bulging eyes, Bazin froze. He knew why the man had come under the cover of darkness. Not to kill him, but to protect his own identity from prying eyes. He was embarrassed to be seen coming here. And that shamed Bazin.

He loosened the tubing from the man's neck. 'Leo.' He didn't try to disguise his gratitude. 'I can't believe you came.'

The man rubbed his throat. 'You're my half-brother, Marco,' he rasped. 'You said you were dying. Of course I came.' His eyes filled with contempt. 'What do you want from me? What could you *possibly* want from a priest?'

Now Bazin's gratitude was mixed with anger and something that approximated love. Though larger and more powerful than his elder brother he had always felt in his shadow. Never good enough, always unworthy. He glanced at the rosary on the bed, then at his brother. 'I want redemption. I *need* absolution before I die.'

The intelligent dark eyes narrowed. 'You're serious?'

'Deadly serious.'

'Then go to confession.'

'I need to do more than say a few Hail Marys, much more . . .' He explained how he had spent his life. 'I must perform some service for the Church, some penance. Tell me what to do.'

His brother's eyes looked deep into his, searching, evaluating. 'It no longer surprises me how many sinners come back to the Church at times of crisis. But you, Marco?' He sighed. 'God never gives up on a lost soul, provided their act of contrition is genuine.'

'Within my power I'll do anything the Church demands.'

Those dark eyes probed his soul. 'Anything?'

'Yes,' said Bazin, collapsing to his knees. 'Anything at all.'

2

New York, five weeks later

As soon as the limousine stopped outside the black glass tower in downtown Manhattan, Ross Kelly jumped out, suitcase in one hand, laptop in the other, and ran to the main doors. He had been cooped up in aeroplanes for the last twenty-four hours, and he was late. He dashed through the lobby, jumped into an empty lift and pressed floor thirty-three.

He studied his reflection in the mirror and frowned. His suit was expensive and, with his tan, height and broad shoulders, should have flattered him, but it looked merely uncomfortable. He had always felt – and looked – better out in the field, wearing Timberlands, jeans and a hard hat, than in the office. He straightened his tie and patted down his unruly sandy hair as the lift pinged and the doors opened. He stepped out and approached a pair of double doors with 'Xplore Geological Consultancy – Specialists in Oil and

Gas' etched into the glass. A man in blue overalls was adding another line beneath it: 'A Division of Alascon Oil'. Ross stepped into the reception area. The rumours had been rumbling for months but he couldn't believe so much had changed while he'd been away in the remote Kokdumalak oilfields of south-western Uzbekistan.

His personal assistant, Gail, was pacing the floor. As soon as she saw him her face relaxed. 'Ross. Thank God you're here. How was Uzbekistan?'

'Good, but I'd have got more data if I hadn't had to rush back for this.' He checked his watch: ten twenty-two. 'Where's the meeting?'

She took his suitcase from him. 'In the conference room. It's already started.'

'Didn't you tell them my plane was delayed?'

'They don't care.'

'What about Bill Bamford?'

'Gone. Ross, *all* the old Xplore board have gone.'

'What about the handover?'

She lowered her voice. 'There's not going to be one. All that talk about Alascon respecting Xplore's specialist expertise and wanting a partnership was garbage. It's a good old-fashioned takeover. Bill Bamford, Charlie Border and the rest have cleared their desks. They were escorted out of the building this morning.'

'How about you?'

'I can get a job anywhere. I only work here because of you.' She smiled. 'So, tell me if you're planning to leave.'

'You'll be the first to know, I promise.'

'Good. Now, if you want to save your ancient-oil project you'd better get going. These guys take no prisoners.' She shrugged. 'But I guess you already know that.'

'Yup.' Ross grimaced. When Xplore had head-hunted him three years ago, he had been working as a geologist in Alascon's respected earth-sciences division. Xplore had offered good money but that wasn't why he'd joined the small oil consultancy. As one of the world's biggest oil companies, Alascon offered excellent training, but they were inflexible, arrogant and risk-averse. Xplore's visionary board had offered him the opportunity for genuine exploration and discovery that Alascon couldn't match. Now he'd be working for Alascon again and that troubled him. He smoothed his hair again and walked down the corridor to the conference room.

As he approached, he heard his own voice. He stopped and peered through the glass. The lights were dimmed but he could see three Alascon executives sitting round the table, watching a plasma screen on which he was presenting his ancient-oil theory. He didn't recognize two of them: an older, bald guy with round glasses, and a freckled man with curly, greying ginger hair. At the sight of the third, a blond man in a charcoal grey suit, his heart sank. George Underwood was the main reason he had left Alascon. As Ross studied his old boss he couldn't help noticing that *his* suit was immaculate.

24

On screen, a sulphurous, molten ball of fire rotated in the blackness of space. Vast meteorites, like red-hot missiles, rained down on it, scarring and deforming its already cratered surface. The charred planet seemed the last place in the universe where life could survive – let alone take hold. Ross heard his voice again, calm and authoritative, describe the computer-generated images: 'In its infancy, four point five billion years ago, Earth was a primeval inferno, bombarded by asteroids and comets, its surface scorched by ultraviolet radiation while volcanic eruptions spewed noxious gases into the primitive atmosphere. But these asteroids and comets that rained down on our planet were loaded with amino acids, vital for the formation of life. Even today, forty thousand tons of meteorites fall to Earth every year. More than seventy varieties of amino acids have been found inside these space rocks, eight of which are the fundamental constituents of proteins found in living cells.'

The screen showed a spectacular impact.

'Like sperm bombarding an egg, these seeds of life rained down on our planet and, amazingly, one – just *one* – of those rocks triggered a reaction, a spark that germinated the earliest forms of bacteria somewhere on Earth. Equally amazingly, they thrived. Evidence now indicates that all life on this planet – including each of us – evolved from that one impact four and a half billion years ago.'

The screen shifted again showing fossil-imprinted rocks from Issua in Greenland and the

Ustyurt plateau in Uzbekistan, near where Ross had just been working.

'These early life forms became fossils, which, in turn, became fossil fuels – oil. We now know that oil can be found in even older deposits than was at first believed. And it's this ancient oil that we should be focusing on.'

'Can you believe this?' said Underwood to the older guy. '*Ancient* oil. I thought all oil was pretty damn ancient.'

His laugh irritated Ross as he entered the room. 'By ancient, George, I mean oil that's a quarter of a billion years older than any previously discovered oil.'

Underwood pressed a button on the remote control and the screen reverted to the company logo. Then the window blinds rose, revealing the skyline of uptown Manhattan, gleaming in the May sunshine. He made a show of consulting his watch, then got up to shake Ross's hand. 'Long time no see.' He smiled. 'Let me introduce you to my colleagues.'

Ross learnt that the greying-ginger guy was Brad Summers, the new financial officer, while the older man was David Kovacs, Xplore's new boss, responsible for assimilating the consultancy into Alascon.

'So, ancient oil, Ross,' said Underwood. 'You *really* believe it exists?'

'Yes, I do.'

'Why, Dr Kelly?' asked Kovacs.

Ross sat down. 'At the turn of the millennium the oldest known oil was one point five billion years old. However, we've recently found deposits in Uzbekistan at least two hundred and fifty million years older than that. The hydrocarbons in this ancient oil are a product of creatures living on Earth at least three point two billion years ago. This indicates that exceptionally old rocks contain untapped reserves that, until now, haven't been a priority for oil prospectors. It's only a matter of time, though, before others in the industry take an interest.'

Underwood looked down at his notes. 'You're working on this with a client, Scarlett Oil. They're a pretty small company.'

'All our clients, here and overseas, are small-to-medium players with limited in-house geological expertise. That's why they use a consultancy.'

'And the odds on finding this ancient oil?'

Ross smiled. 'A lot better than average.' Even with the most advanced technology the average strike rate for finding conventional oil deposits was still only 10 per cent. He pulled a palmtop computer from his jacket, opened it and placed it on the table. A geological map of the world appeared on its screen, highlighting the various rock patterns that indicated potential reserves of trapped oil. It always made Ross a little sad because it demonstrated not only man's knowledge of the Earth's surface *and* what lay beneath but also a world stripped bare of its mysteries. 'My team have developed a software program that amalgamates the seismic, gravity-meter, magnetometer and geological data with satellite imagery and state-of-the-art global-positioning satellite technology to identify the world's most deposit-rich areas. By focusing on ancient rock sites, particularly high-yield cap and reservoir rock combinations, we can increase the odds of finding trapped oil.' Ross paused for effect. 'Our current modelled success rate is approaching twenty per cent. *Twice* the current level.'

Underwood nodded. 'But you've no actual data yet? Only *modelled* data?'

'That's why I went to Uzbekistan. To test the models.' He retrieved a folder from his laptop case and put it on the table. 'We need more time but the initial findings are good. Scarlett Oil's excited.'

'Oh, yes, the *mighty* Scarlett Oil.' Underwood turned to the finance man. 'How much has this cost so far?' He had asked it as if he already knew the answer. Summers turned his laptop round so Underwood could see the screen. 'Wow! Xplore put a lot of time and money into this one. As much as Scarlett Oil.'

Ross clenched his jaw, determined to keep calm. 'George, it's an investment project, based on sound data, which is in the process of being proved in the field. We'll own the search-and-extraction technology, allowing us to offer smaller companies – our client base – the chance to steal a march on their bigger competitors. Including Alascon, unless it embraces this new opportunity.'

Underwood leant over to Kovacs and exchanged whispers with him. Then Kovacs gathered his papers. 'Please don't misunderstand us, Dr Kelly,' he said. 'You have a great reputation within the industry and we want you on our team. But the only reason Alascon bought this small consultancy was because of its excellent contacts and business links with the Far East and the old Soviet republics. And because it was cheap.' He glanced at the finance man's spreadsheet. 'Frankly, given how Xplore spent money, I can see why. Dr Kelly, Alascon Oil doesn't care about speculative ventures with other, smaller, American oil companies. We have little to learn from them.' He pointed at Underwood. 'I'm putting George in charge of oil exploration. You and your team will report to him. I understand you've worked for him in the past.' He turned to Underwood. 'It's your call, George.'

'We want you to focus on developing your contacts in strategically important areas of the world, Ross,' Underwood said, 'in conventional oil. This ancient-oil research has to stop.'

'What about our relationship with Scarlett Oil?'

'What about them? They're small fry.'

Ross gritted his teeth. 'But this *will* make money. A lot of money. Soon.' He had invested two years of his working life on the project and believed passionately in it. He picked up the folder from the table. 'Let me show you. All the new figures are in here. It's a no-brainer.'

Underwood gave a dismissive wave. 'I know it's

your pet project, Ross, but Alascon has no interest in ancient oil, just the good old-fashioned kind.'

'But that's going to run out soon enough.' He slammed the folder on to the table. 'At least look at the latest figures.'

Underwood flashed Kovacs a look that said, 'I told you he could be difficult,' then turned back to Ross. 'I've always admired your talent,' he said. 'You're a brilliant geologist and have a real gift for finding oil. Your one weakness is that you enjoy the adventure of exploration a little too much. To you the mystery is as sweet as the discovery, perhaps sweeter. Alascon isn't about making great discoveries but reducing risk. It doesn't care about excitement, adventure or mysteries, only results. And if you want to stay with this company, earning your very generous salary, you'd better accept that. I want you to direct your team to look for conventional deposits with immediate effect.'

Ross said nothing. Two years' hard work dismissed just as it was about to yield dividends.

Underwood frowned. 'Do you understand, Ross?'

At that moment Ross saw his future career with Alascon in George Underwood's red face and jabbing finger. He was tired and had had enough. He stood to his full height, a head taller than Underwood, and looked down at his former, and would-be future, boss. He held his eyes until Underwood lost his nerve and glanced away. Ross reached for the folder on the desk and tore it into halves, then quarters and finally eighths.

'Do you understand?' asked Underwood again, his voice shaking.

'Take it easy, George,' warned Kovacs. 'Alascon needs guys like Dr Kelly. I'm sure he understands well enough.'

'You *understand*, Ross?' persisted Underwood.

'Perfectly.' Ross kept the torn file in his right hand and retrieved his phone from his pocket with the left. He speed-dialled and Gail answered on the second ring. 'It's me,' he said, into the phone. 'I promised you'd be the first to know.' Staring at Underwood, he dropped the torn file on the man's head. 'I'm resigning,' he said.

'Wait!' said Kovacs, leaping to his feet. 'That isn't necessary.'

Loosening his tie, Ross put the phone and palmtop back into his jacket, then picked up his laptop and walked to the door. As he opened it, he turned back. 'It is necessary,' he said. 'For me.' Then he closed the door and walked away.

3

A few miles from the Xplore offices, the guest of honour was leaving the McNally Auditorium on the Lincoln Campus of Fordham University, the Jesuit university of New York. The priest had ·stayed as long as he had needed to at the conference and was satisfied that he had discharged his duties. Now he was impatient to get away. After thanking his hosts and dismissing his entourage he walked so fast to his official limousine that his limp was barely noticeable.

In the back seat, concealed behind tinted glass, he checked his watch. He had plenty of time before his return flight to Rome tonight. 'Yale University,' he told the driver. 'The Beinecke.'

As the car drove north towards Henry Hudson Parkway, he turned his mind to what had occupied him since he had arrived in America a few days before. He opened his attaché case and began to study the photocopy of a 450-year-old trial document that his office had discovered in the Inquisition files of the Vatican's *secretum secretorum*, the archive of the Church's most sensitive secrets. As he read the hand-written Latin, one of five languages he spoke fluently, his mind whirled with the threats and opportunities it presented.

If what he had heard was true.

An hour and a half later, the limousine pulled up outside Yale University's Beinecke Rare Book and Manuscript Library, one of the largest buildings in the world devoted entirely to rare books. A white oblong structure covered with translucent marble 'windows', which resembled the indentations on a golf ball, it contrasted sharply with Yale's more traditional buildings. The priest, however, ignored the unusual architecture as he climbed the steps.

They were expecting him at the front desk and a senior researcher escorted him to the main hall.

'It's not very busy,' said the priest.

'No.' A flush of excitement suffused the researcher's face. 'But it will be this evening. We're expecting quite a turnout for the open seminars. One of the talks promises to be dynamite.' He pointed to a Plexiglas box, displayed prominently on a plinth in the centre of the hall. It was empty. 'All this week the book's been displayed here, but we've arranged for you to study it in one of the reading rooms for half an hour. If you need more access, digital copies of the pages can be studied on the Internet, on one of the terminals over there.' The man led him to a small, subtly lit room and handed him a pair of white gloves. 'You may only touch it when you're wearing these.'

The priest approached the reading table. 'Thank you.'

The researcher cleared his throat. 'The Voynich is one of my specialist areas. What can I tell you about it?'

'Nothing.' As the priest put on the white gloves, he doubted there was anything the man could tell him that he didn't know already. 'I just need some time alone – to see it in the flesh, as it were.'

'Right.' The man hovered, then moved to the door. 'I'll leave you to it, then. Call me if you want anything.'

But the priest was no longer listening. He was staring, transfixed, at the book. The yellowing document looked unremarkable. Only when his gloved hands slowly turned the pages did its mystery become apparent. They were filled with unrecognizable text, and decorated with crude colour illustrations of bizarre plants that resembled known flora but were actually like nothing on Earth. Other pictures included naked women with unnaturally rounded bellies floating in green liquid.

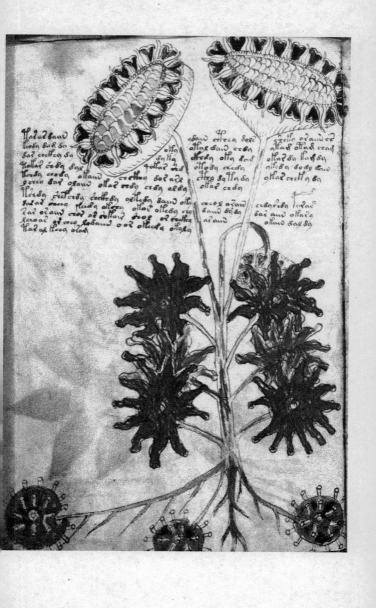

The illustrations were no more sophisticated than a child's, but that didn't detract from their power. The Beinecke Library's catalogue entry lay beside the book: 'Almost every page contains botanical and scientific drawings, many full-page, of a provincial but lively character, in ink washes and various shades of green, brown, yellow, blue and red. Based on the subject matter of the drawings, the contents of the manuscript fall into six sections.'

'Botany' contained drawings of 113 unidentified plant species, accompanied by text. The astronomical, or astrological, section had twenty-five astral diagrams. 'Biology' included drawings of small-scale female nudes, most with bulging abdomens and exaggerated hips, immersed or emerging from fluid, interconnecting tubes or capsules. The pages dealing with pharmaceuticals contained drawings of more than a hundred herbs, while the remaining two sections were composed of continuous text and an illustrated folding page.

The world had been fascinated by it since 1912, when the book dealer Wilfrid Voynich had come across the 134-page volume at the Villa Mondragone, a Jesuit college in Frascati, Italy. A letter dated 1666 had been tucked inside it; the rector of the University of Prague had asked a well-known scholar to attempt to decipher the text. According to the letter, the Holy Roman Emperor Rudolf II of Bohemia had bought it for six hundred gold ducats.

A faded signature on the first page of the manuscript read 'Jacobus de Tepenec'. Records showed that Jacobus Horcicky had been born into a poor family and raised by Jesuits to become a wealthy chemist at Rudolf's court. In 1608 he had been granted the noble name 'de Tepenec' for having saved the emperor's life. His role in the manuscript's history, however, was less clear. Some believed that Rudolf had given it to him to decipher, others that when the emperor abdicated in 1611, and died a year later, the manuscript had come into Horcicky's possession 'by default'. Whatever had happened, the manuscript had found its way somehow to the Jesuit college where Voynich rediscovered it. Many claimed it had come originally from Italy, where it had been stolen from one of the Jesuit libraries and sold to Emperor Rudolf, and that agents of the Catholic Church had eventually reclaimed it, then allowed it to fall into obscurity once more.

The manuscript's illustrations were bizarre but it was the text that had most intrigued Voynich and the countless others who had tried in vain to decipher it. The symbols were teasingly familiar, often resembling roman letters, Arabic numerals and Latin abbreviations. Elaborate gallows-shaped characters decorated many beginnings of lines, while an enigmatic swirl, like '9', could be found at the end of many words.

When Voynich had brought the manuscript to the United States he had invited cryptographers to examine it, but to no avail. In 1961 H. P. Krause, a New York antiquarian book dealer, had bought it, and in 1969 he donated it to Yale University's Beinecke Rare Book and Manuscript Library. In the 1960s and 1970s the National Security Agency had put their best cryptanalysts to work on it, but even they failed.

In the last ten years, researchers employing a battery of statistical methods, including entropy and spectral analysis, discovered that Voynichese – as the language of the text became known – displayed statistical properties consistent with natural languages, which suggested that it was unlikely to be the random writings of a madman or fraud. They also discovered that the text read from left to right and employed between twenty-three and thirty individual symbols, of which the entire manuscript contained around 234,000, which amounted to about 40,000 words, with a vocabulary of perhaps 8,200. Most words were six characters long and showed less variation than those of English, Latin and other Indo-European languages. But still no one was any closer to knowing what the manuscript said, who had written it, or why.

Until now. Apparently.

There was a discreet knock at the door. His half-hour was up. He lingered a moment longer, mesmerized, sensing that the book was about to change his life for ever, and that God was guiding him. He removed the gloves, and allowed his bare fingers to brush the manuscript.

When the door opened and the researcher entered, the priest thanked him, stole one last look at the Voynich, then went back to the lobby.

He paused by a poster announcing that evening's open seminar: 'Solving the Riddle'. Billed as the highlight of Voynich Week, there would be three presentations. A British mathematician from Cambridge University and a computer specialist from MIT were to present the latest techniques for decoding the text. But it was the third that interested the priest: 'The Voynich Manuscript: A Doomed Quest for Eldorado?'

He clutched his attaché case tighter and thought of the photocopied document within it. The original recorded the trial and testimony of a Jesuit priest burnt at the stake for heresy. It also recorded the existence of a book that should have been burnt with him: *The Devil's Book*.

He confirmed the time of the last presentation, satisfied he could still make his flight, then checked the name of the academic giving it: Dr Lauren Kelly.

4

Sitting on the New Haven line train from Grand Central to Darien, Ross Kelly was preoccupied with thoughts of his career. Geology had not been a popular or easy choice for a schoolboy growing up in the Bible Belt. His mother had believed the Earth was created a few thousand years ago and that the Great Flood was the major geologically related event in human history. Creationism might have morphed into Intelligent Design, but things hadn't changed much – and not only in the Bible Belt: the new pope had recently rejected Darwinian evolution in favour of God's guiding hand in all aspects of creation.

But Ross had always fought for his passions. Ever since he was a boy, growing up on his father's farm in the shadow of the Ozark mountains, he had seen geology as a romantic, magical science that charted Earth's history over an unimaginably deep chasm of time. He could still remember the hairs standing up on the back of his neck when he'd first read that Mount Everest was made of rock that had once formed the floor of the oceans. How could anyone not marvel at the sheer pressure and time involved in pushing the Himalayas from the bottom of the sea to the top of the world?

A scholarship to study geology at Princeton, a PhD from MIT and his first years with the earth-sciences division of the mighty Alascon had fuelled his wonder. It was quickly apparent, though, that the oil industry cared more about making profit than exploring the world's treasures. When Xplore, then a lean, progressive search consultancy, had headhunted him, their desire for fresh ideas had rekindled his passion.

But his career there was over now: the visionaries who had recruited him had gone, swept away by men like Underwood and Kovacs, who had more in common with accountants than with explorers. And he had no illusions that other companies in the industry would be any different in embracing anything new.

On the short taxi drive home from the station, Ross contemplated his future. He tried not to think about whether he had made the right decision, or what his wife would say. As the driver pulled into the kerb he saw his ancient Mercedes convertible parked next to Lauren's economical Prius. He had acquired the so-called classic car after he'd joined Xplore. Back then it had seemed to symbolize his success. Now, like his career, its lustre had faded and it looked what it was – an old car covered with bird shit. A third car, small and boxy, was parked alongside. Ross groaned: he was in no mood for visitors. His work took him all over the world, but when he came home he wanted to be alone with his wife. He enjoyed nothing better than a bottle of Pinot Noir, pizza, making love and squabbling over the TV remote – he'd never understand why someone as smart as Lauren preferred reality makeover shows to classic comedies, a good movie or anything by David Attenborough on the Discovery channel. He paid the man, got out and crunched across the gravel to the white clapperboard house he had mortgaged himself to the hilt to buy.

The front door opened and Lauren appeared. In the early-afternoon light, her honey-blonde bob gleamed, her soft green eyes sparkled and her skin glowed. Just seeing her made him feel better. The door opened wider, to reveal another striking woman. While his wife was conventionally beautiful, her assistant at Yale was the opposite. Elizabeth 'Zeb' Quinn resembled a strange blend of punk and geek. Her long, curly hair was dyed henna-red and she wore thick glasses, second-hand jeans, a shapeless hemp jacket and a T-shirt proclaiming: *Gaia's Your Mother! So Stop Killing Her!*

Lauren rushed to kiss him. 'Ross, you're back – God, I'm so happy to see you.'

'Not as happy as me.' He held her tight, enjoying the smell of her hair, then looked over her shoulder. 'Hi, Zeb.'

Elizabeth Quinn smiled and raised a hand in greeting. Ross and she had as civil a relationship as any oilman could have with an eco-warrior who believed everybody in his industry was raping the planet. 'Don't worry, I'll leave you two alone. I was just helping Lauren with her presentation tonight.'

'Presentation?'

Lauren rolled her eyes. 'You know, the Voynich. The translation. My big night.'

'Oh, yes . . .' He'd pushed it to the back of his mind because he hadn't planned to get back from Uzbekistan until the end of the week – just in time for them to fly off on their first vacation in years: two weeks' caving in the jungles of Borneo followed by a week on the beach in Malaysia. He had fought for the time off work – but that, of course, was no longer a problem.

'Welcome home, Ross,' said Zeb, and got into her little hybrid car. 'See you both later. Good luck tonight, Lauren, and whatever Knight says, don't give away any more than you need to.'

'I won't. Thanks.' They waited for her to drive away, then Lauren put her arm through Ross's and led him indoors.

He reached into his jacket pocket and pulled out a small rock. Its opaque metallic surface made it look like gold in the sunlight streaming into the hall. He always brought Lauren an unusual specimen from a field trip. 'It's Schreibersite, a rare meteor stone.'

'It's beautiful. Thank you.' She smiled, eyes

44

bright with excitement. 'I'm glad you had to rush back – I've got amazing news.'

'Great.' He paused. 'I've got some news, too, about the takeover I mentioned on the phone.'

'Tell me.'

'I've resigned.'

Ross wasn't sure what reaction he'd been expecting but it wasn't the one he got. Lauren burst out laughing.

'What's so funny?' He had always admired and envied her relaxed approach to money. She came from a relatively wealthy New York family and didn't equate it with security as he did. Nevertheless, even she had to understand the implications for the mortgage. Then again, she had always counselled him against buying such an expensive house and would probably downgrade quite happily.

She shook her head, trying to control herself. 'I'm sorry, Ross. I'm not laughing at you, just the timing.'

'Why? What's your amazing news? Don't tell me your career's taken yet another stellar turn as I've flushed mine down the drain.'

'It's *our* amazing news. I saw the doctor today. We're having a baby.'

For a second he didn't know what to say. They had been trying for a child for years, but after three unsuccessful rounds of IVF, they had virtually given up. He swept her into his arms. 'That's fantastic! How long?'

'I'm almost three months.'

'Three months.' He stroked her belly, imagining his child growing inside her. 'Why didn't you tell me before?'

'I only just found out. Must have happened when you came back from that long trip to Saudi – you remember how we made up for lost time?'

He smiled.

'And don't worry about your job, Ross. You always feel so responsible for providing us with *everything*. But we're fine. More than fine. If the faculty members don't make me a full professor after tonight, they're bound to when I translate the final section of the Voynich. A Yale professorship might not pay as much as selling your soul to Big Oil but it's enough.'

He kissed her. 'I'm not worried. The only real problem is our vacation. We'll have to cancel the caving expedition – far too strenuous for a woman in your condition – and spend the whole time on the beach.'

'That suits me fine.'

'I bet it does.' He laughed. She always preferred to laze on a beach and read while he got bored after a few days and wanted to explore. Right now, though, spending a few weeks on a beach with Lauren sounded pretty good. He checked his watch. 'What time's your presentation? I was going to get some shut-eye before you shared your *other* amazing achievement with the world but now I'm too excited to sleep.'

5

Yale University

That evening as they arrived at the Beinecke Library, Lauren squeezed Ross's hand and kissed him. 'I want to know you're in the audience,' she whispered, as they got out of his car, 'but don't sit too close to the front or you'll make me nervous.'

Rooms thirty-eight and thirty-nine of the Beinecke had been combined to form a lecture theatre capable of sitting seventy, and Ross took a seat at the back. The room filled fast and he saw Zeb Quinn's red curls at the front. A man in a tweed jacket sat next to her: Bob Knight, Yale's professor of linguistics and Lauren's head of faculty. Ross didn't like him. He had a reputation as a ruthless self-publicist who shamelessly took credit for other people's work. Lauren had tried to keep hers under wraps until she was ready to discuss it, but he had pressured her into revealing details of her initial findings tonight, during Voynich Week.

A priest with sharp features and dark, hooded

eyes took the seat beside Ross. Any member of the public could attend the open seminar, but it was obvious from all of the cord and tweed jackets that most of the audience were academics, researchers and Voynich aficionados. Kelly wondered what a priest was doing there.

The lights dimmed and the first two speakers spoke at such length about spectral analysis, number sequences, polyalphabetic ciphers and other esoteric aspects of the cryptanalyst's dark arts that they made the world's most mysterious manuscript sound tedious and obscure. Torpor descended on the stuffy room and Ross, exhausted and jet-lagged, struggled to stay awake. To his surprise, the priest sat tense and expectant, radiating energy.

Then Lauren stood up and the mood in the room changed. For all her gravitas, she exuded warmth, her full lips constantly on the verge of smiling. Her blonde hair and emerald dress set off her eyes as she gazed confidently at the audience. This was what they had come to hear. The priest took a notebook and pen out of his pocket. As Ross watched Lauren arrange her notes and introduce herself, he felt a surge of fierce pride that she was his wife and would soon be the mother of his child. He was no dullard but he felt ordinary compared to Lauren. Her PhD had been about conserving dying languages, but for the last few years she had focused on the riddle of the Voynich Cipher, and had succeeded where all those before her had failed. Where they had crunched numbers and analysed sequences on a computer, she had used her expertise in her own field.

As a child, Lauren had once written to her parents, 'I don't like this school. It's boring,' in fifty different languages. Her parents had moved her. She still cherished the knowledge that in Amazonia there was a dialect called Tariana, which required a speaker to include a supporting suffix after everything they said, or their listener would assume they were lying; that there was a Caucasian language with no vowels, and a South Asian dialect whose innumerable verbs included *gobray* (to fall into a well knowingly) and *onsra* (to love for the last time). It upset her that of the six thousand languages left in the world more than half would be extinct by the end of the twenty-first century.

Lauren cleared her throat and the room fell silent. She began to read.

' "Welcome, fellow scholar, your efforts have not been in vain. Though your name and mine are insignificant this story is not. Know this: discoveries may excite our blood but mysteries sustain our soul. When we're strong and arrogant, mysteries remind us how little we know of God's world. And when we are weak and desperate, they encourage us to believe that anything is possible." ' Lauren looked up and smiled. 'You've just heard the opening lines of the Voynich, expressed for the first time in English.'

A low murmur rippled through the audience, like wind through a field of barley. Text from the

Voynich flashed up on the screen behind Lauren. She continued, 'With my assistant Zeb's help I've now translated all of the manuscript, except the astrology section. I won't present a verbatim transcript until I've completed it.' She glanced meaningfully at Knight. 'Having been asked to share a synopsis of its contents, however, I can tell you that I found *no* code.' The audience's murmuring grew to a buzz and people were scribbling notes. 'I'm now convinced that Voynichese is a synthetic language. Those linguists among you will know that there are two types: a *posterior* language, which is based on existing languages, the most famous example being Esperanto, and a *priori* language, which is created from scratch. The latter is virtually impossible to translate without knowledge of the creator's rules of grammar and vocabulary, which in this case we don't have. Luckily for us, however, Voynichese appears to be of the *posterior* variety: a blend of two ancient languages, which have then been transliterated into the unique symbols we see in the text.'

A hand shot up from the audience. 'Which two languages?'

The priest's fingers were working at a string of rosary beads.

Lauren shook her head. 'I'm not prepared to reveal the root languages until I've completed the translation. Then I'll make a full announcement and publish all my supporting work.'

'Are you sure there's no code in the text?' asked a woman at the front.

The priest's fingers moved faster on the beads.

'With Zeb's computer models, we realized early on that a code was unlikely,' Lauren said. 'Given the age of the document and the intractable nature of the text, any code would have had to be a poly-alphabetic cipher. But our entropy analyses, which looked at the pattern of symbols in the text, showed that it was too regular, too much like a proper language, to be a code.'

The priest's hand shot up. 'Dr Kelly, before you share with us how you translated the Voynich, per-haps you could tell us what your translation has revealed?' His English was perfect but held the faint trace of an Italian accent.

Lauren nodded. 'First, let me apologize to all those who, like me, hoped the manuscript con-tained some secret. Contrary to certain claims, the Voynich Cipher wasn't written by the medieval monk Roger Bacon and, sadly, it's not an ancient Cathar text, a wizard's treatise on alchemy, a mystic's vision, a message from God, written in the language of angels, or any of the other fanciful things many believed.'

There were audible sighs of disappointment.

'The Voynich is simply the story of a mythic quest in the classic tradition, an allegory of man's greed that shows a prescient awareness of today's environmental concerns. I've purposely translated it without trying to reproduce the archaic language of the time to highlight the sense. It tells of a scholar priest who accompanies a troop of soldiers into a

51

vast jungle in search of Eldorado – the fabled city of gold. His mission is to chronicle their adventure and to claim the souls of the conquered for his church. The gruelling quest decimates the soldiers, leaving them lost in the middle of the forest. Just as they abandon hope, they stumble across a garden filled with strange plants and inhabited by even stranger nymph-like women and other bizarre creatures. It turns out to be both an Eden – and Hell. They find wonders and miracles there, but something terrible too. Only the scholar priest lives to tell the tale.'

As Lauren recounted the story in more detail she used the screen to punctuate her narrative with disturbing illustrations from the manuscript. The audience listened politely. Her synopsis was only a theory until she published and her full findings were accepted. The priest, however, appeared transfixed, his sharp features expressing a blend of incredulity, wonder and concern.

'Our unknown author provides one final twist. Not only does he employ a unique language, present us with bizarre illustrations and an even more bizarre story, but he – and I assume it's a he – claims that the fabulous garden illustrated and described in the manuscript actually exists, and that his story is true. This is how he concludes: "Congratulations, fellow scholar, you have read my story and so proved your dedication, intelligence and wisdom. Whatever your faith, God has now chosen you to do what I cannot: keep His garden safe and ensure its miraculous powers are used for His glory. One day, mankind will doubtless need these powers. I only pray it deserves them. Amen." '

She smiled. 'Because of the extraordinary pains he took to tell his story, it's tempting to think it might be true, and that he created his ingenious language to guard its secret.'

The room was buzzing again.

'You have no idea of the author's identity?' asked the priest.

'No. He doesn't give his name.'

'What do you expect to find in the astrological section you haven't yet translated?' demanded another voice.

'A map?' someone shouted.

Lauren raised her hands for calm. 'Before we get too excited, we must remember that at the time the Voynich was written, in the late sixteenth century, encrypting documents was extremely fashionable. So, sadly, I'm afraid the likelihood is that the author simply possessed an extraordinary intellect, a mischievous sense of humour – and the leisure time to indulge both.'

She waited for the audience's laughter to subside. 'Nevertheless, the Voynich is still a work of genius and if you want to read my synopsis of the translated story I suggest you visit the Beinecke pages on Yale's website.'

In the hallway outside the meeting room, members of the audience besieged Lauren with questions.

Watching her, Ross felt a stab of regret – and envy. After his PhD he, too, could have carved out a career in academia. Harvard and three other good colleges had offered him positions to continue his studies, but he had declined them. If, after graduating from high school, you tell your parents that their only child – their only *son* – has no interest in taking over the struggling farm that's been in the family for generations, but is leaving to take up a scholarship at Princeton, you'd better be successful. To Ross, that meant making money. A lot of it. So he had joined Big Oil. And, if he was honest, he had never wanted to be an academic. He *liked* the buccaneering cut and thrust of oil exploration, journeying to the more inhospitable parts of the world and finding what no one else could.

How quickly things had changed, though. He had once been the shining star with the glittering career ahead of him, while Lauren had been the dedicated academic destined to spend her career in worthy obscurity. Now her star was in the ascendant and, as he watched her fielding questions, he realized she had no idea of how huge her achievement was. She hoped her translation of the Voynich would bring her promotion within her faculty but it was clear to Ross that, once she had completed it, she could take her pick of any job in her field – across the world. Suddenly he had a vision of himself as a house-husband, looking after their baby, while Lauren ascended to even greater heights. He consoled himself with the thought of their three-week holiday. He would worry about finding another job when they got back.

Lauren smiled and beckoned to him, but the priest suddenly engaged her in conversation. Though not a big man he had a commanding presence. Ross watched him introduce himself and, above the hubbub, heard him say: 'I asked if you knew the author's name because I've seen confidential Vatican files that may reveal his identity – and help to unlock the final astrological section.'

Lauren's eyes widened. 'Really?'

'Yes. I rather hoped we might collaborate.'

'I'd certainly love to see the files.'

'We'll happily show you everything in exchange for certain conditions.'

'Such as?'

'The Vatican needs to retain some control over publication to restrict circulation of anything that might be injurious to the Church.'

Lauren flashed her most polite – and dangerous – smile, from which Ross knew the priest would leave empty-handed. 'I'm sorry but I must decline your kind offer,' she said.

'I'm speaking on behalf of the Society of Jesus,' the priest said, as if it was unthinkable anyone could refuse. 'This is for the Holy Mother Church.'

'That's as may be, Father, but this is a personal project and I don't believe in putting *any* restrictions on academic scholarship.'

There was an awkward pause. Then the priest reached into his robes and handed her a card. 'I have to respect your decision, Dr Kelly, but if you change your mind please don't hesitate to contact me.'

As she took the card, Bob Knight intervened smoothly: 'If Dr Kelly's tight-lipped, Father, don't take it personally. She guards the privacy of her work fiercely, keeping most of her files at home. I'm her head of faculty and I barely knew the detail of what she was presenting tonight.' He took Lauren's arm and steered her away. 'Now, if you'll excuse us . . .'

As Knight led Lauren to the end of the corridor the priest stared after them. He was older than Ross had first thought, although his blue-black hair contained little grey and his face was unlined – but for the frown marks between his eyes. Suddenly the man turned, and as the priest's dark eyes met his, Ross saw that he was seething with rage and frustration.

When Lauren returned, beaming with excitement, Ross put his arm round her and escorted her to the exit. 'Congratulations. You certainly got everyone around here buzzing. That priest seemed pretty intense, though.'

She grimaced. 'He said the Vatican had files that might interest me, but he wanted some kind of gag, so I passed.'

'And Knight? He looked pretty excited.'

'He is.' Outside in the cool night air, she gave him a strange pleading smile. 'You want the good news or the bad?'

Ross had never been a fan of bad news. 'The good.'

'Knight's promising me whatever I want at the faculty. I'll be a full professor, significant salary rise, everything.'

'That's great.'

'He wants me to translate the last section as soon as possible. Says there's a lot of interest out there right now.'

Ross knew where this was heading. 'But we're going on vacation for three weeks.'

Again the pleading smile. 'I know. That's the bad news.'

6

Rome, the next day

Because of their power it is said that there are three popes in Rome: the White Pope, the pontiff; the Red Pope, the Grand Inquisitor, now known as the Cardinal Prefect of the Congregation for the Doctrine of the Faith; and the Black Pope, the head of the Jesuits, the Superior General of the Society of Jesus.

The evening after Dr Lauren Ross's seminar at Yale, all was quiet within the walls of the Vatican, and even the surrounding bustle of Rome seemed muted. However, the Black Pope's mind was jangling as he entered the labyrinth of rooms and corridors that adjoined the Apostolic Library. On last night's flight from JFK to Rome's Leonardo da Vinci airport, Father General Leonardo Torino had been unable to sleep, thinking through the implications of Dr Ross's findings. Though exhausted, he had been desperate to rush to the Inquisition Archives and recheck the original document against the photocopy in his case, but first he had had to debrief his staff on his visit to the New York Province of the Society of Jesus and their conference at Fordham University. Then he had had to sit through interminable meetings with the Curia as they discussed plans to set up a second Vatican state in the developing world. Finally, he had updated the Holy Father on the work of the Institute of Miracles – even though all it seemed to do was disprove their existence in the modern age.

Torino had only convinced the new pope to reinstate the ancient institute because the last pontiff had devalued their currency, approving more miracles and canonizing more saints than at any other time in the Church's history. As the largest and most intellectually rigorous order in the Roman Catholic Church, the Society of Jesus was uniquely qualified to prove miracles – to support the canonization of saints and reveal to the world incontrovertible proof of the hand of God. Since its reinstatement, however, the institute had not validated a single one. In fact, Torino had been personally responsible for reversing at least six previously established miracles.

But that might change if what he'd heard at Yale was genuine.

As he reached the *secretum secretorum*, the Church's most sensitive archive, the curator was locking the door for the night. 'Don't close it yet,' Torino ordered. 'I need to check something.'

The old man, head down, continued to turn the

large key in the lock. 'It's late. Can't you come back tomorrow?' He looked up, recognized Torino's black robes and his face flickered with fear. 'Father General, I'm sorry. I didn't realize it was you.'

Torino strode into the dusty, unprepossessing network of rooms and headed for the back chamber. Since the Vatican had opened the Inquisition Archives in 1998 most scholars had focused on celebrated trials, particularly that of Galileo, the scientist who famously shook the Church by claiming – and proving – that the Earth revolved around the sun and not vice versa. However, the obscure case that Torino wished to re-examine was potentially no less controversial.

A year after the reinstatement of the institute, he had despaired of finding a genuine miracle. In this media age, claimants had nothing to lose and everything to gain by falsifying them, so he had instructed the scholars charged with running the institute to look back into the past, to the Inquisition Archives, and seek out those who had braved torture and death to proclaim their miracles. One case they found had fired Torino's imagination: the testimony and trial of Father Orlando Falcon, a fellow Jesuit, who had not just experienced one miracle but discovered a wondrous and terrible place *filled* with them.

The file was tucked away in a corner. Until his scholars had found and photocopied it a few months ago, the contents had probably not been read for hundreds of years. Ignoring the watching curator, and the large sign forbidding the removal of original documents from the archive, the Superior General placed the four-and-a-half-centuries-old manuscript in his briefcase, left the room and headed for his apartment in the Curia Generalizia, the International Headquarters of the Society of Jesus.

7

The high ceilings, antique furniture and ornate rugs afforded the official residence of the Jesuit Superior General a faded splendour, but the ancient air-conditioning made it claustrophobically warm. Exhausted, Torino dismissed his staff, retired to his bedroom and opened the windows.

There were two framed photographs on the bedside table. One, of himself as a child at the Jesuit orphanage in Naples, reminded him of where he had come from, and the other of what he had achieved: in it, Torino stood in the black robes of his office beside the Holy Father. Above the bed hung a crucifix and beside the desk two gilt-framed diplomas: a medical degree from the University of Milan and a PhD in theology. He placed his laptop on the bed and emptied his briefcase beside it.

Torino's hand trembled as he poured himself a glass of cold water from the jug on the table. He gulped it, then sat at the desk and opened the ancient file.

As he turned the yellowed vellum, the Latin text seemed to greet him like an old friend:

On the day of Thursday 8th of the month of July 1560 in the presence of His Excellency, the Grand Inquisitor, Cardinal Prefect Michele Ghislieri. Being summoned to the Holy Inquisition, there appeared Father Orlando Falcon, a Jesuit Priest, charged with heresy.

. . . It was asked him, 'Father Orlando, what was the mission of the one hundred conquistadors?'

'To conquer new lands, Your Excellency, and discover Eldorado for King Charles of Spain.'

'What was your mission in accompanying them?'

'To save the souls of the conquered and to claim a share of the gold for the Holy Mother Church.'

'But there was no City of Gold? You found something else instead?'

'Yes, Your Excellency.'

'Tell me again what you found, so we may record it here . . .'

Torino's excitement mounted as he read again the description of Falcon's discovery of a magical garden, the creatures he had encountered there. When he reached the finale in which the remaining conquistadors had met savage deaths, leaving only the scholar priest alive to tell the tale, he could barely contain himself. The story was virtually identical to Lauren Ross's synopsis of the Voynich. The only significant difference was that Falcon's

Inquisition testimony contained an additional reference to something he called *radix*, which in Latin meant 'root' or 'source'. Although vague about it, Falcon had regarded it as potentially more powerful even than the miraculous garden. Torino wondered if it featured in Lauren Kelly's verbatim translation of the Voynich, or the yet-to-be-translated section.

He flicked through to the end of the file.

... After Father Orlando had recounted the full nature of his discovery, it was asked him, 'Why do you persist in this heresy? A miraculous Eden such as this cannot exist in the New World among heathens and savages. You must be mistaken, lying or possessed.'

Father Orlando replied, 'I am telling the truth. I want only to claim it for the Holy Mother Church.'

'You are a respected priest, a favourite of the founder of your order, the Blessed Ignatius Loyola. You must realize that your heresy threatens the Church.'

'How can the truth threaten the Holy Mother Church?'

'If you persist I can only express my regret and sadness that Satan should have claimed so fine a priest. I vow, however, to do everything in my power to reclaim your soul.' His Excellency instructed the clerks to present the heretic with a written confession, and said, 'Recant, Father Orlando. Renounce your claims. Sign the confession.'

The heretic refused and was taken to the cells where his feet were burnt over hot coals. He did not recant. The heretic was given into the care of a nun who was instructed to soothe his wounds and encourage him to choose again the path of righteousness. The next morning the nun reported that the heretic's feet had miraculously healed.

His Excellency asked the heretic, 'How do you explain this sorcery?'

He answered, 'It proves my claims are true.'

His Excellency replied, 'This proves only that Satan has taken possession of your body and soul.' Father Orlando was returned to the cells where wooden boot vices were placed round his feet and tightened until the bones broke. He still did not recant.

The next morning, the nun reported that the heretic's feet had not healed and that Father Orlando's bones remained broken. There was no more sorcery. After examining the priest, His Excellency concluded that the Devil had been driven from him. The heretic was again handed the document and again His Excellency asked him, 'Now, Father Orlando, will you sign the confession and recant your heresy?'

He again refused and was imprisoned for many months. After this time a manuscript was found in Father Orlando's cell, written in the Devil's language, bearing images of a perverted Eden. The heretic was condemned to death. Even at the end, moments before his execution, he still refused to recant. His book of the Devil was ordered burnt . . .

Torino read the last lines again: . . . *a manuscript was found in Father Orlando's cell, written in the Devil's language, bearing images of a perverted Eden.* The current Church authorities had long since forgotten Falcon's forbidden volume, but less than a hundred years ago the Curia had recorded its suspicions that it might be the document the world now knew as the Voynich Cipher Manuscript. Yesterday, in New York, he had stolen away to the Beinecke Library to see the original and hear Lauren Kelly's talk. The pre-publicity, including the subtitle of her presentation, 'A Doomed Quest For Eldorado?' had been enough to pique his interest and, having listened to her, he was now convinced that Falcon's Devil's book was indeed the Voynich.

He reached for his notes and felt again the bitter frustration he had experienced when Dr Kelly had refused to collaborate with him on completing her research. Apparently she would take a three-week vacation, then finish the translation. He powered up his laptop. The Internet was infested with individuals and communities obsessed with unravelling the manuscript's secrets. Any Google search of 'Voynich' threw up thousands of websites, forums and chat rooms dedicated to the document. Most were hosted by crackpots, amateur sleuths, writers and researchers selling their own particular theory about it. When the Beinecke homepage appeared on screen he clicked on Voynich Synopsis, laid the Inquisition Archives document next to the screen and again compared the story in both sources. The parallels were uncanny.

Despite the still-enciphered astrological section, the translation was a towering achievement. There had been some journalists at the Beinecke, but he was surprised and relieved that she had chosen to reveal her findings in an obscure open lecture on linguistics rather than a full-blown press conference. Then he reminded himself that Dr Lauren Kelly hadn't yet proved what she had accomplished. In academic terms, until she completed the translation and published her findings in full, her work would be classed only as a theory – one in a long line. There was no doubt in Torino's mind, however, that her translation was accurate.

Understandably, she assumed that the fantastical story was an allegorical fantasy, but the Church's hierarchy had once viewed it as a blasphemous attempt to rewrite Genesis and a threat to everything they stood for. Their ruthless response proved nothing, but it raised a question. Why had Father Orlando Falcon not only created the incredibly complex Voynich but endured torture and a hideous death rather than recant his story if it was fiction?

Might his miraculous garden exist?

Torino stood, stretched his tired muscles and limped to the open window. As a child at the orphanage, he had been small, conscientious and clever, the priests' favourite but an easy target for the other boys. One particularly vicious beating had crushed his sciatic nerve, permanently disabling him.

As he breathed in the evening air, the mighty dome of St Peter's before him, he was convinced that God had entrusted him with unravelling the enigma of Falcon's garden. He thought again of Dr Lauren Kelly and frowned. By refusing to collaborate on the final section she had shown she was no friend of the Church. A sudden notion chilled him. *What if she had already deciphered the final section and it not only explained Falcon's mysterious* radix *but was also a map? What if she planned to publish the complete translation and prove the existence of Falcon's garden by revealing its location?*

The implications for the Holy Mother Church – to which he owed everything – were unthinkable. Forget Galileo. Forget Darwin. If the garden existed, it could bestow supreme power on his beloved church. Or destroy it in an instant.

He considered sharing his fears with the Holy Father, or the Cardinal Prefect of the Congregation for the Doctrine of the Faith, but both were unimaginative old men. They would laugh at his theory or not understand it – either way they would do nothing. Apart from their plans to found a second Vatican state in the southern hemisphere, they were taking no radical new steps to promote and protect the Church's waning influence in the world. He would need more evidence before he involved them. He had to find out what Lauren Kelly knew and her intentions.

As he limped back to his desk his eyes focused on

the photograph of himself as a child. He checked his watch. The time difference was in his favour. He rummaged through his papers until he found an anonymous card with a phone number on it. He hesitated for a moment, knowing he was about to cross a line, then reminded himself that these were desperate times and, to serve and protect God's Church, he must use whatever resources presented themselves. Indeed, the Lord Himself might have engineered this unorthodox opportunity. He picked up the phone beside his bed and dialled.

A voice answered on the third ring. 'Yes?'

He stared at the larger boy in the photograph. 'Marco,' he said.

'Leo, thank God. I've been waiting—'

Torino's eyes moved to the file on the bed. 'Is your treatment over?'

'Yes.'

'Do you still want absolution?'

A sharp intake of breath. 'Yes.'

'You're prepared to do any penance for the Church?'

'Anything.'

'Good.' Torino told himself again that this was the right course of action. 'I think it's time the left hand of the Devil became the right hand of God.'

8

Six days later

It was almost midnight when Ross turned the Mercedes into the driveway of their Darien home. The long weekend in Vermont had been Lauren's idea, consolation for postponing their holiday and celebration of her pregnancy and the Voynich. He had been looking forward more than he'd realized to getting away from everything so the long weekend now seemed a poor substitute for the planned three weeks in the Far East.

As the car slowed, Lauren leant across to kiss his cheek. 'Thanks, Ross, I had a lovely time.'

'So did I. It could have been longer, though.' He flashed a lopsided smile. 'Say, about three weeks.'

She laughed. 'Stop trying to make me feel guilty. I know you're disappointed, but the insurance covered the cost. We haven't lost any money.'

'You know it's not about the money,' he said. 'This was planned months ago, and we haven't had a real holiday together for years.'

She raised an eyebrow. 'That's because *you* were always too busy with *your* work.'

'*Touché.*' It was ironic that when he had time on his hands Lauren had a deadline to meet. 'But you've been working on the manuscript for more than seven years. What difference will three weeks make?'

'All the difference between being the first to complete it and letting someone else get there ahead of me. I'm so close, but the last section isn't like the rest. It's more difficult.' As he parked she put her hand on his. 'I'll make a deal with you. I'll still be able to fly in two months and we'll take our holiday then, whether I've cracked the manuscript or not.'

He smiled at her, thinking how much he loved her. 'Sure. But by then I'll probably be up to my eyeballs in a new job.'

'Fine by me.' She placed his hand on her belly. 'Pretty soon we're going to have another mouth to feed.'

Ross got out of the car and pulled their bags from the back seat. He opened the front door, turned on the lights and followed Lauren into the hallway. 'I'm sorry for giving you a hard time. I guess I'm feeling—'

But she wasn't listening to him. She was looking up at the darkened landing. 'You heard that?' she whispered.

'What?' He put the bags down on the polished cedar floor and moved to the foot of the stairs. 'Where?'

'In my office. I thought I heard something.'

He hadn't. He walked quietly up the stairs.

She followed him to the top, put a hand on his arm. 'Why don't we just call nine one one?'

'Because it's probably nothing. Wait here. I'll check it out.'

He walked across the landing to the door on the left: the smallest bedroom of five, which Lauren used for her work. He had the study. He stood by the closed door and listened, but heard nothing. He relaxed, turned back to his wife and shook his head.

'Be careful,' she mouthed.

He smiled at her and she smiled back.

He turned the knob, opened the door and sensed that something was wrong. He heard Lauren hiss: 'Don't go in, Ross. I always lock the door. Someone must be in there.'

Then his world exploded.

A force slammed the door back on him, smashing into his face, throwing him backwards on to the landing, his head striking the balustrade. Blood clouded his vision and through it he saw a masked figure towering over him. A weaker man would have been knocked out, but Ross dragged himself up, turned to his wife, standing frozen at the head of the stairs, and yelled, 'Run, Lauren! Run!' The intruder lashed out with his heel, catching Ross hard in the temple.

Lauren ran, but as Ross lapsed towards unconsciousness, he saw that she wasn't running away but towards him. 'Leave him alone!' she shouted.

The figure stepped over Ross and made for the stairs, Lauren in his path. Vision blurred, Ross reached up and grabbed the intruder's trouser leg, exposing a thick scar above the right ankle. The man barrelled past him, shoving Lauren against the balustrade with such force that the rail broke and she plummeted to the floor of the hall below. There was a thud and a sickening crack. Then she was silent. The last sound Ross heard before darkness claimed him was the click of the front door closing.

9

Uganda, Africa

Thousands of miles away, in a small town near Lake Victoria, the Jambo Internet café represented an outpost of extraordinary technology, its air-conditioned interior a refuge from the sweltering heat. Amid its young clientele of locals and tanned backpackers, drinking coffee and tapping at computer terminals, one pale elderly face stood out. Sipping a sweet *latte*, Sister Chantal studied her screen.

Every month she took her walking-stick and strolled into town from the Aids hospice on the hill, ordered a *latte* and a pastry, then sat at one of the terminals. Every month her frail fingers entered the same keyword in the major search engines and scoured the Internet, and every month she found nothing new. When she had finished her pastry and the *latte*, she would return to the hospice and tell herself that next month things would be different. Next month her burden would be lifted.

She had lived at the hospice for the last twelve years and she enjoyed her work there, but she knew it would soon be time to leave. It wasn't just that the mother superior and the Church authorities would eventually start asking questions – as they had done in every other hospital and hospice where she had worked. Her precious supplies were running low and to continue her lonely vigil she had to replenish them. It was hard to believe she was running out of time. A stab of self-pity pierced her serene self-discipline. She pushed it away and concentrated on the computer screen.

First, she scanned the BBC and CNN. As usual, the news wasn't good. A story about Alascon Oil's new pipeline project was particularly worrying. When she had read enough she went to Google and entered her search word. She scrolled down the first four pages, dismissing each hit.

Then something caught her eye.

She paused, coffee in hand, but remained calm: she had found encouraging items before, all of which had come to nothing. She clicked on the entry and studied the website. Then she placed her untouched coffee on the desk. As she read, her heart beat faster and her palms moistened. She reached up and loosened her wimple, suddenly short of breath. Struggling to control her rising excitement, she visited two more websites, gaining more background information, then sent the relevant pages to the printer. Next she accessed the Banque Genève secure site, then entered her password and account number. She barely glanced at the large balance. The money was a means to an end. Nothing more. She paid for a plane ticket and transferred funds to the nearest bank, in Jinja. Finally she stood up, settled her bill and rushed out, leaving her coffee on the desk.

When she returned to the hospice it was quiet. Most of the nuns were in the chapel or tending the abundant crops in the small garden of fertile red earth. She went straight to her spartan room and packed everything she owned into a small suitcase. Before closing it she retrieved an old wooden box and undid the padlock. She took out a smaller, ornately carved box, opened it and examined the contents. The leather drawstring pouch was almost empty. A rush of relief and elation flooded her. It had once been full to bursting but it no longer mattered that her supply was almost exhausted. Her wait would soon be over.

A hesitant knock made her spin round and slam the box shut. Two small, painfully thin boys stood in the doorway. 'What are you doing, Sister?'

She smiled at them. '*Jambo*, Samuel, Joshua.' Samuel and Joshua Jarimogi were twins, born with Aids. After a long struggle, their mother had died six months ago and, according to the doctors, it was inevitable that the boys would soon join her. Sister Chantal tried not to get too involved with the patients – over the long years she had seen too many die. But Samuel and Joshua were her favourites.

'Can we play?' asked Samuel.

Sister Chantal glanced at her case, then at the box. She should leave, before the mother superior or one of the other sisters challenged her, but her vigil was almost over and the euphoria she felt compelled her to do something reckless: a small act of rebellion after a lifetime of discipline, obedience, patience and self-sacrifice. 'Yes. Let's have a tea party.'

She took the carved box and led the boys to the deserted kitchen. She put on the kettle and told them to fetch two cups and saucers. She opened the leather pouch and emptied most of its contents into the box, saving only the barest minimum for her final task; she was growing weak and would need her remaining strength to complete her vigil and pass on her burden. She had been forced to see so many die. What harm could this do now? She prepared the contents and tilted the box so they collected in one corner, shook half into one cup, half into the other, then poured in the boiling water. As she put the box down, Samuel reached for it, fascinated by the unusual carvings.

'Can we have it?' he asked.

Her first instinct was to take it back, but as she had no more need of it, she pocketed the leather pouch and nodded. 'Yes, Sam, you can share the box. But it's very old and very precious so take care of it.' She added sweet condensed milk to the cups and waited for the liquid to cool. 'Now drink your tea.'

10

Rome, three days later

Breathing in the soothing fragrance of pine and orange trees, Marco Bazin looked down on the dome of St Peter's, rising above the dawn mist of the eternal city. At such an early hour the Aventine Hill was deserted and he enjoyed the illusion that he was alone in the world. Then a man appeared in the distance. Bazin recognized his gait instantly. As he braced himself for the encounter he pondered the irony of what had happened. In all his years as an assassin, *la mano sinistra del diavolo* had never failed in an assignment. Until three days ago, the one time he had been ordered *not* to harm anyone.

Bazin cast his mind back to the night when the priest had visited him at his alpine retreat, then to his childhood and the hot, dusty courtyard of the old Jesuit orphanage in Naples. There had been no smell of fresh pine or oranges in that place, only the stench of sewers, sweat and fear. Half-brothers, born of the same whore, he and Leo had been each other's only friend, opposites bonded by a common need to belong and survive. His older, smarter, smaller half-brother had helped him with his studies, while he had protected Leo when the others had picked on him for his size and cleverness.

Then they had left the orphanage and everything had changed.

The Jesuits had always valued Leo's intellect. They had encouraged him to join the order and further his studies. The Church had become his salvation. Bazin, however, had hated the priests and they had had no time for his rough ways, so he had turned his back on the Church and joined the Camorra, the Neapolitan branch of that other Italian institution: the Mafia. Over the years the brothers' paths had diverged further, one becoming a powerful priest dedicated to saving souls, the other a feared assassin paid for taking lives.

When Bazin had discovered he was dying, however, he had called the only person he knew who could save his soul. To his surprise, gratitude and shame, Leo had offered him a way to absolve himself of his sins. But now, as he watched Father General Leonardo Torino approach in the early-morning mist, Bazin knew he had failed him.

Torino didn't smile or greet him, just tapped his watch. 'Let's keep this brief, Marco. I'm a busy man and I don't want my people to come looking for me.' He frowned. 'What happened in America? I thought you were meant to be good at this. The plan was to go in, get the information and leave, not to jeopardize Dr Kelly's work in case she hadn't finished it. I certainly didn't tell you to hurt anyone and get the police involved.'

Bazin couldn't meet his eye. 'You told me they'd be away for three weeks, Leo.'

'You will address me as "Father General".' He paused. 'They should have been away on holiday. The point is you were supposed to be discreet.'

'I was, Father General. I covered my face and left no trace. The police will assume I fled before I had a chance to take much. If they'd been away like you said no one would've known I was even there. But I had to use force to escape – or you wouldn't have got what you wanted. In the end, I took a few valuables to make it look like a normal burglary.'

For a while Torino said nothing, just glared at Bazin as he stared bleakly into the distance. 'You've disappointed me, Marco. Your journey to absolution has not begun well. But we can salvage something from this. *If* you got what I asked for.'

Bazin reached into his jacket pocket and pulled out a La Cie portable hard drive. 'Before I was interrupted, I downloaded most of the relevant folders you told me to look for.' He handed it to Torino. 'But not all of them.'

'This better have what I want on it. I'll contact you when I need more.' Torino concealed the hard drive in his robes, turned abruptly and walked away.

Bazin thought of what he had done to acquire what Torino had asked for. 'Are you sure this is what the Church wants, Father General?' he called after Torino. 'That this is how I'll gain absolution?'

Torino stopped, and Bazin saw his shoulders tense as he turned. 'You dare to question me?' he said, his face white with rage. 'If I want advice on killing, I'll come to you. But I'll be the judge of what the Church wants and needs.' He narrowed his eyes and stepped close enough for Bazin to smell mint and garlic on his breath. 'You *begged* for my help. Remember?' Before Bazin could answer, Torino had grabbed his half-brother's crotch.

'What the *fuck* are you doing?' Bazin pulled at his wrist but Torino only gripped harder.

'Listen to me, Marco. You demanded *my* help. Never forget that.' He squeezed. 'You know why God let the surgeons cut off one of your balls? Because they represent your two lives: the one you live now and the one you live beyond death. God took the first because of your past sins, and if you want to keep the remaining one, the one that represents your eternal future, you must follow Him – and His Church. God's got you by the balls, Marco. You said you wanted absolution. The question is: how much?'

'I told you. I want it. I *need* it.'

'In medieval England, when a man gave evidence in court, he didn't put a hand on the Bible. He held his testes. The word "testimony" comes from that practice. And as I hold your last precious one, Marco, know that this is God's testimony. We're on a crusade, the Church is fighting for its very existence and God demands you help His ministry by doing *whatever*'s necessary.' He paused to let his words sink in. 'You no longer work for the Mafia. You're no longer *la mano sinistra del diavolo*, a base assassin who kills for money, but a crusader, a holy warrior, God's right hand wielding a cleansing sword against Rome's mortal enemies. From this day forward, *whatever* I tell you to do in His name is sanctioned, pure, righteous. You understand?'

'Yes.'

Bazin did understand. Despite the pain – or because of it – relief swamped him. Finally he had found his purpose and he would surrender to it. Torino was showing him the uncompromising path that led to redemption and he would follow it to the end, come what may.

As if reading his mind, the Superior General released his grip. 'Are you prepared to do whatever I say the Church needs? However delicate? And will you pledge to help without asking questions?'

'Yes.'

'If you tell anyone of this, the Church will disavow everything. *I* will disavow everything. You understand?'

'I want only absolution, Father General.'

'Then you must earn it.'

11

Back in his quarters, Torino plugged the drive into his laptop. As he examined the contents, he felt little remorse for what had happened to Lauren Kelly and her husband. He had offered her the chance to collaborate and she had declined. Though he had not intended Bazin to harm the couple, it was vital that he learn what Lauren Kelly knew. Perversely, what had happened might even prove beneficial to the Church. With the woman silenced, it would be easier to protect the discovery outlined in the Voynich – assuming she had completed the translation. His greater concern was the Holy Father and others in the Curia. Until he had evidence, they would never condone what he was doing, especially his unholy alliance with Bazin.

On screen, the computer files documented most of the successes and failures on Lauren Kelly's tortuous path to decoding the Voynich. He read how, with Elizabeth Quinn's help, she had quickly discounted a complex polyalphabetic cipher and used her impressive breadth of linguistic knowledge to deduce that the text was a posterior synthetic language based on two existing languages. Torino had learnt this much from her talk at Yale but now he had the details.

Voynichese was apparently a hybrid of highly structured Latin and Mandarin Chinese, in which characters didn't just represent letters but whole words and phrases. The relevant letters of the Latin alphabet and the key Chinese symbols had then been transliterated into the unique characters used in the Voynich text, further disguising the blended language. Apart from this transliteration, however, the translated part of the manuscript contained no cipher. The use of Chinese tallied with Torino's research on Father Orlando Falcon. A favourite of Ignatius Loyola, Falcon had been sent on one of the first missions to China as a young Jesuit in the late 1540s.

Torino already knew from the Inquisition Archives that the author had possessed a phenomenal intellect; it was one of the reasons the Church had taken his claims so seriously, and why he had been punished so severely. Torino was equally impressed, however, by the depth of Dr Kelly's scholarship, and the counter-intuitive way in which she had burrowed into the author's brilliant mind to unlock his story.

Or most of it.

Scanning the files, Torino found her verbatim translation of the Voynich story. It was even more

vivid and terrifying than the synopsis had been –
but it didn't include the remaining astrological
section. And there was no mention of Father
Orlando's *radix* or 'source'. In one of her earlier files
Kelly had written:

> *From what I've learnt, I believe the final astrological
> section may contain a series of compass bearings,
> geographical landmarks and star signs. My creeping
> suspicion is that the more I discover the more I'll be
> forced to revise my assumptions about the document
> and its mysteries . . .*

What had she meant by that? Had she decided
that the story was not an allegory but a chronicle of
what its author had actually discovered? If so, had
she since unravelled the final astrological section –
and the map it might contain? It was tantalizingly
inconclusive.

Cursing Bazin for failing to complete his task, he
searched the rest of the files, but found no clear
evidence that Lauren Kelly had yet deciphered the
final section. Perhaps it was in the files that Bazin
had been unable to download before he was
interrupted. If so, Torino must claim it for the
Church.

But how?

He wanted to rush out and order Bazin back to
check the rest of her computer. But the Kelly house
was now a crime scene and possibly under
surveillance. As the Superior General of the Jesuits,

he couldn't afford to be incriminated. He would have to be patient and bide his time until the right moment presented itself. He didn't feel patient, though. He felt as if a clock was ticking, counting down the seconds until his beloved Church either fulfilled its rightful destiny as God's sole ministry on Earth, or disappeared, dismissed as an obsolete relic.

12

Three weeks later

Death had brought them together. They had met at
the funeral of a mutual friend in Boston, while he
was at MIT and she was at Harvard. She had said
later that she had taken an instant dislike to him,
thought he was too physically confident, too sure of
himself. Then they had begun to talk – really talk –
and discovered that they had both recently lost a
parent, she her father and he his mother.

Death had bonded them.

They agreed on little: she was religious and
believed passionately in conservation, he was an
atheist and had no qualms about working for Big
Oil, but each loved the way the other thought. He
also loved the nape of her neck and her smell. She
loved his strength and the way he listened. Soon
they loved each other. They joked that they were
going to live for ever or die in the attempt. Nothing
would separate them. Ever. If one got lost, the
other would go to the ends of the Earth to find them.

Now Ross found himself staring into the darkness, gripped by panic, unable to find his soulmate. Lauren was lost to him.

Death threatened to separate them.

'Ross, Ross, Ross.'

His heart skipped. He could hear her calling to him in the dark. She was trapped and needed his help. He had to find her and do whatever was necessary to rescue her . . .

'Ross.'

A hand on his shoulder shook him gently.

'Ross, wake up.'

Ross opened his eyes, and when he saw her his first emotion was relief: it had been a nightmare. Lauren was fine. She was there.

But it wasn't Lauren. It was her assistant, Zeb Quinn. The sickening sadness flooded back.

'Ross, it's about three o'clock in the afternoon. I let you sleep for a few hours after lunch while I watched over Lauren. I'm off back to Yale now but your dad and Lauren's mum are coming up soon. Mr Greenbloom, the neurosurgeon, said he wants to talk with you all. You okay with that?'

'Yes.' He rubbed his eyes and stood up beside Lauren's bed. He was wearing jeans and a faded sweatshirt. Dazed with sleep, he checked his watch. 'Thanks, Zeb. Thanks for everything.'

'If you need me for anything – anything at all – call me. You got my cell number. Right?'

'Right. Thanks.' Zeb left, and he went to the adjoining bathroom to splash his face with water.

Three weeks had passed since the burglary and in that time he had aged visibly. His face was pale, his blue eyes were bloodshot and his hair – partially shaved where they had sutured a gash with twelve stitches – was flecked with new silver. The doctors said the hairline fracture on his skull was healing well and his dislocated shoulder had made a full recovery. But that was only half the story.

Lauren's room in the Sacred Heart Hospital outside Bridgeport, Connecticut, was clean and bright. A large window looked out over Long Island Sound, and if he peered to the right he could just see the distant towers of Manhattan. Flowers and cards adorned the broad window sill. Friends had showered him with messages, but those who had come to visit had been awkward, unsure how to respond to Lauren's injury. Ross was grateful that few had known of her pregnancy and now preferred to be left on his own; it was difficult enough to handle his own shock and grief without managing theirs. The exception had been Zeb Quinn. Though she and Ross had never been close, she had proved herself a true and practical friend.

The two orchids on the sill were from Lauren's sisters, who lived abroad, one in London, the other in Sydney. They had flown in and stayed for two weeks to help and support their mother. In the last week they had gone home. One of the larger bouquets was from Xplore. After making the right sympathetic noises, Kovacs had told Ross that they wanted him back and were prepared to wait until he was ready to discuss terms. But right now Ross couldn't have given a damn about his career.

Lauren's bed was in the middle of the room. She had been turned to prevent bedsores, and lay partially on her left side. Wires and tubes connected her to a bank of monitors and intravenous drips. A white tube extended from her trachea to a ventilator, whose rhythmic sound dominated the quiet room. The bandages had been removed from her head, and her blonde hair was growing back after the surgery. Her eyes were closed. She looked frail but beautiful, a sleeping princess. He fantasized that if he kissed her in just the right way he could wake her – and mend her broken body.

As he gazed at her, he felt a surge of irrational hatred for the Voynich manuscript. If she hadn't felt compelled to complete it, they would have been returning from their holiday now. Instead he had spent the last few weeks in Hell, rattling around in their empty house, which Lauren – and Lauren alone – had made into a home. Every detail in it reminded him of her and happier times. There was a suggestion that the intruder had been after her files, though there was no proof and no leads. The police had speculated about motive, but all they knew with any certainty was that Ross and Lauren had disturbed him and she had got in his way.

So arbitrary. So meaningless.

Lowered voices outside the door interrupted his thoughts. There was a knock, then Henry Greenbloom entered holding a manila folder. He was a thin, pale, angular man who kept his eyes fixed on the bed as he greeted Ross. Lauren's mother, Diana Wharton, followed with his father. Sam Kelly was a big man, a farmer with calloused hands and a craggy, weathered face, while Lauren's mother was an elegant, alabaster-skinned academic from Manhattan, yet they had become friends. They had lost their partners at about the same time, but the reason for their mutual liking was simple. They were decent people who respected each other and loved their children.

Greenbloom pointed to the chairs arranged by the bed and met Ross's eye for the first time. 'Shall we sit?' His tone was clinical and detached. 'It's important you all fully understand the situation. The fact of the matter is that even if Lauren does come out of her coma, which is unlikely, given the head injuries she sustained, she may well be brain-damaged and paralysed. Her spinal cord hasn't been severed, but the damage between the C3 and C4 vertebrae may have left her paralysed from the neck down. She needs a ventilator to breathe and that may not change.'

Ross glanced at his wife and wondered if she could hear the surgeon's bleak description of her future – or lack of it. Through the window, he heard a car start, someone say a cheerful farewell, and laughter. It was difficult to accept that outside this room life was continuing as normal.

Greenbloom went on: 'The better news is that because Lauren's head and neck absorbed much of the impact the baby is still viable.' Ross felt a painful jolt of hope. Greenbloom produced a scan from his folder. 'According to Obstetrics, the foetus is about the right size for sixteen weeks, measuring around four and a half inches from crown to rump and weighing two point eight ounces. Ultrasound examination reveals clear activity. There's a long way to go, and we'll need to monitor the situation constantly, but it's possible that the baby will reach full term in Lauren's uterus.'

'What about Lauren? What are the options?' said Ross.

'Barring a miracle, there are two. We wait indefinitely for Lauren to come out of her coma, hoping she won't be paralysed or too brain-damaged.' A pause. 'Failing that, after an agreed period of time, we turn off the ventilator.'

'And let her die?' Ross said, horrified. 'What about stem-cell therapy and all the other cures you guys are meant to be working on? I've read there might be a breakthrough in healing spinal-cord injuries in the next few years.'

'There *might* be, Ross, but I can't see Lauren waking again, never mind walking. The bitter truth is that there's not much more that we or any medical team in the world can do for her. It's the baby we have to focus on.'

Diana Wharton wiped her eyes and reached for the scan. 'Is Lauren suffering?'

'No.'

'And there really is hope for the baby?'

'Yes.'

She turned to Ross and his father. 'That's something, isn't it?'

Sam Kelly rested a hand on hers and smiled. 'That's a lot. There's always hope.'

Ross felt a rush of admiration for his father. A hardworking farmer, beset by disappointment and tragedy, he had learnt to accept and look beyond both. He remembered the day when his father had told him his new baby brother wasn't coming home, and that his mother couldn't have any more children. He had gone on to say he felt blessed that his wife had survived and that Ross should feel glad he still had a mother. Even when cancer had taken her a few years ago, his father still counted himself fortunate for the time he'd had with her. But Ross couldn't be so stoical. He couldn't just accept what was going to happen. Was Lauren at peace in a dark, dreamless sleep or, as in his nightmare, was she calling to him, desperate to be rescued?

Greenbloom stood up. 'We'll do everything we can for the baby. I just wanted to make sure you knew the facts of the situation so you could prepare yourselves for every eventuality.'

Ross blinked back tears of grief and frustration. He had made a career of finding what others couldn't but now, when it mattered most, he was useless. Her mother passed him the scan and he saw his own grief reflected in her face. Then he saw his father's sadness and compassion. In both he witnessed something else: resignation. They were already making their peace with whatever would happen to Lauren and pinning their hopes on their grandchild.

Ross couldn't do that. He studied the scan. The foetus *looked* like a baby: there was fine hair on its head; its fingernails were formed; the legs were longer than the arms. He wanted a child more than anything in the world, and he wanted it to have the brothers or sisters he had never had, but he didn't *know* the baby. He did know and love Lauren. He realized guiltily that he would gladly give up the baby to save his wife. His chest tightened and the blood pounded in his head. Whatever the doctor had said about Lauren, and whatever hope there was for their baby, Ross wasn't ready to give up on her. Not yet. Not ever.

13

Yale University, that evening
'Could you please tell me where Dr Lauren Kelly's office is?'

The young student shook his head. 'Sorry, Sister. Yale's a big place. You'll need to ask at Administration. They'll point you in the right direction. Go to the red-brick building, turn left through the arch and it's the big stone place on the other side of the green.' He checked his watch. 'It's getting late but someone should still be there.'

'Thank you.'

'You're welcome.'

As she walked off, leaning on her stick for support, she could feel herself tiring, but soon she'd be able to rest. She enjoyed strolling through the campus. Yale's leafy academic calm contrasted agreeably with the rush of the modern world, and reminded her of a more reflective age. The quiet didn't quell her excitement, though. Her heart was fluttering like the wings of a hummingbird. She was to be rewarded for her patience. The wait was over.

She smiled, suddenly grateful for the technology of the modern world. Jet planes had whisked her from Entebbe to London to Geneva. There, she had finalized her financial affairs and retrieved the item she kept in the bank's safe-deposit box, then flown on to New York. Without the Internet she couldn't have learnt so quickly of Dr Kelly's achievement. God had been smiling down on her that day at the Jambo Internet café when she had found Lauren Kelly's synopsis on the Yale website.

She opened her case, ignored the vacuum-sealed parcel she had retrieved from Geneva, and took out a creased printout. She reread the first lines of Dr Kelly's synopsis and crossed herself. She had forgotten how many times she had despaired of this day ever coming. It was appropriate that it should happen here, a few hundred yards from where the original lay in the Beinecke Library.

She walked into the stone building the student had mentioned and approached the reception desk. The two women behind it were collecting their handbags, getting ready to leave for the night. 'Can I help you?' asked the younger.

'I hope so. Where can I find Dr Lauren Kelly?'

The young woman looked down at her screen. 'I'm sorry. She hasn't been on campus for some days and we've no date for her return—'

'It's okay, Maisie. I'll deal with this,' interrupted the older woman. She adjusted her spectacles and smiled sympathetically. 'Maisie's new here. Is this to do with all that's happened, Sister?'

Sister Chantal fingered her crucifix, dismayed that Lauren Kelly's achievement was already making waves. 'Yes . . . yes, it is.' She had hoped the translation would attract little attention until it was completed. And without her help she was confident that that would never happen. 'Do you know where I can find her?'

'Yes. I'm sure we have the name of the hospital on the computer.'

'Hospital?'

'I assumed you wanted to visit Dr Kelly there because of her injury.'

An icy hand squeezed Sister Chantal's heart. 'Injury?'

The woman frowned. 'You don't know what happened?'

14

A few miles away, Ross Kelly was still trying to process Greenbloom's chilling prognosis. As he left the Sacred Heart Hospital, he felt curiously drawn to its small chapel.

If the total life of Earth was scaled down to a twenty-four-hour day, then mankind had turned up in the last few seconds – so it was odd that God should have created man in His own image. It made much more sense that man, with his evolved consciousness, had created God. It was one of the things Ross and Lauren had argued about from the very first time they met. He envied the comfort her faith brought her, and marvelled at how believers always credited God with the good things but never blamed Him for the bad.

His mother's faith had comforted her, too, in times of crisis. When she had miscarried, she didn't blame God but sought Him out. And when she developed cancer, she had prayed to Him to give her strength. Even Ross's father found solace in accepting adversity as God's will. But Ross couldn't. He wanted to believe there was some divine order in the world: it made it so much easier to accept everything. But there was no evidence. Over the last few weeks, he had prayed for Lauren, but he had sensed only a void. The few times Ross had glimpsed a spiritual dimension, it had been in the wonders of the natural world: the crystal formations in the vast cave of Lechugia, the Ozark mountains at dawn near his father's farm. Even the awesome history of the planet could make him reconsider his place in the scheme of things.

If God did exist, Ross had no time for the religions that had claimed Him as their own. It amazed him that believers – Christian, Jew or Muslim – could ruthlessly dismiss all other religions and not understand why he might want to dismiss theirs. Religion had done him one small service, though: as a boy he had joined the church choir and from that had learnt he had inherited his mother's perfect pitch.

Perhaps it was those happier memories that now drew him to the silence of the empty chapel. With its faint smell of incense, the pale wood pews, smooth white walls and contemporary stained-glass windows it offered a peaceful haven from the worries of the world. He took a seat at the front, looked up at the cross and wondered why religions cared more about a person's faith than what he or she did with their life. Why did we have to believe in God to be saved? Was He so vain, insecure and petty that He needed us to recognize Him? Why couldn't we just live good, worthwhile lives? Why did He allow Lauren to suffer when she believed in Him, but spared Ross who didn't?

'May I sit here?'

Ross jumped. He turned to see a priest standing in the aisle. There was something familiar about him. 'It's your chapel,' he said. 'I'm not a believer.'

The priest smiled. 'We all believe in something. Faith is what separates us from beasts.' He sat down beside him. 'And this *is* your chapel. It was intended for people in your predicament, Dr Kelly.'

'You know my name.'

Another smile. 'I'm a great admirer of your wife and her work, which deserves to be more widely appreciated. *She* deserves to be more widely appreciated.'

At that Ross remembered who he was. 'You were at the Beinecke when Lauren presented her translation of the Voynich.'

The priest held out his hand. 'Father General Leonardo Torino. Yes, I was at the Beinecke. When I learnt what had happened to your wife I had to approach you about her work.' He paused. 'May I explain? Or would you prefer me to leave you alone?'

Since Lauren's lecture, many academics, journalists and general Voynich fanatics had crawled out of the woodwork, demanding to know if she would recover, and when she expected to publish the complete translation with full supporting documentation. Some had even camped outside his house for a few days. He had changed his phone number to stop the calls, but still had to sift through a vast pile of mail each morning. Two days ago Bob Knight had demanded access to the files and notes Lauren had stored at home so that the university could validate and complete her work. Ross had refused, telling him that she, and no one else, would finish it. It angered him that people were waiting like vultures for her to die, desperate to pick over her discoveries. 'You came about the Voynich?'

'Yes.'

'What's your interest in it?'

'It's very simple. I'm the Superior General of the Society of Jesus, and Vatican records show that a priest from my order, a Jesuit, wrote the Voynich Cipher Manuscript more than four centuries ago, but we haven't yet been able to translate his text or understand his illustrations. And although the original manuscript is here at Yale, we feel possessive of it. The story may only be a simple allegory, a parable, but we regard the Voynich as a valuable document created by one of our own and we want to reclaim its meaning. When we learnt of your wife's translation I approached her and suggested we combine our records with her excellent work to complete it. She declined, said she had problems with our making conditions on what she could publish. I was disappointed but respected her wishes. I kept the offer open.' A pause. 'Then I learnt of her injury and discreetly followed her progress. When my work brought me back to America I decided to make time in my schedule to visit you. It's hard to explain, but my order feels indebted to and responsible for her. We want her to be rewarded for her service to the Church, in this world and the next. We will, of course, pray for her and ensure she takes her place in Heaven.'

The word 'ensure' annoyed Ross. 'That's kind of you – but how do you know *you* hold the keys to Heaven?' Something flickered in the priest's dark eyes – hurt or possibly anger – then was gone. 'No offence intended,' he added. 'It's just that I'd prefer your prayers to help Lauren in this world rather than prepare her for the next.'

'We *can* help her in this world. That's why I'm here. Our scholars are confident of completing the manuscript in due course, but with your wife's notes they could do it in a fraction of the time. Out of respect for her scholarship and wishes, we'd waive all conditions of publication. Naturally we'd give her full credit for the translation and compensate her financially – whether she recovers or not. The Holy Mother Church has significant resources and we'll do whatever's necessary – financial or other-wise – to help you both through this testing time.'

'You just want access to her notes?'

'Yes. Digital copies will suffice. As a matter of interest, do you know if they contain any mention of something called the "source" or its Latin equivalent, "*radix*"?'

He shook his head. 'I couldn't tell you. My wife kept her cards – and her notes – pretty close to her chest. Why?'

The priest made a dismissive gesture. 'It's not important. What *is* important is that her notes would allow us to finish translating the manuscript, and give her the recognition she deserves. I don't expect an answer now but please give it some thought.' He pulled out a card, handed it to Ross, then checked his watch. 'I have some business in New York tomorrow morning but must return to Rome in the evening. I'd be grateful if I could visit you before then to answer any questions. I want you to feel comfortable with entrusting your wife's work to us. May I call on you tomorrow afternoon? Say, about four?'

Ross nodded. 'That should be okay.' He found it reassuring that scholars who not only shared and appreciated Lauren's passion but also felt an ownership of the manuscript would complete her work. And it was important to him that she would receive full acknowledgement. He suspected that Knight would eventually claim her original files for Yale, and most of the credit for her work. Ross would talk to Zeb Quinn but he suspected she would agree to sharing the notes with Torino. If nothing else, it would keep Knight honest. He gave the priest his address.

'I'll leave you to your thoughts, Dr Kelly. Until tomorrow.'

Ross glanced at the Superior General's card. He

couldn't help but be impressed that a man in his position had made time to visit him personally. Further proof that he was committed to Lauren's work. As he watched the priest leave the chapel, he noticed he had a slight limp.

15

The next morning

Sister Chantal had done everything within her power to fulfil her duty. But now, as she was about to pass on her heavy burden, all was lost. After everything she had endured this was too much to bear.

She had told the Sacred Heart Hospital that she wanted to pray for Lauren Kelly, but when she had seen her lying prostrate on the bed, attached to wires and tubes, she wanted only to pray for herself. She walked to the bed, collapsed to her knees and wept. For the first time in her long vigil she felt true despair. But she didn't pray. Instead she focused on what to do. It couldn't end like this. There was only one way to put things right. Even as she thought it, she bowed her head in disbelief – and regret.

'If only I hadn't been so foolish,' she said bitterly, glancing at her case, then at Lauren's feeding tube. 'If only I'd saved it all.' She glanced behind her, then opened her case and searched for the leather pouch. When she saw how much remained she knew the gesture was futile. But she had to do something.

It took her six minutes. Then, as she put the empty pouch back into her case, she heard the door open.

Ross still wasn't used to having the bed he had shared with Lauren to himself. Throughout their marriage he had often been away, but he could only remember a handful of nights when he had slept alone at home.

Last night he had drunk a bottle of wine and watched TV into the early hours, careful not to disturb his father who was staying in one of the guest bedrooms. Free to watch any channel he chose, he eventually fell asleep in front of one of the reality makeover shows that Lauren liked, and when he woke he had been curled up on her side of the bed. After breakfast, his father had gone to Manhattan to visit her mother, and Ross had made his daily pilgrimage to the hospital. When he'd arrived, mildly hungover, the last thing he had expected to see was a nun kneeling at his wife's bedside.

'Who are you?' he demanded. 'What are you doing here?'

When she turned he saw that she had been crying. Despite that, she possessed a serene, ageless beauty and the most amazing eyes he had ever seen – piercing sky-blue irises ringed with violet. 'I am

Sister Chantal. I came to see Dr Lauren Kelly.' She spoke English in the precise way that well-educated Europeans often do. 'Who are you?'

'Ross Kelly, Lauren's husband. Are you with Father General Leonardo Torino?'

Fear flickered in the nun's eyes. 'No.'

'Then how do you know Lauren?'

'Through her work. We've never met but I *feel* I know her because she understands the mind of a man I admire.' She struggled to stand, and Ross helped her to her feet. 'How did this happen to your wife?' she asked. He explained about the intruder in Lauren's office, and the beautiful eyes flickered again. 'Was anything taken?'

'Some cash, jewellery and a video camera, maybe something from her computer. Why?'

'Has anybody else contacted you about Father Orlando's manuscript?'

'*What* manuscript?'

'The manuscript you know as the Voynich Cipher. You mentioned the Father General. Has he been to see you about the manuscript?'

This was too weird. 'What's going on? What's this about?'

Those striking eyes stared at him, unblinking, assessing. 'I need your help.' She gestured to Lauren. 'And you need mine.' Beneath the brittle calm he detected a fierce desperation now. 'Time is running out. I'm getting weaker and there's much we need to do.'

'We?'

'Yes. You, your wife and I.'

'My wife? What are you talking about? She's—'

Sister Chantal gripped his arm with surprising strength. 'Let me explain. It's important. For *all* of us. Can we talk somewhere we won't be disturbed? Somewhere private?'

As Ross looked into those disconcerting eyes, every rational instinct told him to ask her politely but firmly to leave. Yet something about her passion and desperation chimed with his own. And what did he have to lose? He made a decision that would change for ever his already shattered life. 'Come with me,' he said.

16

Later that day

As Father General Leonardo Torino stepped out of
the limousine and walked up the gravel drive to the
Kelly house he felt confident of the outcome. He
prided himself on knowing the hearts and minds of
men, and his meeting with Ross Kelly in the
hospital chapel had gone better than he had
hoped.

He rang the doorbell and waited. He heard raised
voices, then the door opened. When he saw the
guarded expression on the geologist's face, his
confidence evaporated. Kelly led him into
the kitchen, where Torino saw an elderly nun sitting
at the table, an empty coffee cup in front of her. His
surprise at her presence was compounded by the
fleeting panic he saw in her eyes as Ross introduced
them. As he processed this he noticed her slip an
opaque plastic bag into the case beside her. 'Good
afternoon, Sister.'

'Father General.' She fingered the large crucifix

that hung from her neck, then bowed her head and rose from the chair. 'I'm sorry, I'm tired. I must leave.'

Kelly moved towards her and a look passed between them. 'Sister Chantal, let me show you to the lounge. You can rest there while I talk with the Father General.'

Sister Chantal grabbed her small case and cane, and put her arm through his.

Her name further piqued Torino's interest. He was sure he had come across it recently but couldn't remember where. He waited in the kitchen until Kelly returned. 'I'm surprised to find a nun visiting you, a non-believer.'

Kelly frowned. 'As you said, we all need to believe in something.' The frown deepened. 'Tell me, Father General, why are you *really* interested in my wife's translation of the Voynich?'

'I thought I explained yesterday. It was written by one of our own. We regard the document as ours. We want to complete the translation.'

'Why?'

'Because it's part of our heritage. And it's a puzzle. Which is why your wife wanted to translate it.'

'You told me yesterday that you thought the manuscript was a parable – a simple story.' Kelly was studying him now. 'Is that what you really believe?'

The question bothered Torino. Yesterday the man had trusted him. Today he didn't. What had he been told? He thought of the package the nun had hidden and a frisson of excitement ran through him. What had Kelly *seen*? 'Of course it's a parable. It can't possibly be true, if that's what you're suggesting. Can it?'

'Tell me about the source you mentioned yesterday. Tell me what you think it is.'

'Why? What do *you* know about it, Dr Kelly?'

Kelly ignored his question. 'Tell me, Father General, what do you know about a priest called Orlando Falcon?'

Torino hid his thoughts better than most men but he knew his face betrayed him now. Only he knew about Father Orlando Falcon and his link with the Voynich. 'As I told you yesterday, we believe a Jesuit priest wrote the Voynich. And that priest may have been Father Orlando Falcon. What do *you* know about him?'

Kelly said nothing.

'I assume this has something to do with Sister Chantal's visit. Why don't you tell me what's troubling you? I can be a powerful ally. Like I said yesterday, the Church has resources. If you suspect there's more to the Voynich than you originally thought, it would be in your best interests to share it with us and come under the umbrella of the Church's protection.'

'Protection? From whom? I'm not giving Lauren's notes to anybody until I find out what's going on. I'm beginning to suspect that whoever broke into our house and harmed Lauren wanted

111

her notes – badly.' Kelly was glaring at him now. 'How badly do *you* want them, Father?'

Torino valued self-control above all things, but at that moment almost lost his. To come so close to possessing what he most desired only to be thwarted was intolerable. Anger and frustration welled within him. 'You think I tried to steal your wife's notes? I don't need them. We have files in the Vatican, Inquisition Archives that will give us all the information we need. I only came here to expedite our translation and help you.'

'To help me? Are you sure you didn't want to use Lauren's notes for your own ends, whatever they may be?'

'Be careful, Dr Kelly. You have no idea what you're getting involved in. I'm offering to share the burden of this perilous knowledge before it's too late. Don't refuse it.'

'Why not? What will you do?'

Torino clenched his jaw and allowed his rage to cool into something harder. It was pointless saying more – he had already said too much. Kelly's mind was made up. What had the mysterious Sister Chantal said to him – or shown him? 'You'll regret this,' he said coldly, left the house, walked across the gravel and stepped into his limousine. As he sat back and considered his options, he suddenly remembered where he had last heard of Sister Chantal. He called his office in Rome and told them to put him through to Father Seamus Dunleavy at the Institute of Miracles. 'That letter from the Ugandan hospice you brought to my attention last week.'

'The spontaneous healing of the two brothers with Aids?'

'Yes. What was the name of the nun who went missing at around the same time?'

'Sister Chantal.' Torino was about to ask another question when Father Seamus continued: 'I don't know if it's relevant, Father General, but the hospice sent us something else linked to the case.'

'What?'

'A wooden box with ornate carvings. The cured boys claim the nun gave it to them.'

'Describe the carvings.'

'I'll take a photo and send it to you.'

As the image appeared on Torino's phone, his mouth dried. It confirmed that Sister Chantal was somehow linked to Orlando Falcon's Garden of God, and could be crucial to finding it. 'Thank you, Father, that's very helpful. Tell me one more thing. How much do we know about the nun, Sister Chantal?'

'Very little.'

'I want you to find out all you can. Who she is, how long she's been in her order, where she comes from – everything.'

As he hung up he knew he had to manage the next stage carefully. If the geologist and the nun did as Torino predicted, they would become invaluable, unwitting pawns. Otherwise Torino would have no choice but to intervene – aggressively.

He pressed a number on speed dial: 'Marco, it's me. There's something the Church needs you to do.'

17

Ross Kelly didn't know what to think. What Sister Chantal had told him before Torino arrived was so ludicrous, so insane, that he couldn't believe it. When he had challenged Torino, he had expected the Black Pope to confirm his scepticism, but the priest's veiled threats had done the opposite. They had bolstered the nun's credibility.

Immediately Torino had left, Ross checked on Sister Chantal, who was asleep on the couch. He draped a blanket over her, took the opaque plastic bag from her hands and went up to Lauren's office. He powered up Lauren's computer, input her password and opened her private Voynich folder. Before he went into any files, however, he found himself staring at the nun's bag. He wanted to believe the story she had told him, recalling their earlier conversation, because it offered him hope where there was none . . .

'Ross, do you know who wrote the Voynich?'

'No idea. No one does, do they?'

'A Jesuit priest, Father Orlando Falcon, wrote it in the latter half of the sixteenth century, some years after the Spanish conquistador Pizarro conquered the Incan Empire of what is now Ecuador and Peru. It chronicles an ill-fated quest to find Eldorado, the legendary city of gold, for King Charles the Fifth of Spain. And it tells of what Father Orlando and the conquistadors discovered instead.'

'I thought the Voynich was an allegory – a piece of fiction.'

The nun shook her head. 'It was an account of what Orlando Falcon found. When he returned from the New World, the papal Inquisition was at its height. No less than three Grand Inquisitors became pope during the second half of the sixteenth century. The second, Pius the Fifth, was in power when Father Orlando returned to Rome, claiming to have found a miraculous garden that challenged the story of Genesis. Obviously this disturbed the pope and his cardinals. The story went against the prevailing dogma and undermined the scriptures. It threatened everything they and the Church stood for. There could only be one Eden and that must be in the Holy Land, or in Christendom. A second Garden of God couldn't exist in the New World among heathens and savages unless it was the Devil's work. They couldn't ignore Father Orlando, though, because he was a respected Jesuit, a one-time *protégé* of the great Ignatius Loyola. So they pronounced him a heretic. A once fine priest who had become possessed while in the New World.'

'What did they do to him?'

'They demanded he recant. When he refused they handed him over to the torturers, who burnt his feet on hot coals. The next morning his feet had healed. He claimed this miracle was proof of his discovery, but it only confirmed the Grand Inquisitor's conviction that Satan had possessed his soul. The torturers then placed his feet in a wooden vice and crushed the bones. This time his body didn't heal and the Grand Inquisitor concluded the Devil had been driven out. But Father Orlando still refused to recant. For many months they held him in a cell while they decided what to do with him. He was not idle during that time.'

She paused to sip some coffee. Despite his scepticism, Ross was impatient for her to continue.

'When he realized that even the Church couldn't be trusted, and his miraculous discovery might die with him, he decided to record it for a time when it would be better appreciated and understood.' She stared into her cup. 'You must understand one thing. Father Orlando Falcon was an exceptional man. To record his discovery and protect it from those who would exploit it, he created a hybrid language, complete with its own characters. Apart from a few meaningless symbols, which he inserted to confuse those trying to decipher his work, most of his text and illustrations described the wonders he witnessed. And he did all this from memory, while lying in a tiny cell, crippled by torture, using materials smuggled in to him.

'Of course, they eventually found the manuscript, which sealed his fate. They called it *The Devil's Book* because of its unintelligible writing and pictures of a perverted Eden. He was sentenced to be burnt at the stake, the manuscript with him.'

'What happened?'

'He was executed, but an accomplice hid the manuscript in one of the Jesuit libraries. Father Orlando wanted the book hidden in plain view so that one day it would be found, deciphered and his miraculous garden rediscovered.'

'You really believe it existed?'

She looked at him as a patient teacher might at a slow pupil. 'It exists.'

'But what's this got to do with Lauren?'

'Father Orlando wrote most of the manuscript in a hybrid language of two existing tongues so it could eventually be translated. But only by a scholar who was intelligent, dedicated and wise enough to understand his mind and grasp the significance of his discovery. Someone worthy of the garden.'

Ross remembered the night of Lauren's talk at the Beinecke when she had recited the final words of the Voynich: 'Congratulations, fellow scholar, you have read my story and so proved your dedication, intelligence and wisdom. Whatever your faith, God has now chosen you to do what I cannot: to keep His garden safe and ensure its miraculous powers are used for His glory.' He was overcome by wistful yearning. Earlier that day he had resigned from Xplore and been told of Lauren's pregnancy. His only problem then had been his career. Oh, happy days. 'Someone like my wife?' he said.

'Exactly. But Father Orlando always intended one key section of the manuscript to be impossible to translate. Although he used the same text characters as the rest of the document, its language was invented. Without knowing his grammar or vocabulary it could *never* be translated.'

Ross nodded. 'So, though she didn't realize it, my wife had already completed as much of the translation as anyone possibly could?'

'Yes.'

'So we'll never know what's in the last section.'

She seemed unsure how or whether to continue, but eventually said, 'When Father Orlando returned to Rome, he vowed to tell only the pope of what he had found. But when he discovered he couldn't trust even the highest authority with his secret he told the Inquisition he had burnt his chronicles. But he hadn't. He had placed them for safekeeping in a box with his personal effects, and before he was killed he told his accomplice where this box could be found. In it, a notebook gave detailed directions to the garden and outlined the natural hazards that protected it.'

'A separate notebook?'

'A separate notebook, written in his own tongue.' Her unblinking eyes didn't leave his. 'He also gave the accomplice a translation of the last section of what you call the Voynich.'

'What was in it?'

'An account of something even more mysterious than the garden. Something Father Orlando called the source and claimed was the power behind the garden.'

Ross sat back in his chair and crossed his arms. 'How can you possibly know this?'

'Because I am the Keeper,' she said, as though her statement needed no explanation.

'The Keeper?'

'The Keeper of the Garden. My duty is to watch over Father Orlando's discovery until someone dedicated, intelligent and wise enough to understand what to do with it deciphers the main part of his manuscript. When this happens I am to seek out the scholar responsible, confirm that they are worthy, then deliver the book to them and pass on my burden. Father Orlando prophesied that this would come to pass when the garden was under its greatest threat – and it's never been under more threat than it is now.'

Her voice grew more impassioned. 'Every year mankind gets closer to abusing the garden and its source. Each month on the news I see that loggers, farmers, roads and oil companies are encroaching on what was once remote, virgin jungle. I despaired of the document's ever being deciphered until I read about your wife's translation on the Internet, researched her background and discovered her love of conservation. I knew she was the one.' Sister Chantal reached into her case and pulled out a vacuum-sealed plastic bag. As she did so a leather pouch fell on to the floor. It was dusted with fragments of crushed rock. Their metallic iridescence reminded Ross of the Schreibersite rock sample he had given Lauren on his return from Uzbekistan, but their crystalline translucency was different – unique. He studied the fragments but couldn't identify which rock they came from – and he knew most rocks.

He switched his attention to the plastic bag. As she opened the seal, a faint, musty smell tainted the air. 'This is Father Orlando's book of directions to the garden.' She pulled it out and opened it carefully. The last few pages were a different colour from the rest. 'To keep them together, the translation of the Voynich's astrological section was bound into the back many years ago.' She passed it to him. The small book's grained leather had been carefully preserved but it was undeniably ancient. 'It's proof of what I say. If your wife could read it she'd have no doubt.'

He opened the book. The yellowed pages were covered in neat calligraphy. To his surprise, he could understand most of it. 'It's in Spanish.'

'Orlando Falcon's native tongue. He wrote it before his return to Rome, but it's appropriate that it's not in Latin, the language of the Church. After they betrayed him he vowed never to trust Rome again. We shouldn't either.'

'But you're a nun.'

'As a nun I'm able to stay anonymous, occupying my time in performing good works around the world. Father Orlando never lost faith in God, only in those who wield power in Rome. They don't serve God, only themselves and the power of the Church. They are dangerous, Ross. Ruthless.'

'I'm no fan of the Catholic Church but I can't believe—'

'There are those in Rome who would do *any-thing* to protect and promote their precious church – even if it went against Christ's teachings.' Again he glimpsed desperation in her serene gaze.

He went back to the book and carefully turned the pages. The first few were covered with drawings that made him take a sharp breath. They were crude but familiar: an oval flower unlike anything in nature and a drawing of an oddly shaped naked woman, similar to the illustrations in the Voynich. Even the neat Spanish script had echoes of its text.

He flicked to the end, to the mismatched pages: the translation of the impossible section of the Voynich that Lauren had delayed their holiday to solve. It was also in Spanish, with many instances of '*el origen*' – the source. The more he studied the book, the more his eyes told him what his head couldn't accept: that Orlando Falcon's garden might be genuine. The implications made his heart beat faster and filled him with questions: 'Where did you get this? Who gave it to you?'

'The last Keeper.'

'How long have you had it?'

Again those unsettling eyes locked on his. 'Whatever I tell you won't change what you believe. Let the book be my proof. Just accept that if your wife saw it she'd know it was genuine.'

'You want Lauren to take over as the Keeper? Is that it? How long have you been the Keeper? How many were there before you? How were *you* chosen?'

She gave him a weary smile. 'No more questions. You'll discover everything for yourself in due course. But I promised to protect Father Orlando's legacy and I can't rest until I hand over his notebook to the translator of the Voynich – your wife, Lauren. Now that his prophecy has come to pass, Lauren's destiny is to be the new Keeper, but before she can fulfil her role the garden's miraculous powers must first cure her. Only then can she take over my burden and protect his legacy. Don't you see, Ross? We have no choice. We have to get back to the garden.' She reached across the table to place her hand on his. 'Ross, you and I need the same thing. You want your wife to wake. And I can't sleep until she does.'

18

Now, sitting in Lauren's office, Ross stared at the opaque plastic bag he had taken from the sleeping Sister Chantal and reflected on how she had hidden it when Torino, an officer of Rome, had appeared in the kitchen. It was clear that, whatever Ross thought, they both believed the Voynich was more than a fairytale.

He unsealed the bag and re-examined the ancient notebook. Apart from a few damaged pages it was in remarkable condition. He retrieved a Spanish/English dictionary from Lauren's bookshelf, and studied the neat Spanish text. For some minutes he pored over the last mismatched pages, fascinated by the vague references to *el origen*. Father General Leonardo Torino had also mentioned the term, using the Latin *radix*.

He turned his attention to the main part of the notebook. It contained a set of directions, including landmarks, compass settings and astronomical data with charts that showed which stars to follow at different times of the year. There were pages and pages of instructions detailing how to find the garden, but no map, and there was no way of drawing a useful one from the contents: only one place was mentioned by name, the town from which the quest had started. All subsequent directions related to that point and relied on compass settings, the position of the stars and key landmarks. It was as though Father Orlando Falcon had viewed his quest into the jungle as a voyage on an uncharted green ocean and navigated accordingly. One would have to go to the starting point and follow the directions wherever they led. Though they were detailed, the few physical landmarks had vague, poetic names, including the endpoint, which Falcon called El Jardin del Dios, the Garden of God. Even if they were genuine, and the garden existed, the chance of finding it was dauntingly slim.

Ross referred back to the Voynich translation in Lauren's notes, and compared the beginning of the story, which described the journey to the garden, with Falcon's notebook. When he looked at the general sequence of events in conjunction with the more detailed stages mentioned in Falcon's notebook they tallied.

He went on the Internet and researched the Inquisition. Just as Sister Chantal had told him, three Grand Inquisitors had become popes in the late sixteenth century, and the second had indeed been Pius V. He searched for Orlando Falcon and found nothing, but when he checked historical references to Pizarro's conquest of the New World the chronology tallied with when Sister Chantal claimed that Falcon had undertaken his quest.

Yet however much he wanted to believe in Orlando Falcon's Garden of God, he couldn't. Ross was a scientist, a geologist. How could such a place exist? It was too fanciful to be credible. His head ached. He was too close to this. He needed perspective, to speak to someone he could trust, and who knew something about the subject. What had Sister Chantal said? *Let the book be my proof. If your wife saw it she'd know it was genuine.* Lauren couldn't read it, but he knew someone who could.

He picked up the phone and dialled.

19

Many people misunderstood Elizabeth Quinn. Some called her a dyke because she didn't have a boyfriend, but she wasn't a lesbian. She just found most men uninteresting. In fact, though she professed to love mankind, she often found *people* uninteresting. Her lens on the world had two settings: wide angle and close-up, with little between. She cared passionately about big-picture issues, such as the fate of the planet, and she loved the honesty and purity of a detailed mathematical problem, but for an expert in linguistics and the daughter of a diplomat who had travelled the world, she cared little for the small talk of day-to-day life.

Lean and statuesque, she looked like a warrior queen. Even when you factored in the thick glasses, second-hand jeans, hemp jacket and T-shirts proclaiming her outspoken views on saving the planet. Beneath the red curls, however, was a first-class analytical brain. And beneath her *Save Gaia!* T-shirts there beat a passionate heart. For all her impatience with people there was one person she did care about – idolized, even: the brilliant, compassionate, articulate and beautiful Lauren Kelly. She even forgave her for marrying an oilman.

'This is amazing. It's *definitely* genuine,' she pronounced, after flipping through a few pages of Orlando Falcon's book. She had come over immediately Ross called, and had listened avidly while he told her about Torino and Sister Chantal.

'How do you know?'

'I helped Lauren with the computer and mathematical stuff, but I'm a specialist in linguistics and literary forensics, and I've spent a lot of time studying the Voynich. This is by the same hand. I'm certain of it. Look at the *i* and the tail on the *g*. Lauren and I often wondered if this garden could exist.'

Ross stopped pacing. 'Even though it's impossible?'

'Why's it impossible? Are you saying you geologists have discovered *everything* on the planet? Guys are finding new things all the time. Remember a couple of years ago when they found a new species of gorilla in the Congo, and those pigmy humans in Indonesia? Not to mention the countless new plants and animals being discovered in jungles all the time. Why couldn't a garden like this be hidden away somewhere?'

'A garden of miracles? Don't you think someone would have found it by now?'

She tapped the notebook. 'Hello. Someone did, apparently, four and half centuries ago. Orlando Falcon.'

'But I'm a scientist.'

'So am I. And our job's to unravel mysteries, not dismiss them. Use the scientific method, Ross. Develop a hypothesis. Here's a challenge. Let's assume the garden does exist. Can you, as a geologist, build a hypothesis to explain it?'

'Some of it, of course.'

'Okay, go for it.' She reached for the computer mouse and, as she scrolled through the beginning of Lauren's translation, Ross sat down beside her and together they read what was on the screen:

. . . Our quest was ill fated from the outset. We began in the cloud forests high in the mountains. The mist was so dense we could not see our feet. In the first week, seven soldiers fell to their deaths, disappearing into the ghostly white void. When we eventually descended to the plain, an impenetrable jungle awaited us, pierced only by a mighty river. We built rafts and let the current carry us deep into the green unknown.

For days the river took us where it willed, through violent rapids and rocks, until it drove us towards a waterfall. Two rafts were smashed, drowning all on board. Those craft remaining to us were propelled headlong through the waterfall, then along a narrow waterway, inhabited by dragon-like creatures. More of our number were taken.

*We left the rafts to cut our way through the jungle.
By now the conquerors had become the conquered.
Infested with beasts and disease, the forest was so
dense that time lost any meaning. Day and night
became one. As we marched, snakes bit the soldiers'
feet and legs, then disappeared into the thick undergrowth, while unseen beasts lurked in the viridian
depths. I soon despaired of finding any city of
gold. Death was the only thing we would discover
there.*

*Lost, our numbers depleted, I showed the captain
my chronicle in which I had recorded key landmarks,
compass bearings and the position of the stars. It will
lead us home, I told him. But the captain could not
return without gold.*

'Nothing too controversial so far,' Zeb mused.
'Carry on.'

*We struck deeper into the infernal jungle. Weary and
in despair, we endured many obstacles before entering
a vast cave, a cathedral of rock, seamed with gold. We
followed the gold downward to a towering chamber,
as hot as any oven, lit by a single opening in the high
ceiling. The gold led us lower to a river of fire bridged
by a causeway of black rock. We traversed the causeway and entered more caves. The air was poisonous,
heavy with brimstone, and the walls dripped burning
rain. We covered our mouths, shielded our eyes and
went on, but terror gripped me because I feared I was
about to enter Hell. Finally I saw light. Then a sweet,*

eerie sound filled my ears. I rushed to the light and was almost blinded by the beauty of what I saw. This was not Hell, but Heaven on Earth, the Garden of God . . .

Zeb paused the mouse. 'Still okay?'

'I think so. The seam of gold could have been either true gold or pyrites. The subterranean lava stream and sulphur caves dripping with sulphuric acid are possible geological features and often found together.'

'Okay. A light leads them outside into a garden filled with strange plants unlike any in the outside world, and walled on all sides by steep cliffs. What about the plants?'

Despite his scepticism Ross was responding now to her enthusiasm. 'If the enclosed garden is ringed by lava it could possibly have evolved its unique ecosystem, entirely independent of the jungle outside. A teenager recently discovered a complete prehistoric ecosystem in Israel, sealed off for millions of years. The Ayalon Cave is pitch black, two and a half kilometres long, has its own lake and lies deep under layers of impermeable chalk. Its ecosystem is powered not by the sun but by creatures that oxidize sulphur as an energy source. At least eight new species, which date back millions of years, have been found there.'

'There you go. This ain't so hard, is it?' She scrolled down the text. 'How about the perfectly circular lake in the middle of the garden fed by a stream of glowing water from the forbidden caves at the far end of the garden?'

'A circular lake's not uncommon: there's a perfectly round lake in the middle of the Congo rainforest. The glowing water could be phosphorescence.' Reaching over Zeb's shoulder, he pointed out a picture on Lauren's desk. 'What about these round-bellied naked women who live in the forbidden caves and sing in pure voices?'

'Scholars have always called them the nymphs but in the Voynich they're the Eves.'

'Okay, what are they doing there? And the other creatures featured in the Voynich?'

'You said the garden could have its own unique ecosystem where plants and animals evolved independent of the outside world. The nymphs and other creatures may be like the pigmy humans found on the isolated Indonesian island, or those new species in the Israeli cave.'

'I suppose it's possible.'

Zeb shrugged. 'That's all a hypothesis needs to be.'

He tapped the screen. 'Okay, but this is the part where I start to have problems.' He read aloud: ' "When the injured soldiers fed from the plants and drank from the lake, their wounds and broken bones healed miraculously. Even those close to death revived and recovered full health." '

Zeb ran her fingers through her red curls. She wanted to believe in the garden. She loved the idea of its being the core of Gaia's nurturing goodness,

Mother Earth's heart, within which anything was possible. But she knew that simply wishing something didn't make it so. She needed a reason to believe. 'Okay, we're still playing hypothesis. What could explain a unique, isolated garden, with its own ecosystem in which the water and plants have miraculous healing properties?'

Ross shrugged. 'Orlando Falcon thought it was a divine place – the Garden of God.'

'But he was a priest. You're a scientist. How do *you* explain it?'

He looked up at the framed print on the wall above Lauren's desk: a centuries-old map of the world. Large swathes of the ancient chart were marked '*Terra Incognita*', unknown land, and its oceans featured drawings of sea monsters with the warning 'Beware! Here Be Dragons.' As Ross studied it, a strange expression appeared on his face, as though he had seen, or thought of, something he couldn't quite believe.

Zeb caught the excitement in his eyes. 'What is it, Ross?' she said. 'Tell me.'

20

Ross didn't answer immediately. He kept staring at the ancient map above Lauren's desk, contrasting it with Xplore's precise geological map of the globe, which showed not only the surface of the entire planet but also what lay beneath. The insight that excited him came from the last time he had used Xplore's map to present his ill-fated ancient-oil theory to Underwood and Kovacs on the day he'd resigned.

He grabbed the mouse from Zeb and returned to the description in Lauren's translation of the lava stream and poisonous caves dripping with burning rain. It reminded him of the toxic conditions prevalent when the world was young, sparking a connection in his mind that was so outlandish it couldn't possibly be valid. Could it? Despite his scepticism, his heart beat faster. It was the one hypothesis that might explain everything. He scrolled forward to the end of the story where the soldiers die while searching for something mysterious, hidden deep within the forbidden caves at the far end of the garden, convinced it's treasure. The scholar priest tries to stop them but all are killed and the stream runs red with their blood.

Ross grabbed Orlando Falcon's book of directions and flipped to the last pages, with the translation of the final section of the Voynich. As he scanned the text he kept seeing, again and again, the words '*el origen*', the source. Everything pointed to his hypothesis – however outlandish it seemed.

'What?' Zeb demanded again. Her eyes were huge behind her thick glasses. 'What is it?'

He tried to organize his jumbled thoughts. 'Fact: there was a moment on Earth before which the planet was barren and after which it wasn't. And once you consider the significance of this improbable, miraculous but undeniable moment in its history, *anything* is possible.'

'You're talking about the time when life began on Earth?'

'Not just when the miraculous spark of life happened, but how it happened and, crucially, *where*.'

Zeb nodded slowly. 'Okay, so we're talking about when and where life began on Earth. Go on.'

'*If,* as a growing body of evidence suggests, the seeds of life came from asteroid-borne amino acids hitting the planet four billion years ago and *if* the place where the seminal asteroid hit the Earth's crust has been preserved – in the same way that three-point-eight-billion-year-old Issua supracrustal rock in west Greenland and four-billion-year-old crust of Acasta Gneisses in north-western Canada have been preserved – *then* Orlando Falcon's Eden-like Garden of God could be the epicentre of life, the original point of impact from which all life began, somehow frozen in space and time. In the final section, Falcon even mentions something he calls *el origen*, the source.' He paused, but Zeb said nothing. Her face had paled. 'What's more,' he continued, '*if* the garden, or its source, does exist and *if* it's the point at which all life began, *then* it might still contain the original primordial soup, the life-giving concentrate, the precursor of DNA – which might explain its strange flora and fauna and its miraculous healing properties.'

There was a beat before Zeb spoke. When she did it was barely a whisper. 'So, like the nun said, something in the garden might cure Lauren?'

'Yes,' he said slowly, as hope seeped through him. *If* – and it was an enormous *if* – this bizarre garden was what his hypothesis supposed it might be, not only could he save Lauren but he would uncover one of the holy grails of geology, perhaps the holy grail of all science: the origin of life.

Zeb sat back in her chair, held her head in her hands and gave a nervous laugh. 'Fuck. The Garden of God in the Voynich is the womb of Gaia, the cradle of all life on Earth. Fuck, Ross, that's one hell of a hypothesis. No wonder that priest's got his panties in a twist.'

He laughed with her. 'We've still got to prove the hypothesis.'

'There's one way to do that,' Zeb said, reaching for Orlando Falcon's notebook. 'Find the garden.'

Ross thought of Lauren and the baby and his excitement evaporated. 'I can't leave Lauren to go on a wild-goose chase. Not when she needs me most.'

'It's not a wild-goose chase,' said a voice behind them.

Ross swivelled round. 'How long have you been there?'

'Long enough to hear your theory.'

'You must be Sister Chantal,' said Zeb, standing up. 'Hello, I'm Zeb Quinn. I worked with Lauren on the manuscript.'

Sister Chantal walked across the room and clasped Zeb's hand in both of hers, then picked up Falcon's notebook from the desk and clutched it to her chest. 'Are you both coming with me to find the garden?'

'You can count me in,' said Zeb.

'Whoa, not so fast,' said Ross. He pointed to the notebook. 'Even if the garden does exist — and it's a big if — some of the clues are pretty cryptic, to say the least.'

'I can interpret them,' said Sister Chantal.

'Really? How come you're so confident?'

'I'm the Keeper. I've followed them in the past.'

'To get to the garden?' Ross frowned in disbelief. 'You've *been* there?'

'Yes.'

'So why do you need us to help you go back?'

'Because I'm old, the journey is difficult and it was a very long time ago.' She tapped the notebook. 'To find our way we'll need to follow this step by step.'

Ross rubbed his temples in frustration, unable to determine if the old woman was telling the truth or was a delusional fantasist. 'Sister, I want to believe your story. I really want to believe there's a miraculous garden out there that can save my wife. But if you think I'm going to leave Lauren in her current state, just because you say this garden exists and you've been there, you're wrong.'

'But what about your theory?'

'This isn't a science experiment. I can't leave my wife to check out an improbable hypothesis. I need more. I need proof.'

'I showed you the book.'

He shook his head.

She paused. 'I did have something that might have convinced you of the garden's healing power, but not enough. I used the last of it . . .' she levelled her beautiful eyes on Ross '. . . for Lauren.'

Ross's heart jumped. 'What are you saying?' Suddenly he remembered how he had found Sister Chantal kneeling by Lauren's bed – near the feeding tube. Then he remembered the nun's empty leather pouch. He felt sick. 'You gave her something?'

She gazed evenly at him. 'Only what I had left, which wasn't much. It was a futile gesture but I wanted desperately to make her well. I'd have given her more if I'd had it. I'm sure it'll have had some effect, but it won't cure her, I'm afraid.'

'What exactly did you give her?' demanded Zeb.

Ross jumped up and reached for the phone. Not only was the old nun delusional but she had poisoned his wife. 'What have you done? For Christ's sake, what have you done?' The phone rang as his hand touched it. He put it on speaker and glared at Sister Chantal. 'Ross Kelly.'

'Ross, it's Diana.' Lauren's mother sounded breathless. 'I'm calling from the hospital.'

Zeb's face turned pale and something cold uncoiled in Ross's stomach. 'What's wrong? What's happened?'

'Don't worry, Ross, it's good,' she said quickly. 'There's been a small but significant improvement. Lauren's off the ventilator. She's breathing for herself and the baby's getting oxygen. They've warned me not to get too excited because her prognosis hasn't really changed, but the baby's doing well.'

He was flooded with relief and shock. He continued to glare at the nun. 'When did they discover she was doing better, Diana?'

'Less than an hour ago.'

'Do they know how it happened?'

'Not yet. They're running tests – but the doctors said it was *very* unusual to get such a sudden improvement. Frankly it's a minor miracle, Ross.'

'I'll come over.'

'You don't need to. It's late and, like I said, they're

running tests. I'll stay with her till midnight. Why don't you come in first thing tomorrow morning?'

He glanced at his watch. It *was* late, and he wouldn't know any more until the test results were through. 'I'll do that, Diana. Thanks for letting me know.'

'See you tomorrow. Good night.'

He hung up, trying to process what had just happened. He didn't know whether to feel angry or grateful for the nun's meddling.

It was Zeb who broke the silence. 'You gave Lauren something from the garden?'

'Yes.'

'What?' demanded Ross.

'It doesn't matter. What matters is that it was all I had left, and it wasn't enough. We need more. A lot more.' She seemed suddenly very tired. 'Ross, I don't care how you explain Father Orlando's garden – religiously, scientifically, spiritually. Just know that it has the power to cure your wife and a lot more besides.' She slumped on to the chair beside him. 'And we haven't much time to find it. The medicine I gave Lauren was what I had saved for myself to help me make the arduous journey. I'm frail, and without me to interpret the directions I fear you'll never find it.' She smiled. 'So, whatever decision you make, Ross, make it soon. Because, with or without you, I'm going.'

21

That night, Ross slept on his decision, dreaming of his fragile family: Lauren and the baby, clinging to life; the baby trying desperately to enter the world, the mother fighting not to leave it.

While he slept, the assassin who had once been *la mano sinistra del diavolo* stealthily carried out his master's instructions.

First he attached digital taps to Ross's home phone lines.

Later, in the early hours of the morning, he entered the deserted corridors of the Sacred Heart Hospital wearing an orderly's uniform and carrying a black bag. When he was sure he was alone he entered room thirty-six of the spinal-injuries unit. As he approached the bed he checked the name on the chart and opened his bag. For a long moment he stared at the patient's inert form, listening to the rhythmic sound of the instruments that kept her alive. All the time his face remained expressionless, betraying no hint of what he was thinking.

Eventually, he reached into the bag and did what the Father General had instructed him to do.

Then he cast a final glance at the bed and left. No one registered his presence, and if the bed's occupant had seen him she was in no position to tell.

22

Ross had hoped to wake having decided on a course of action, but he was as conflicted as he'd been when he'd gone to bed. And when he got to the hospital with his father, Lauren's neurologist didn't help matters.

'She's certainly improved,' said Greenbloom, 'although we don't know why. She can now breathe unaided and the swelling round the brainstem has lessened. The scans also revealed that some fractures on her damaged vertebrae are no longer visible, which again we can't explain. All this is good, but she's still in a deep coma, level one on the Rancho, and level three on the Glasgow coma scale.'

'How about the baby?'

'Its prognosis is marginally better,' the neurologist said cautiously.

'So what you're saying is, there's been a sudden improvement but the outlook hasn't changed?'

'Yes.'

Though Ross welcomed the removal of the

ventilator, Greenbloom's analysis made it hard to feel upbeat. As he ate breakfast with his father in the small hospital canteen, he kept thinking about Father Orlando's garden. He waited for his father to finish his eggs and hash browns, then told him about it. He expected no-nonsense Sam Kelly to demand why he was even considering 'all that garbage'. Instead, he cradled his coffee cup in his large, calloused hands and frowned thoughtfully.

'All I know as a farmer is that nature's got a funny way of surprising you. So I'm not going to sit here and say there's no way the garden exists. Son, you're the one who left the farm to go to college. What's your education telling you? Could it exist?'

Ross considered his hypothesis again. 'I guess it's possible, in theory.'

'Could it help Lauren? I read somewhere that the jungles of the world are full of medicines and cures modern science doesn't yet know about.'

Ross thought of Lauren's improvement. 'Again, it's possible.'

'Possible sounds pretty good right now,' said his father. 'A hell of a lot better than what Dr Greenbloom keeps telling us.' He looked hard at Ross. 'Son, you've never been one to sit on your rump and wait for something to happen. What's stopping you now?'

'Leaving Lauren and the baby. If I search for this place I could be away, in the middle of nowhere, for at least a couple of months.'

Fire ignited in his father's usually calm eyes. 'I'll

tell you one thing, son. If there was anything I could have done, however long a shot, to save your unborn brother all those years ago, or your mother when the cancer took her, I'd have done it in a heartbeat.' He smiled sadly. 'You're lucky, son. You *can* do something. I don't know your profession too well, but I understand it involves finding stuff. It's what you do and you're good at it. If there's even the slightest chance this garden exists then *you* can find it. And if saving Lauren and Junior means leaving them for a few months, then go ahead. I'll be here to mind things. I'm selling the farm, anyway. My heart ain't in it any more and you don't want it. Old Lou Jackman's made me a decent offer and I'm going to retire. So, don't you worry about Lauren and my grandchild. Let Lauren's mother and me watch over them for a while.'

Ross felt a rush of gratitude and hope. Here was something he could do at last. 'You sure, Dad?'

'Hell, son, I've never been more sure of anything in my life. Say goodbye to Lauren, explain why you're going, then do your damnedest to save her. If you do nothing, you might regret it for the rest of your life.'

Filled with new purpose, Ross strode to Lauren's room and reached for his phone. The enthusiasm in Zeb Quinn's voice made him smile. 'Hey, Ross, have you decided yet?'

'Are you still in?' he asked.

'You bet. Are we going or what?'

'Yes,' he said. 'We're going.'

Her tone changed. 'You're okay about leaving Lauren?'

'Yes.' He tried to quash his doubts and match her enthusiasm. 'But only because I'm doing it for her.'

23

Overalls discarded, Marco Bazin sat on his bed in the Best Western Motel, a few yards from the Sacred Heart Hospital, and waited for Ross Kelly to reappear on his screen. The pictures on his laptop and the sound in his earphones came from the wireless surveillance camera and microphone he had concealed last night in the picture frame above Lauren Kelly's bed. Torino believed that whatever plans Ross had, he would open his heart to his comatose wife.

When the Superior General had called yesterday evening Bazin had been waiting in a Manhattan hotel. His instructions had been both cryptic and explicit: a treacherous nun had joined forces with the atheist geologist and together they posed a mortal danger to the Holy Mother Church. They threatened to expose and abuse a sacred place of great power that rightfully belonged to the Church – and *only* the Church. At first, Ross was simply to be followed, but if he threatened to publicize any details of his quest Bazin was to apprehend the nun and silence him. Permanently.

After he had placed a simple digital listening device on the Kellys' home phone line, Bazin had gone straight to the hospital and concealed the surveillance equipment. In the last two decades the demands of his profession had become increasingly sophisticated. No longer was it sufficient to be expert in handling lethal weapons. Survival now depended on proficiency in a range of relevant technologies.

Bazin sat up straight, suddenly alert.

On screen, Ross entered the room and sat beside his wife. The tender way he held her hand aroused in Bazin a spark of emotion, which he quickly suppressed. He pressed the record button on the laptop and accessed Torino's private email, sending him the encrypted video files in real time. If Ross revealed anything it would be now.

There was a knock at his door.

The sound penetrated his headphones. 'I don't need Housekeeping. My room's fine,' he called.

Knock, knock.

'I said no, thanks.'

Knock, knock.

Frowning, Bazin took off the headphones, reached for the Glock beside his bed and walked to the door. He peered out of the peephole. The person was standing too close, blocking his view. He slipped the latch and opened the door. 'I don't need—'

Click.

Before Bazin could step back into the room, a gun, not unlike his own, had been levelled at his temple.

'Drop the piece. Nice and slow.'

Bazin did as he was told.

'Oh, my, this is too easy. I heard you got the big C, lost a nut or something. Didn't figure *la mano sinistra del diavolo* had become a total pussy, though. Step back into the room.' The man kicked Bazin's gun through the door then closed it.

It was Vinnie Pesci, the Gambini family's American enforcer. Don Gambini had hired Bazin in the past. Since he had pledged his allegiance to Torino, Bazin had kept a low profile, careful to use a variety of passports and identities, but he had always known the day would arrive when his old life caught up with him. 'What do you want, Vinnie? I've retired. I paid back the money the Gambinis gave me for the last hit.'

'That's not how it goes. No one retires until Don Gambini says so. Anyway, he figures you're full of shit and working for the Trapanis now.'

'I told you, I've retired.'

'Oh, yeah?' Pesci indicated the laptop and headphones on the bed. 'You're working for *someone*. Here's the thing. The old man wants the left hand of the Devil – in a bag. And what Don Gambini wants, Don Gambini gets.'

Bazin said nothing. In the past Pesci would never have dared come alone.

Pesci reached into his jacket and drew out a surgeon's saw and a folded plastic sheet, which he threw on to the floor. 'I always admired your style so you can see this as homage to *la mano sinistra del diavolo*. You know the score. Lay out the sheet and I'll do it quick. Just like you used to. Fuck about and I'll cut off your hand while you're still breathing.'

'Don't do this, Vinnie. Don't make me kill you.'

Pesci laughed at that. 'Kill *me*? What the fuck you talkin' about?'

'I can't let you kill me before I've had absolution.'

Pesci levelled his gun at Bazin's groin. 'I'll give you absolution, pal. Lay out the plastic and kneel like a good Catholic boy. Or I'll *make* you kneel. You hear what I'm saying?'

In his mind – and nightmares – Bazin had gone through this moment many times, wondering what he could do to save himself if ever *la mano sinistra del diavolo* came for *him*. His answer was always the same: not a lot. Unless the killer made a mistake.

Fortunately Pesci had. A big one. He hadn't unfolded the plastic before he'd dropped it on to the floor. Bazin picked it up and threw it out in front of him. It billowed like an opaque sail, momentarily screening him from Pesci. In that instant Bazin leapt low and hard at the other man. Before Pesci could get off a shot Bazin had located his solar plexus with his left hand and his windpipe with the right. The blow to the solar plexus incapacitated him. The one to the windpipe killed him.

Standing over Pesci's body, Bazin felt no elation. Not only was he in more need of absolution than ever now but he knew Gambini would send another Vinnie Pesci to hunt him down, then another, until sooner or later he would be wrapped in black plastic and buried. If he wanted to live long enough for absolution he'd have to find somewhere on Earth where Gambini and his other enemies from his old life couldn't find him.

One of the two phones by his bed began to ring. He wondered who could be calling him. Then he realized it was the phone Torino had given him. Only the priest knew the number.

'Are you watching?' His half-brother sounded breathless with excitement.

Bazin glanced at the laptop. 'I can see Kelly talking to his wife.'

'You haven't been listening?'

'I've been kinda busy.'

'Listen to what they're saying, then go back over the recordings but tell no one what you hear. After that I need you to do something. And if you do this right I promise you that the Holy Father himself will absolve you of your sins.'

Bazin gazed down at Pesci's still twitching corpse. 'What do I have to do?'

'Kelly and the false nun who visited him yesterday are leaving the country. They're taking someone with them – an academic called Quinn. I have matters to arrange in the Vatican, but I want you to follow them and not let them out of your sight.'

'Where are they going?'

'Listen to what Ross is telling his wife. It explains everything. Stay with him and the nun wherever they lead you. They'll be going off the beaten track, into the jungle. Can you handle that?'

Bazin thought of Gambini's people and the countless others who would be hunting for him. He thought of disappearing into the jungle. Then he thought of the Holy Father offering him redemption. He smiled. 'Yes,' he said. 'That works for me.'

PART TWO

Terra Incognita

24

Peru

South America's third largest country lies just south of the equator, on the north-west coast of South America, and is divided into three main areas: the narrow Pacific coastal strip to the west, which includes the capital, Lima; the central mighty Andes mountain range, which runs like a distorted spine down the western side of the continent; and the eastern section, which covers more than half of the country and forms the western part of the fabled Amazon basin.

Overlapping the borders of nine countries and covering a significant proportion of South America, the Amazon basin dwarfs even a relatively large country like Peru. Its legendary river cuts across the entire continent, from the Peruvian Andes in the west to the Atlantic Ocean in the east, a distance of more than four thousand miles. The Amazon, including its tributaries, holds an astonishing fifth of the world's fresh water — more than the next six largest rivers combined – and its flow is so powerful that it dilutes the salt water of the Atlantic more than a hundred miles from the shoreline. Manau, an island in the river's mouth, is as large as Denmark.

The Amazon jungle is no less awe-inspiring. It extends over 1.2 billion acres – of which only a fraction has been explored – and accounts for more than half of all the rainforest in the world. Teeming with life, it hosts a diversity of organisms found nowhere else on Earth: more than two million insect species, a hundred thousand plant, two thousand fish and six hundred mammal – and these are just the ones that are known. New species are discovered every year. The Amazon is also the source of many rare and valuable minerals.

Reading these facts in his guidebook both discouraged and encouraged Ross Kelly as his domestic Aerocondor flight flew across the Andes from Lima's Aeroporto Internacional Jorge Chávez to the Northern Highlands. The sheer scale of the Amazon emphasized how difficult it would be to find what he was seeking, but it also promised that *anything* could be lost in its massive, uncharted forest, including Falcon's magical garden. Most of all, though, it made him grasp the enormity of his task.

After he had decided to seek out the garden, he had allowed himself a rush of hope, but now he felt flat and alone. At Xplore he had been able to draw on all the company's resources: surveys, tests and field personnel. Now he was in a strange country with only a frail, possibly insane nun, an intense PhD student and an ancient notebook of cryptic clues to help him.

He glanced to his left, where Zeb was engrossed in a history of Peru. Beside her, Sister Chantal lay back in her seat, mouth open, snoring. She had forsaken her habit and wimple for practical cotton trousers, walking boots and a fleece.

Zeb nudged him. 'You okay?'

'Yeah.'

'Don't worry about Lauren. She's in good hands.' As soon as they'd arrived in Lima, Ross had called his father, and again just before the domestic flight had taken off. Of course, there had been no change in Lauren's condition, but he couldn't stop worrying about whether he had done the right thing in leaving her. His nightmare was that before she died she would wake momentarily, call him, and he wouldn't be there to comfort her and say goodbye. Zeb tapped her book. 'This'll cheer you up. I know where Falcon started his journey.'

'We knew that already – in Cajamarca. That's why we're flying there.'

Zeb flashed him a withering look. 'I mean I know *exactly* where it started.'

He reached into his crumpled linen jacket and took out his notes. Falcon had written that the quest began in Cajamarca outside a place called La Prisión del Rey, the king's prison. 'You know where La Prisión del Rey is?'

'Yep.'

It did cheer him. If the first cryptic clue tallied with the real world, independent of any interpretation from Sister Chantal, it lent credibility to the other clues. Particularly as he hadn't yet found any place called La Prisión del Rey in his guidebook.

'It goes back to the conquest of Peru by the Spanish, one of the most bizarre events in history. In 1532 Francisco Pizarro crossed the mountains from the coast, with fewer than two hundred men, and established himself in the great Inca plaza in Cajamarca. The Inca emperor, Atahualpa, with an unarmed retinue of thousands entered the plaza in good faith to meet the strange white men.

'Pizarro didn't meet Atahualpa, though. Instead he sent his chaplain, who approached the Inca and informed him that a certain God the Father had sent His Son, part of a Trinity, to Earth, where He was crucified. Before that happened, the chaplain explained, the Son, whose name was Jesus Christ, had conferred His power upon an Apostle, Peter, and Peter had passed that power, successively, to other men, called popes, one of whom had commissioned Charles the Fifth of Spain to conquer and convert the Inca and his people. Atahualpa's only hope of salvation, the chaplain concluded, was to swear allegiance to Jesus Christ and acknowledge himself a subject of Charles the Fifth.

'When he heard this, Atahualpa informed the chaplain that he, the Inca, was the greatest prince on earth and that he would be the subject of no man. This pope, he said, must be mad to talk of giving away countries that didn't belong to him. As for Jesus Christ who had died, the Inca was sorry, but – and here he pointed to the sun – "My God still lives in the heavens and looks down on His children."'

Ross smiled. He liked Atahualpa's style.

Zeb continued: 'The waiting conquistadors were hiding in the massive buildings that surrounded the square and, when the chaplain returned with the Inca's reply, Pizarro, his foot soldiers and cavalry erupted into the plaza. Muskets and cannons firing, they slaughtered between two thousand and ten thousand unarmed people that day and took the emperor prisoner.'

'All in the name of God and the Catholic Church, no doubt,' said Ross.

'No doubt. In captivity, Atahualpa spoke often with the Spanish and soon understood that, despite all talk of popes and Trinities, it was love of gold that brought the white men to his country. To gain his freedom he offered Pizarro enough gold – tears of the sun, as the Inca called it – to fill a room measuring seventeen by twenty-two feet to a height of nine feet. Soon afterwards Atahualpa was executed, but the king's ransom was paid and the chamber where it was measured, El Cuarto del Rescate, was said to be the one in which the Inca king was imprisoned – La Prisión del Rey.'

Ross thumbed through his Lonely Planet guide-book and there, on page 336, was the major tourist attraction in Cajamarca, the only Inca building left standing in the town – El Cuarto del Rescate.

Just then, the captain announced that the plane was starting its descent and, out of the window, Ross saw Cajamarca sitting high on the slopes of the eastern Andes, above the clouds and surrounded by forest. Beyond, in the far distance, he glimpsed what looked like the shore of a great green ocean: the Amazon.

As he dreamt of what he might find in its midst, he didn't notice a man staring at him from five rows back.

25

Rome

The Vatican's Sala Clementina was a tall room with a marble floor, the upper walls and high ceiling decorated with a fresco that seemed to stretch to Heaven itself. The Congregation for the Causation of Saints often used it to plead the case for their candidates. Today only three men occupied the large space: the three so-called popes, the most powerful men in Rome.

On the left, resplendent in the scarlet robes of his office, sat Cardinal Prefect Guido Vasari, the Red Pope. Tall and lean with a hooked nose and dark, hangdog eyes, he was head of the Congregation for the Doctrine of the Faith, the oldest and most powerful of the nine congregations in the Curia. Originally called the Inquisition, and tasked with ruthlessly protecting the Holy Mother Church from heresy, its role had evolved to promoting and safeguarding Catholic doctrine throughout the world. Many, however, still referred to the Cardinal

Prefect by his original title: the Grand Inquisitor.

On the right, in sober black robes, sat Father General Leonardo Torino, the Black Pope, the Superior General of the Society of Jesus, the order founded by Ignatius Loyola and famed for its intellectual rigour and asceticism. Centuries ago, during the Counter-reformation, when the Inquisition had employed fear and torture to stem the flow of Protestantism, the Society of Jesus had favoured intellect and argument. Jesuits prided themselves on understanding the beliefs, customs and languages of potential converts better than they did themselves. This included the newest religion of all: science.

A stout, white-robed man sat at the head of the table, between Vasari and Torino: the pontiff.

Torino glanced at the other two and felt a surge of sympathy for Orlando Falcon. He imagined his brother Jesuit standing before these old men's predecessors, and *his* predecessor, trying to tell them what he had discovered. It must have been impossible. The Lord's emissaries on earth should be visionaries, not cautious old men who saw only obstacles. Torino rested his hands on the laptop and box file in front of him, hoping he had enough evidence to convince them to do what was necessary to reverse the Holy Mother Church's declining fortunes.

The Holy Father's watery blue eyes settled on his. 'You requested this meeting, Father General. Why?'

Torino opened his file and placed the pages on

Father Orlando's trial and testimony before them. 'Four hundred and fifty years ago, our predecessors condemned a respected Jesuit priest to be burnt at the stake. His crime? He claimed to have discovered a garden of miracles for the Holy Mother Church.' He proceeded to summarize Falcon's trial and testimony.

'I don't understand, Father General,' said the pope, when Torino had finished. 'Since you became head of the Institute of Miracles you've been merciless with every claim. You're constantly telling me that although the Church needs miracles to show God's hand in the world, they must be scientifically proven examples that no one can deny. During your time in office you haven't ratified one miracle. Why are you interested in this priest's ancient claims?'

'Because I don't believe the Holy Mother Church should be forced, like a dog scrabbling for food, to seek out miracles. Instead she should be their inspiration, the wellspring from which they flow.' Torino held up a printout of Lauren Kelly's translation of the Voynich. 'This is a Yale academic's translation of the so-called Voynich Cipher Manuscript.'

'The Voynich?'

'The document that Father Orlando Falcon wrote while imprisoned by the Inquisition more than four centuries ago. The same Devil's book that the Church, especially the three men who held our positions at the time, denounced as the dangerous ramblings of a possessed man. The translation is

163

almost *identical* to Falcon's original testimony recorded in the Inquisition Archives. It would appear that the text he wrote all those centuries ago was a coded language that has only now been understood. Why would Father Orlando have bothered to invent a complex language if his story was a lie, a heresy?'

'You walk in dangerous territory, Father General,' counselled the pope.

'Now is not the time to tread carefully, Your Holiness. Now is the time to be bold. If this miraculous Garden of God exists it has massive implications for the Church.'

'But it can't exist,' Cardinal Prefect Vasari said, reaching for Falcon's testimony. 'Father Orlando claimed, essentially, to have discovered the Garden of Eden in a primitive jungle, in the midst of savages. Eden *can't* have been in the New World among heathens. And his strange creatures and bizarre plants are far removed from any description in the Bible. He tried to rewrite Genesis, for heaven's sake.'

Torino nodded. 'If it exists, though, its power could restore the Holy Mother Church's standing in the world.'

'It can't,' insisted the Cardinal Prefect. 'It goes against doctrine, undermines the scriptures and threatens the Church.'

'All the more reason why we can't allow anyone else to find it,' countered Torino. He turned to the pope. 'Holy Father, many people currently believe that the Voynich records a harmless myth. But if they knew it had been written by the sole survivor of a mission to find Eldorado, a Jesuit priest who was tortured because of what he claimed to have discovered, then it would, at the very least, embarrass the Church. At worst, it might encourage others to find this garden. Its existence might undermine the Bible and our doctrine. It could erode the Church's already declining relevance. Think about the miraculous healing powers Falcon claimed for his garden. Who needs the Church if people no longer fear death or disease?'

He raised a finger. 'But if *we* found it, we could mould it to fit our doctrine and bring glory to Rome. We could claim its power as our own. The Holy Mother Church would no longer need to seek out miracles as proof of God's hand on earth. She would control them. Rome would again be a dominant force in the world.'

'Why are you so sure this place exists?' the pontiff asked.

'Because Orlando Falcon wrote directions to his garden in a separate notebook, which, unfortunately, is now in the possession of an atheist, Dr Ross Kelly, the husband of the academic who deciphered the Voynich. Dr Kelly is a geologist and has already flown to Peru to search for the garden.'

'What?' The pope and the Cardinal Prefect sat forward.

'Of course, he may find nothing, but what if he does discover something?'

165

Torino briefed them on all he knew, omitting any reference to Bazin. He had always kept his assassin half-brother secret and now was not the time to reveal their relationship. He explained that Lauren Kelly had translated the Voynich manuscript, except for one key section, which she believed contained a map. She had been injured in a burglary, jeopardizing publication of a complete translation. He had subsequently approached her husband and gained his verbal agreement to see her notes. 'But the nun changed his mind.'

'What nun?'

'A Sister Chantal. She visited Dr Kelly and convinced him that Falcon's garden wasn't a fantasy and might contain a cure for his wife. She gave him Father Orlando's notebook.'

'How did she get hold of it? Who is this Sister Chantal?'

Torino reached into his box file. He took out a letter and a small carved box. 'A few days ago my office received this request from one of our Aids hospices in Uganda. They want the Institute of Miracles to investigate an apparent intervention. Two of their terminal patients, twin boys, have been cured simultaneously and spontaneously. On the same day, one of the nuns disappeared from the hospice. When questioned, the boys claimed that she had made them tea, using something from this box.' He handed it to the pope. 'Look at the carving.'

'I see flowers.'

'They're not ordinary flowers. You'll see flowers like that in only one place: the Voynich Cipher Manuscript.'

Silence.

'According to our research, the sister who disappeared had been with the hospice for twelve years, and two other hospices before that, but her order has no record of her earlier life. None. Her name? Sister Chantal.' The two men remained silent but Torino had their complete attention. 'All we know with certainty is that she's linked to Father Orlando and the Voynich. Whoever this mysterious rebel nun is, Dr Ross Kelly now has the notebook containing the directions, and is already searching for the garden to find a cure for his wife.'

He powered up his laptop, turned the screen towards them and played scenes of Ross Kelly in his comatose wife's hospital room: explaining that the garden revealed in Lauren's translation of the Voynich might hold a cure for her; telling her that they were going to find the garden; kissing her goodbye and asking for her blessing.

'How did you get this?' demanded Vasari.

'I have an ally, a servant of the Church, who keeps me informed.'

The Holy Father frowned. 'You have someone *spying* on Dr Kelly?'

'I prefer to see it as watching and listening. He wants only to serve the Church, as we all do.'

'Take care you do nothing to shame Rome, Father General,' said the pope.

'I'd never do anything to harm the Holy Mother Church, but if Kelly finds this garden and tells the world of its existence, he could destroy Rome.'

Vasari leant forward. 'You really think the geologist will find a miracle cure for his wife?'

'I fear he'll find a great deal more than that.'

'Like what?'

Torino narrowed his eyes. 'The miracle of creation. The scientific answer to the Book of Genesis.' He turned again to the pope. 'Holy Father, six months ago you announced the Holy Mother Church's revised position on evolution. You rejected Darwin's theory and embraced intelligent design. You enshrined in doctrine the Roman Catholic Church's belief that God, not evolution, is behind the creation and development of life.'

'Yes.'

'In the Inquisition Archives, Father Orlando spoke of something he called the *radix*, the source. In the garden its brilliance attracted the gold-hunting conquistadors and got them killed. Falcon was vague about what exactly it was, but he claimed it was the power behind the miraculous garden.'

'Your point is?'

'On the video, Kelly mentioned a theory – a hypothesis – to explain scientifically how Father Orlando's miraculous garden could exist,' Torino said. 'Kelly's theory is even bolder than the one Father Orlando dared in his blasphemous testimony: that this Garden of God and its source might be the origin of all life on earth. Forget Darwin and evolution. If Kelly finds this garden, he won't just be able to save his wife, demonstrating that miracles are independent of any church, he might also be able to show where, when and how life began on earth. He may be able to *prove* scientifically the theory of evolution – make it fact. Our doctrine will be in shreds. Religion relies on mystery, on faith. These revelations will render the Church as we know it, and all of us, redundant.'

The horror on the pope's face was almost comical but Torino didn't laugh. 'So what do you suggest we do?' demanded the pontiff.

'We turn the threat into an opportunity. We find the garden first and control it.'

'How?'

Torino had considered every option: from kidnapping the nun to stealing the book to threatening Ross Kelly. But he couldn't tell the pope any of this. So he lied: 'My scholars have managed to translate most of the final section of the manuscript. It gives directions to the garden and, with your blessing, I intend to seek it myself.'

'But you have duties.'

'None greater than this. I will set aside two months. No more. I have already arranged for Father Xavier Alonso to fulfil my responsibilities in that time.'

'You intend to race the geologist to the garden?'

'Yes.'

'Let's say you find it,' said Vasari. 'What do we do with it?'

Torino reached into his box file and pulled out three copies of the same document. He handed one to each man and kept the last for himself. 'These are a list of options, depending on what is found.' He smiled as he watched them read the bullet points. Their fear had been replaced with excitement. 'As you can see, the opportunities are limitless. So long as we manage everything carefully.'

The pope's pale eyes locked on to Torino's. 'I demand only one thing, Father General. Regardless of what you find, I as the Holy Father must see and hear *nothing* that contravenes doctrine. Doctrine must be sacrosanct. I must not be put in a position where I have to deny anything. Papal infallibility cannot be compromised. You understand?'

'Perfectly. I assure you that if the garden exists it will bring only glory to you and the Holy Mother Church.'

The pope nodded slowly. 'Good. How do we control this place? Surely, it will belong to whichever government owns the land.'

Torino smiled. 'The Cardinal Prefect has already supplied an excellent solution to that.'

Vasari raised an eyebrow. 'I have?'

'Yes. Your brilliant plan to bolster our presence in the world by founding a second Vatican state in the southern hemisphere.'

Vasari understood immediately. 'You can claim to be searching for the ideal location to build the

Vatican of the New World. Even if Falcon's garden doesn't exist and you find nothing, the Church won't suffer. We've nothing to lose.'

'And everything to gain,' said the pope, slowly. 'If you do find something we can incorporate it into the new Vatican and legally claim it as our own.' Torino remained silent, letting them own the plan. The pope turned to Vasari, who shrugged and gave an almost imperceptible nod. Then the pontiff levelled his unblinking gaze on Torino. 'Take whoever and whatever you need. Do whatever's necessary, but keep us briefed. And be careful, Father General.'

'I understand, Your Holiness.'

'Go then,' said the Holy Father. 'Do God's work.'

26

Cajamarca, the next day

Ross, Zeb and Sister Chantal spent the night in the Hotel El Ingenio, the best in Cajamarca. Since they would soon be roughing it in the jungle Ross had decided they should enjoy the comforts of civilization while they could. After a surprisingly good night's sleep, he showered and dressed in jeans, T-shirt and a light fleece: the morning temperature was cool but forecast to hit the low seventies, with humidity in the eighties. After breakfast, he and the others walked into the town centre in search of a guide.

They didn't have to look far. Outside the hotel they were approached by a man sharpening a huge knife on a leather belt. 'You want guide? My name is Chico,' he informed them proudly, grinning and exposing toothless gums. Before Ross or the others could reply, Chico was tapping his razor-sharp knife on Ross's shoulder and reassuring him he could take them anywhere so long as they put down a deposit of ten thousand US dollars and signed a blood chit absolving him of responsibility should they be murdered, raped, kidnapped, imprisoned or go missing. He closed his compelling sales pitch by boasting that he had only lost two gringos in the last few years.

Ross and the others declined four times, but had to walk a whole two blocks before the man got the message and went in search of other prey.

Despite being steeped in history, set in the spectacular Andean cloud forests, and surrounded by the magnificent ruins of ancient pre-Incan cities, Cajamarca didn't boast many tourists. It was too far north of the popular trail and its world-famous sites: Machu Picchu, Cuzco and Lake Titicaca. Nevertheless Cajamarca still had its fair share of tour companies. After a frustrating day spent in most of them, they ended up in Amazonas Tours.

'Are you *haqueros*?' The man with the bad suit and worse teeth spoke loud enough for everyone in Amazonas Tours to hear.

Ross gestured to his companions sitting alongside him: the frail Sister Chantal in her olive fleece and pressed khakis, the red-haired, fresh-faced Zeb in jeans and a baggy sweatshirt. 'Do we look like grave robbers?'

'Are you gold hunters?'

'No.'

'Are you oil prospectors?'

Ross shook his head.

The man from Amazonas Tours scratched his

head. 'Then why do you want to explore outside the usual tourist areas and national parks? The Amazon is a dangerous place. People who leave the known trails get lost and are never seen again.'

'That's why we need an escort.'

The man frowned. 'It's not just the danger to you. This area is full of ruins and graves, and in the past people plundered our treasures. The government has made laws to protect our culture. If you want to go outside the designated tourist areas you will need a permit. Amazonas Tours can arrange one within four to six weeks.'

Ross glanced up at the ceiling fan, exasperated. He was sitting before one of three desks in the open-plan office. The others were busy with tourists and a queue of four people was waiting by the large window, which overlooked the gardens of Cajamarca's scruffily elegant Plaza de Armas, the town square where Pizarro's men had slaughtered the Incas and captured the Emperor Atahualpa all those centuries ago. 'I don't see the problem. We just want to hire some equipment, transportation and a guide to help us navigate the cloud forest, the river and the rainforest.'

'But, señor, you don't know where you want to go. How can a guide help you?' He lowered his voice marginally. 'Unless you are *haqueros* and you have an illegal map.'

'We're not *haqueros*.'

'Then why do you need to go outside—'

Ross didn't let him finish. He stood up and

shook the man's hand. 'Thank you, Señor Hidalgo, you've been a great help.'

As he led the other two out of the office, he brushed past a dapper man in a safari suit.

'God, this place is so bureaucratic,' said Zeb, as they emerged into the late-afternoon sun bathing the square. 'Perhaps we should use an unofficial guide.'

Ross groaned.

'That's the fourth tour company who've told us we can't go off the beaten track without permits,' Zeb said. 'They want to know what we're looking for.'

'Which we can't tell them,' said Ross, 'so we need to agree on a cover story. It seems they don't like grave robbers or treasure hunters, so I suggest we're oil prospectors.'

'I'd much rather be a treasure hunter,' said Zeb. 'Sounds way more romantic.' She turned to Sister Chantal. 'You said you'd been here before. What did you do?'

'It was a long, long time ago. I was younger and things were very different.'

I bet, thought Ross. He reached into his rucksack and took out a small palmtop computer, complete with geological maps and a global-positioning satellite system. 'We could follow the directions ourselves,' he said. 'Stock up on provisions and equipment, hire a car to the river, then a boat from there.'

'Do you even know what provisions and

equipment to take? Or how much? What about when we're in the middle of the jungle?' said Zeb. 'Do you have any experience of surviving out there?'

'Some,' said Ross, miserably aware that a few weeks ago he and Lauren had planned to be caving in the jungles of Borneo – before she'd learnt she was pregnant and before . . . 'I know the basics – how to hang a hammock and net to protect us from insects, and I know most of the dangers, like the fer-de-lance.'

'The what?' said Zeb.

'Snakes,' said Sister Chantal, calmly. 'Very poisonous small ones you can easily step on if you're not careful.'

'I rest my case,' said Zeb, crossing her arms. 'I'm not going anywhere without an expert jungle guide.'

It seemed that their desperate quest was about to fizzle out before it had even begun. Perhaps this was a sign that he should go home to Lauren and accept whatever was going to happen. He glanced back at Amazonas Tours. A couple stood outside, holding hands. A little girl sat on the man's shoulders, twirling his hair in her fingers. Ross remembered the numerous occasions when Lauren had pointed out similar family units. 'That'll be us one day, Ross,' she'd said. Not any more, he thought. Not if she doesn't recover. Not if the baby dies.

He was about to launch into a speech about how he was going on whether the women joined him or not, when the man in the safari suit stepped into view. He was shorter and stockier than Ross with a cleanshaven ruddy face and immaculately combed hair. He exuded the subtle smell of soap. 'I apologize if I'm intruding,' he said, in a very English accent, 'but I couldn't help overhearing your predicament in Amazonas Tours. I believe I may be able to help.' He extended his hand to Ross. 'The name's Nigel Hackett, and I have a proposal. May I suggest we retire to that bar over there and discuss it?'

27

Nigel Hackett couldn't help himself.

'Please don't do that. Your towel's *sucio*,' he said to the waiter in the Heladeria Holanda Bar as the waiter placed a bottle of Inca Kola on the table and wiped his glass. Hackett noticed his three potential clients watching him and smiled apologetically. 'I do hate it when they wipe a freshly washed glass with a filthy towel.'

All his life, Nigel Hackett had done everything that was expected of him. As a sickly child, beset by allergies, he had gone out of his way to please his ambitious parents. When they had invested in a first-class education for their precious only child – Holmewood House in Kent, then Charterhouse and a medical degree at Cambridge – he had passed all his exams and met their expectations. He had qualified as a doctor, completed a short service commission in the British Army Medical Corps, then settled down as a GP near Guildford. He married a girl his parents approved of, then did everything to please *her*: earning enough money and status to give her a comfortable life as the wife of a Home Counties doctor.

Despite his apparent conformity, however, Nigel Hackett harboured a secret. Ever since he was a boy, when the legendary adventurer Matt Lincoln had visited his school to lecture on the lost pre-Incan civilizations of Peru and the Amazon, he had dreamt of becoming an explorer. He wanted to discover the fabled lost city for which Lincoln had searched in vain, the mother megalopolis in the heart of the Amazon Basin from which all South American civilizations sprang. Hackett had told no one of this dream, though. Not until his thirty-first birthday, when his wife had left him for her salsa-dance teacher and broken his heart. Three years ago, he had sold up, paid off his divorce settlement and set up a river-running outfit on the Amazon. The plan was to live on the boat, support himself by ferrying tourists to the great sites and use his spare time to follow his dream: exploring the jungle to discover lost cities – and their gold.

Dreams rarely come true.

Hackett wasn't a natural explorer. His allergies and obsessive fear of dirt were manageable in England – even when he had been in the army – but not in the jungle. The soil made his nose itch and his eyes water. He had to wear thick glasses, rather than contact lenses, to correct his poor eyesight. Though he had made some good contacts and friends, who got him government permits and offered to sell any gold he found without involving the authorities, his river-running business was barely viable. The locals were squeezing him out and he was only surviving by ferrying oil geologists into the jungle and offering himself as their on-board doctor. As for his dream, he had had precious little time to look for any ruins – most of which had been discovered anyway. He had come to Cajamarca in a last-ditch attempt to link up with local tour companies and offer visitors a one-ticket tour of the cloud forest *and* the Amazon. But none of the tour operators in Cajamarca or nearby Chachapoyas was biting: the status quo suited them just fine.

Hackett needed a change of fortune. Unless he earned some money soon he faced the unthinkable: selling his new boat and the Land Rover to return to the grey skies of England with his tail between his legs. When he had overheard the frustrated trio of travellers in Amazonas Tours – the tall American, the young, disconcertingly attractive red-haired woman and the elegant elderly lady with striking eyes – he had listened.

Introductions made, he smiled at his potential clients, wondering what had brought together a geologist, an academic and a nun. 'So, you want equipment, provisions, transport and a guide?'

'Yes,' said Ross.

'For how long?'

'Up to two months.'

'Two months? That's not going to be cheap.'

'Obviously.'

'All of you are going?'

'Yes,' said the elderly sister, who wore none of the trappings of a nun, save the large crucifix he glimpsed at her neck. She smiled as she sipped her *latte*. Something about her eyes made Hackett decide against underestimating her.

'But you don't know exactly where you want to go,' he observed.

'Not exactly,' said Ross. 'We know where to start and we've got directions that lead to the river, then into the jungle.'

Hackett's eyes widened. 'Let me guess. You're looking for gold.'

There was a pause as the three glanced at each other. The attractive young woman, Zeb, dipped her finger into some spilt coffee on the table by her cup and licked it off. He shuddered. Had she no idea how many germs she had just ingested? 'Yes,' she said. 'We're treasure hunters.'

'Aren't we all?' he said drily. God, there was one born every minute. 'Don't tell me, someone sold you a map.'

'No,' said Ross.

'You *have* a map, though, haven't you? Where did you get it? Someone sold it you in Lima, no doubt. Told you it leads to lost treasure, Inca gold.' He laughed. 'I'm warning you, there are thousands of maps flying around and they're all nonsense. I know. I've checked out a few myself.' Hackett studied them again. The bizarre trio didn't resemble the Yank tourists who came, in their loud shirts and ironed denims, for safe adventure. 'Take my advice, my friends, don't waste your time and money. Enjoy Peru. See the amazing Chachapoyan ruins here. Go south to Cuzco and Machu Picchu, travel east to jungle-locked Iquitos, then north to the beach in Máncora. Paint the town red in Lima and go home.'

'Mr Hackett, we don't have a map,' said Ross. 'What we do have is a very old document, written by a Jesuit priest, shortly after Pizarro's conquest of Peru.'

Hackett almost laughed again, but the other man's expression cut through his scepticism. This was no holiday adventurer seeking easy gold. 'Where did you buy it?'

'I didn't buy it,' said the nun, 'but it contains directions and we need your help to follow them.'

'Directions to where?'

'The Jesuit priest accompanied a troop of conquistadors into the jungle.' Her beautiful eyes crinkled in an enigmatic smile. 'To find Eldorado.'

'The fabled city of gold.' An electric surge of excitement rippled through Hackett. 'And he found something?'

The trio nodded.

Hackett sat forward. 'What?'

'That's what we want to check out,' said Ross.

'Can I see the document?'

Sister Chantal handed him a book. Hackett opened it carefully. Its leather binding and yellowed vellum pages appeared authentic. There were some mismatched pages bound into the back but they looked equally old. He turned to the first pages; the directions were in Castilian Spanish and in a cryptic style. He felt three pairs of eyes assessing him. He registered the start point, La Prisión del Rey, and read the first direction. He flicked through the next few pages, digesting as much as he could. After a few minutes he looked up, trying to appear unimpressed. 'Are all the directions in here?'

The nun took the book from him. 'All of them.'

'Do they mean anything to you, Mr Hackett?' asked Zeb.

'I think so,' said Hackett, licking his lips. He wanted to reach for his asthma inhaler, but instead he slowed his breathing to calm his racing heart. Was this yet another pipe dream, more castles in the air? Or, as he was about to give up and go home, was it the real thing?

'Can you, for example, tell us exactly where the quest starts?' asked Ross.

They were testing him now. Hackett checked his watch. Good, it would soon be dark. He rose from his chair and threw some money on to the table to cover the drinks. 'Come with me.' He moved to the door. 'I can do better than tell you where your priest started his quest.' He opened the door and walked out into the dusk. 'A lot better.'

As they followed Hackett across the town square and down a side street to the only Inca building left standing in Cajamarca, Ross had no idea that he, too, was being followed. The small chamber where the Inca emperor had been imprisoned by Pizarro was unremarkable inside, except for what Hackett assured Ross were signs of Inca construction: trapezoidal doorways and niches in the inner walls. It smelt of dust and the past.

'This is it,' said Hackett. 'The tour guides call it El Cuarto del Rescate, the ransom chamber, but your priest was right. This was actually La Prisión del Rey.' He looked Ross in the eye. 'But you already knew that, didn't you? Would you be more impressed if I told you where the first direction leads?'

'Yes,' said Ross. 'I think we would.'

When Hackett led them outside it was dark, and as Ross's eyes settled on a bright star, he tried to remember what the charts in Falcon's notebook had said about the night sky in June. Hackett followed his gaze then said to Sister Chantal, 'Tell me again the first direction in your book.'

She read it aloud: '"With the cross as your guide, march two days to an ancient lost city on the eyebrow of the jungle."'

Hackett smiled. 'Oh, yes, the Eyebrow of the Jungle, La Ceja de la Selva.' He pointed up to the bright star. 'That's your cross – Crux, also known as the Southern Cross.' He flashed a boyish smile. 'But we don't need to follow it because I already know where it leads. The ancient city on the Eyebrow of the Jungle may have been lost when

184

your priest wrote his book, but Juan Crisóstomo found it in 1843. It's called Kuelap.' He pointed to a spotless silver Land Rover parked nearby. 'And it won't take us two days in that.' He smiled at Ross. 'More impressed?'

Ross couldn't suppress a grin. 'A little.'

Hackett indicated the notebook in Sister Chantal's hands. 'From what I read, most of the early directions seem pretty straightforward. The important thing is to find where on the river they lead you. Once you take a boat and head up the Amazon I suspect the clues will be harder to follow. Fortunately, June's the beginning of the drier season and the riverbanks won't be flooded. Most landmarks should be visible.'

Ross couldn't help liking the Englishman. 'Will you help us, then? Can you provide transport, a guide to keep us out of trouble and whatever supplies we need to survive the trip? We'll pay whatever you think is fair.'

For a while Hackett didn't say anything. Then, 'Does anyone else know about this?'

'No.'

'Let's say I get a guide, equip the expedition and come with you. And let's say we do find Eldorado. Do we share everything? I know a man who can sell the gold for us.'

'I don't see why not.' Ross turned to Chantal and Zeb, who nodded. 'The way we see it, a percentage of something is better than all of nothing. We'll split any gold we find four ways. Equal partners.'

He and the women extended their hands, which Hackett shook.

'Have you got a good guide?' asked Zeb.

Hackett nodded. 'Juarez helps me with the boat. He's Quechua and knows the Amazon as well as anybody.' He reached into a pocket and brought out an inhaler. 'But this isn't just about gold for me. The area of dense cloud forest is littered with the remains of great pre-Inca civilizations, thousands of years old, and one of the great mysteries is what caused people like the Chachapoyans to live in that high mountain jungle. Where did they come from? Many archaeologists believe that the Chacha migrated overland through the jungles of the Amazon Basin and that the cradle of the continent's civilization, the great metropolis with its massive towers, battlements and plazas, is still out there, hidden in the Amazon rainforest. Some say *that* could be Eldorado.' Hackett smiled. 'I've wanted to find it for as long as I can remember.'

Ross felt a stab of guilt for allowing him to believe they were looking for Eldorado, then reminded himself that there was probably more chance of finding Hackett's lost city than Falcon's miraculous garden. 'What about the permits everyone keeps talking about?'

Hackett waved a hand dismissively. 'This government doesn't care about preserving its culture, only the money it brings in from tourism. Back in 2003 they granted the oil companies *carte blanche* access to indigenous ancestral lands throughout almost the entire Peruvian Amazon – and we all know how much the oil industry cares about conservation. If something valuable is out there we'd better find it quick before they destroy it. If it's big enough and valuable enough it might even make the government stop churning up the jungle.'

'When can we leave?' demanded Ross.

'Today's Monday . . . Thursday?'

'No sooner?'

'It'll take a little time to arrange supplies for a month or two.' He pulled out a pad, scribbled some notes, then tore off a sheet and handed it to Ross. 'I'll collect most of what you'll need but here are some personal items you must have in the jungle – sunscreen, sun hats, rucksacks, that kind of thing, if you haven't already got them.'

Ross scanned the list. They had most of the items already, but one surprised him. 'Condoms? I'm married.'

Hackett laughed. 'They're not for sex. They're for the jungle. And buy the smallest you can find – however proud you are of what you've got. The water in the Amazon isn't as warm as you think and you need a nice tight fit.'

'I don't understand.'

'You will, trust me. Where are you staying?'

'El Ingenio.'

'I'll pick you up first thing on Thursday. Before dawn. Say, four thirty? We'll have a long day ahead of us.'

'We'll be waiting,' said Ross, wondering how he

was going to fill the time once he'd bought the remaining few items.

From where Marco Bazin stood in the shadows, he didn't need the discreet earphone connected to the directional microphone in his hand. He had heard everything, both in the bar and out on the street. Now he knew when and where Kelly was setting off on his quest, he had time to meet Torino and tell him his plan.

Despite his fatigue, Bazin felt good as he watched Kelly and the others shake hands with the Englishman and go their separate ways. In the sun his olive skin was already losing its sallow pallor, his hair was growing back and he felt strong for the first time in months. He had been tailing Kelly, the nun and the student with bright red hair all the way from the States, and had let them out of his sight only when they'd checked into their hotel yesterday evening. Then he had wandered around the bars on the seamier side of town, recruiting help.

He preferred to work alone but in the past he'd occasionally brought in jackals and vultures for preparation, back-up and clean-up work. This was one of those occasions, except now he was doing it for a higher purpose.

'Is the notebook a treasure map?'

Bazin stepped out of the alleyway, adjusted his Panama hat and turned to the man beside him. The Peruvian's greedy eyes gleamed like jet. 'Let me worry about the book, Raul. You worry about getting the equipment, guns and men. You can have them by Wednesday noon?'

'*Sí*. You will pay the men how much, señor?'

'What we agreed. No more, no less.'

For a second, Raul looked as if he might try to renegotiate, then he nodded. The man was an amateur but Bazin had no choice. He had to use him. He had no contacts in the area and time wasn't on his side. This might be God's work but it was the Devil's job finding reliable men willing to steal and kill for money.

28

Lima, the next day

The two anonymous black limousines left the Jesuit Residence and made their way through the wide boulevards of Lima. Tinted windows concealed the two passengers in the back seat of the lead car. A soundproof screen separated them from the driver.

'What if it doesn't work?' demanded Torino, as he listened to Bazin's plan.

Bazin smiled. 'It has to. And if anything goes wrong, I've built in a few contingencies.' He handed Torino a palmtop computer and explained how the device worked. 'The transmitter's global-positioning satellite technology will allow you to pinpoint their exact location on the map to within a few feet.'

Torino sensed new confidence in his half-brother. He was no longer simply accepting his tasks but embellishing them. 'We can't afford any mistakes. This must succeed.'

'It will.'

Torino pressed an intercom button and told the driver to stop. The car pulled into a side street and came to a halt. 'Do it, Marco,' he said. Bazin got out and Torino leant out of the window. 'But keep me informed.'

The car drove off, entered Prolongacion Avenue and parked by a large colonial building bearing a brass plaque: Ministerio del Interior. His entourage emerged from the second car – his reed-thin, bespectacled personal assistant, and four tall men in anonymous grey uniforms. Before they reached him he told them to wait in the limousine. He entered the building alone.

The Peruvian Minister for the Interior afforded Torino the respect worthy of a visiting head of state. He greeted him personally, then escorted him into his imposing office and introduced him to the only other man in the room: the Peruvian government's lawyer. They exchanged pleasantries, then got down to business.

'First, let me assure you that we've signed the confidentiality agreement your lawyers sent from Rome. Whatever is discussed in this office stays here.'

Torino pulled a document out of his briefcase. It was sealed and stamped with the papal seal. 'That reassures me. I cannot stress enough how delicate this is. Though we favour Peru for our initiative, nothing has yet been officially decided. If this is leaked before the deal is finalized the Vatican will deny all knowledge. You understand?'

'Of course. We'll do nothing to jeopardize this opportunity. I spoke to our president earlier and he instructed me to give you every assistance in this matter. He would be here himself but he's on a trade visit to China.'

Torino handed the sealed document to the minister. 'This confirms that I speak for the pope.'

The minister broke the seal, scanned the letter and passed it to the lawyer. 'How can we help you, Father General?'

'As you know, the Vatican is an independent state within Italy. Ever since the Lateran Treaty of 1929 its unique sovereign status has been enshrined in law. This gives the Roman Catholic Church precious independence and authority to do as it thinks morally right, regardless of the host nation's politics.

'The Holy Mother Church is keen to extend its moral presence in the world. To that end we wish to found a second Vatican in the southern hemisphere, away from the staid conventions of Europe. In contrast to the ancient, urban splendour of Rome, this new Vatican will be a brand new eco-state. A spiritual retreat from the corruption of the modern world, the new Vatican state will be ecologically responsible and self-sufficient. This vision of the future will act as a beacon and an example to the world.'

'A new Eden?' said the minister.

Torino smiled. 'Exactly. Our preferred location is in Roman Catholic South America, and Peru is an excellent candidate. It's stable, neither too big nor too small. However, we are aware that a few years ago you agreed that the oil companies could develop swathes of the Amazon and build a pipeline. We are also aware that your country's international image has suffered because of this perceived neglect of the rainforest in pursuit of oil money.'

The minister shuffled in his seat. 'How can we help you decide on Peru?'

'We would found the new Vatican in the Amazon, within a protected perimeter of virgin forest that will be maintained and conserved as God intended. You will cede this land to the Vatican and enshrine in perpetuity its status as a sovereign nation state in both international and Peruvian law. You will also undertake to protect its sovereignty.

'In return you'll receive competitive payment for the land and, as hosts of the second Vatican, you'll enjoy enhanced international status within the region and the world. You'll also restore your image by showing the world you care about conservation. In effect you'll be surrendering land of limited economic value in exchange for capital, prestige and international goodwill.'

The minister glanced at the lawyer, who nodded. 'That sounds reasonable.' The minister rose and approached a map on the wall.

'Is any part of the Peruvian rainforest off limits or earmarked for the oil companies?' asked Torino.

'Not specifically. If you wanted a particular tract

of land we'd give you precedence over the oil companies.' He pointed at the map. 'In any case I can advise you on a prime parcel—'

'That won't be necessary. I'll know the land when I see it. The Lord will guide me to it.'

'Father General, you surely don't want to go into the jungle yourself?'

'I must.'

'It's a dangerous place, Father General.'

'God will protect me, and the Holy Father has supplied me with four Vatican soldiers.'

'The Swiss Guard?' The beginnings of an incredulous smile formed on the minister's lips. 'With all due respect, every government minister who goes into the interior is always accompanied by a team of *highly trained* Special Forces soldiers.'

'And I will be doing the same. They might wear colourful ceremonial dress and wield halberds but the Swiss Guard are anything but toy soldiers, Minister.'

'I meant no offence. It's just that if anything happened to the Superior General of the Society of Jesus while a guest in our country . . .'

Torino raised a hand. 'I understand.' Many underestimated the Vatican's small army, which had been made up of Swiss mercenaries since the sixteenth century. When Hitler's army had entered Rome in the Second World War, Swiss Guards had donned subdued grey uniforms and taken up positions behind machine-guns and mortars. The Germans did not move against the Vatican but the Guard, though vastly outnumbered, had been prepared to sacrifice their lives for the Holy Father. All members of the modern Swiss Guard were Catholics, aged between nineteen and thirty, over five feet eight inches tall, and trained in the professional Swiss army. Competition was fierce and the Vatican selected only the best. Each recruit vowed to defend the pope and the apostolic palace with his life. The four Swiss Guards assigned to Torino were élite soldiers who spoke Spanish and had relevant jungle training. 'Be assured, Minister, my men are more than capable of protecting me. But I would appreciate your co-operation in authorizing access to any weapons or equipment they may require while in your country.'

'Of course.' The minister took a piece of paper from the lawyer and handed it to Torino. 'This letter guarantees you safe passage through the country. It also authorizes you to requisition any equipment and transport you might need in your search, including any weapons or supplies for your men. Tell the local authorities your requirements and they'll arrange everything.' He gestured again to the lawyer, who produced three copies of a thick document. 'This is the agreement your lawyers in Rome finalized with ours yesterday. It gives the Vatican the right to claim up to twenty thousand hectares of virgin Peruvian rainforest at the price agreed.'

'Any land I choose?'

'So long as it's virgin forest and doesn't belong to anybody else.'

'What about native tribes?'

'We'll move them.'

'If I require more than twenty thousand hectares?'

'We just add a supplementary agreement.' The minister smiled. 'As you'll discover, Father General, there's a lot of jungle out there.'

29

Cajamarca, Thursday, 4.30 a.m.

Lauren had always accused Ross of being impatient, but he had never felt as impatient as he did kicking his heels in Cajamarca waiting for Hackett's return. Sister Chantal had retreated into a world of her own, using the opportunity to sleep and gather her strength. Zeb kept trying to reassure him, between reading everything she could find – as Lauren used to do when she was on holiday. But he couldn't relax. After he had purchased items on Hackett's list and explored Cajamarca for the third time he had pored over Falcon's notebook, trying to guess how long it would take to find the garden, if it existed. He was in limbo – neither by his wife's side nor on the trail seeking her cure – and desperate to move. Every day he called his father, every day Sam Kelly reported that there had been no change in Lauren's condition, and every day Ross had considered flying home.

Finally, Thursday morning arrived and Hackett

picked them up outside the hotel in his silver Land Rover. It was still dark and the Southern Cross was visible in the sky.

Hackett was attired in pristine khakis, safari jacket, Indiana Jones hat and thick glasses. He greeted them, then stowed their bags on the roof rack. 'Please wipe your feet before getting into the car, then wind up the windows. I'm allergic to dirt. I'll put on the aircon when we're all in.'

Allergic to dirt? Ross exchanged a glance with Zeb, but said nothing as he sat in the front passenger seat while Zeb and Sister Chantal made themselves comfortable in the back. He had to admire Hackett for choosing a vocation for which he was so apparently ill-suited: running tours into the Amazon jungle, probably the largest source of dirt in the world. Ross liked the eccentric Englishman, though. For all his reserve and odd habits, Hackett exuded old-fashioned integrity.

The journey to Kuelap took six hours. The rough road cut across the cloud forest and over a three-thousand-metre-high pass, then dropped steeply to the Río Marañón. Eventually, they stopped at a village called Tingo, south of Chachapoyas.

'We walk from here,' said Hackett. He looked at Sister Chantal. 'It's a pretty steep climb. Do you want to wait in the car?'

Sister Chantal didn't bother to answer, just got out, took Zeb's arm and began to walk. It was warm with a light, humid breeze and Ross could smell the red earth beneath his feet as they climbed. It took two more hours to reach the ruins, a thousand metres above Tingo, but when he saw the lost fortress he forgot his exhaustion and stared. The place was massive. According to Hackett, the fabulous ruined city was the largest pre-Inca construction in Peru. High above the left bank of the Río Utucamba the fort was set on a crumbling ridge. The battlements rose some sixty feet and stretched for nearly half a mile.

'This is Kuelap,' said Hackett, retrieving his inhaler from a pocket and taking a puff, 'the keystone of known Chachapoyan culture. Most Chachapoyan fortresses were built on high ridges like this one. They tower over the cloud forest and are known locally as La Ceja de la Selva, the Eyebrow of the Jungle.' Ross was surprised to see that they were virtually alone. He would have thought a place as spectacular as this would be teeming with tourists. While Zeb and Sister Chantal sat down to regain their breath, Hackett beckoned him to a tower situated at the highest point in the fort. It was twenty-seven feet high with crumbling steps to the top.

Standing atop the ancient fortress, almost ten thousand feet above sea level, he looked east. The jungles of the Amazon stretched out below him as far as he could see and, in the far distance, a ribbon of gleaming silver wound its way through the green. This vast, open space felt a million miles from home and the claustrophobic confines of Lauren's hospital room. His constant sadness and guilt at leaving her were compounded by the wish that she could see this. But he felt something else too: the stirring of hope. He allowed himself to imagine that Falcon's garden might be somewhere in the viridian expanse – and a cure. From that ancient vantage-point anything seemed possible.

Hackett pointed to a well-worn road that led down to the basin. 'Your priest's next few directions lead us east towards the river. That road's been the only passage down to the Amazon for centuries so I suspect the trail will follow it to Tarapoto, then on to Yurimaguas on the Río Huallaga, which eventually connects with the Amazon itself. I'm in radio contact with Juarez, our guide, and when we know exactly where on the river your priest's directions lead, I'll call him and get him to pick us up for the next leg of the journey.' He pointed towards the Amazon. 'I suspect the directions will come into their own when we find ourselves in that uncharted sea of green.'

For some moments both men stood in silence, gazing across the vast expanse, lost in their thoughts.

'Can you hear it?' said Hackett, eventually.

Ross listened to the breeze. 'Hear what?'

'The call,' Hackett said, a smile forming on his lips. 'The call to adventure.'

As the gleaming silver Land Rover drove away from Tingo, a mud-spattered Toyota Land Cruiser set off behind it.

'Why we follow these gringos? They know where to find gold?'

Marco Bazin put down the binoculars. 'You're following them, Raul, because I'm paying you to. Keep your distance but don't let them out of your sight.' He took off his Panama and scratched his head. In the rear-view mirror he caught sight of the man sitting behind him, oiling his gun. More boy than man, his long, dark face was ravaged by acne. 'You know what to do? All of you?' He had to keep the contempt from his voice.

'*Sí*,' they mumbled, and smirked at each other.

Bazin locked eyes with the man-boy oiling his gun. 'Remember, you only get the rest of the money when the job's done.' He was grateful to be unknown in these parts, but his reputation had had its uses in the past. If these amateurs had known who he was – who he had once been – they would show him more respect.

Bazin checked his expensive new phone for a signal, then cursed his stupidity: though no bigger than a cellphone, it used state-of-the-art satellite technology so it should work anywhere on the planet. He called Torino's identical phone. The Jesuit answered on the third ring.

'They're on the move,' said Bazin.

'Don't let them out of your sight. I'll follow when I've finished in Lima.'

30

Yurimaguas

'Which is your boat, Nigel?' asked Zeb, in a bored drawl. 'Let me guess.' She pointed to a gleaming white vessel that stood out from the other grubby ferries and dilapidated steamboats berthed in the sleepy river port. 'That one.'

'How did you know?' said Hackett.

'Call it a wild guess.'

The journey from Kuelap to Yurimaguas had taken the best part of two days, and the roads had been as rough as any Ross had encountered. Even in the Land Rover the last six-hour stretch from Tarapoto had been an unpaved, gut-wrenching ride. It wasn't just the length of the journey that frayed tempers but being stuck for so long together in a car. Zeb might have had an ordered mathematical mind but she cared nothing for tidiness and liked to stick her feet on the dashboard when she took her turn in the front. She seemed almost to enjoy provoking

Hackett, who was too polite to retaliate.

Hackett parked by the boat, and when Ross opened the car door the air was a good five to ten degrees warmer and more humid than it had been in the mountains. He got out and stretched his legs. Looking at the immaculate boat, he understood for the first time what 'shipshape' meant. Brass letters spelt out the name *Discovery* on the blindingly white hull, and when they boarded every surface was polished brass or varnished teak.

'What a lovely boat,' said Sister Chantal.

Hackett beamed with pride. 'The *Discovery*'s a custom-built seventy-footer, powered by two hundred-and-fifty horsepower Detroit diesels.'

'How many berths?' said Ross.

'Six cabins.'

Ross breathed a sigh of relief. Everyone would have their own space.

A small, wiry man with smiling brown eyes, honeyed skin and thick black hair stepped from the engine room. His white T-shirt and blue jeans were as spotless as the boat.

Hackett introduced him as Juarez. 'The irony is that I left England to come to the jungle and seek out ancient ruins, whereas Juarez comes from the jungle and wants to visit the great cities of Europe and North America. He hates ruins, regards them as dead places. Nevertheless, he helps me with the boat and acts as our guide. He speaks fluent English, Spanish and Quechua and knows the Amazon – river and jungle – as well as anyone. He's also a damn good cook.' Hackett pointed down one of the side aisles. 'Follow me. I'll show you to your cabins.'

As Hackett took them round the boat, no one noticed a tall man in a Panama walk past the *Discovery*. Twice. The second time he came so close to the edge of the dock that when he bent to tie his laces, he could easily have touched the hull.

Each tiny cabin was as neat and clean as Ross had expected, and had an adjoining shower room. A neat pile of equipment and supplies was laid out on each bed, including a tightly rolled hammock and mosquito net, with cans of full-strength insect repellent. 'Use it liberally,' said Hackett, 'even in your cabin. Before we leave the boat and go into the jungle Juarez will explain how to use the hammock and the mosquito net to stop yourself being eaten alive.'

'This boat looks expensive. How often is it chartered?' Ross asked, when Hackett had shown the others to their rooms.

'Not often enough. I survive by renting it to the oil companies and occasionally the pharmaceutical giants. It seems everyone's looking for treasure in the Amazon, whether it's gold, oil or the next cure for cancer.' He pointed to a chest on the deck. 'That's full of tennis balls and baseball caps with company logos on them. Tennis balls are all the rage with the kids around these parts and the oil companies give them out as freebies. It's good PR, apparently. Alascon Oil's red ones are the current craze.'

Ross groaned inwardly at the thought of Underwood and Kovacs.

'I'll leave you to freshen up,' said Hackett. 'Yurimaguas is one of the gateways to the jungle. If my reading of the next directions is correct we'll follow the Río Huallaga through Lagunas, then join the Río Marañón and head east. Eventually we'll join the main river, the Amazonas, which will take us into the heart of the jungle.'

Hackett left and Ross slumped on to his bed. He reached into his wallet for a photograph taken on his honeymoon: Lauren smiling in the glow of a Hawaiian sunset. She had a flower in her hair and looked tanned and well. He wondered if he would ever see her smile again. The rumble of the boat's powerful diesel engines interrupted his thoughts. He got up and looked out of the porthole. As the brown river water churned below him, the faded, raffish charm of Yurimaguas receded into the distance and the river snaked into the heart of the largest jungle on earth.

As Ross gazed down the winding waterway, he felt his quest had truly begun.

Bazin watched the *Discovery* leave Yurimaguas, then checked his handheld computer screen, which showed a map of north-east Peru. When he activated the GPS transmitter he'd attached to the boat's hull, a beeping dot appeared on the screen, moving out of Yurimaguas. He adjusted his Panama, then turned to the others in the dinghy.

'I like the girl with the red hair,' said the one who had been oiling his gun in the Land Cruiser.

Bazin glared at him. 'Forget her. You know what you have to do. I can't allow any of you to make a mistake. Understand?'

Raul laughed. 'You worry too much.'

Bazin suspected he wasn't worrying enough. He gunned the powerful outboard and the boat sped off in the wake of the *Discovery*.

31

A bullet hitting the human head makes a particular sound. Once heard, it is never forgotten. The next morning, after a fitful sleep, Ross heard it for the first time – more than once.

The incident happened some hours after the *Discovery* had passed Lagunas, where the deserted Río Marañón was half a mile wide. He was reading Falcon's notebook, mentally ticking off the landmarks they'd passed and counting the ones that remained, when he heard Juarez call to Hackett. Ross followed Juarez's pointing finger and saw a dinghy floating near the riverbank with three men on board. Two were waving while the third held up a broken paddle and gestured to the outboard.

'We help them?' said Juarez.

'Of course,' said Hackett. 'If we can't fix their outboard, we'll tow them upriver to the nearest town.'

The *Discovery* pulled up alongside the dinghy and one of the passengers, a larger man wearing a white Panama hat, held up a bottle in his left hand. '*Usted ha conseguido agua potable?* Have you any water?'

Hackett pushed the ladder over the side while Juarez threw them a line to secure their dinghy to the *Discovery*. Despite the heat, the men wore coats when they climbed aboard. Ross assumed they contained their valuables but soon realized he had been wrong.

Very wrong.

The man with the Panama pulled a pistol from his jacket with his left hand and pointed its oily black muzzle at Hackett. The other two were levelling larger semi-automatics at the passengers on deck. Panama counted each of them, as though he knew how many should be on board. 'I want you to raise your hands and stand in a line.' He turned to Ross and Sister Chantal. 'Which of you has the book?'

'What book?' said Sister Chantal.

Panama shook his head wearily. 'The notebook with the directions.'

How did he know about Falcon's book? Ross glanced at Hackett and saw, from the shock on his face, that he knew nothing of this. One of the men, with acne-scarred skin and small beady eyes, touched Zeb's red hair. 'I like her,' he said.

'I told you, forget the girl. We want the notebook,' said Panama.

'Don't give them anything,' said Zeb. 'Pizza Face doesn't scare me.'

'Shut up, Zeb,' said Ross.

Hackett stepped closer to her. 'Steady on. Let's keep calm.'

Ross turned to Sister Chantal. 'Give it to him,' he said. He was on this quest to save Lauren's life, not to risk anyone else's.

Sister Chantal gazed calmly at the man in the Panama. 'No.'

'Give him the book,' Ross said again.

'No.'

Pizza Face laughed and reached for Zeb's left breast. Zeb recoiled and Hackett shoved him away. 'Take your hands off her,' he said.

Pizza Face twisted round and struck Hackett across the head with his gun, sending the Englishman sprawling to the floor, blood pouring from his temple, glasses clattering across the deck. As Zeb knelt to help him, Pizza Face took aim at him. 'I kill him,' he spat.

'Wait,' said the third man, wiping his forehead while keeping his gun trained on Juarez.

'Give him the goddamned book,' Ross shouted at Sister Chantal.

'They'll kill us anyway,' she said, with glacial calm. 'I will not make it easy for them.'

'Killing you is easy,' said Panama, raising his left hand and pointing his weapon at her forehead. 'Let me show you.'

As soon as he heard the *Discovery*'s engines, the man cutting his way through the thick jungle sheathed his machete and rushed to the riverbank. He took cover when he saw the men from the dinghy climb on board the boat and pull out their weapons. He watched for a moment, considering his options, then raised his rifle, nestled the butt in his shoulder and took aim.

He waited for as long as he could, reluctant to intervene, until the man in the Panama levelled his pistol at the old lady's forehead.

He knew then that he had to act.

He slowed his breathing, checked his aim and squeezed the trigger.

As Ross watched Panama's finger whiten on the trigger, he knew the man would shoot Sister Chantal, and some futile impulse made him lunge forward to stop him.

His face was a kiss away from Panama's when the shot rang out, sending brilliantly coloured parrots flying from the trees. When the bullet struck its target it sounded like nothing Ross had heard before. Movies sometimes used the metaphor of a bullet exploding a watermelon, but this sounded crisper, sharper: the shattering of brittle bone as the bullet entered and left the skull, counterpointing the explosive impact on soft tissue and brain. Despite the hot, humid air, the expelled blood and flesh felt warm on his face.

In his horror he turned to Sister Chantal and couldn't understand why she was still standing. Why she was unharmed. Then he realized that

Panama had been shot. The force had thrown him to the deck, where he lay dead, his white hat and head merged into a bloody pulp that pooled, red and sticky, on the polished wood.

A second shot rang out and Pizza Face fell backwards into the river, a large hole in his forehead, surprise on his face. A third shot collapsed the last man, like a marionette with cut strings. He toppled overboard.

In the eerie silence that followed, Ross and the others stared at each other. Then Ross saw a figure on the nearby riverbank, waving a rifle. '*Hola,*' the man shouted. 'You okay?'

Ross looked at Hackett, who nodded, while Zeb picked up his glasses, then dabbed at his wound. Sister Chantal smiled serenely at their saviour. 'God certainly moves in mysterious ways,' she said.

'Can I come aboard?' the man asked.

Juarez rushed to the wheelhouse and retrieved a rifle and a black pistol.

'Bit late for those now,' said Hackett.

Juarez put away the rifle but kept the pistol close to hand as he steered the *Discovery* to the bank. The man boarded, carrying his rifle over his shoulder and a large rucksack. He was tall and athletic with a handsome, world-weary face and sad eyes, his olive skin burnished by the sun. He didn't seem fazed to have dispatched three men. Waving away their thanks, he approached Hackett as if he was an old friend. 'Señor Nigel Hackett.'

When Hackett rose to his feet he resembled a

provincial bank manager beside the swashbuckling stranger. 'Have we met?'

The man raised an eyebrow. 'Osvaldo Mendoza. I also have a boat that ferries tourists down the river. We met once in Lagunas.'

'Of course,' said Hackett. Ross almost smiled. It would be impolite and unBritish to snub the man who had just saved your life. Hackett extended his hand and Mendoza shook it. 'I don't know how we can repay you for coming to our assistance.'

'You can give me a lift to Iquitos, my friend. My boat is not as grand – or as memorable – as yours. That's why I'm here. It sank, and I was waiting to flag down the ferry to Iquitos when I saw your difficulty.' He gestured to the body still on board. 'Bandits don't usually operate so far from the drug fields of the Huallaga valley. What did they want?'

Hackett turned to Sister Chantal. 'Why didn't you give them the notebook? They would have killed us if Señor Mendoza hadn't turned up.'

'As I said before, they would have killed us anyway,' she said.

Mendoza grimaced. 'I fear she's right, señor. Those men don't let you live to complain to the police. What notebook did they want? It must be valuable.'

'It contains directions,' said Hackett, glaring at the nun.

'Directions?'

Hackett turned to Ross. 'How the hell did they even know about it? You told me no one else did.'

No one else should have known about the notebook, thought Ross. But one other person knew of Falcon's garden. Torino. The priest could have seen the book when he'd met Sister Chantal at Ross's house, then put two and two together. Ross found it hard to believe that a senior officer of the Church would hire murderous bandits to steal it but there seemed no other explanation. 'Perhaps one other person knows what we're looking for, but he can't find it without the notebook.'

'You mean—' started Sister Chantal. Ross flashed her a look and she stopped. Now was not the time to explain to Hackett and the others why a senior Catholic priest was involved.

'So we've got serious competition?' said Hackett.

'We *had* serious competition,' said Ross. 'With those men dead, there's no way he can follow us into the jungle.'

'What about the police?' said Zeb.

'What about them?' said Mendoza, quietly.

All eyes turned to him.

'She means the bodies,' said Ross.

Mendoza bent down to the remaining body on the deck and rolled it into the river. A red stain marked where it had lain. 'What bodies?' He pointed to three large crocodiles moving through the water. The other two had already disappeared. He took a handkerchief from his pocket and passed it to Ross. 'Wipe your face.' Ross did so and Mendoza looked him in the eye. 'I killed three men to help you. The police here are not as they are in

America. They'll ask us a lot of questions – questions I don't need, questions you don't need. They'll take your book of directions and keep it. If you're in a hurry, señor, and want to find what you seek before your rival, don't involve the police. You understand?'

'I'm afraid I agree with him, Ross,' said Hackett. 'The police won't do us any favours.'

Ross looked at the women, who stared blankly at him, ashen-faced, eyes wide with shock, then at the churning river where a crocodile was already pulling the last body under the murky water. He had always had his doubts about this quest but now the stakes were even higher.

Mendoza's eyes met his. 'Where you're going you need a man who knows how to use a gun. When I left the army my boat was my future, but now it's gone. I have no insurance, no prospects. Give me a share of whatever you seek and I'll come with you.'

'You don't even know what we're looking for.'

'It must be valuable.'

Ross tried to judge the man standing before him. Mendoza had saved their lives and proved himself a powerful ally, but he might also make a dangerous enemy. He turned to the others. Zeb and Juarez nodded uncertainly. Sister Chantal lowered her eyes and said nothing. 'Nigel, you're the captain. It's your boat. What do you think?' Hackett hesitated. 'Now's not the time to be polite,' Ross pressed. 'Señor Mendoza says you've met him before. Have you?'

Hackett grimaced. 'I don't know. I've got an appalling memory for faces, but he has no reason to lie and we might easily have met. I've certainly been to Lagunas a number of times and met many river-runners. Anyway, I'd say Señor Mendoza's earned his passage.'

'That's settled, then. Now let's get the hell out of here.'

32

The Sacred Heart Hospital, Bridgeport, Connecticut

Ross and Lauren Kelly's unborn baby was now five months into its development, over halfway through the pregnancy. Its length from crown to rump was more than seven inches, its weight about ten and a half ounces. Though its rapid growth rate had slowed, the baby's organs were maturing and developing.

Yesterday her grandchild's progress had filled Diana Wharton with hope. Now she sat in the dark beside her daughter's bed, drifting into and out of sleep. She had intended to leave at midnight but had changed her mind: she preferred to be with Lauren than alone in her bed at home.

Something snapped her awake. Disoriented, she peered round the darkened room, silent except for the rhythmic beat of the instruments. According to the luminous clock on the wall it was almost three in the morning. As her eyes grew accustomed to the gloom she did a double take, unable to believe what she was seeing: Lauren's eyes were open.

Diana Wharton jumped up and bent close to her daughter. For a second she allowed herself to believe a miracle had happened – the miracle she had been praying for every day and every night. But Lauren's eyes were closed. It had been an illusion, a trick of the light, a cruel dream.

Tears streaming down her cheeks, knowing she would not sleep again that night, Diana stroked her daughter's face.

33

Iquitos

The remote capital of the Department of Lareto is unique. Linked to the outside world only by air and river, Iquitos is the world's only large city totally surrounded by jungle and unreachable by road.

Founded as a Jesuit mission in the 1750s, a century after Falcon had written the Voynich, Iquitos had to fend off constant attacks from Indian tribes who didn't wish to be converted. The tiny settlement survived and grew slowly until by the 1870s it had 1,500 inhabitants. Then came the great rubber boom and the population increased sixteen-fold. While the barons became fabulously rich, the rubber tappers, mainly local Indians, suffered virtual enslavement. During the Second World War the rubber market collapsed. Then, in the 1960s, a second boom revitalized the area, this time in oil. Iquitos was now a thriving frontier town, violent but prosperous, attracting oilmen, adventurers and tourists alike.

When the *Discovery* pulled alongside the other boats in Puerto Masusa, a couple of kilometres north of the city centre, Ross saw the influence of oil everywhere. Small children ran around in grubby oil-company T-shirts playing with logo-stamped tennis balls. A huge poster by the docks depicted a lush, idyllic jungle scene, complete with bright parrots, flowers and a cooling spring – not an ugly oil rig, pipeline or sump in sight. Beneath it was a discreet oil-company logo and the tag line *Ayudamos Perú a utilizar sus recursos naturales.* Helping Peru use its natural resources.

When the boat had docked, Hackett asked the group to gather in the galley. 'After what happened I realize some of you'll be nervous about going on. Iquitos is the last outpost of civilization from where you can board a plane back to Lima. Here, we'll take on final supplies and then we'll be on our own, in virgin jungle, for the next month or so. Once we leave no one will be able to return unless we all do. If you want to bail out, now's the time to do it.'

As Ross heard these words, his anxiety peaked. This was the point of no return, his last chance to fly back to Lauren. He looked around the group but no one raised a hand.

Except Juarez.

Hackett glared at him. 'We need you, Juarez. You're the only one of us who knows the jungle.'

'But why should I come with you, Señor Hackett?' Juarez asked. 'It is dangerous. People have tried to kill us. I don't even know what you're look-ing for.'

'The ruins of a lost civilization,' said Hackett.

'But I don't like ruins,' Juarez said mournfully.

'We're looking for gold,' Zeb said. 'Treasure.'

'How much?' asked Mendoza. He was rubbing his temples as if he was in pain.

'We don't know,' Ross said carefully. 'We're not sure what we'll find.'

'But you guys think there's something?' Mendoza said.

'I know it,' said Sister Chantal.

'That's good enough for me,' said Mendoza, shooting Juarez a meaningful look.

'Come on, Juarez,' said Zeb, with her most winning smile. 'You're a fit young man. You surely can't be scared when a girl like me and an old lady like Sister Chantal are prepared to go.'

Juarez reddened and shuffled uncomfortably in his chair. 'I'm not scared. I just want to know *why* I should go.'

'For glory and gold,' said Hackett. 'Come on, Juarez. You've always said you wanted to leave the jungle and visit the great cities of Europe and America. Well, with this gold, you could go to New York, Paris, London, wherever you want.'

'I only go if we share everything equally,' said Juarez.

'Agreed,' confirmed Ross, wondering how these people were going to react when they eventually discovered they hadn't been looking for gold but for a garden, which probably didn't exist. Sister Chantal didn't seem to worry about this, but he did. At that moment his GPS-enabled phone rang. When he heard his father's voice his pulse quickened. He walked out on deck. 'Hi, Dad. How's Lauren?'

'Stable. Her mother thought she saw something last night but it was nothing. I rang to ask about you. How's it going in Peru?'

'Early days,' said Ross. He decided against telling him about the attack. 'We're just about to head off into the jungle proper. The boat's got a radio but it'll be difficult to keep in touch.'

His father laughed. 'That may be no bad thing, son. Might stop you calling in every day.' He paused, as if hearing Ross's indecision. 'Son, whatever you think about what you're doing in Peru, you've got to choose. Either come home now and accept whatever happens, or commit to finding the garden. There can't be any half-measures. If you stay, you'll come home knowing you did all you could. If you don't you'll never find peace.'

As Ross put away the phone, he knew his father was right. Zeb and Sister Chantal came out on deck. 'How's Lauren?' asked Zeb. 'If you need to go back,' she checked her watch, 'we can be home by this time tomorrow.'

Sister Chantal said nothing.

'Is there a problem?' said Hackett, strolling out to join them. 'Bad news from home?'

'My wife's not been well.'

'So what the hell are you doing in the Amazon hunting treasure?'

'It's a long story, Nigel.'

Hackett hesitated, clearly balancing the desire to know more with his natural courtesy. 'I hope she'll be okay. Juarez and I are going ashore for supplies. We'll set off again in about six hours.' He looked meaningfully at Ross. 'You okay with that?'

Mendoza appeared suddenly, still rubbing his temples. He walked over to Hackett. 'You got some strong painkillers?'

'A few in my medical bag. Why?'

'Bad migraine.'

'I'll write a prescription. You can pick up some pills in town.' Hackett turned back to Ross. 'Are you in?'

Both Zeb and Sister Chantal were watching him closely. If Lauren died while he was away he'd feel terrible guilt. But if he went back and she died anyway, which she almost certainly would, he'd feel guilty for not having done everything in his power to save her. He had come this far and had to go on. Even if the garden was a myth, it offered the only chance to save his wife and he had to take it. Unlike Hackett, Mendoza and Juarez, he wasn't seeking mere treasure. He was seeking something far more precious and elusive. Hope. 'I'm in, Nigel,' he said. 'All the way.'

Six hours later

Yesterday's flight from Lima to Iquitos had been

222

uneventful, and Torino had spent a comfortable night at the Hotel Eldorado Plaza in the centre of the city. After dismissing his private secretary and the rest of his entourage in Lima, he was travelling alone – except, of course, for his guards. The fewer people who knew of his mission the better. His only concern related to Bazin. He had sent him a number of texts on his satellite phone, but had not yet received a response. He had also heard rumours in town: fishermen had found a half-eaten body in the river south of Iquitos, with a bullet through its head. There was also talk of gunfire and an abandoned dinghy.

However, as Torino stood on the deck of his requisitioned boat, he refused to worry unduly about his half-brother. If Bazin was dead, he had died performing a service for the Church. And his death had not been in vain: he had put contingencies in place. Torino blinked in the dying sun and raised a pair of binoculars to his eyes. He watched the *Discovery* leave Puerto Masusa and cruise downriver until it disappeared round the bend of the vast waterway. Then he looked at the palmtop computer Bazin had given him in Lima. The onscreen map showed a dot moving north-east down the Amazon.

Now four soldiers in jungle fatigues were loading his boat. Three were fair-haired, which, with their height, made them stand out among the smaller, darker locals. Historically, the Swiss Guard were recruited from the German-speaking Swiss cantons.

Two passed him with an open case of rifles and ammunition. 'Why are those coming with us?' Torino demanded.

Fleischer, the sergeant – the *Feldwebel* – frowned. 'Please, Father General, we're going into the jungle. My orders are to defend you. Guns may not sit well with your sacred office but we need them.'

'You misunderstand me, Feldwebel. I don't mind you bringing weapons. I'm only concerned to know – is that all you're taking?'

'I don't understand, Father General.'

Torino thought of the story in the Voynich, and Father Orlando Falcon's testimony in the Inquisition Archives. He considered the treacherous route to the garden's source, the *radix*, in the forbidden caves, and reflected on how the last conquistadors had been butchered, their blood colouring the stream a deep red. 'Assume you'll be confronted by forces far stronger and fiercer than you expect, Feldwebel. Arm yourselves with the best, most advanced weaponry you can. You must be capable of protecting us against every eventuality.' Then he remembered his agreement with the Holy Father. 'There are at least two more pieces of equipment you will need to bring.' He told Fleischer what they were.

'But, Father General, this will delay us by a day. Are you sure they're necessary?'

'I understood from the Holy Father that you were committed to helping me fulfil my mission *unquestioningly*. Is that your understanding, too, Feldwebel?'

'Yes, it is, Father General.'

'Then I suggest you do exactly as I ask. And, trust me, these extra precautions are as much for your benefit as mine.' Torino glanced up at the sun and basked in its warmth. The Lord was smiling down on him. Then his eyes dropped to the screen in his hand, the dot moving north-east. 'Hurry,' he said. 'I want to leave within twenty-four hours.'

34

Over the next few days, as the *Discovery* sailed down the Amazon, Ross became increasingly concerned about Sister Chantal. Since the attack she had been steadily withdrawing into herself. As each day passed, she was increasingly distant and spent more and more time in her cabin.

Every day they navigated by the compass bearings in Falcon's book, and every night they followed his star charts. On day three, they reached two small headlands that appeared to curve towards each other as they rose above the jungle: Los Cuernos del Toro, the Bull's Horns.

Here, Falcon's directions instructed them to turn off the reassuring main river into the maze of tributaries. Directly linked to the Amazon, they were large rivers in their own right, and bore signs of man's encroachment. In small villages, which a few years ago would have been untroubled by the modern world, they saw children wearing baseball caps and T-shirts, playing with the ubiquitous oil-company tennis balls. Even further into the forest they saw vast areas being cleared for oil pipelines: men wearing bright yellow hard hats were operating bright yellow earth movers, cutting swathes through the emerald green jungle, exposing earth as red as a bloody wound.

'Bastards,' said Zeb. 'Can't they see what they're doing? Why is everybody in the oil business so fucking short-sighted?'

'Because the world needs oil,' retorted Ross. 'Almost everything we use – everything *you* use, Zeb – comes from petroleum products. Shampoo, toothpaste, lip balm, non-stick frying-pans, CDs and DVDs, golf balls, not to mention everything made from any type of plastic.'

'But what about the consequences? When will the world decide that the remaining jungle is more precious than oil?'

He couldn't answer that. If Lauren could see this she would be as horrified as Zeb was. It shocked him, too. He knew that man had eroded a vast proportion of rainforest in the last few years; he had read the statistics. But seeing it at close quarters, how efficiently their machines cut through the trees, made him understand why Sister Chantal had been so concerned about preserving the garden. How much longer would it be before those yellow earth movers reached it? Assuming, of course, it existed.

Eventually they found themselves in virgin forest, and as the boat wound through the narrowing waterways Juarez called from the wheelhouse: 'Don't swim in the water here.'

'Why?' asked Zeb. 'Piranha?'

'Worse. Candiru.'

'What?'

Hackett grimaced. 'Tiny catfish. They're really nasty creatures, especially if you're a bloke. That's why I put condoms on your list.'

'I don't understand,' said Ross.

'A candiru will swim up the urethra, open the spines on its head like an umbrella and anchor itself halfway up the penis, blocking it so you can't piss. Forget the horrific pain. Without surgery – major surgery – your bladder will burst and you'll die. Not a nice way to go.'

Unconsciously Ross crossed his legs – as did every man on board.

As they moved deeper into the maze, the back of his neck tingled, as if unseen eyes were watching him constantly from the jungle. Not one pair but thousands. He flapped at flies and mosquitoes the size of small birds, all apparently immune to insect repellent. A brace of blind river dolphins passed the boat. He saw a giant anaconda make its way lazily through the water and slither up the riverbank, its scales glistening in the sunlight before it disappeared into the jungle. He checked his phone. No signal. His father couldn't contact him if Lauren's condition changed. He felt a sudden surge of anxiety, followed by a strange elation. He had no choice now but to focus on the job in hand.

Nevertheless, this beautiful, dangerous paradise would be an easy and inhospitable place to get lost.

Suddenly he was acutely aware of the importance of Falcon's directions and found himself looking for Sister Chantal. Though she hadn't helped much so far, they would need her to clarify the more cryptic directions. Mendoza lounged on the shaded part of the deck, holding his head, Zeb was reading in the galley, Hackett and Juarez were at the helm. It was almost four in the afternoon. Sister Chantal liked a siesta after lunch but she was usually around by three.

Zeb glanced up from her book. 'What is it?'

'Have you seen Sister Chantal?'

'She's probably in her cabin. Why?'

He lowered his voice. 'I want to ask her about the directions.'

'I'll come with you.'

Zeb knocked on Sister Chantal's door and heard, 'Is it time?' She opened the door to reveal the blinds drawn, the cabin in half-darkness and Sister Chantal lying on the bed. Her eyes were closed. 'Is it time?' the nun asked again, apparently half-asleep or in a trance. 'Is my burden to be lifted?'

'It's okay, Sister. We'll come back later. Sorry we disturbed you.'

35

The following morning, the *Discovery* reached another of the landmarks featured in Falcon's book. Zeb looked at the distinctive sugarloaf-shaped mound, rising above the skyline of forest trees, and consulted her compass. 'We should head in that direction,' she said, pointing to a channel where the water was rougher.

Juarez ran to the front of the boat and used a long pole to sound the depth of the swirling river. 'Okay, Señor Hackett,' he shouted to the wheelhouse, then pointed downriver to where the water frothed white. 'Mind the rocks.'

Ross studied the geological map on his palmtop computer and felt a frisson: they were entering a part of the jungle where the on-screen information was extrapolated but not known. They were now in true *terra incognita* where the earth's crust was probably ancient pre-Cambrian rock, unchanged for billions of years. The model supported his hypothesis for Falcon's garden and gave him hope.

Zeb came over to him and pulled him away from the others. 'From here this river gets more and more wild until it comes to what Falcon warns is La Boca del Inferno, the Mouth of Hell. He's written PELIGRO, danger, then told us to rush into the Mouth of Hell to pass beyond El Velo de la Luz, the Veil of Light, whatever that means. Perhaps the Mouth of Hell is a waterfall.' She thumbed through the translation. 'Yes, he talks about one here.'

Ross nodded. 'But what's the Veil of Light? We've got to warn Hackett.'

Hackett and the others agreed that the Mouth of Hell probably was a waterfall.

'What do we do about it?' asked Mendoza.

'Go carefully,' said Hackett, grimly. 'And where's Sister Chantal? I haven't seen her all day.'

'She's tired,' said Zeb. 'Catching up on some rest.'

'You'd better warn her it'll get pretty bumpy soon.'

When Ross and Zeb knocked on the door, they heard, 'Come in.' Once again Sister Chantal was lying on her bed with the blinds drawn. 'Sister,' said Ross, 'we've got to ask you about the directions. About La Boca del Inferno. It's important.'

'Come closer,' she said, in a faraway voice.

Ross stepped into the room. 'I also need to ask you about El Velo de la Luz. Father Orlando Falcon said there was danger. Do you know why?'

'Come closer,' she said. 'Let me see your face.' A fine sheen of perspiration beaded her forehead and

her eyes seemed focused on a point beyond his face.
'You're here,' she said, with a smile. 'I knew my
sacrifice would be rewarded.'

'Sister, are you okay?'

'I'm fine,' she said. She touched his cheek.
'Everything's fine now you're here, Father Orlando.'

36

That night

The knocking woke Torino from a deep sleep.

'What is it?'

He roused himself from his bed and saw Feldwebel Fleischer standing in his cabin doorway. 'Father General, I have Cardinal Prefect Guido Vasari on the radio in the wheelhouse. He is calling from Rome and demands to speak with you.'

Demands? thought Torino. 'What time is it?'

A faint smile. 'In Rome it's nine in the morning, Your Excellency. Here it's two.'

Torino clambered out of his cabin and made his way along the deck. The wheelhouse, lit up like a lone lantern, made the vast river and the chattering forest fringing its banks seem even darker. The close, warm night was black with only the faintest glow from a cloud-obscured moon.

In the wheelhouse, the soldier piloting the vessel handed him the radio. Torino wiped the sleep from his eyes. 'I need privacy, please.' He waited for the soldiers to leave, then put the radio to his lips. 'Cardinal Prefect?'

'Father General, where are you?' Vasari sounded angry. 'You haven't called in for days. I had to be patched through to your men by the Minister of the Interior.'

'I am on the Amazon and it's the middle of the night.'

'I don't care what time it is. You are to return immediately.'

'Why?'

'When we sanctioned this venture you expressly told the Holy Father and me that your scholars had translated the final section of the Voynich. You said you had directions to this garden. However, when I requested a copy from the scholars in your office, they knew nothing of any directions.'

It was Torino's turn to be angry. 'Cardinal Prefect, you have no right to question me or to pry into matters of the Society of Jesus. The Jesuit order is not under your jurisdiction.'

'It is, however, under the Holy Father's. He's as concerned as I am. You said you could find Father Orlando Falcon's Garden of God, and do it discreetly because you had a map. We thought you *knew* where it was. It's becoming increasingly obvious that this garden is a myth, a personal obsession of yours.'

'It's not a myth.'

'Even if it does exist, how do you expect to find it without a map?'

'By following Dr Kelly, who does have one.'

'*Following* him? Can't you see that Dr Kelly is only doing this because he's seeking a miracle to save his wife? *You* are a senior officer of the Holy Mother Church, a man of God. You set an example for Rome.'

'But what if Dr Kelly finds something? I can take it from him, claim it for the new Vatican. I have the legal authority and the soldiers to enforce it.'

'You're talking about a direct confrontation, a very *public* one. The very thing we agreed we must avoid. Father General, this madness must stop. You will jeopardize the Church's reputation *and* the new Vatican project. You and the soldiers must return immediately.'

'Since when has the Superior General of the Society of Jesus taken orders from a cardinal?'

'These aren't my orders.' Vasari was almost apoplectic with fury. 'They come directly from—'

'I can't hear you, Cardinal Prefect, the radio's breaking up.'

Vasari was screaming now. 'You must come back, Father General. That is a direct order from the Holy Father.'

Torino listened to him for a moment longer, then turned off the radio. He rose and called Fleischer. 'Feldwebel, I want there to be total radio silence from now on. No incoming or outgoing calls.'

'But, Father General, the security protocol is to call in our position every two days.'

'In that case, change it. The Holy Father demands total discretion. There are those who want to stop my mission and no one must know where I am.' He handed the radio to Fleischer. 'Tell the Peruvian authorities you'll not be receiving any more calls, and that you'll only call in if there's an emergency. When you've done that I want this radio temporarily disabled.'

'Yes, Father General.'

'Good. Wake me at dawn.'

So, Cardinal Prefect Guido Vasari was sabotaging his mission, he thought. No doubt he was already pouring poison into the Holy Father's ear. That was the trouble with the Roman Catholic Church today: the leaders had no vision. But when he found the Garden of God and presented it to the Holy Father, they would understand. Then they would recognize him as the saviour of the Holy Mother Church.

37

The next morning
They heard it first: a rumble like distant thunder.
Despite Falcon's warnings and Hackett's vigilance,
the Mouth of Hell still took them by surprise. As
the *Discovery* turned into a narrower, winding
stretch of river the rough waters appeared calmer.
Juarez leant over the prow and lowered the sounding pole, expecting the water to get shallower, a sign
that rocks, rapids and a waterfall were imminent.
But the water wasn't shallower. It was deeper.

Much deeper.

And the current was stronger. So strong that he
had to grip the sounding pole to keep it in his grasp
and trust in the harness he was wearing to avoid
falling in. The current hauled the boat along and as
Hackett struggled to slow it, the rumble became a
roar. They turned a tight bend but even when they
straightened and looked beyond the giant trees that
lined the river they couldn't see anything. There was
too much spray.

Then the waterfall was before them, and Ross heard Hackett mutter, 'Bollocks.'

It wasn't the drop into Hell they had expected but *above* them. The stretch of river ended abruptly. The *Discovery* was heading straight for a towering cliff from which water cascaded into the river. But that wasn't the only reason why Hackett was swearing. Between the boat and the waterfall there was a whirlpool as fierce as any Ross had ever seen. *This* was the Mouth of Hell and Ross understood now why Falcon had so christened it. At that moment, it appeared that anything caught in its vortex would be sucked into the underworld.

'What do we do?' Juarez shouted.

'Pull into the bank,' yelled Mendoza.

'Too many rocks,' replied Hackett, 'and I've got no control of the boat, anyway.'

'So what do we do? Jump off?' Zeb pointed to the two rowboats at the back. 'We could take those.'

Hackett laughed. 'If the *Discovery*'s engines can't escape it—'

'Go faster,' ordered a voice behind them.

Sister Chantal was standing by the wheelhouse, frail and dishevelled. Her eyes were red-rimmed but clear.

'I've got it on full throttle. I can't go any faster.'

'Not backwards,' she said. '*Forwards*. Go full speed towards it.'

'Sister, are you mad?' said Mendoza.

'If you want to live, do as I say. And do it now.'

'No way.'

'Do it,' said Ross. 'The direction tells us to *rush* into the Mouth of Hell.'

Hackett shook his head in disbelief. 'Have you seen that cliff? It's solid rock. If we manage to get past the whirlpool and avoid getting crushed by the waterfall we'll smash into the rock.'

'Go forward,' insisted Sister Chantal, 'as fast as you can. Head for El Velo de la Luz.'

Ross pointed at the cliff as the sunlight caught the waterfall, causing it to sparkle like a curtain of blindingly brilliant diamonds. 'El Velo de la Luz, the Veil of Light. Aim for the waterfall. Full speed ahead.' Hackett hesitated. 'Unless you've got a better idea?'

Hackett changed gear and steered the boat straight for the Mouth of Hell and the waterfall. 'Everyone, get under cover and hold on to something firm. This isn't going to be fun.'

The engines roared and the boat shot forward as though surfing a wave. Ross stood with the others in the galley as she sped towards the whirlpool's boiling waters. For one sickening moment, it appeared that the Mouth of Hell would swallow them whole but as the *Discovery* entered the whirlpool centrifugal forces pushed her to the outer lip, then threw her into the waterfall, where she was deluged. The jolt threw Ross to the floor, smashing his left hand. The pain was excruciating as he scrabbled to his feet. From their wide-eyed expressions he could tell that the others were as terrified as he was. To his surprise, Mendoza's eyes were closed and he was crossing himself. Even Sister Chantal looked frightened. Then everything darkened and he braced himself for the impact.

It never came.

Instead the sound fell away, became muffled, as if someone had closed a door. He moved to the deck. They were no longer under the waterfall but in a tunnel inside the cliff. The river evidently didn't end in the whirlpool and the cliff face, but continued into the rock. He guessed that this area of the jungle was riddled with subterranean rivers, the lower ones fed by the whirlpool.

As if on Charon's ferry to the underworld, they travelled down the dark waterway. No one spoke. Ross's main fear was that the river would descend deeper and spill them into an abyss.

They emerged, eventually, into a small pool. When Ross looked back he saw they had come through a ridge of rock that curved round on both sides as far as he could see, resembling the edge of a large crater. The contours were disguised beneath trees and thick foliage but from this angle its shape was clear. Ahead, a narrow stream meandered into the jungle.

'Let me see your hand,' Hackett said. Ross winced as the doctor felt it. 'Looks like you've fractured your wrist. It's nastier than it looks and could take a while to heal.' He went to his cabin and returned with a black medical bag. 'Ideally, you'd have an X-ray to find out if you need surgery and then we'd put it in plaster, but that's not an option here. If I put it in a tight bandage and you limit the use of the hand, it should be okay for now.'

'Señor Hackett,' said a voice from the wheelhouse.

'What is it, Juarez?'

'The radio's not working. I can't find anything wrong with it but it's dead. Probably got damaged back there.'

Hackett was bandaging Ross's hand and wrist. 'A buggered radio means we're stuck out here with no means of communicating with the outside world. We're on our own. Be grateful you haven't broken a leg.'

Zeb was studying Falcon's directions and a copy of the Voynich translation. 'We've got to carry on down that stream, but even I can see it's too narrow for the *Discovery*.'

Ross pointed to her two dinghies, each about eight feet long. 'How about those?'

Hackett nodded. 'Three to a boat. And whatever we need to take with us.' He turned to Juarez and Mendoza. 'Why don't you two get them down and start transferring supplies and equipment? Take the guns and machetes, too.'

'I'll help,' said Zeb.

Sister Chantal was sitting in the galley, eyes closed. Ross rested his good hand on her shoulder. 'You okay?'

She opened her eyes, focused on him and smiled. 'Yes,' she said. 'I'm fine.' He studied her anxiously.

Falcon's directions were even more cryptic from this point.

For the next hour and a half they transferred all they needed from the *Discovery* to the two dinghies. Ross, Sister Chantal and Hackett would travel in one boat, Mendoza, Zeb and Juarez in the second. Finally, as they were boarding, Hackett returned to the *Discovery*. He had a key in his hand.

'What are you doing?' asked Mendoza. 'You've already battened down the hatches and locked the doors.'

Hackett inserted the key in a black box by the wheelhouse and turned it. 'Arming the alarm.'

Zeb laughed and Ross couldn't restrain a smile. Hackett had been so stoic in handling the attack by the bandits and negotiating the Mouth of Hell that Ross had almost forgotten his obsessive habits. Genuine crises seemed not to faze the Englishman, but minor concerns elicited disproportionate anxiety.

Zeb got into her boat. 'Nigel, I can understand you closing her up to keep out animals, but an alarm? Who the fuck's going to steal her out here?'

'You can't be too careful,' said Hackett. He sounded hurt.

'But who the hell's going to *hear* the alarm out here?' said Zeb.

'It's a deterrent, and it's *my* boat,' he said.

Zeb returned to her notes and the Voynich translation. 'Our guiding priest warns us that this waterway is filled with dragon-like creatures.'

'Crocodiles,' said Sister Chantal.

'Makes sense,' said Hackett calmly.

'Shit,' said Zeb.

'Juarez, you know about Amazon crocodiles,' said Hackett. 'They shouldn't trouble us in the boats, should they?'

'No,' said Juarez, with reassuring confidence, as the two boats set out in convoy. Then, after a pause: 'But we must be careful if there are many of them.'

Ross shifted uncomfortably on the small seat. The wooden planks that formed the boat's hull seemed thin and insubstantial. 'How many crocodiles might there be in an infested river?'

'Two or three,' said Juarez.

Ross relaxed a little.

'Hundred,' clarified Hackett.

38

In idle moments Zeb found herself comparing Nigel Hackett with Osvaldo Mendoza and discovering, to her surprise – and concern – that the quirky Englishman intrigued her. Hackett was infuriating and a right royal pain in the ass, but undeniably interesting. How could he worry about the *Discovery*'s being stolen in the middle of the jungle but row calmly down a narrow river infested with crocodiles?

Zeb wasn't calm, far from it. Not much scared her and she revered Mother Nature in all her diversity, but she hated crocodiles. Even more than snakes. And snakes scared the crap out of her. After the first few miles, though, she stopped counting the crocodiles. There were too many.

And it was getting dark.

She wasn't sure whether she preferred being able to see the beasts in all their hideous glory or just their shapes in the dusk. As night fell, the stars were reflected in the dark water and Zeb would have been lost in the beauty of the place, had it not been for the glassy eyes that broke the surface like twin periscopes, glowing ruby-red in the reflection of her torch. They remained motionless, but her light stirred up a hollow grunt. There were many such pairs of eyes and, as the boats passed them, the warning grunt arose. Zeb could barely see her companions and no one spoke. It was as though she was alone in the velvet dark.

Gradually, Zeb grew aware of light above and behind her. Over the jagged horizon of trees an orange disc appeared. She knew it was the moon but it felt like sunrise on another planet. As the stars dimmed, the water turned silver, and she became acutely aware that she was the alien in the unfamiliar environment.

In the half-light, she heard Juarez's voice, hushed but clear: 'Every crocodile has a different eye colour. Green and orange are common. This is the black caiman. Its eyes are clear but they look red because the light reflects off their blood vessels.'

Silence fell, only to be broken by another grunt. This time when Zeb moved her torch she saw that it had come from Juarez, crouched in the front of the boat. He was answered by a grunt from near the shore. 'I have confused them,' he whispered. 'They don't know if we're intruders or one of them.'

The river fell silent again.

Then Zeb heard a deeper grunt directly behind her. She twisted away, rocking the boat, and aimed her light in its direction, revealing a pair of eyes wider apart than any she had seen, red lights mounted on the end of a thick black log. If the distance between them was proportional to the size of the animal the creature had to be massive. Suddenly, there was a hard bump against the boat. It tipped alarmingly and Zeb lost her balance.

There was another bump, harder than the first.

She was going to fall into the river and called to Juarez for help but he was holding the oars. The water's chill made her gasp and she went under, kicking, panicking, desperate to get back into the boat. She had read that crocodiles didn't bite off limbs as a shark did, but gripped you in their crushing jaws and rolled you until you drowned or were too weak to fight. Then they dragged you to a submerged hollow in the riverbank and left you there with their other prey. Eventually, they returned and ate you. She had read stories of victims regaining consciousness in the reptile's watery lair, surrounded by rotting flesh . . .

Frantically she reached up to the boat, to where Mendoza was holding out his hand. Something touched her leg and she screamed. She kicked harder, adrenalin pumping through her.

Then she heard a deeper, louder grunt. Right behind her. The creature had to be huge. She had never felt such raw terror. Something gripped her shoulder, pulling her away from Mendoza. She screamed again and at that moment she knew she was close to death. She fought like a madwoman, trying to squirm out of the grip.

The grunt sounded again, close to her ear, chilling her, and she felt herself pulled out of the water. She struggled, but the grip was too tight. Then, through her panic, she heard, 'Calm down, Zeb. You're safe.' It was Ross. 'Nigel and I have got you. The big croc's moved off.'

As they laid her in the bottom of the boat, she found herself looking up into Hackett's concerned face. Despite the warm air, she was shivering. 'Gave us a bit of a scare there,' he said, wrapping a blanket round her.

She sat up. 'Gave *you* a scare?' she said, teeth chattering. 'Fuck! What happened? I could have sworn it got me. I heard it real close.'

Hackett pointed at Ross. 'The last couple of grunts weren't a croc. It was Ross.'

'Ross? But it was so real and so loud.'

'I thought I'd better make it sound bigger than the crocs in the water with you. Scare them off. You okay?'

'I guess.' She took a deep breath. 'Thanks. The water's refreshing but it's not a good night for a swim.'

Juarez navigated them through the infested waters until eventually they reached a clearer stretch of river. When he seemed satisfied that it was free of crocodiles he directed them to the bank where there was an elevated section, reached by a set of natural rock steps. 'We build a fire there and rest for the night.' He looked back at the dark river and its myriad red eyes. 'A *big* fire.'

Earlier

La Boca del Inferno took Torino's party by surprise, just as it had Ross's. However, when the soldier piloting the boat tried to slow down and throw it into reverse Torino said, 'Go straight ahead. Don't flinch. The Lord will protect us.'

Feldwebel Fleischer shook his head. 'But, Father General, it's dangerous. It'll soon be dark and your safety is our primary responsibility.'

'Have faith. We're on a sacred mission and the Lord is guiding me. No harm can come to us. Head straight for the waterfall.'

Torino could not know what fate awaited them. He had, however, studied the Voynich and the Inquisition Archives, and on the screen in his hand he could see the dot of Bazin's GPS transmitter somewhere beyond the whirlpool and the waterfall. Most importantly, Torino was convinced he was on a righteous mission for God, and it was not yet his time to die.

For a moment, as the boat thrashed in the churning water, he thought the sergeant would overrule him, but the pilot held his nerve and his course.

After the boat had thrust through the whirlpool, Torino breathed a sigh of relief. He wasn't surprised, though. Even as the boat travelled down the dark, subterranean river within the cliff he knew God was protecting him. He also knew that Falcon and the conquistadors had survived the ordeal on simple rafts with nothing but faith to sustain them and that, according to the flashing dot on his palmtop screen, Ross Kelly's boat was somewhere ahead.

Soon they saw the *Discovery* neatly tucked against the left bank. The gleaming modern vessel was incongruous in the virgin-jungle setting and the soldiers raised their weapons.

Feldwebel Fleischer gestured at the computer in Torino's hand. 'This is the boat you've been tracking, Father General. Who are they?'

'The vessel belongs to enemies of the Holy Mother Church, who would do anything to stop my mission.'

'What is your mission, Father General? All we've been told is to escort you into the jungle and bring you back safely.'

'All will become clear, Feldwebel, but for now we must follow these people and ensure they do not thwart the Lord's purpose.'

'But how will we follow them? They're no longer on board and you were tracking the boat.'

Torino studied the blinking dot on his screen, his face grim. 'The Lord will guide me.' His eyes settled on the narrow stream winding its way into the jungle. *Dragon-like creatures*. 'Check there's no one on board, then disable their boat.'

Fleischer frowned. 'Is that necessary?'

'Are you questioning me?'

'No, Father General.'

'Then do as I say. Fill the boats with the weapons and supplies, then let's make our way down that stream.'

39

'That's incredible. Do it again,' said Hackett, lifting another bottle of beer from the cool river. Ross marvelled at how clean and uncreased Hackett's khaki safari suit was, despite all they had been through. Juarez did another of his long grunting crocodile noises and Ross copied it.

'How do you do it, Ross?' asked Mendoza. 'I can't make the same sound as Juarez and I've been trying for ages now. You did it first time.'

'I have perfect pitch, which means I can identify and reproduce any note I hear. I discovered it when I was in a church choir. It's not very useful, really, just a party trick.'

They had pulled the boats on to the bank and had had supper – tinned beans, rice and fish. They were now sitting round the fire drinking coffee and beer, letting off steam after the excitement of the day. Only Sister Chantal was asleep, curled up a few feet away.

'You used to sing in a church choir?' asked Zeb, astonishment written on her face.

'Only as a kid.'

'I used to go to church,' said Mendoza, popping a painkiller into his mouth. He sounded wistful and Ross remembered him crossing himself when the *Discovery* was in the Mouth of Hell. 'I still believe in God as my saviour.' His companions gawped – this was the man they had witnessed shoot three dead – but Mendoza ignored them. 'You believe in God, Ross?' he asked.

'I believe in good, not God.'

'How will you find absolution for your sins?'

Ross thought about this. 'By trying to take responsibility for my actions, I guess. I don't believe you can be absolved of your sins, as you put it. You can only try to make amends with good deeds. Overwrite the bad with the good.'

'Only the Church can wipe away your sins,' said Juarez, with an emphatic nod.

Ross laughed. 'You can't just go to church and ask some priest to wipe the slate clean. When you wrong a man you ask *him* for forgiveness, not God. You prove your remorse by your deeds, not prayers. We are what we do. One good deed can make a lot of difference to the world.'

'A good deed in the eyes of God or man?'

'Man, of course.'

'But how does man know good without the guidance of God?' asked Juarez.

'And how does man know God's guidance without the Church?' said Mendoza.

'Enough!' said Hackett, taking a swig of beer. 'Where were you brought up? Don't you know it's simply not done to discuss religion, politics or sex over the dinner table?' He turned to Mendoza. 'Let me ask you a much more interesting question. I don't mean to offend you, señor, but you were a soldier and we all saw what happened on the river near Iquitos. What's it like to kill a man?'

'What sort of question is that?' said Zeb, shocked.

Hackett raised his hands defensively. 'I qualified as a doctor, made a vow to do no harm, but I also served in the British Army and had military training. I've often wondered what it's like to take a life.' He flashed a crooked smile. 'Christ, during my divorce I fantasized about it. So tell me, señor, what's it feel like?'

For a long moment Ross thought he wasn't going to answer. Then Mendoza said, 'Killing one man is difficult. Killing the second is easier, the third easier still. Soon it's so easy life has no value any more. And when life has no value, nothing else does. Only what you believe. Your faith.' He smiled, almost sweetly, at Hackett. 'Stick to your Hippocratic oath, Dr Hackett. You'll sleep better for it.'

Hackett digested this. Then he turned to Ross. 'Since we're getting to know each other, tell us how you came by the priest's notebook.' He pointed at

Ross, Zeb and the sleeping shape of Sister Chantal. 'And what brought you three together.'

'It just happened,' said Ross, evasively.

Juarez rescued him. 'Why you gringos always want to find old ruins?'

'Because of their history,' said Hackett. 'And their gold.'

'You don't care about the curse of *el abuelo*?'

'The what?' said Ross.

Hackett raised an eyebrow, sneezed, then took a hit on his inhaler. 'The curse of *el abuelo* – the grandfather. Juarez's people believe it's dangerous to enter ruins because the curse of *el abuelo* will strike you. It's an unpleasant transference in which all the diseases of the gathered dead enter and infest the interloper's body.'

They laughed, but Juarez was indignant. 'It's true,' he protested.

Suddenly they were silenced by a distant, high-pitched wail.

'What the hell was that?' exclaimed Zeb.

Hackett's face had paled. 'The alarm on my boat.'

It stopped as abruptly as it had started.

'Must have been an animal or a malfunction,' said Mendoza.

'You're probably right,' said Ross. What else could it have been? No other human had reason to come this way. Except Torino. And he had no way of knowing where they were headed.

A rifle shot rang out, startling them.

'What the hell—'

Mendoza was standing, rifle nestled in his shoulder. 'Got him,' he said. 'That'll keep them away better than any grunting.'

Hackett arced the beam of his torch towards the river, and Ross saw, reflected in the light, countless unblinking eyes staring at them.

40

The next day they reached El Halo, a twenty-foot-diameter circle of black stone, veined with quartz that sparkled in the sun. According to Falcon, El Halo was the place where they should leave the boats and continue their journey on foot. From here, in Falcon's notebook, the directions became more cryptic – not least the next one: At El Halo use the arrow to set your course, then follow it through the jungle to La Barba Verde, the Green Beard.

After a sleepless night spent listening to the crocodiles, some had changed places on the boats before continuing on their voyage. Sister Chantal waved away Ross's concern for her. 'I'm okay.' Now, as they reached the distinctive circle of stone, Ross knew that the nun's interpretation would be of crucial importance. The lead boat had already reached the bank and was obscured by El Halo. When Ross's boat joined it, Hackett and Mendoza were unloading. He couldn't see the nun.

'Where's Sister Chantal?' he asked.

'She must have walked off,' Hackett suggested. 'She can't be far.'

Ross panicked. They were in the middle of the jungle and the one person who could direct them was missing. Then he saw her behind the black stone with her back to him.

'Where do we go from here, Sister?' he asked. She didn't reply. 'What does the next clue mean?'

Still no reply.

She stared at El Halo blankly, then began to stroke the stone. His heart sank.

When he stepped closer, he saw that she was studying marks carved into the stone, gate marks such as those a prisoner scratches on a cell wall to count the days, four vertical strokes crossed with a diagonal, representing five. Beside it was a single vertical stroke, indicating a total of six. There were also six sets of roman numerals. It took Ross a moment to work out that they represented dates, the most recent more than seventy years ago. Before he could process what he was seeing, Sister Chantal brushed her hands over them.

'I know where we are,' she said, to no one in particular, eyes sparkling. She clutched her crucifix. 'Give me a compass.'

Ross reached into his pocket and handed her his. She stroked the stone again. 'Feel it, Ross,' she said.

He touched the stone and felt a raised area, disguised by moss. His fingers described the shape of a triangle with a tail.

'What is it?' said Zeb.

'An arrow.'

'And it points south by south-east,' said Sister Chantal, studying the compass.

Ross checked the map on his GPS palmtop and tried to work out where the arrow might be pointing, but his screen showed only a blank expanse of uncharted virgin jungle.

'Follow me,' said Sister Chantal.

'Wait,' said Mendoza, turning back to the boats. 'I've got to get something.'

'Hurry,' said the nun, showing no trace of her earlier exhaustion. 'We're getting closer. I can sense it.'

41

The jungle was everything described in the Voynich. Noisy, hellish and hot. Juarez made everyone wear heavy shoes and watch each step because of the constant threat of fer-de-lance and other poisonous creatures. Cutting through the steaming undergrowth with heavy packs was slow, exhausting work. Sister Chantal leant on the others for support but led with almost manic vigour.

That night, after a hasty supper of fish and rice, they slept in hammocks suspended above the forest floor, shrouded in nets to keep out insects and other inquisitive jungle creatures drawn to their body warmth. Exhausted, listening to the constant chatter of the forest, Ross held his aching wrist and wondered about Lauren, his sadness tempered by excitement. Then he fell into a deep, dreamless sleep.

The next afternoon they reached a small lagoon backed by looming cliffs that blocked their path. Covered with trees and dense foliage, the high ridge of rock was another apparent dead end. Then the reinvigorated Sister Chantal called, 'Over here!'

She had walked fifty yards to their right and was pointing up at the cliff. Its fissures reminded Ross of the famous 'face' on Ayers Rock in Australia, with eyes, nose and mouth. Below the mouth a mass of vines and other greenery stretched to the ground like a beard: La Barba Verde.

Using machetes, Hackett and Mendoza cut through the greenery to reveal a large opening in the cliff face. Ross checked his watch, and when he led the others through the gap, he noted it was 1.58 p.m. The passage took them through a series of unusual caves, marbled and striated with fossils, minerals and ores. Under different circumstances he might have stopped for samples.

Eventually, they emerged on to a high shelf, over-looking a narrow valley that stretched to the far horizon. In the afternoon light it was a lush green paradise, splashed with exotic blooms of red, blue and other primary colours. There were fewer trees than there had been in the jungle and on the terrain above the valley. Ross had read once that when trees are burnt or chopped down in a forest, an abundance of other growth quickly fills the rich soil, exploiting the space and the sunlight filtering through the thinned canopy to the forest floor. What had thinned the trees here?

He checked his watch again and noticed it was only two minutes past two, which was impossible. Many more than four minutes had passed since he'd last checked his watch, more like thirty. He then realized that the second hand had stopped. The rugged and expensive Tag Heuer had been a Christmas gift from Lauren, and Tags didn't just stop. He shook his wrist and turned to Zeb. 'What time do you make it?'

'Two minutes past two.'

Ross frowned. 'Nigel?'

Hackett glanced at his wrist. 'The same.' Then he tapped his watch. 'Hang on, it's stopped.'

'So has mine,' said Ross. 'It appears all our watches stopped at exactly the same time.' He pointed back at the ridge. 'Perhaps there was something magnetic in the caves we walked through.' He reached into his pack and checked the GPS on his palmtop computer. The screen gave a quick reading then fizzed, like a television with a faulty aerial. 'Wow,' he said. 'Whatever force it is, it's powerful enough to stop satellite signals too.' From this point on, then, they would be blind. Lost in space and time with no idea of where or even *when* they were. They were now totally dependent on Falcon's notebook – not just to find the garden but also their way back. 'Zeb, what does Father Orlando say we do next?'

Zeb glanced at her notes. 'We keep left and walk along the high shelf, with the valley on our right.' She pointed to the dense forest above it. 'We head over there.'

But Sister Chantal turned right, scrabbled in the undergrowth and began to walk down a narrow, sloping path into the valley. Ross's heart skipped a beat.

'Where are you going, Sister?' asked Zeb, echoing his thoughts. 'The directions don't lead down there.'

Sister Chantal carried on, then stopped on a natural viewing platform.

'Have you seen something?' asked Hackett. 'What's down there?'

She beckoned. 'If you come here, Mr Hackett, I'll show you.'

Ross and Hackett clambered down, leaving the others with the packs and equipment. Perhaps it was the angle of the setting sun, or the perspective from the lower ledge, but as Ross stood beside her and Hackett the valley's secret was revealed: a regular pattern of geometric structures.

It was too much for Hackett, who collapsed to his knees. 'This is it,' he said. 'We've only gone and found it.' Tears streamed down his face. 'This is the mother metropolis.'

Ross, too, was awestruck. The ruins of Kuelap had been vast but they were dwarfed now by the lost city laid out below him. Despite the greenery that covered everything, he could clearly see the contours of what had once been a mighty metropolis. The streets, the plazas, even the few remaining pillars that matched the mighty trees in the surrounding jungle were clearly visible. As he peered down he saw two spotted jaguars lope through the boulevards. This once great city had been reclaimed by nature.

'This place has probably been lost to mankind for more than a thousand years. Those circular habitations are typical of the Chachapoyan cloud people. I bet this is where their civilization was born, and many more besides – Christ, this could be the cradle of *all* South American civilizations. This is fantastic. A life's dream come true.' He called up to the others: 'We're here! We've found it! The mother of all lost cities!'

'Will there be gold?' asked Mendoza.

'There's a simple way to find out. Let's go down and take a look.'

'But what about *el abuelo*?' wailed Juarez.

'Where's your courage, man?' growled Mendoza.

Hackett laughed. 'Trust me, my friend, these ruins are worth the risk. They'll make us rich and famous. All of us.'

When Hackett led Juarez and Mendoza down into the valley, Ross and Zeb hung back with Sister Chantal. 'What is this place, Sister?' said Ross, quietly.

She did not reply.

'It's not in the Voynich or Falcon's book,' said Zeb, flicking through her notes.

'Perhaps it really is Eldorado,' said Ross, 'and Father Orlando missed it. Perhaps he and the conquistadors walked right past the very thing they were seeking.'

'Look at them,' said Zeb, watching Hackett and the others rushing down the path. Ross detected fondness in her eyes. 'Nigel's like a kid. Who'd have thought the tight-ass could get so excited? For his sake, I hope there is gold here.'

'There is,' said Sister Chantal, emphatically. 'So much that they'll stay here while we go in search of something infinitely more valuable. We should be able to reach the garden and be back in a week. We'll leave them a note.'

Ross realized he had seriously misjudged her. 'You had this little diversion planned from the start, didn't you?'

'The fewer people who know about the garden the better.'

Ross stepped round so he could see her face. 'How did you know this place was here?'

When she met his gaze her eyes were ruthlessly clear. 'I'm the Keeper,' she said, and walked down into the lost city.

42

The breeze dropped as they descended into the valley. By the time they reached the city, there was no movement in the warm, humid air, and the sheen on Ross's skin had developed into rivulets of sweat. As they passed the crumbling gate towers, the sounds of the jungle were replaced with an eerie quiet. Ross listened intently but heard only the occasional drone of insects. Among the vine-clad ruins and the surrounding slopes of the deep, lush valley, he had the surreal impression that he was on the floor of the ocean in a vast, verdant Atlantis. The impression was heightened when he looked up, beyond the towering pillars, to the sun refracted in the hazy blue sky above.

'I don't like this place. It's dead,' said Juarez, as he shuffled along behind Hackett. 'Something bad happened here.'

'Shut up,' said Mendoza.

'Yes, Juarez. Will you relax, for Christ's sake?' added Hackett.

But as they walked down the main boulevard, dwarfed by the towering rock edifices that lined their passage, stepping over thick vines and passing narrow side streets, Ross noted that both Mendoza and Hackett had spoken softly when they admonished the other man, as if wary of disturbing some malevolent presence. Despite the silence, the sensation of being watched was even more acute than it had been in the jungle. Ross didn't like the place and he suspected that even Hackett, despite his passion for antiquity, wasn't happy. An intangible sense of foreboding reminded him of the time he and Lauren had visited the Colosseum in Rome, which had shared a similar atmosphere of dread and despair. He glanced at Sister Chantal, who kept her eyes straight ahead. Zeb was clutching herself as if she was cold, despite the oppressive heat.

'I don't see any gold,' said Mendoza.

Hackett pointed to the end of the boulevard, flanked by two rough-hewn pillars. 'From what I saw on the ridge, the public and civic areas will be over there. That's where we should search.'

'Screw the gold,' said Zeb. 'I want to know where we're going to spend the night.'

'Me too,' said Juarez.

'The public areas and the main plaza should be more open,' said Hackett, 'less claustrophobic.'

'You mean less creepy,' said Zeb.

Hackett was right. The boulevard led to a large plaza. Its vast paving stones were cracked and uneven where plants and trees had grown through them. To the right a large diamond-shaped area – twenty feet wide – was bordered with heavy stones. The earth within it, covered with vegetation and dark blooms, had sunk many feet below the surrounding stones, giving the impression of a vast pit of flowers.

To the left they saw a stepped pyramid, extravagantly overrun with plants. Each of the three steps was the height of a modern house with a steep staircase carved into the front face, leading to a portal in the top tier. The structure was about sixty feet high and reminded Ross of the Aztec and Mayan pyramids he had seen on the Discovery channel. He couldn't help but be impressed by its scale. Just assembling the massive rocks to form the steps would be an amazing feat with today's technology, let alone at the time it had been built.

'Did you know there are more pyramids in Peru than there are in Egypt?' said Hackett. 'And that stepped ziggurats like this are also found in the Middle East and the Mediterranean?'

'How old is it?'

Hackett was cutting away vines. 'I'd say at least a thousand years old.'

'How the hell did they build it?'

Hackett wiped the sweat from his brow. 'With the one resource they had in abundance. Manpower. Ancient civilizations had no unions, but they did have pulleys, levers and armies of men. Durham Cathedral in northern England and the amazing temple Angkor Wat in Cambodia are both almost a thousand years old. The Colosseum in Rome's almost two thousand, while Stonehenge and the Great Pyramid at Giza are more than four thousand.'

'Check this out, Ross,' shouted Zeb, from across the plaza. She stood at the edge, pointing at a ring of stones that surrounded a stone bowl. In its centre a pillar about four feet high had been carved into the shape of an exotic flower.

Ross went over to her. The pillar was sunk deep into the ground, and the splayed stone petals formed multiple spouts. 'Looks like there was once a natural spring they directed into a communal fountain.'

But Zeb wasn't listening. Instead her eyes were fixed on the side of the ziggurat. 'Ross,' she whispered, pointing a shaking finger. 'Over there. You see it?'

He blinked. The vines obscured most of the stone but he could see something carved into it. An image he recognized. 'Yes,' he said, mouth dry. 'I see it.'

He rushed over to the ziggurat and, with his good hand, began to hack away the vines, exposing a carving at least six feet high. Zeb reached into her pack, pulled out her notes and flipped through the photocopied pages of the Voynich. She stopped at one and held it up.

'Look, Ross! This is page ninety-three of the Voynich.'

Ross stood back from the ziggurat and took it

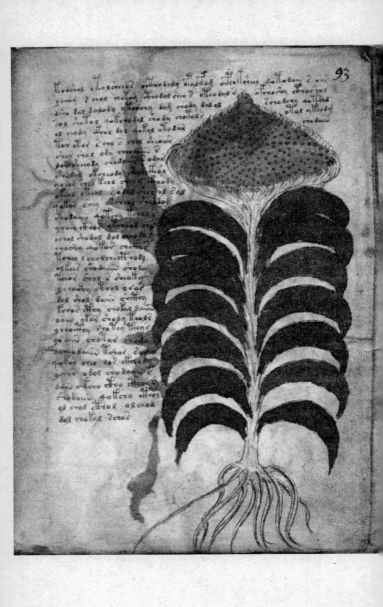

from her. The carving had been done with more skill than the drawing but otherwise it was identical. He rushed to the next block of stone and cut back the vine, revealing another carving of a strange plant, then another. He reached for Zeb's photocopies. Each of the strange plants carved into the stone was the same as one of those illustrated in the Voynich.

'I thought Father Orlando and the conquistadors never found this place,' she said.

'Perhaps they didn't,' said Ross. He felt dizzy with the heat and the possibilities of what he was seeing. He looked about for Sister Chantal and the others, but they were nowhere to be seen.

Then he heard his name. 'Ross!' He stepped away from the ziggurat as Hackett poked his head out of the portal at the top and waved. 'Ross! Zeb! Come up here. You've got to see this.'

43

The steps up the pyramid were easier to climb than they looked from the ground, even though thick vines obstructed many of them. As Ross led Zeb upwards, he tried to process the images he had seen and what they might mean. He caught himself searching the vegetation for any sign of the flowers and plants depicted in the Voynich and on the ziggurat, but there were none.

At the top of the stairs he entered a portal crowned with a trapezoidal lintel, similar to the one in the ransom chamber at Cajamarca. It led into a cool, gloomy room that smelt like a zoo but was remarkably clean and well preserved. Sister Chantal caught his eye. 'Did you know about the carvings down there?' he hissed.

She said nothing.

'What carvings?' said Hackett. 'Are they anything like these?' He stepped aside and shone his Maglite torch on the walls. Zeb gasped. The walls were decorated with intricately carved, three-foot-square frames, each of which contained a scene, like a storyboard or comic strip. 'Neither the Incas nor their predecessors had a written language,' he said. 'It wasn't until the Spaniards chronicled their conquests and discoveries that anything was written down. This was how the ancients who once lived here recorded events.'

'And what events they were,' whispered Zeb.

'I told you something bad happened here,' said Juarez.

Even Ross, with no training in language or symbols, could follow the narrative. The first carved image depicted the flower-shaped fountain in full flow, surrounded by a circle of human figures kneeling before it, as if in worship, while a benign sun shone down from above. The second image was of the same fountain, this time surrounded by a circle of human figures dancing and eating strange plants, like those in the Voynich. In the next image the fountain was dry and the flowers were dying. The fourth showed figures digging the diamond-shaped pit and throwing piles of human bodies into it. In the next a figure was laid on top of the ziggurat and another was pulling out its heart. The sixth showed the fountain again with two drops falling into it: from the sacrificial heart and the sun. The last image was of a line of humans of varying sizes, men, women and children, leaving the city and going into the jungle.

'I don't understand,' said Hackett.

'Isn't it obvious, Nigel?' said Zeb. 'When the

fountain dried up people became sick and died. They performed sacrifices to bring the water back but they didn't work so the city died and the survivors left.'

'I understand the story,' said Hackett. 'I just don't understand why they were so dependent on a fountain. This isn't the desert. It's a rainforest – and it's been one for thousands of years. They wouldn't need a small fountain to stay alive and healthy.'

'Unless it wasn't ordinary water,' said Zeb.

Ross thought again of the unusual plants depicted in the carvings and the Voynich. Had they grown here because of something in the spring water, something unique to Father Orlando's garden? Excitement coursed through him. Had the water contained some unusual chemicals or minerals on which the people had relied? 'The water probably came from a subterranean stream with a source not far from here,' he said. 'Then something happened – a geological shift, a subterranean landslide – which dammed the stream and dried up the spring.'

'So, although the spring's dried up its source might still exist?' asked Zeb.

'Yes.' He returned her smile. Orlando Falcon's garden was seeming less and less like a myth. 'And it might be pretty close.'

'Whatever they thought was in the water,' said Hackett, pointing at the penultimate image, 'they offered two sacrifices to bring it back.' He tapped the drops. 'Human blood and the tears of the sun.'

He smiled a wide, boyish smile. 'And do you know what that is? Gold.'

Ross thought of the ore-riddled caves they had walked through to reach the valley. Perhaps they contained seams of gold, once mined by the inhabitants of this place.

'Where would the gold be?' said Mendoza.

'In a sacred place.' Hackett pointed again at the carvings and tapped the image of the ziggurat. 'Somewhere in *here*.'

Just then, Juarez's voice cried, 'Sister Chantal's found something!'

Ross and the others followed Hackett's Maglite beam to the far recesses of the chamber where Juarez stood with the nun, pointing his torch down a flight of dark steps that disappeared into the depths of the pyramid. The stairs descended one flight, levelled out, then turned back on themselves, descending further into the darkness. The zoo smell wafted up from the bowels of the stone ziggurat. Animal droppings lay on the rough-hewn steps. Large ones.

Mendoza cocked his weapon, Hackett pulled a pistol from his backpack, and Juarez took the rifle from his shoulder.

'If there's gold it'll be down here,' said Hackett, moving to the stairs.

'I go with you,' said Juarez, eyes bright with uncustomary bravado. 'You said we share everything. I want to see this gold.'

Hackett prodded a vine, which slithered away. A

snake. 'Whatever you say.' He checked his pistol, then glanced nervously at Ross and Mendoza. 'You're coming, too, aren't you?'

Mendoza nodded. Ross hesitated, holding his broken wrist. He hadn't come for gold or to explore any ancient lost city, and he wasn't armed, but he felt compelled to see what was down there. 'I'm coming,' he said.

'I'm not,' said Zeb. 'I'll stay with Sister Chantal.'

'Let's go.' Hackett adjusted his hat, then headed down the stairs.

44

Juarez and Hackett went first down the wide steps, followed by Ross and Mendoza. Before he descended into the pungent darkness, Ross glanced back at the nun, trying in vain to read her inscrutable expression. *Had she been there before? Did she know what was down there?*

At the end of the first flight, the air was cooler but the smell stronger. Ross took out his own torch and shone it into the darkness. They followed the steps down three more returns until they came to a small antechamber and an open portal. Stone brackets that had once held flaming torches lined the walls. In the Maglite beam, Ross saw that the portal led into a large chamber with a passage down the centre, lined on each side with rows of stone shelves, stacked six high. Each contained what appeared to be a stone coffin. He shuddered.

'They were probably for the bodies of the more prestigious sacrificial victims,' said Hackett. 'Minus the hearts, of course.'

Ross saw Juarez's shoulders tremble. The Peruvian hated ruins, so to him this place must be terrifying. And at that moment, in the claustrophobic tomb surrounded by the remains of those who had died in agony more than a thousand years ago, he had some respect for the curse.

Suddenly Juarez yelped and Ross almost dropped his torch. '*Mirada! Mirada! Oro! Oro!*' Look! Look! Gold! Gold!

'Fuck!' said Hackett.

Ross turned his beam to meet Juarez's – and saw it. Not piles of treasure strewn around in decadent abandon, as the movies showed, but blocks, each one laid out with architectural precision. The ingots formed a six-foot-high version of the ziggurat they were standing in. A few were missing. Who took them? he wondered. The survivors fleeing to found new cities and new civilizations? Sister Chantal?

Mendoza whistled. 'How much is this worth?'

Hackett was wheezing with excitement. He patted his jacket for his inhaler, took a puff and collected himself. 'The last time I checked, gold was about six hundred and fifty dollars an ounce.' He picked up an ingot. 'Each of these must weigh at least four or five hundred ounces and there are hundreds, if not thousands.'

'So we're all rich, yes?' said Juarez.

'Very,' said Mendoza. 'Hundreds of millions of dollars rich. But how do we move it?'

'The river's only a day and a half away,' said Hackett, replacing the ingot. 'We take some now and get suitable transport, then come back for the rest.'

Ross felt strangely detached from the find. It was thrilling, and he wasn't immune to the giddy prospect of limitless wealth, but this wasn't the treasure he was seeking. He thought of how the ancient inhabitants of this place had spilt blood and presented their gold to save what they regarded as far more precious: the fountain, their city and their lives. He, too, would gladly give up his share of gold to save what he loved.

'Ross, where are you going?'

'To get some fresh air and tell Zeb and Sister Chantal what we found.'

'But don't you want to stay and talk about what to do with it?'

'It's not going anywhere.'

Hackett frowned. 'This is an amazing discovery, Ross, yet you don't seem excited.'

'Of course I'm excited. I just think we can decide what to do with it outside.'

'I come with you,' said Juarez. 'I like gold but I don't like this place.'

'Me too,' said Mendoza.

'We may as well *all* go, then.' Hackett sounded sulky.

Ross walked back to the stairs. As he passed the coffins, he felt Juarez tense. At the same time, he sensed something to his right: a sudden shift in the air, and a feral smell that raised the hairs on the back of his neck. He swivelled round.

Juarez was frozen to the spot, staring into the dark recesses behind the coffins. '*El abuelo*,' he rasped, as if his vocal cords no longer obeyed him.

In the beam of Ross's torch a black shape moved behind the coffins and two hungry, malevolent eyes stared at him.

Then it roared and sprang.

Ross dropped to his knees as the creature leapt at Mendoza. Then Juarez, the man who was seemingly scared of his own shadow, jumped in front of Mendoza and fired off a shot. It missed and the beast hit the Peruvian, knocking him to the ground and ripping at his throat. Juarez screamed and Ross felt something warm splash his face. As Hackett levelled his pistol and Mendoza raised his rifle, both trying to get a clear shot without hitting Juarez, Ross kicked at the beast with his Timberlands. His steel toecaps connected with hard muscle and the black creature growled in the torchlight, then shot past him.

Hackett rushed to Juarez, who was clutching his throat, eyes staring into the dark. The pyramid of gold was spattered with blood.

'I need a gun,' said Ross, grabbing Juarez's and racing after the animal.

'Where's it gone?' said Mendoza.

'Up the steps,' said Ross. 'To Zeb and Sister Chantal.'

45

Zeb had been grateful for the time alone with Sister Chantal. She had no desire to go down those dark stairs into the fetid bowels of the ziggurat and she wanted to quiz the nun on the forsaken city. 'What will they find down there?' she asked.

'Gold.'

'How do you know?'

'Because I do.'

'How? Have you been here before?' Zeb's frustration was growing. 'Why can't you ever just give a straight answer?'

'Because whatever I say won't change what you believe. What does it matter how I know anything? You now know that water from Father Orlando's garden once flowed here. You and Ross have seen the fountain, the carvings of the story and the plants from the Voynich. You have seen *proof* of the garden's existence, and once the others have found the gold we can leave them and go in search of it. That's all that matters.'

'How close is it from here?'

'A few days' walk.'

'You're sure it's still there?'

A look of fear crossed the nun's features. 'It *must* be.'

Zeb was studying the carved image of the dried-up fountain. 'But what if—'

She was silenced by a muffled scream and a gun-shot that issued from the darkened stairs. She stood up and pulled Sister Chantal to her feet. Another scream. Sister Chantal walked to the stairs and Zeb followed her. As she looked down into the gloom, a black shape leapt, snarling, at the nun, slashing with its claws, throwing her to the floor. Then Ross appeared and fired a shot into the air. The huge cat darted for the doorway and disappeared outside.

As Zeb rushed to Sister Chantal, Ross ran to the exit, raised the rifle and fired into the fading light.

'You get it?' Zeb called.

'It was too fast.' He ran back to help Zeb prop Sister Chantal against the wall. Blood flowed from a cut on her cheek and she had a large contusion on her forehead. Her right shoulder bore two shallow slashes where claws had torn her cotton shirt but, luckily, her shredded backpack had taken the brunt of the attack.

'What the hell was that?' said Zeb.

'A melanistic jaguar.'

'A what?'

'A black-pigmented jaguar. A panther.'

He sounded distracted and Zeb stared up at

him. 'There's blood all over your face. You okay?'

'It's not mine,' Ross said, in a monotone. He was holding Sister Chantal's wrist. 'She's out cold and her pulse is weak.'

Zeb helped him lay her on her back, then loosened her collar. 'We'd better get Nigel.'

When she turned, a dazed Mendoza and an ashen-faced Hackett were walking up the stairs, carrying Juarez between them.

This wasn't how it was supposed to happen. As Hackett tried to staunch Juarez's bleeding, he knew his friend was close to death, and that he was powerless to prevent it. As he opened Juarez's shirt to examine the wounds in his throat and chest, he thought of all the times over the last three years they had sat together on the *Discovery*, drinking Cusqueña beer and talking about their dreams.

Juarez had been born in a remote Amazonian village close to the Ecuadorian border but had always longed to see Europe and North America. Hackett had promised that when he returned to London, having found fame and fortune in the Amazon, he would take Juarez with him. Only last night, asleep in his hammock, Hackett had dreamt of lecturing to the Royal Geographical Society. As the great and good applauded, the beautiful Zeb Quinn – who no longer mocked his idiosyncrasies but understood, admired and *desired* him – stood at his side.

But now his friend would never leave the jungle

to live his dreams and, although Hackett had discovered his lost city and its gold, his own dreams of glory seemed hollow too.

Juarez gripped his arm and tried to speak. 'I'm not scared,' he rasped. 'I'm not a coward.'

'I know, my friend,' said Hackett.

'No, you're not,' Mendoza concurred. 'You're the bravest man I ever met. You saved my life.'

Juarez gripped Hackett's arm tighter, a smile playing on his lips. Finally his face relaxed. Hackett closed his eyelids and laid him on the floor. 'He's gone.'

'I'm sorry,' said Ross.

'So am I,' said Hackett. Zeb was kneeling over Sister Chantal, tears in her eyes. As he watched, she put a hand to her mouth.

'What do we do now?' asked Mendoza.

Hackett sighed. 'I don't know.'

Ross laid a hand on his shoulder. 'Nigel, there's nothing more you can do for Juarez. Why don't you attend to Sister Chantal while Osvaldo and I bury our friend? Then we'll build a fire.'

Hackett nodded numbly. 'I want him buried deep,' he said fiercely. 'I don't want any animals getting to him.'

'We'll make sure of it, señor,' said Mendoza. 'I'll say a prayer, and we'll put a stone on top of the grave.'

Hackett hesitated a little longer, then relinquished his friend to them and moved to examine Sister Chantal.

282

'How is she?' said Zeb.

Hackett checked Sister Chantal's cuts, contusion and breathing. 'She's concussed, but she appears to be breathing regularly. Her cuts are superficial and the bump on her head looks nastier than it is.' He reached for his medical bag. 'I'll check her blood pressure, then we'll make her comfortable and let her rest.'

'It'll be dark soon,' said Ross. 'I vote we spend the night on the flat top of this pyramid. We can build a fire there and it should be easier to keep away any more unwelcome visitors. If you guys can get Sister Chantal and our baggage to the top, Osvaldo and I'll look after Juarez.'

46

'You want some strong painkillers for your wrist?' asked Mendoza, popping a tablet into his mouth.

'No, thanks,' said Ross, welcoming the pain as he helped Mendoza lower Juarez's body into the hole they had dug in the soft earth behind the pyramid. It distracted him from the gathering dusk and from what they were doing. In burying Juarez he felt as if he was burying a part of himself. He had come here to save Lauren but already his quest had cost four lives: those of the three bandits who had tried to hijack them and now Juarez. As he shovelled earth into the grave, he thought of the strange carvings at the base of the ziggurat and felt a little consoled.

He was close now to either realizing his dream of saving Lauren, or confirming his worst fear that this trek into the jungle had been a waste of precious time and lives. Sister Chantal claimed that from here they could reach the garden and be back in a week, and had seemed confident of doing so without a guide – without Juarez. Depending on how quickly they returned to civilization he could be back in the States in two or three weeks with whatever he found in the garden. His main concern now was the enigmatic Sister Chantal, the key to interpreting the final directions.

Mendoza coughed. 'I still can't believe what Juarez did for me.

'He was a brave and selfless man,' said Ross.

'But I'd thought he was a coward.'

'We are what we do,' said Ross, almost to himself. 'His last act defined him.'

Mendoza patted the earth with his hand. 'This man will go to heaven.'

'I won't argue with you on that one.'

After filling in the hole, they dragged a slab from the plaza, placed it over the mound, and Mendoza assembled a small pile of stones to mark the grave. Then they called to the others. Hackett came down, then he and Mendoza said simple prayers, while Zeb watched over Sister Chantal.

Later, they made a fire on the flat top of the ziggurat and prepared food. No one was hungry but they went through the motions, picking at their tinned beans and meat stew.

'How's Sister Chantal?' Ross asked.

'She's stirred a couple of times, but she's still out of it,' Hackett replied. 'Her blood pressure's okay, though. I think she just needs rest.'

Zeb was sitting by the baggage, frantically rooting through Sister Chantal's shredded pack. 'You okay, Zeb?' Ross called to her.

Zeb's eyes were bright and red-rimmed from crying. 'No,' she said quietly. 'I'm not.' She held up a pile of shredded, bloodstained paper, then Father Orlando's notebook, what was left of it. 'The backpack saved Sister Chantal's life but the notebook was in it. The jaguar tore it to pieces.'

Ross felt sick. 'Show me.'

The cruel irony was that the first pages were still legible and the last mismatched section had survived virtually untouched. It was only the middle of the book, the end pages of the first section – the crucial final directions to the garden – that had been obliterated. He took the torn pages from Zeb and knew immediately they couldn't be salvaged. He thought again of the strange plants carved at the base of the ziggurat and the story of the fountain. The metallic taste of disappointment flooded his mouth. The carved images had encouraged him earlier, but now they taunted him. Just when he was beginning to believe in Father Orlando's garden, just when he was getting close, it was to be denied him. 'The last directions are gone.'

'So?' said Hackett. 'We don't need them any more.'

'We do,' said Zeb. 'They were the most critical.'

'But this is it. This lost city is what we were looking for.' Hackett paused. 'Isn't it?'

'No,' said Ross. 'It's not.'

'What are you saying? Finding this place was a bonus? What's going on?'

Ross looked at Sister Chantal in her sleeping bag.

'I don't know if it was a fluke or not but this isn't where Father Orlando's directions lead,' he said. 'In fact, he made no mention of this place in any of his writings.'

'But this is one of the biggest archaeological discoveries in history,' Hackett expostulated. 'Not just in South America, but the entire world. How can it not be where his directions lead? What could possibly be more important than this?'

'Or more valuable?' demanded Mendoza.

Zeb pulled some photocopied sheets out of her backpack and passed them to Hackett, then summarized the story in the Voynich. 'We're looking for a garden where plants like this grow.'

'You came all this way, into the largest rainforest in the world, to find a *garden*?' said Hackett.

'Yes.'

Hackett studied the photocopies. 'These plants are like the ones on the carvings here.'

'Exactly,' said Ross. 'Which means we're probably close.'

Hackett frowned, trying to understand. 'The garden must be pretty special.'

'That's what we're hoping,' said Zeb. 'Father Orlando called it the Garden of God.'

'How is it special?' asked Mendoza.

Ross kept his eyes focused on Hackett. 'We're hoping it has healing properties, as in the Voynich story.'

'Healing properties?' Hackett snorted. Ross recognized his own initial scepticism in the doctor's face. Hackett stared into the fire. 'Let me guess, you think the plants are somehow linked to the water from the fountain here. You think the spring once came from this miraculous garden.'

'It fits,' said Ross. 'The spring could have been fed via an underground stream, which flowed from the garden and then got blocked. Perhaps the people were dependent on the water, or whatever was in it, and became sick when it dried up.'

Hackett was shaking his head.

'You think the garden is close to here?' said Mendoza, clearly intrigued.

'Yes,' said Ross.

'If it exists,' said Hackett, 'what do we do about this place and the gold? Which, by the way, *does* exist.'

'The gold will wait for us,' said Mendoza. He gave a decisive nod. 'I'm coming with you, Ross.'

'You don't have to. It'll be dangerous. According to the story, all the surviving conquistadors died in the garden. Only Father Orlando survived to tell the tale.'

Mendoza laughed. 'If it's safe enough for an old nun, a man with a broken wrist and a young woman, it's safe enough for me. I'm coming.'

'Hang on,' said Hackett. 'This is madness. We've already lost Juarez in finding this place. Why put anyone else at risk looking for some mythic Shangri-La?'

'None of you has to come with me,' said Ross. 'I'm sorry about Juarez, I really am, but finding this garden was the reason I came here.'

'And you, Zeb?' demanded Hackett. 'You're committed to finding it, too?'

'Yes.'

'Then I've no choice but to go too, I suppose,' said Hackett, and gave a weary sigh. 'The garden sounds like a load of guff, but we should stay together.' He looked at Zeb. 'If it's dangerous you'll need someone to take care of you.'

For the first time that evening Zeb smiled. 'Someone like you, Nigel?'

Hackett bristled. 'Someone *exactly* like me – someone careful and cautious. I'm not losing anyone else on this trip.'

'This discussion is academic, anyway,' Ross said quietly. He held up Father Orlando's damaged notebook. 'The crucial section, containing the final directions to the garden, is unreadable.'

'Can't you remember any of them?' said Mendoza.

'All I can remember is one of the last landmarks, something called La Sonrisa del Dios, the Smile of God. After that I think we find ourselves in a cave system. But I've no idea how to find La Sonrisa del Dios, whatever it is.' He turned to Zeb. 'How about you?'

'I remember it being a good three days' walk from La Barba Verde to La Sonrisa del Dios, with only the stars to guide us. But I've no idea which stars.'

'So, what are you saying?' said Hackett. 'We're stuffed?'

'Yes.' Ross was suddenly desperate to get away from the cursed city. 'That's exactly what I'm saying.'

That night on the ancient ziggurat, sitting under the stars surrounded by the ruins of a civilization that had been dead for more than a thousand years, was the loneliest Ross could remember.

While the others slept by the fire he kept watch, Juarez's rifle cradled in his lap. Despite his exhaustion, he knew he wouldn't sleep. It wasn't his aching wrist that kept him awake but the suffocating feeling of time crushing him. He thought of Lauren in the States and of the life growing inside her womb. In a few weeks it would be six months, two-thirds of the way through the pregnancy. In another three months it would be due. These next weeks were critical, and yet they seemed insignificant against the centuries of history that surrounded him.

Turning away from the crackling fire, he stared into the humid, enveloping dark, wishing he could believe in some merciful higher power. Tomorrow he would leave this forsaken place, go home and accept whatever happened. His great quest was over.

47

Ross woke with a start. A pearlescent moon still hung in the sky, but, when he looked over the lost city to the horizon, a soft glow told him dawn was imminent. He couldn't remember falling asleep but he felt alert and fresh. He also felt compelled to act.

He stood up, stepped round the sleeping Hackett and Mendoza, passed Zeb's still form and knelt beside Sister Chantal. He shook her gently until she opened her eyes.

'Wake up,' he murmured. 'We've got to go.'

'Where?' She touched the bruise on her head, dazed, disoriented and frightened.

He kept his voice soft but firm. 'You get up now and take us to Father Orlando's garden, or we turn back and go home.'

She reached out her hand. 'Where's the notebook?'

'It's ruined. There are no more directions. It's up to you now. You say you're the Keeper, that you've been to the garden before. Now's the time to prove it.'

'What about the others?'

'They'll be with us.'

'But they can't—'

'I don't care about secrecy any more. Your plan to use this place to distract them didn't work. Juarez is dead.'

Her eyes widened. 'Juarez is dead?'

'The jaguar that attacked you killed him. We're in the middle of nowhere – literally – and there are two choices. We go on to the garden together or we go home. We're depending on you. Lauren's depending on you.'

'All the directions are destroyed?'

He handed her the notebook. 'See for yourself.'

She rubbed her head, thinking. 'The others can come only if they vow to tell no one of the garden and to take nothing from it.'

'They'll make that promise.'

'There might be one other way to find the garden, but I need a compass.'

'Here's mine.' He reached into his pocket. 'I doubt it'll work, though. There's some strange magnetic field here. The GPS is out and our watches have stopped.'

'Give it to me.'

He glanced at it, then at the rising sun. Wherever the needle was pointing, it sure as hell wasn't magnetic north. 'Like I said, it's not working.'

She took it, sat up and smiled. 'Follow the needle.'

'What do you mean?'

'Follow the needle. It should lead us to the garden.'

He took the compass from her. Normally when a compass wasn't working correctly the needle became erratic. This one wasn't. It pointed firmly in one direction. It wasn't north but it was steady. His pulse quickened. Was the interference coming not from the ore-riddled ridge they had passed through but from the garden – or the source? 'You sure this will lead us there?'

She nodded, eyes sparkling.

'Good.' Ross hardly dared to believe they were continuing the quest. 'In that case, I'll wake the others.'

Within an hour they were ready to leave. They climbed the path out of the valley to the high shelf above, then turned in the direction of the compass needle. As they were about to re-enter dense jungle, Ross looked back. From this elevation, the valley again seemed lush but unremarkable, its secret concealed beneath the vegetation. He strained to glimpse the ziggurat to no avail.

Then he caught a glint of light, the reflection of the sun on metal or glass, coming from the high shelf near the ridge. He wondered what it could be, then pushed it from his mind and followed the others into the jungle.

Father General Leonardo Torino lowered his binoculars and squinted in the early-morning sunlight. For the first time since Iquitos he could see Ross Kelly and the others. It took all his self-control to prevent the relief showing on his face.

'How did you know they would be here, Father General?' said Fleischer. 'We found their trail in the jungle but how did—'

'I told you, Feldwebel, we're on a sacred mission. The Lord is guiding us.' Torino fixed him with his most intense stare. 'Did you doubt me?' Fleischer and his men bowed their heads and crossed themselves. Torino raised his binoculars and focused on the spot where he'd seen Kelly. 'However, the Lord may need our help from here, Feldwebel. We must follow our quarry and not lose them in the jungle.'

'I understand, Father General.' He pointed to one of his men, a shorter, muscular man with thick eyebrows and a jagged scar on his right cheek. 'Weber, keep close, but make sure you aren't seen. Leave a trail for us to follow. If your pack's too heavy, share its weight with Petersen and Gerber.'

'It's fine, sir. I can move fast enough to track them.'

'Good.' Fleischer reached into his pack, pulled out a pair of basic two-way radios and handed one to Weber. They switched them on and both crackled into life, unaffected by whatever force had stopped their watches. 'Keep us informed.'

As Torino and the others watched Weber hurry along the high shelf after Kelly's party, not one noticed the lost city in the valley below, slumbering beneath its blanket of green.

48

Juarez was in their thoughts as they hacked their way through the steaming jungle over the next two and a half days. They missed his alert presence and nimble ability to thread a path through the densest forest. Even the immaculate Hackett was dishevelled. They slept by night, suspended above the forest floor in hammocks, sheltered beneath tarpaulins to keep out the rain. By day, they moved at a slow but determined pace, oblivious of any trail they left.

Ross lost count of the exotic creatures they encountered: golden-pelted monkeys, brilliantly coloured snakes, spiders the size of a man's hand. He was sure some must have been unclassified species. When he thought of the strange plants and animals he had seen since entering the Amazon, how commonplace the bizarre had become, Falcon's garden, with its exotic flora and fauna, seemed less and less inconceivable.

On the third day another ridge blocked their

path. It was concave and topped with tooth-white rocks. Immediately Ross knew it must be the one other landmark he remembered from the notebook, La Sonrisa del Dios, the Smile of God.

It occurred to him then that the garden was protected by a number of concentric circles of high rock, like ripples when a stone is dropped into a pond. They had passed through the first via the fierce waterfall of El Velo de la Luz and the second by La Barba Verde. As Ross gazed at La Sonrisa del Dios, adrenalin surged through him. Was this the final barrier protecting Father Orlando's mythical garden?

As if reading his mind, Hackett asked, 'Are we almost there?'

'Yes,' Sister Chantal said. 'The cave system that leads to the garden cuts through the ridge beneath those white rocks.'

Ross checked his GPS again, hoping to determine his exact location, but two words filled the screen: Signal Error.

The sun was setting and, though Ross and Sister Chantal wanted to press on, the others decided to rest and tackle the caves in the morning. Ross feared his racing mind would keep him awake, but when he collapsed on to his hammock he fell instantly into a deep, dreamless sleep.

Only Sister Chantal did not sleep that night. Clutching her crucifix she lay awake in the dark, listening to the sounds of the forest, waiting for dawn to break. Though she was consumed by fatigue, and her body ached, she couldn't relax. Not yet. She burnt with the need to reach the end of her long journey. She yearned to finish her ordeal, fulfil her promise and reap her elusive reward.

49

The next morning, Ross, Zeb, Hackett and Mendoza followed Sister Chantal to the cliff beneath the white rocks of La Sonrisa del Dios. She led them to a vertical fissure crowned with a natural arch and, one by one, they squeezed through the opening until they found themselves in La Catedral, the cathedral-like cave described in the Voynich. Shafts of sunlight illuminated the vast space and Ross saw dozens of small openings hundreds of feet above their heads, which shone like stars among the stalactites on the soaring vault of the roof. The shafts of sunlight picked out glittering, gilded veins in the rock walls.

'Gold,' said Mendoza, with greedy eyes.

Ross studied a vein. 'It looks like gold but I'm afraid it's pyrites, fool's gold.'

'Whatever it is, this is the band of gold that Father Orlando and the conquistadors followed to the garden,' said Sister Chantal. 'We must follow it, too.'

They had entered the vast cave on what amounted to a mezzanine level. Its ceiling, with the star-like apertures, rose above, and its floor was over an abrupt edge to their right, many feet below. A Boeing 747 could have parked in it with ease. Hell, a fleet of them could land and take off in it, Ross thought. The air was surprisingly hot, and tainted with a foul smell, which worsened as they went deeper. Ammonia made his eyes water and Hackett, sucking at his inhaler, was scrabbling in his medical bag for a surgical mask.

Deeper into the cave, the ground sloped down and the passage became narrower until they were walking in single file along a ledge. Now Ross could see the source of the overpowering stench. Over the abyss to his right there was a conical mountain of bat droppings. At least forty feet across and easily as tall, it rose from the floor below to its peak, a few feet from where they were standing. A rustling, clicking sound came from the mound and its dark surface was constantly moving. Every inch was beaded with writhing cockroaches, feeding on the waste. Zeb covered her face. The sight was almost worse than the smell, and Ross put his hand over his mouth to stop himself retching. Above the surgical mask Hackett's eyes showed his disgust. For a man who hated anything remotely dirty or *sucio* this was a nightmare.

In the darker corners of the ceiling, Ross spotted thousands of bats hanging from the rock. He dreaded the possibility of their waking suddenly and overwhelming them as they fled the cave in their thousands. He pointed upwards to warn the others, who instinctively pushed themselves closer to the wall, putting as much distance as they could between them and the edge.

The danger, however, came from below.

Hackett saw the sandy-coloured snake first, wriggling along the ledge, trying to evade them, but Zeb almost stepped on it. It reared and struck her thick walking boot. As it prepared to strike again Hackett kicked it away, inadvertently towards Mendoza, who jumped out of its path and lost his footing. Trying to regain his balance, he fell on then rolled off the ledge. He scrabbled frantically for a handhold on the sharp rock but gained only a momentary grip before he dropped into the seething mound of filth. He sank fast. Cockroaches covered his boots and lower leg, then swarmed up his body.

By the time Ross was on his knees and holding out his good hand, Mendoza was up to his neck in bat faeces. As his head sank below the cockroaches, he stared up at Ross, lips sealed, eyes wide with terror. Ross hung further over the ledge but couldn't reach his flailing right hand. Then an arm circled his waist and a rope tightened over his shirt.

'You're okay,' said Hackett. 'Zeb and I've got you.'

Eyes watering, nostrils stinging, Ross edged over till his face was inches from the filth and grabbed Mendoza's hand just as it disappeared. Mendoza's other hand reached for him and the sudden weight almost yanked his face into the mire. 'Pull me up!' he shouted.

His arm jerked so hard that Ross had to use his broken wrist to avoid dislocating his shoulder. Gritting his teeth against the pain, he felt the rope tighten round his waist and drag him up. Gradually, Mendoza emerged, and when his head cleared the surface he breathed out and gasped.

As they dragged him on to the ledge, Sister Chantal sprayed him with insect repellent. Lying there, he writhed like a madman, knocking Hackett's glasses and medical bag into the filth. His panic only abated after Hackett patted down his clothes, scattering the remaining cockroaches. As Mendoza recovered his composure and changed his clothes, Ross watched Hackett's medical bag and spectacles sinking beneath the seething cockroaches. He also saw the snake, writhing in its death throes. After a few seconds the mound had consumed it.

Zeb patted Hackett's shoulder. He was rubbing his hands as if to erase any trace of the cockroaches he had brushed off Mendoza. 'Thanks for kicking the snake away from me.' She gestured to his usually clean, pressed trousers and grinned. 'You should regard this as aversion therapy.'

Hackett smiled thinly. 'I've lost my glasses. I'm almost blind without them.'

'I can't believe a man like you doesn't have a spare set,' said Zeb.

'I do,' Hackett said. He pointed at the mound. 'It was in my medical bag.'

Mendoza stood up and helped Ross to his feet. 'That's the second time someone's saved my life. How's your wrist?'

Like my hand's coming off, he thought. 'It's fine,' he said.

They continued along the pyrites seams, descending until they reached another vast chamber, not as wide or as long as before but taller, illuminated by a single, distant opening above. A Manhattan skyscraper could have stood in that cavern and not protruded from the hole.

'Look,' said Hackett.

Ross's heart skipped a beat. A few yards from where they were standing, half concealed by stones, corroded but still recognizable, lay a metal helmet of the same peaked design used by the Spanish conquistadors, and a pewter goblet.

'Surely they can't be from Falcon's quest,' said Zeb, as Hackett picked up the goblet, rubbed it clean and put it into his backpack.

The heat was oppressive now and Ross could see a causeway of black pumice stepping-stones ahead, leading across a chasm through which a stream of molten lava flowed: the river of fire mentioned in the Voynich. Beyond, they would encounter an unwelcoming network of dank, dark, dripping caves.

They were now at the threshold of the garden, and for the first time since he had embarked on his quest, Ross allowed himself to believe that Falcon and Sister Chantal had been telling the truth. He might indeed find something remarkable and miraculous here to help Lauren.

'These are the last obstacles,' said Sister Chantal. 'Beyond the river of fire lie caves of burning rain and poisonous gas, but if we follow the veins of gold we will reach the garden.' She paused, glanced at Ross, then focused on the others. 'Remember your vows. Tell no one of this place and take nothing from it.' She looked at each in turn, only moving on when they nodded.

Hackett didn't look happy. 'Mountains of bat shit, cockroaches, rivers of fire, burning rain, poisonous gas. I hope this garden of yours is worth it. Good God, it's like one of those old adventure stories.'

Ross put on his sunglasses. 'There's only one way to find out.' He pointed to the causeway. 'I'm going to cross that. Then I'm going to hold my breath, cover my skin and eyes, and rush through those caves, following the pyrites to the other side. When you follow me, you mustn't breathe the air or let the liquid dripping off the ceiling touch your skin or eyes. It's basically concentrated sulphuric acid.' He put on his waterproof and pulled up the hood, leaving as little skin exposed as possible, then walked to the causeway. 'You guys ready?'

Sister Chantal smiled.

'You, Zeb?'

Zeb nodded, eyes bright. 'Yep.'

Mendoza stepped forward to join them but Hackett hung back.

Ross's heart was beating fast. He couldn't remember the last time he had felt so excited. He realized then that this was no longer just about saving Lauren and their child. His passion for geology, stifled for so long by Big Oil, had reawakened. He called to Hackett, 'What are you waiting for? Want to discover what drove a priest to write the most mysterious manuscript in the world? Want to see a place even more amazing and magical than your precious Eldorado?' He began to walk across the causeway, heat wafting up to him from the lava. 'If you do, follow me.'

PART THREE

The Garden of God

50

After he'd crossed the causeway, Ross checked that the others were following him, then turned on his torch, took one last breath, grasped Sister Chantal's hand and led her, with Zeb, through the dripping caves. Even with the sunglasses his eyes watered. A drop from the acidic ceiling touched his right hand and he felt it burn before he rubbed it off with the opposite sleeve. This was the burning rain described in the Voynich. That, and the toxic smell of brimstone, or sulphur – a substance associated with the Devil – had made Orlando Falcon fear he had entered the portals of Hell.

Right now, Ross sympathized with him.

Holding his breath, he glanced round the system of toxic subterranean caves and passageways. From the heat under his feet, and the river of fire behind them, he guessed there was magma beneath. He felt as he had in the caves of Cueva de Villa Luz in southern Mexico, as though he had gone back billions of years to when the young Earth was a toxic incubator for the most primitive forms of life. Even here there was life: he could see small extremophiles feeding off the sulphurous walls.

Following the gilt seams, he dragged Sister Chantal and Zeb through the labyrinth for so many seconds that he feared they would not find their way out before they had to breathe.

Then the pyrites stopped. All he could see ahead of him was solid wall. A dead end.

Sister Chantal's face was pale, her eyes bloodshot. She looked on the verge of death. Was this where they would die?

Then she smiled.

She took his torch and Zeb's, and, with her own, switched them off. In the sudden darkness, needing to breathe, he felt close to panic. Then a hand gripped his elbow, turning him. In the darkness, uncorrupted by torchbeams, he discerned a faint vertical line of light down the right-hand side of the apparently solid wall. He moved closer and saw that two separate walls ran parallel to each other, a thin gap between them forming a passageway. He moved into it and walked towards the light.

Outside, he gulped fresh air. When his eyes grew accustomed to the glare he saw he was in a place unlike any he had seen before. Where the air in the caves had been poisonous, it was now sweet, fresh and perfumed. If the toxic caves were Hell, this was Heaven on Earth. He turned to Sister Chantal, but before he could say anything, she nodded.

'Yes,' she said, with an ecstatic smile. 'This is the garden.'

Ross stood at one end of a deep elliptical basin, more than a thousand yards long and many hundreds wide, completely enclosed by a funnel of rock so deep that the sun's rays barely reached its verdant floor. He seemed to be inside a huge eye, the pupil a perfectly circular lake in the centre. At the far end, where the ground was higher, he could see another cave. A stream flowed from it to feed the limpid lake. The clear water had a green glow, as though fireflies were swimming in it.

Around the lake grasses were growing, with trees and exotic plants unlike anything in the jungle they had just walked through – unlike anything he had ever seen in nature.

'Look, Ross.' Zeb held open her photocopied pages of the Voynich with the illustrations, then waved at the trees, flowers and plants around them. 'They're just like in the book, and the descriptions of this place are spot-on.' She pointed to the far cave. 'That must lead to the forbidden caves Falcon wrote about, where the nymphs lived.'

And where the conquistadors died, thought Ross. To his left, at the base of the cliff, he saw a pile of perfectly spherical rocks, and more half-formed spheres emerging from the cliff. They reminded him of the Moeraki boulders on New Zealand's South Island. But it was the plants and the glowing water that captivated him.

And the air.

It had a subtle fragrance and taste, a delicious blend of floral, vanilla and citrus notes that was sweet yet not cloying.

The others were equally enraptured. Sister Chantal bent down beside the lake, cupped her hands in the water and drank, her face radiating joy. If she had been a cat she would have purred. Ross noticed that the water in her cupped palms contained microscopic glowing particles, similar to those he had spied in her leather pouch when they had first met.

Suddenly an eerie sound filled the air, like a choir singing. There were no discernible words or phrases, just a series of almost mechanically perfect notes. Beautiful yet soulless, it came from the cave at the end of the garden and made the hairs stand up on the back of his neck. The sound stopped as abruptly as it had started.

'What was that?' he said.

Sister Chantal laid a hand on his arm. 'Wait, Ross,' she said. 'The caves at the far end of the garden, no one must go into them without me.'

Hackett rubbed his eyes. 'Why not?' he said.

'Because I'm the Keeper,' she said.

'The what?' said Mendoza.

'Just do as she says,' Ross told them.

'What is this place?' said Hackett.

Sister Chantal placed a finger over her lips. 'No more questions. It'll be dark soon.' She knelt by the lake, filled her cupped hands with the phosphorescent water and proffered it to them. 'Drink from the stream and the lake. Eat fruit from the trees. Get some sleep. You may see small creatures in the garden but they're harmless. Just don't go into the caves. Tomorrow everything will become clearer.' She smiled at Ross. 'Much clearer.'

She walked away from them to a raised area with a neat mound of small stones. Ross watched her kneel beside it to pray. He wanted to ask her more questions, but he knew better than to intrude now. Like the others, he knelt and drank from the lake. The water had a distinctive sodium taste that reminded him of a French mineral water he had never liked: Badoit. He ate strange fruit from the trees, which tasted better. Their flavours were familiar but hard to place – like packaged mixed-fruit juices. In one fruit, the size of an apple, he thought he could taste pomegranate, passion fruit and cherry.

As dusk closed the eye of the garden, he realized he was exhausted. He didn't bother with the hammock or the mosquito net, just rolled out his sleeping bag on the soft grass and lay down. The others did the same, as if they understood that they were safe.

Before he closed his eyes he looked once more into the dark, still lake and saw countless stars reflected in it. Then he noticed that the night sky at the top of the funnel was cloudy. The bright spots in the water were shards of crystal lying at the bottom, their luminosity revealed by the darkness of the night. Their beauty filled his mind with more questions. Then, mercifully, he slept.

Sister Chantal slept better than she could remember. Curled up beside the mound of stones, away from the others, she dreamt that she was free.

Released from her vow.

Recompensed for her sacrifice.

Reunited with the one she had lost.

She woke once during the night, when everyone was asleep, and wandered to the lake. As she drank she indulged her vanity for the first time since she had made her vow and inspected her reflection in the water. What she saw saddened her. Where once the face had been young, beautiful and full of hope, it was now old and spent.

Would he still care how she looked? The thought made her smile, and joy surfaced through the sadness. Her wait had been so long, but the hardest part was over. Soon she could surrender her burden and rejoin him.

She sighed. 'Soon,' she whispered, as she returned to her sleeping bag. 'Soon.'

51

The next morning Osvaldo Mendoza woke first. He staggered to his feet and went to a corner of the garden, concealed by bushes. Before he had opened his fly, he realized that the constant pain in his head had gone. When he stopped peeing he noticed something even more remarkable. Something that made him stand rock-still for more than a minute, stunned. He fell to his knees and prayed.

Ross woke during a dream he couldn't remember, except that it had involved Lauren and made him happy for the first time in weeks. He didn't want to wake, but Hackett was shaking him.

'Wake up, Ross.'

He blinked. 'Why? What's going on?'

'You've got to see this place. It's amazing.'

Ross rolled over. Why, when he was having the best sleep in ages, had Hackett chosen this moment to get overexcited? 'I know it's amazing. I'm here. I can see it.'

'But, Ross, *I* can see it, too.'

'Nigel, what the hell are you talking about?'

'Give me your hand.' Hackett grabbed at his broken wrist but instinctively Ross snatched it away. 'Give me your hand,' Hackett insisted. 'Trust me.' He began unwrapping the expertly applied bandage. 'How does it feel?'

'Okay.'

Hackett squeezed his wrist. 'How does that feel?'

'Like I said, okay. Now leave me alone.'

'It shouldn't feel okay. What I just did should have made you scream.' He paused a beat. 'If your wrist was still broken.'

Ross sat up and looked at his hand. The swelling and bruising had gone. So had the stiffness and pain. 'Perhaps it wasn't broken.'

'It was a classic break and it's healed months before it should have done. It's not just you. I've had dodgy eyesight since childhood. Now it's perfect. Cured overnight. Twenty-twenty vision. And I haven't used these since I got here.' He took his ventilator and antihistamine pills out of his pocket. Then he took two deep breaths. 'Listen to that. Clear as a bell. With all these flowers my allergies should be having a field day, but my chest and sinuses have never been so clear.'

Hackett pointed to Mendoza, who was sitting by the lake, legs crossed, eyes closed, hands clasped as if in prayer. 'Osvaldo's having some kind of spiritual experience. Keeps crossing himself and muttering thanks. Since Iquitos the guy's been holding his head in pain and chewing painkillers like they're sweets. Not your bog-standard aspirin either, but prescription-strength codeine, which is an opiate, the same family as morphine. Kept telling me he was okay whenever I quizzed him, but he's obviously been in a lot of pain. This morning I woke up and found him crying. Imagine that – a man like *him* crying! When I asked him what was wrong he said there was nothing wrong with him. He was fine. *Really* fine. Keeps calling it a miracle.'

Hackett swept his hand round the garden. 'It must be something in the water we drank or the fruit we ate. God, I wish Juarez had made it here. This place is incredible.' He reached for his backpack. 'This is pretty amazing too.' He took out the pewter goblet he had picked up yesterday and handed it to Ross. 'Look inside.'

'I can see a watch.'

'It's mine. I left it in there last night. Look at it.' Ross peered at the face. The second hand was moving – slowly and erratically, but it was moving. 'Now take it out,' said Hackett. Ross did so and the second hand stopped. He dropped the watch back in and it started again. 'Isn't that weird?'

Ross took off his Tag Heuer and placed it in the goblet. Its second hand also came back to life sluggishly. He studied the goblet. 'Old pewter like this has a high tin and lead content. My guess is the tin's high magnetic permeability and the lead's radioactivity-shielding properties give some protection against whatever forces stopped it.'

Ross replaced his watch and flexed his bad wrist. No trace of the excruciating pain he had felt yesterday after he'd pulled Mendoza from the mound of bat droppings. He remembered the passage in the Voynich: the conquistadors had arrived with broken bones and been cured. A shiver ran through him.

Zeb walked over to them. She was barefoot, in jeans and a red T-shirt with *Gaia has feelings too* emblazoned across her small breasts. Her red hair was dishevelled and her face creased with sleep, but otherwise she looked fresh and rested. 'There's something wrong with my eyes,' she said, squinting behind her thick lenses.

'No, there isn't,' said Hackett, smiling. He took off her glasses. 'You just don't need these now.'

She blinked and her eyes opened wide. 'That's incredible!'

'Isn't it?' agreed Hackett, laughing. 'Bloody incredible.'

Ross left them to marvel and washed his face in the lake. He studied the particles in the water but they were too small to tell him anything. Then he peered down, trying to detect the crystals he had spotted last night. In the daylight, however, they were invisible. He got to his feet and walked round the garden. He saw a small lizard scamper on its hind legs towards a copse. It was vaguely familiar and then he remembered a drawing in the Voynich of what he had supposed was a dragon. How deceptive scale could be.

In the early morning the garden seemed even more magical than it had bathed in yesterday's late-afternoon light. There was a cool dampness in the air and a thin mist hung over the lake, partially shrouding the far cave and the stream flowing from it. He guessed that the sun's rays would burn off the mist when they eventually reached into the garden. He watched Zeb and Hackett go to Mendoza and sit down beside him, sharing their wonder and amazement.

Ross didn't join them. He needed answers. He walked round the garden, studying the cliff walls. The rock wasn't soft like the limestone prevalent in these parts. It was harder and impermeable, almost certainly volcanic. He guessed that it formed a bowl within which the garden sat, surrounded by magma, a ring of fire, sealing it off from the outside world. But it hadn't always been sealed. If his theory was correct there had been a time, billions of years ago, when this place had leaked its life force into a then barren planet, seeding all that was to follow. Then the ring of fire had closed, the bowl of volcanic rock had cooled and hardened, locking everything within. The last leak had been sealed off a thousand years ago, when the spring in the lost city had dried up.

As he wandered round the perimeter, large oval sunflowers and huge bulbous artichoke-like blooms reminded him of South Africa's proteus flower. He saw dog-like creatures in the undergrowth and odd insects, all recognizable from the Voynich. He

317

imagined Orlando Falcon lying in his cell, mentally retracing the steps he himself was now taking, drawing their likenesses in his manuscript. What struck Ross most, though, was not how different everything was from the outside world but how similar. Even though the plants and creatures in this basin had evolved independently of anything outside, it appeared that evolution had arrived at similar solutions: petals, seeds, leaves, eyes, legs. He hadn't yet seen anything completely alien. Especially when he considered the creatures and plants he had discovered on his journey through the Amazon.

He looked back to the mound of stones where Sister Chantal had slept but she wasn't there. A moment later he spotted her standing by the stream at the far end of the lake, near the entrance to the forbidden caves.

Sister Chantal looked different. She wore sandals and a white blouse over a white skirt, and she had undone her hair so it fell below her shoulders. The early-morning light lent her an ethereal air and she seemed younger, stronger. Her wrinkles hadn't disappeared and her hair was still streaked with grey, but the contusion on her head and the surface wounds from the jaguar attack had gone. Also, the weariness had left her eyes and her translucent skin glowed. A small bag was slung over her left shoulder. As he approached, she took his hand. 'Your wrist's better.'

He clenched his fist. 'It's fine. That's what I want to ask you about. And about Lauren.'

'Come,' she said. 'Let me explain a few things.' She pointed to the stream and the lake. 'As you've discovered, the water and any produce from the plants in the garden will not only rebalance and refresh the body, but heal any ailments.'

He thought of Lauren's broken neck. 'Heal anything?'

'Most things, it would appear.' She touched her face and smiled sadly. 'The one thing it can't do is make us younger. It can slow, even halt, the ageing process, but not reverse it.'

'Can it cure Lauren?'

'Of course. That's why I brought you here.' She spoke with such confidence that Ross had to blink back tears.

'So what do I do? Take her a bottle of the lake water or some fruit?'

She shook her head. 'I tried that once but when the water or plants are taken from the garden they lose their power. No living thing here can survive outside. The fruit rots and the water goes stagnant. I don't know why. It's as though everything has become so dependent on this place that it must die immediately it leaves. But creatures like us, who have evolved to survive outside its orbit, are revitalized here. However, we can only gain the benefits by drinking the water or eating the produce in the garden.'

'So I have to bring Lauren here?'

She smiled. 'No. There's another way.' She pointed behind her to the dark opening whence the stream came. 'Come, I'll show you.'

She took his hand and led him into the forbidden caves.

52

As Ross followed Sister Chantal along the stream to the forbidden caves trepidation must have shown on his face.

'The antechamber's harmless,' she said. 'The forbidden, dangerous part lies beyond.'

The first thing he noticed was a faint smell: a musky, damp, mustard-seed aroma – like the aftermath of sex. The space was high and deep. The cave floor rose in steps as he entered, culminating in a high ledge, behind which an ascending tunnel disappeared into the heart of the surrounding rock. The stream that fed the lake flowed down the tunnel to a small waterfall, which dropped from the ledge, forming two pools, then eddied into the garden. Inside the tunnel, alongside the rushing stream, there was a path wide enough for two men. When Ross looked closely he saw that it was made up of glittering crystals. In fact, the whole tunnel was encrusted with them.

He could see all this from the entrance because

the interior of the antechamber was bathed in an ethereal glow, which emanated from deep within the tunnel, amplified by the crystals and the stream. The path emitted its own glittering phosphorescence, presenting an irresistible temptation to enter the tunnel and discover the source of the strange light. A potentially deadly temptation, Ross remembered, from a passage in Lauren's translation of the Voynich:

Though the conquistadors could not communicate directly with the Eves, the scholar priest understood that it was forbidden to enter their cave. For many days they rested after their gruelling journey and enjoyed the beautiful garden. But soon, like all idle men, they grew curious and greedy, wondering what could be in the cave. It must be valuable, they reasoned. Gold.

The scholar priest counselled them to obey their hosts but the captain was a proud man who obeyed only his king. That night the conquistadors ventured into the cave. They found the Eves bathing in pools, filled by water flowing from a vaulted tunnel in the raised back of the cave. As well as water, light issued from deep within the tunnel bathing everything in a golden glow. Alongside the rushing stream, a path climbed and twisted into the rock. It appeared to be encrusted with diamonds, which sparkled in the light. Convinced that its source must be a vast treasure trove, the conquistadors were drawn to it like moths to a flame.

When they approached, the Eves emitted a high-pitched wailing and blocked their path. The scholar priest begged the men not to enter. But they pushed him and the Eves aside and began their ascent. The scholar priest watched each of them disappear into the tunnel and for many minutes nothing happened.

Then the screaming started.

And the stream turned red with their blood.

Twenty-one men entered the tunnel, all the surviving members of the original troop. Not one came down. Every conquistador died. The scholar priest understood then that the Eves had not been protecting whatever was in the tunnel from their greed but the conquistadors from whatever was in the tunnel. After witnessing the horrors of that night, he concluded that only man could turn Heaven into Hell.

The tunnel of blood also featured in the last pages of Falcon's notebook: the translation of the Voynich's astrological section that Lauren had not yet unravelled. According to this section, Falcon later went up the tunnel himself and discovered '*el origen*' – the source, what Torino called the '*radix*'. Ross took the damaged notebook from his backpack and studied the relevant pages, but apart from a typically cryptic reference to something called El Árbol de la Vida y de la Muerte, the Tree of Life and Death, they told him little. He pulled out his compass and watched the needle rotate furiously, then point up the tunnel.

'What's up there?' he asked.

'I don't know. Only Father Orlando lived to see *el origen*.'

'But in his notebook he doesn't explain what it is. Only that it's the power behind the garden, is incredibly beautiful and the path leading to it is dangerous.' Ross was burning to know more but something moved in his peripheral vision. He shifted his focus and saw that the glowing tunnel was not the only remarkable thing in the cave.

In the far recesses, white shapes moved in the shadows. He stepped closer and saw a creature staring back at him, a biped, about four feet high with translucent alabaster-white skin. It had two arms, a distended belly and two mounds on its chest, with no nipples. Its face was round with large, attractive eyes, a small nose and a wide mouth. On top of its head there was a cluster of strand-like growths, entwined with flowers. The creature seemed as fascinated by Ross as he was by it.

'Father Orlando was many things,' Sister Chantal said quietly, 'but, as you can see, he was no artist.'

It was one of the Voynich's nymphs – one of Orlando Falcon's Eves – though it looked nothing like Ross had expected. He had heard of sailors mistaking manatees for mermaids, and this, perhaps, explained why Orlando Falcon had depicted the creature as a female human.

Similar creatures were emerging from the shadows now, but his eyes were drawn to writhing, serpentine growths on the ceiling and walls at the back of the cave. The tubular tentacle structures appeared to grow from the rock like thick vines. Grotesquely beautiful, with veins that throbbed like blood vessels, they seemed a strange blend of plant and animal. The tentacles ended in variously shaped pods. Ross glimpsed some nymphs reclining in them while others straddled the vines. They seemed to have a strange symbiotic relationship with each other.

'What are they?' he asked. 'Those tubular growths?'

'Like the Eves, they've been here since Father Orlando discovered the garden. They run through much of the cave.' She retrieved a torch from her bag, switched it on and led him towards the far recesses of the antechamber. The space was even deeper than it appeared from the entrance and led to a warren of other caves and tunnels deep within the rock. As they approached, the nymphs either melted into the tunnels or hissed threateningly. Sister Chantal held up her crucifix and began to hum a two-note refrain. Immediately the nymphs became less agitated and copied the sound. When she stopped they appeared calmer, accepting their presence. She left the crucifix hanging outside her blouse. 'It reassures them,' she said.

In the beam of Sister Chantal's torch the tubular tentacles seemed to be everywhere, like ducting in the basement of a large building. He followed a number of thicker ones down a passage to the right

where the air felt warmer until he saw a fiery red glow ahead.

'Careful, Ross.'

Suddenly he was hit by a wall of heat, and stopped where the tunnel ended in an abrupt ledge. Magma boiled many feet below. A thin, broken rock bridge led across it to more dark caves.

'In Father Orlando's time that bridge was wider and unbroken,' said Sister Chantal. 'He claimed it was another way out of the garden, that it led to the other side of the ridge that surrounds this place.'

You'd have to be pretty desperate to take that exit, thought Ross. It made the poisonous caves through which they had come seem like a walk in the park.

Sister Chantal turned. 'Let's go back to the antechamber. I want to show you something *really* impressive.'

When they reached it five nymphs were bathing in the pool directly beneath the small waterfall. Wherever he looked, he saw pages of the Voynich come alive.

Sister Chantal led him on to the ledge towards the tunnel and bent down by the stream. She put her cupped hand into the rushing water, as if it was a gold prospector's pan, then brought it out and displayed it to Ross. 'This is what we've come for. This is what can cure Lauren.'

53

Her hand was full of small, luminous, crystalline rock particles, larger than the microscopic ones in the water he had drunk from the lake but smaller than the shards he had seen last night. She moved her hand and the crystals sparkled many colours. 'These are the only things I allow myself to take out of the garden, but these crystals are too small. Any power they have will dissipate once we leave. They need to be of a certain size to retain their potency. You can grind them down when you're outside but the crystal's got to be big enough to start with.'

'Where can I get a large enough one? From the bottom of the lake?'

'No. Those are smaller than they look. Something to do with the magnifying effect of all that water.' She reached into the stream again and picked up a large shard, which had broken off from the lattice of crystal encrusting the tunnel. She handed it to him.

He looked at it, mesmerized. It was beautiful,

part opaque, part clear, and glowed as he turned it in his hand. He imagined he could feel its power. 'You're sure this will cure Lauren?'

She hesitated for the briefest moment, glanced up the tunnel, then said, 'Yes. So long as you keep it whole until you need to use it, it should retain much of its potency.'

'I'd love to analyse it.'

She smiled guiltily. 'Though my main concern is to fulfil my vow, a few years ago I had a sample analysed blind by a lab in Geneva. I was desperate to be relieved of my responsibility. I wanted them to synthesize it, take the pressure off the garden – and off me.'

'What did they find?'

'The laboratory report claimed it was unusually, but not dangerously, radioactive and contained every key amino acid building block necessary for life – including phosphorus, which was relatively rare. But they found nothing else unusual, certainly no hint of its ability to heal. They replicated it exactly, creating an identical clone of its constituent ingredients, but it had none of the original's power. Whatever spark makes the combined constituent parts heal in the way you've all experienced is beyond their instruments.' She pointed at the crystal in Ross's hand. 'But that should work. Take it home, grind up a good quantity, mix it into a drink and feed it to Lauren. I like it in tea with condensed milk.' She smiled. 'But I have a sweet tooth.'

'You've used this stuff?'

She clutched her crucifix. 'It's been my lifeline. How do you think I've maintained my vigil for so long? So *very* long.'

Now, looking into her eyes, unguarded for the first time since they'd met, he saw her pain and loneliness laid bare. Suddenly he understood the depth of her dedication to the garden, and the extent of her sacrifice. A tremor ran through him. 'There haven't been any other Keepers before you, have there?' he said.

'No. Only me. I was the novice nun who cared for Orlando Falcon. I was the accomplice who hid his Devil's book. It was I he charged with reclaiming his possessions, including his notebook, and protecting his garden.'

'But why?'

'*Why?*'

'Why did you help him? Why did you make your vow?'

'Because I fell in love with him. I loved him more than the Church. I loved him more than life.' A small shake of the head. 'I loved him more than the release of *death*. When he made me vow to protect his garden until someone deciphered his manuscript and proved themselves worthy to take over his legacy, I had no idea how long I would have to wait.' She patted the crucifix. 'He gave me this cross and told me that whenever my burden seemed too great I would always find salvation in it.' She paused, as if lost in thought. 'Before they burnt him at the stake he also made a vow to me.'

'What was it?'

'That he would wait for me.' A small smile played on her lips. 'He said, "For you I will wait for ever."' She pointed out to the garden, to the mound of stones. 'His remains are buried there. I brought his ashes from Rome. One day, soon, I hope, our waiting will be over and we will be reunited.'

'You were there when he died?'

She looked away. 'I watched.'

He studied her once beautiful face. 'You've lived for more than four and a half centuries?'

'I've *existed* for that long, yes. It hasn't always felt like living.'

'But that's impossible!' he gasped.

She laughed. It was a humourless sound. 'Feel your healed wrist. Look at the crystal in your hand. Then tell me it's impossible.'

'But how did you live? How did you support yourself for so long?'

'Father Orlando came from a wealthy Castilian family. When he died he left me a sizeable amount, which kept me going for some years. Then I stumbled on the lost city and its gold, some of which I invested – over a *long* period of time. Money is the least of my worries.'

He remembered that some of the gold ingots in the ziggurat had been missing. 'But what about the authorities, your passport, your identity?'

'Remaining a nun has helped. Sister Chantal is a given official name. My Catholic order bestowed it on me when I was seventeen. I chose to keep it and over the long years it's now become who I am. But throughout my life I've had numerous legal identities – all borrowed from children I treated in hospices. When they died, their names lived on in me. I've held various passports, French, Italian, British – but not yet American.' A smile. 'Your country's still young – only half as old as I am.'

He remembered the six dates scratched on El Halo, each about seventy years apart. 'You returned here at regular intervals, to refresh yourself and replenish your supplies, before assuming another identity, another life, in a different part of the world.'

She nodded. 'I aged so slowly that I had to keep moving to avoid drawing attention to myself. So far, I think I've already lived six life spans, six three score years and ten. As well as checking on the garden, I returned here to replenish my supplies of the crystal so I could continue my vigil. As I said, the crystals slow my ageing but they can't reverse it. I sometimes wonder if I'd stayed here the whole time whether I would have stopped ageing and stayed for ever young. But I needed to be in the world to do my duty and fulfil my vow. I had to keep track of Father Orlando's manuscript – as it travelled across Europe, returned to Italy and finally ended up in America – to discover if anyone had deciphered it. And, for my own sanity, I had to do good in the real world.'

She patted Ross's arm. 'Anyway, I'm now in my seventh lifespan. The last, I hope. I've done all I can. You have the means to cure your wife. Once you've done so, I can pass on my burden to her. My vow will have been fulfilled. We both have what we wanted. We should leave tomorrow.'

'Tomorrow?'

She tapped the crystal in Ross's hand. 'We need to get this to your wife as soon as possible.'

'You're *sure* it'll cure her?'

Again she hesitated and looked back at the glowing tunnel. 'I'm as sure as I can be. Over the years, apart from two recent exceptions, I've only used its powers to slow my ageing and restore my health, but I'm confident it will cure your wife. The last few granules I gave her had an effect.'

'It was *negligible*.'

She frowned. 'Have faith, Ross. This crystal will be enough.' She pointed to the tunnel. 'The only way to *guarantee* a cure would be to take a sample of the source itself, which Father Orlando believed had limitless power. But getting to it is impossible.'

'Father Orlando went up and survived.'

'I don't know how, though. Anyway, it's irrelevant. What you're holding will be enough to save Lauren and your unborn child. Come, Ross,' she said, leading him back into the light of the garden. 'Let's return to the others and tell them we're leaving.'

As Ross clasped the crystal he knew he should feel grateful. But as his eyes strayed back to the tunnel, doubt nagged at him.

54

That night

Hackett shook his head at Sister Chantal. 'Do you know how many expeditions the big pharmaceutical companies have sent into the jungles of the world, looking for plants with healing properties? Hundreds. Thousands. They've found a few things but never a real breakthrough. Nothing like this. This place is incredible. It's got everything. It's a comprehensive medicine cabinet. It's our duty to share it with the world.'

Sister Chantal shook her head. 'Nothing living here can survive outside. The water and the plants are useless. More importantly, you all made a vow before you came. You promised never to speak of this place or to take anything from it.'

'But it's too amazing to be kept secret.'

'You made a vow and vows must be kept.'

'And I'll keep it. It's just that as a doctor—'

Sister Chantal's passion flared. 'You can't equivocate with a vow. A vow is black and white.

335

There's never a plausible excuse or justifiable reason to break it. You either keep a vow or break it. There's no middle ground. A vow is for ever.'

The sun had set and they were sitting round a small fire towards the top of the eye. They had had dinner and were now drinking coffee, arguing about the place in which they found themselves. Ross could sympathize with Hackett's view but earlier, when he'd shown Zeb the crystal concealed in his backpack and told her about his experience in the cave, she had sided with Sister Chantal. 'Ross, Lauren translated the Voynich. She deserves to be saved by the garden. In return, Sister Chantal will expect her to protect it. If Falcon and Sister Chantal believe that whoever translated the Voynich should determine what happens to this place they couldn't have chosen a more responsible person than Lauren. And I'll tell you now: the last thing Lauren would do is tell the world about it. Not until she knew what the world would do with it.'

Sister Chantal turned to the others. 'You will all honour the vow.' It was a command.

'Yes,' said Zeb, quickly.

Sister Chantal looked at Mendoza. 'And you?'

Mendoza met her gaze. 'People would pay anything to come to this place and be cured. But we have enough gold in the lost city. I'll keep my vow,' he said solemnly.

'But, Sister, why don't you want to tell the world about it?' pleaded Hackett. 'Think of the good it could do.'

'For whom?' said Zeb.

Hackett turned to her, surprised. 'For humanity, of course. This place will save lives.'

'But who will save this place?'

'What do you mean?'

'This place is a resource and not just for humanity. What do you think man would do with it if he found it?'

'Use it to heal, of course.'

'This small garden to heal the whole population of the Earth? Who chooses who to save first? Who takes priority before it's depleted and destroyed? And what do we do after we've exhausted it and killed all the living creatures here just to prolong *our* lives?'

'We could conserve it,' said Hackett.

Zeb laughed. 'The only thing mankind conserves are ruins – and I use the term *man*kind advisedly. We're crap at conserving living resources. Not until we've used them up or turned them into ruins. Only then, when it's too late, do we suddenly get all misty-eyed. Sister Chantal's right to keep this place secret.'

'But what if the pharmaceutical industry could analyse what's here?' demanded Hackett. 'We saw how important the spring water was to the lost city. It could contain stem-cell regenerators, electrolytes, amino acids. They could synthesize it. Make a limitless supply.'

Zeb laughed again. 'We also saw what happened to the lost city when the water dried up. Even if they could unlock this place's power, do you suppose the pharmaceutical industry – that paragon of ethics, morality and altruism – would give it away free?'

'They could make it affordable, at least.'

'Have you ever known any pharmaceutical company make anything affordable – particularly something as valuable as this – let alone give it away free? Just look at what's happening with HIV drugs in Africa. Even if they did give it away would that be a good thing? Think about it: a world with no more death or disease, just an ever-growing population, everyone needing their fix to keep them healthy and alive. Anyway, this place would put the pharmaceutical industry out of business overnight. They'd have to destroy it before it destroyed them.'

For all Zeb's pessimism, Ross feared she was right. If this was an alternative to oil he knew what his industry would do: exploit it or bury it.

Hackett was about to respond when Sister Chantal raised a hand, like a referee in a fight. 'Nothing in here can be synthesized,' she said. 'I had a sample analysed a few years ago and, apart from some amino acids and a low level of radio-activity, they found nothing. The synthesized version was useless.'

'They found nothing?' said Hackett. 'No stem-cell promoters? Nothing that might explain how it repairs DNA?'

The nun shook her head.

'I suspect that what drives life in this place is a precursor to DNA,' said Ross.

Hackett thought for a moment. 'You mean this whole place could be working on something like RNA? Or something even more primitive?'

'Whatever's the *most* primitive form of life,' said Ross. 'As a geologist the only way I can explain this place is if it's a throwback to when life first began on Earth. It may even be *the* place where life began. If DNA is like the Microsoft Windows software of life, then whatever's behind this garden is DOS or whatever came before that. This is the base programming behind DNA. The stuff that *makes* DNA. It might not exist anywhere else in the world. That's why labs can't detect it. They've never seen it before. They've no idea what they're looking for.'

Hackett was nodding. 'It seems as if every organism here has evolved different phenotypes from those in the outside world. Part of that could be environmental, due to its isolation, but a greater part could be that it stems directly from a more primitive genotype.'

'What the hell's the difference between a phenotype and a genotype?' asked Zeb.

'A genotype is an organism's genetic makeup, its book of instructions,' said Hackett. 'A phenotype is its physical form, what it looks like, determined by genes and environment. For example, your hair, skin and eye colour are largely determined by your genotype but expressed in your phenotype. The point is most creatures have evolved *separate* genotypes and phenotypes. The human genotype, for example, uses its phenotype to survive – by making our bodies want to have sex so we pass on our genes. But many evolutionary biologists believe that the first living organisms were so basic they were just bundles of instructions. The genotype *was* the phenotype. The software was the hardware. There was no secondary body. If life here is as primitive as Ross believes, then the base genotype, the original instructions for life, might still exist in its primal form, whatever that is.'

'This place can't be explained by science,' said Mendoza, solemnly. 'It's sacred. It's too important to be left to scientists or businessmen. Only the Church can know what's best for a place like this.'

'Which church?' said Sister Chantal.

Mendoza frowned disapprovingly. 'You're a Roman Catholic nun. There's only one church that can decide what's best for this place.'

Sister Chantal shook her head. 'A great man, a priest, once said that this place was the Garden of God and I believe him. It *is* sacred. Too sacred for any church or religion to control.' She gave a weary sigh. 'Let me tell you how this place was discovered and why my friends, Ross and Zeb, accompanied me here.' For the next few minutes she talked about Orlando Falcon, the Voynich, Lauren Kelly and Father General Leonardo Torino. Hackett and Mendoza listened, rapt, until she was finished.

But Mendoza was unconvinced. 'Sister, you'd rather entrust the future of this garden to a woman lying unconscious in hospital than to your own church?'

'Once Lauren Kelly has been cured I can hand over my burden. I'm simply fulfilling my vow. No more, no less. All I ask is that you fulfil yours.'

Hackett turned to Ross. 'You think the Father General could have been behind your wife's injury?'

'I've no proof, but I wouldn't put it past him after what happened with the bandits on the river.'

'But he's a senior officer of the Roman Catholic Church!' said Hackett.

'Then I guess they must really want this place.'

'So when do we leave?' asked Zeb.

'Tomorrow. We'll return first to the lost city.' Sister Chantal turned to Hackett and Mendoza. 'For your gold. Then Ross, Zeb and I shall go back to America.'

Hackett laid a hand on Ross's shoulder. 'We may have lost Juarez,' he said sadly, 'but it appears our trip into the jungle wasn't totally in vain. We all found what we were looking for.'

'Yes, I suppose we did.' But even as he said it, Ross thought of the light emanating from the tunnel of blood: the source. It was now clear that the garden and its unusual life forms were merely physical expressions of the miraculous powers that

341

had drawn him here. The true source of the miraculous garden, and possibly life itself, was what Hackett had called the base genotype. And when he thought of its power and his desire to *ensure* Lauren's recovery, he realized that, despite the crystal in his bag, he might not have everything he had come for. Not yet, anyway.

55

The next morning Ross woke early and while the others slept he stole into the forbidden caves. He wasn't sure what he hoped to achieve, only that he had to explore the caves one last time before he left. As he entered, he wondered how old they were. He guessed that radioactive dating would place them at, or near, the dawn of creation.

In the half-light he saw two white figures in the pool, picking shards of crystal rock from the water and gnawing at them with small but impressively sharp teeth. Their translucent flesh seemed to pulse in the gloom. Immediately they saw him, they stopped and opened their mouths in song. Their voices filled the cave, building in a crescendo, then stopped abruptly. They didn't move, just watched him. So he mimicked their singing, note for note.

They opened their mouths again. This time they sang a higher, more complex sequence of notes.

Again Ross copied it.

One of the nymphs came closer. It had red

flowers in its frond-like hair. Its mouth widened and a chattering sound came from it, like laughter. Close up the creature was disconcerting. Its large eyes reminded him of a Disney cartoon, but when he looked into them he couldn't see any emotion – any connection. Its mouth, full of sharp animal teeth, confirmed that it was no human. And yet, when he copied its sounds, it responded. He wondered if Orlando Falcon, the brilliant linguist and communicator, had done something similar all those centuries ago. Had he formed a bond with these creatures, especially after the conquistadors had been killed? Were they his only companions while he was stranded in this strange, dangerous paradise? Had he come to see them as a simpler, more innocent version of humanity, harking back to a time before we were corrupted?

Ross tried an experiment. He created his own sound – but as soon as he uttered the first note he knew it wasn't original. He was unconsciously reproducing the alien scales from Spielberg's *Close Encounters of the Third Kind*. But when he stopped, the nymph copied him. Perfectly.

He tried another tune: the James Bond theme. Again the nymph reproduced it immaculately. Now more of them were emerging from the gloom, all keen to watch the parlour game.

He waited and his new friend, the nymph with red flowers in its hair, made another series of sounds. Unlike Ross's movie scores, the nymph's notes sounded random with no discernible tune or melody, the difference between prose and poetry. Nevertheless, he repeated the sequence and the nymphs resumed their laughter-like chattering.

He had begun to hum the *Pink Panther* theme, when a scream stopped him. The short, piercing sound made his skin crawl. The nymphs fell silent and turned as one to the back of the cave. Ross followed their gaze. In the gloom, among the mass of tubular stems, he saw one of the pods open to reveal a nymph with a huge, distended belly. Between its spread legs, curled in a foetal ball, was another nymph, greyer in colour but not much smaller than the mother – if that was what it was. The 'child' moved, and three of the watching nymphs lifted it from the pod and carried it to one of the pools, where they ground up shards of crystal between their teeth and fed it to the new-born, mouth-to-mouth. As it swallowed their offerings, it brightened to the radiant white of the others.

Four other nymphs walked to the pod and lifted the mother. Its colour was also changing, darkening, like that of a dead fish losing its freshness. The musky, mustard-seed smell he had detected yesterday was stronger now. The creature seemed barely alive but the other nymphs made no attempt to revive it in the pool, as they had with the new-born. Instead, they lifted it on to their shoulders and carried it towards the entrance to the tunnel of blood, where they stopped.

Six other nymphs rushed from the cave and

returned with fruit and plants. There was a lull as they formed a procession behind the quartet bearing the dying mother. As if on some invisible cue, they began to sing, a fractured, haunting melody, as they entered the tunnel and climbed the path beside the rushing stream.

Ross looked around the cave. The other nymphs were occupied with the newborn. He hesitated, heart pounding, feeling the crystal in his bag, knowing he should be grateful for what he had and walk away. He couldn't, though. Not yet. He followed the procession into the tunnel of blood.

56

Ross hung back, keeping a discreet distance from the nymphs. The meandering path was wet and uneven but his Timberlands held their grip on the crystal-encrusted steps. As he climbed he became aware of two things: the tunnel was long, and it appeared to get brighter the further he went.

He estimated he had been walking for about fifteen minutes when the nymphs stopped singing. The light was now so bright it seemed to bleach everything. Unable to see without squinting, he pressed himself into a recess in the wall and put on his sunglasses. Now he could marvel at the gilded crystal rock that surrounded him. It was more dramatic even than the amazing formations in the vast Lechugia caves of New Mexico.

Peering out of the recess he saw that the tunnel ahead curved and widened to form a chamber with a small waterfall. The ground there was flat but beyond it the path rose to another level, leading to the light above. On this higher level, by the top of the waterfall, the tunnel widened again to form another small chamber to the right of the main path, its walls pockmarked with a warren of small holes and tunnels. Each was pitch black, beyond the reach of the light, but as he stared at the holes he thought he saw dark shapes writhing within them. Two spots of red flickered, then disappeared into the shadows, reminding him of the crocodile-infested river. A shudder rippled through him.

The nymphs had congregated at the base of the waterfall. Three, laden with the fruit and plants, approached the path to the higher level. As they climbed, the others again burst into song. This time it was more a chant, an incantation: two notes repeated again and again.

As the sound reverberated round the walls, the three nymphs reached the upper level and walked to the right, into the centre of the chamber. They placed the fruit and plants on the ground in front of the holes. Then, as soon as they'd returned to the others, the chanting stopped. Within seconds the upper chamber exploded into a writhing orgy of violence. Long dark shapes shot out of the holes and tunnels and attacked the food. They didn't linger, just tore at the fruit and plants and retreated to their lairs. Then they launched another attack, repeating the frenzied process until there was nothing left. It was over so fast that it was hard to make out what had happened.

When the food was gone and the creatures had retired to their holes, Ross could still see them shuffling restlessly, red eyes staring. The nymphs started their chant again and the creatures froze. This time four nymphs carried the dying one to the same spot where the fruit had been left. It whimpered but didn't struggle when the others laid it down and retreated to the lower level. Again, when the chanting stopped, the creatures twisted out of the walls like missiles, their long worm-like bodies never leaving the holes entirely. This time the feeding frenzy took longer and Ross watched in horror as the dark, armour-plated beasts drilled through their prey, extracting circular chunks of flesh from the nymph, then retreating to their holes and propelling themselves forward again. In seconds the screaming nymph had been shredded. In a little more than a minute it had been consumed.

When it was over the nymphs made their way back down the tunnel, reverting to the same fractured melody they had sung on the way up. Ross pressed himself deeper into the recess to watch them pass. It seemed that even in this miraculous paradise nature had to maintain a balance, however cruel. For every birth there had to be a death. One in, one out.

As soon as the singing receded, he ventured out to where they had been standing and looked up to the next level. Ahead, he could see the tunnel leading to the source of light. To its right was the dark chamber, its walls pocked with tunnels and holes. A jutting shape, which didn't fit with the crystalline rocks, caught his eye. It took him some seconds to see that it was a sword. Its blade was encrusted with crystals but the handle and hilt were clearly recognizable. He looked round and saw, encased within the rocks, a breastplate punched with holes and half of a helmet. All lay only a few yards from the dark holes and in that instant he knew they had belonged to the ill-fated conquistadors who had climbed this passage to what they thought was treasure. He thought again of the passage in the Voynich.

The scholar priest watched each of them disappear into the tunnel and for many minutes nothing happened. Then the screaming started. And the stream turned red with their blood.

If they had kept to the path on the upper level the conquistadors would still have fallen prey to the rock worms. Their armour and weapons, invincible against the Inca, were useless against such predators. He shuddered at the image of twenty-one men being butchered like the nymph. No wonder it had been a bloodbath.

He looked up the passageway towards the beckoning light. Unlike the conquistadors, Ross knew it wasn't the glow of treasure but something far more valuable. A famous quotation from Louis Pasteur came to mind: 'I am on the verge of mysteries and the veils are getting thinner.' Excitement and frustration pulsed through him.

Just out of reach was what promised to be the holy grail of geology, of *all* science, the point of origin for life on this planet – and a certain cure for Lauren. He watched the shapes moving in the dark, guarding the passage to whatever was up there. He was tantalizingly close to the most incredible discovery in Earth's history – something that had given birth eventually to humanity, although only one man had ever seen it – yet he couldn't reach it. If only he had more time to find a way to get past the creatures, as Father Orlando had.

Ross licked his dry lips, opened his mouth and replicated the nymphs' two-note chant. Immediately, the movement in the holes stopped.

He fell silent and the movement started again. Some of the creatures shot out of the holes, jaws snapping. It seemed that the chanting not only stilled them, but also primed them to expect food. He sang the notes again. The creatures instantly retreated to their holes and froze. He stopped and they sprang into life once more.

Was this how Father Orlando had eventually reached what he had called *el origen*?

Ross wondered how much further away the source was. He also wondered how long the creatures would stay immobile if he maintained the chant, and whether, once he got past this section, he would be safe. He thought of the crystal in his backpack. Sister Chantal was convinced it was enough to cure Lauren, and she had almost as much at stake as he did. He should be grateful for what he had, hurry home and not look back. And yet—

Bang.

The sharp report was muffled but unmistakable.

Bang.

Another report. Then silence.

He turned, horrified, and ran back to the antechamber.

Why would anyone be firing a high-powered rifle in the garden?

57

Moments earlier

For an orphan bastard born in the gutters of Naples, Leonardo Torino had experienced many triumphs in his life, not least the day he became Superior General of the order that had moulded him. Nothing, however, came close to the elation he felt now. After stumbling through caves filled with bat filth and sulphur, he breathed in the fresh, scented air, wiped his stinging eyes and stared. Everywhere he looked there were plants from the Voynich and before him the circular lake described in Falcon's testimony, the forbidden caves too. An ecstatic tremor ran through him. Father Orlando's mythic garden existed and Torino would claim it for the Holy Mother Church. He would save the Church that had saved him. The whole world would bow down before her majesty and power, and depend on her for their salvation.

Torino turned to the soldiers. All were staring, open-mouthed, struggling to believe the vision before them.

'What is this place?' asked Fleischer.

Torino smiled. 'This, Feldwebel, is what we must claim for the Holy Mother Church. This is the Garden of God.'

Weber, the soldier who had followed Ross's party, raised his rifle. 'They're over there, to the right of the lake, and they've seen us.'

Torino raised his binoculars and saw a man and two women three hundred yards away. One was the red-haired student from America, the other the nun, Sister Chantal, but he didn't recognize the man. Ross Kelly wasn't with them. They were standing by a pile of backpacks, preparing to leave. He had got here just in time.

'They're armed,' said Fleischer, shouldering his weapon.

Torino saw the man bend to the backpacks, then pull out a revolver and a rifle. He handed the revolver to the red-haired woman and raised his rifle. Torino imagined how threatening armed soldiers must look, appearing suddenly in this isolated place.

'What are your orders?' said Fleischer.

Torino took in the situation. He could easily defuse matters. Tell the soldiers to lower their weapons, approach Kelly's party and show them the legal documents granting him possession of the garden. But then what? He couldn't let them leave. Aside from the soldiers, they were the only people who knew of this place's existence. They would undoubtedly tell others about it. Kelly certainly wouldn't go quietly, not without a cure for his wife and the opportunity to tell the world of his geological discovery. It wasn't in the Vatican's interests for anyone to know about the garden yet, not until Torino had learnt more about its power and decided how best to use it. Far better to stoke the conflict. Use his superior force to cow and control Kelly and his friends.

'These people are dangerous and can't be trusted,' he said. 'You must disarm them. Take no chances. Fire a warning shot.'

Weber did so. The man stood his ground and gestured for the women to run to the caves.

Weber fired another shot but the man still didn't flee or return fire. He edged backwards, gun raised, covering the women's retreat.

Weber pulled the rifle closer into his shoulder, peered down the sight and squeezed his finger on the trigger. 'I can disarm him from here.'

Torino raised his binoculars and scanned the garden for Kelly. He couldn't see him or anyone else. 'No, leave him. Let them gather in the caves. It'll make it easier to round them up.'

'It might be difficult to flush them out,' said Fleischer.

Torino smiled to himself. 'That won't be a problem, Feldwebel. Trust me.' He walked into the garden and headed for the caves. 'Come. Let's do God's work.'

58

The first thing Ross saw when he scrambled out of the tunnel was Mendoza crouching by the antechamber's small waterfall, gripping his rifle. 'Where the hell have you been?' he hissed.

Ross pointed back to the tunnel. 'I've been trying to find out what's behind this place. You won't believe what's up there.' He glanced anxiously to the back of the cave where the nymphs watched from the shadows. 'What were you shooting at?'

Mendoza shook his head. 'It wasn't me.' He pointed to the cave's entrance. 'Seems we've got company. We were packing to leave, getting a last look at the place, and I came to fetch you. These guys appeared out of nowhere.'

Ross crouched behind a boulder and peered out. Zeb and Sister Chantal were running towards him as fast as they could, Zeb clutching Hackett's revolver in her right hand. Hackett covered the rear, rifle raised, retreating at a more dignified pace towards the cave. Ross couldn't see who they were running from so he stood up. His blood ran cold. 'How the hell did he get here?' he muttered.

Father General Leonardo Torino looked different out of his robes but Ross knew him instantly. Dressed in thick boots, canvas trousers, a white cotton shirt and sleeveless jacket, he was flanked by four uniformed men, all armed and carrying large backpacks. They were clearly confident that their quarry couldn't escape.

When Zeb and Chantal reached Ross, they slumped down, panting, behind the next boulder. 'Give me the gun,' Ross said. Zeb was only too happy to hand it over. She looked scared but Sister Chantal's face was white with fury. Just as she had been about to fulfil her vow and surrender her responsibility for the garden, everything she had striven for, every sacrifice she had made, had come to nothing.

Hackett rushed in, cradling his rifle. He crouched beside Ross. 'Is our visitor your dodgy priest?'

'Father General Leonardo Torino.'

'What's he doing here?' Sister Chantal hissed. 'How did he find this place?'

'We must have led him,' Ross said.

'But how?' demanded Hackett. 'I thought we'd lost him when Osvaldo killed his pirates on the river.'

'I don't know,' said Ross. 'What happened out there? They just appeared?'

'Out of nowhere and began firing.'

'If they'd wanted to shoot you, you'd have been hit by now,' said Mendoza, from deeper within the cave. 'They wanted to contain us here.'

Hackett turned and glanced round the cave. 'Is there another way out?' He pointed to the tunnel. 'Where does that lead?'

'You don't want to go up there,' said Ross. He thought of the exit across the magma pool behind the antechamber. 'There's a possible way out at the back of the cave but it's not a route I'd recommend.'

'What do we do?' said Zeb. 'Fight them?'

Hackett grimaced. 'Those soldiers are well armed. And judging by their backpacks they've brought a mini arsenal with them.'

'We can't just let them take over this place,' said Sister Chantal.

Torino's voice boomed out across the lake. 'Dr Kelly, you and your party are trespassing.' He held up a leather attaché case. 'I have the required legal documentation to claim this land. We mean you no harm but these soldiers are here to enforce my rightful claim.' The priest approached the forbidden caves, flanked by the soldiers. 'Show yourself. You have nothing to fear from us.'

Yeah, right, thought Ross. As he looked at the men's hard faces and weapons, the exit across the magma pool seemed more appealing. As Torino neared them, Hackett raised his rifle and Ross fingered his Glock. It seemed so puny. This was madness. They couldn't win. They'd only be killed. They had to accept defeat. Behind him, he heard the metallic click of Mendoza's rifle bolt engaging and Ross remembered how he had dispatched the three bandits on the river.

'Put your guns down or I'll shoot,' Mendoza ordered.

'You're a bit hopeful,' said Hackett, peering out of the cave. 'And you'll have to speak a lot louder than that if you want them to hear you.'

'Not them. *You.*'

Ross turned. Mendoza's rifle was trained on his chest. 'What?'

'You can't be serious,' said Hackett.

'Drop your guns. Now.'

Hackett and Ross did as they were told. Mendoza stepped closer and kicked the guns behind him. 'I don't understand,' said Ross.

'You will.' Mendoza raised his voice. 'Father General, can you hear me?'

A pause. 'Is that you, Marco?'

'Yes. They're here, all accounted for. I'm sending them out.'

'Marco?' said a stunned Zeb. 'I thought your name was Osvaldo.'

He ignored her. 'Raise your hands and step out of the cave.'

'You made a vow,' said Sister Chantal, stunned.

After the initial shock, nausea swirled in Ross's gut. He couldn't believe what was happening. He had allowed this man, who had pretended to be his friend, to undermine his already impossible quest to save Lauren. Now, when against all the odds he had found what he sought, he was to be denied. All the anger, frustration and grief he had suppressed since the night of her injury erupted within him. He had never known rage like it. He leapt at Mendoza, lunging for the rifle, taking him by surprise.

'What have you done?' he roared, as he flung the man to the ground and wrestled him for the rifle. 'What the *fuck* have you done?' In his rage, he had no idea how long they fought, but when he had finally wrested the gun off Mendoza and pointed it at the man who had betrayed them, his whole body was trembling.

Then he glanced at Mendoza's right leg and froze.

Mendoza's jeans had ridden up over his boots, revealing a transmitter strapped to his shin. But it was the thick scar above his right ankle that stunned Ross and revealed the full extent of Mendoza and Torino's duplicity. He had seen that scar once before, through a haze of blood on the night Lauren had been injured, moments before she had been thrown from the landing and broken her neck.

Ross had never wanted to kill anyone before but in that instant, as he looked down at the man who had destroyed Lauren's life, he wanted to kill Mendoza – or whatever the bastard's name was. As his finger tightened on the trigger, a soldier rushed in behind him, rifle butt raised, and bludgeoned him across the head. Ross collapsed, the pain so intense he clamped his eyes shut to dull its white glare. A second blow turned the white to black.

59

As Feldwebel Fleischer and his soldiers dragged Kelly away and led his companions out of the caves at gunpoint, Torino smiled at the man who, for the last few weeks, had used the name Osvaldo Mendoza. At that moment, in the euphoria of triumph, he felt genuine affection for his half-brother. 'You did well, Marco.'

'Who are the soldiers, Father General?'

Torino waved a hand dismissively. 'Swiss Guard. The Holy Father sent them to protect me in the jungle. Now, tell me everything, Marco. What happened on the river before Iquitos? I was worried until I got your satellite text warning about La Boca del Inferno.'

'Things didn't go as planned. The three men I hired to frighten Kelly's party were supposed to flee when I fired a warning shot. Make me look a hero. But they were amateurs and got greedy.'

'Greedy?'

'Their leader, Raul, heard Kelly talking about the

priest's book and assumed it led to treasure. He and the other two tried to get it for themselves.'

Torino frowned at his half-brother. 'You killed them?'

'I had no choice. Raul was going to shoot the nun and you said she might be valuable.' Bazin shrugged. 'In the end it made me more credible with Kelly and the others. And I had contingencies in place.'

Torino nodded. 'They worked well, Marco. Both the GPS transmitter on the boat and the one on your ankle worked like a charm. I was a little concerned, though, when the satellite signal began to break up. One of the soldiers had to track you over the last few days. But he says you left a good trail, especially through the sulphur caves.'

'Did you find the lost city?'

'What? No.' Torino had no interest in lost cities.

'There's gold there.'

Torino shook his head. 'This is more valuable than gold.' He turned back to Kelly and the others, who were being corralled by the soldiers into an area enclosed by rocks and trees. 'What can you tell me about this place? What have you learnt?'

'It's incredible. Just drinking the lake water and eating the plants can cure you.' Bazin paused for a moment, as if overcome. 'When we got to Iquitos I was getting excruciating headaches, one of the symptoms the clinic told me to watch for if the cancer spread to the brain. They were the worst I've known, even with powerful painkillers. I had them all day every day. Then I drank the water here and the next morning the pain had gone. I've never felt better. I'm cured. I know it.' He lowered his voice. 'Even the testicle the surgeons removed is growing back. The scar has virtually disappeared. It's like God laid his hand on me, washed away my sins and gave me a second chance. And it's not just me.' Torino listened as Bazin told him how the garden had healed Kelly's broken wrist and corrected Nigel Hackett's and Zeb Quinn's eyesight. 'Drink the water. Eat the fruit. See for yourself.'

'I will,' Torino said. 'What else?'

'Speak to the nun. She knows most about this place. According to her, any living thing dies when it's taken out. Even the water goes stale.'

'It loses its power to heal outside the garden?'

'So she says.'

'How was Kelly going to heal his wife, then?'

'Last night I heard him and Zeb talking together. He showed her a strange rock that Sister Chantal gave him. It's in his backpack.' Bazin pointed into the caves. 'She got it from in there.'

Torino walked into the damp cave and his excitement increased. The pools, the waterfall and the tunnel of blood were exactly as they were in the Voynich. He peered into the gloom and saw white shapes flitting in the shadows. The Eves that Falcon spoke of in his manuscript and his testimony, he thought. As he had feared, this place presented problems for the Church as well as opportunities. He turned to the glowing tunnel and remembered the passage that described how the conquistadors had died.

Bazin pointed to the tunnel. 'When I came in here this morning Ross was up there.'

Torino didn't disguise his surprise. 'Up there? Are you sure?'

'I saw him climbing down. Said I wouldn't believe what he'd seen up there.'

Torino's eyes followed the glittering path until it disappeared and anticipation coursed through him. He approached the tunnel and studied the crystals encrusting the entrance. Then he bent down and put his hand into the rushing stream, noting the crystal rocks on its bed, the shards in the pools and the phosphorescent water flowing out of the cave into the lake. 'What did Dr Kelly see up there?'

'There wasn't time to ask him. But he said he was trying to find out what was behind this place's miraculous powers.'

'We *know* what's behind the garden's miraculous powers. God.' Torino thought of the mysterious *radix* in Father Orlando's testimony to the Inquisition. 'But it won't do any harm to understand the agent God might be using. I must talk with Dr Kelly and Sister Chantal. But first I want to make a few observations of my own.'

60

The next morning

'If we're trespassing, why don't they just kick us out?' Zeb demanded.

'I know,' said Hackett. 'They've no right to keep us here.'

'The Father General can't let us leave,' said Sister Chantal, bitterly. 'Not until he's decided what to do with this place – and us.'

Ross had slept fitfully, drifting into and out of consciousness. When he finally woke, the excruciating pain in his head had gone. The soldiers had corralled them within a copse of trees near to where Father Orlando's remains were buried. The trees and four boulders formed a natural enclosure, over which the soldiers had erected a tarpaulin. Within this makeshift pen, each had been laid out on the mossy ground, their ankles and wrists secured with plastic ties. The soldiers had fed them and allowed them to use the latrines they had dug in the corner of the garden, but there was no doubt that they were prisoners. When he opened his eyes Ross saw two soldiers unpacking and stacking an arsenal of weapons beneath another tarpaulin shelter.

'Christ, look at the stuff they've brought with them,' said Hackett, craning his neck for a clearer view.

'What are those things with fuel tanks attached to them?' asked Zeb.

'I think they're flame-throwers,' said Hackett. 'But what about those yellow parcels? One of their packs was full of them. Christ, what the hell did they expect to find here? They can't have thought we were that dangerous.'

'I don't think the weapons were meant for us,' said Ross, thinking of the Voynich and what had killed the conquistadors in the tunnel of blood.

'You okay? How's your head?' Zeb asked him.

'Fine.' Ross almost missed the pain. It had helped focus his rage and, right now, rage would have felt a hell of a lot better than despair.

'This place is amazing. Your swelling and bruising's already gone.' She cocked her head. 'There's Osvaldo – or whoever the hell the son-of-a-bitch really is. You sure he was the guy who hurt Lauren?'

Ross shifted as Mendoza stepped out of one of three tents by the lake. He felt his fury return. 'Positive.'

'The priest called him Marco – Marco Bazin,' said Hackett. 'The bastard's going through our backpacks now.'

As Ross lay on the ground, he thought of Lauren,

helpless on her hospital bed. God, he missed her. He yearned to call his father and ask how she and the baby were. He had come so close to saving them; he had held their salvation in his hand. He no longer cared about the source or the caves. He only wanted Lauren back. As he watched Bazin retrieve the rock crystal and Father Orlando's damaged notebook, he stoked the rage burning within him. He still found it hard to believe Torino's duplicity: a so-called man of God offering him sympathy and requesting his wife's notes – in a hospital chapel of all places – after *he* had ordered the burglary responsible for Lauren's injuries. There was no way Ross was leaving this garden without the one thing he had come for: the means to save his family. If Torino wanted war, then so be it.

Bazin turned towards them, stepped over Hackett and pulled a knife from his belt.

'Come to stab us in the back again, have you?' said Hackett.

Bazin ignored him and turned to the soldiers. 'Gag them. The Father General doesn't want them communicating.' He knelt down and cut the plastic ties on Ross's and Sister Chantal's ankles. 'He wants you two to talk, though.' He grabbed their wrists and pulled them to their feet. 'Come.'

61

'Tell me something, Osvaldo,' Kelly demanded, as Bazin led them to Torino.

'My name is Marco.'

'Okay, Marco, my loyal and trustworthy friend, tell me how much Torino's paying you. How much does a lowlife bag of shit like you cost?'

The other man's tone infuriated Bazin. The scientist, an atheist who believed in nothing, had no right to assume he was superior to him. 'The Father General's paying me nothing. I'm doing this to cleanse my soul. This is God's work.'

'No,' said Sister Chantal. 'This may be the Father General's work but it is *not* God's.'

'What would you, a traitor to the Church, know about God's work?' said Bazin.

Kelly stared at him. 'You're doing this because you think it's right?' Bazin pushed him on, but Kelly hadn't finished. 'Remember our chat about deeds being everything? You said that only God and the Church can judge if a man's deeds are good or bad. Tell me one thing. How the fuck does your God justify you putting my wife into a coma?' He clenched his teeth so hard that his jaw muscles bunched. 'I can't believe Juarez died saving your life. His was worth infinitely more than yours. Christ, I can't believe *I* saved your fucking life. Instead of pulling you out of the bat shit I should have left you to your fellow cockroaches.'

Bazin burnt to make the geologist understand the righteousness of his deeds. 'You weren't supposed to be in the house, and I didn't mean to hurt your wife but the Superior General needed her files. She got in the way.'

'Really? And those men you killed on the boat? The ones you set up to join our gang, to spy on us? Did you intend to kill them?'

'No.'

'Christ,' said Kelly. 'In that case, I hope you *do* intend to kill *me*.'

Bazin sighed. 'No, my friend, you don't. I was once paid to kill. I was good at it, too. Some said I was the best. I've lost count of how many men I *intended* to kill but I know they're all dead.'

'Is that you speaking now, Marco, or the Scourge of God? It's getting hard to tell the difference.'

The geologist's refusal to understand him, and his arrogant assumption that only he was right, incensed Bazin. He had been justified in betraying Kelly and the others. Having seen the garden, and experienced its power, he knew it was too important to be left in the hands of men like him. Or those

369

who had betrayed Rome, like Sister Chantal. Even Hackett would let the drug companies exploit it for money. Only the Holy Mother Church could and should channel its power. Only his half-brother, the Black Pope, was qualified to know how best to use it. Bazin reassured himself that he had served the Church well, and that his redemption was certain.

As he pushed Kelly and the nun through the entrance to the forbidden caves, he saw his half-brother emerge from the dark recesses of the antechamber. The Superior General held a folder in his right hand and was smiling.

'Look,' Torino said, as he walked closer. 'No limp. This place is truly miraculous. I want you both to tell me all about it.' He waved the folder towards the glowing tunnel. 'I especially want to know what's up there.'

'Why should we tell you anything?' Kelly asked.

Bazin frowned at him, unwrapped the crystal and handed it to Torino. 'Ross, the Superior General holds the fate of your wife in his hands. If I were you I'd tell him whatever he wants to know.'

Torino studied the shard. 'Have you the notebook?'

Bazin passed it to him. 'It's damaged, but most of it's still legible. The part you asked about is at the end.'

'Thank you, Marco. Please wait outside. I'll call if I need you.'

62

Torino had never felt so empowered and sure of his destiny. When he had woken this morning, cured of his limp, it was as if God's own blood flowed in his veins. And now, when he opened Father Orlando's notebook and scanned the last section, he knew he was close to exceeding even his most lofty ambitions.

'When did the Catholic Church start employing thieving, deceitful murderers?' said Kelly.

Torino glanced up from the notebook and watched his half-brother leave the cave. 'Marco has proved himself a loyal servant of the Church.' He smiled. 'Please, Dr Kelly, let us put any unpleasantness behind us. It was never my intention to harm your wife and unborn child, and if this crystal is as powerful as Sister Chantal believes, the damage can be reversed. There's no reason for any more animosity between us.'

'No reason for any animosity?' Kelly held up his bound wrists. 'You're holding us captive.'

'That's a precaution. To make sure we all under-stand each other before I let you return home.' Torino turned to Sister Chantal. 'Sister, you need feel no anger either. Father Orlando Falcon's original intention was to tell the pope of his dis-covery. He believed only the Holy Mother Church could be trusted with his garden.' He frowned. 'Regretfully, Rome didn't appreciate his discovery then, but now the Holy Father himself wants to embrace it within the bosom of the Church.'

'He's sanctioned all you've done?' she said incredulously.

Torino ignored her question. 'Sister, Father Orlando wanted the garden to be in safe hands, and now it will be. You should be satisfied.'

'What the hell are you going to do with it?' demanded Kelly. 'Turn it into a miraculous theme park? A Lourdes that *genuinely* cures people? Grant admission to people if they convert to Catholicism?'

'He won't do that,' said Sister Chantal. She spat the words. 'He can't let the world know about this place. It doesn't fit with Rome's doctrine.'

Torino's eyes narrowed. 'What do you know or care about Rome's doctrine, Sister? You betrayed the Holy Mother Church.'

'I betrayed no one,' she replied, with venom. 'If I've learnt anything over my long life it's that the Church should *serve* faith, not be its rigid master. I don't need this miraculous garden to fit with doctrine to know it's a place of God. Everything here contradicts the biblical Garden of Eden and the scriptures. Not only is it thousands of miles away from the Holy Land but it's also nowhere near the geographical origins of *any* major religion. The creatures and plants here prove that miraculous life can be created and evolve in parallel with humanity, independent of mankind and God's Church.

'And yet there are miracles in this godless place. How can that be? Are there perhaps alternative ways to interpret God's word, which go against the pope's infallible doctrine? Father Orlando thought so. And I do, too. I don't fear the strange creatures here, or the questions they raise about creation and evolution. Nothing here challenges *my* faith, only my understanding of it. This place might even be *the* Garden of Eden for all I know.' She laughed bitterly. 'But you, Father General, are a *slave* to your infallible doctrine. You put it before everything. You'd rather change the truth to fit what you believe than change what you believe to fit the truth.'

For a moment Torino said nothing. He had only contempt for the nun. She spoke of vows, but she had broken hers to the Church. 'You're right,' he said eventually. 'The Church does need to treat a discovery like this carefully. There are those who could misinterpret the garden and its creatures.' He gestured to the nymphs in the shadows. 'They might see them as contradicting the scriptures and the pope's recent decrees denying evolution. And, yes, I can't allow anything here to play into the hands of those who would destroy the Holy Mother Church, which embodies the hopes and dreams of millions of believers worldwide. I make no apologies for protecting their faith. But the truth is, I don't care about this miraculous so-called Garden of God or its exotic creatures.' He pointed up the tunnel. 'Not nearly as much as what's up there.'

He turned to Kelly and smiled at his surprise. 'And I suspect you don't either, Dr Kelly. As an atheist and a scientist, how do *you* explain this miraculous garden? Is it the cradle of evolution, the origin of life on Earth, a scientific Eden? Or are the garden and its creatures merely a sideshow to the main attraction?'

Kelly said nothing.

'Come on, Dr Kelly. We both know that the garden and its creatures are an irrelevant aberration, a distraction.' He raised the shard of crystal. 'Even this is a peripheral by-product of the *real* power behind this place.' He gestured to the glowing tunnel and tapped the notebook. 'Father Orlando wrote about it in the section of the Voynich your wife couldn't translate. He called it *el origen*.' He opened his manila folder and showed Kelly the relevant passage. 'His testimony in the Inquisition Archives records it by its Latin name: *radix*. Both mean "the source". Neither document explains what it is, instead describing it in philosophical and spiritual terms. In his notebook he mentions El Árbol de la Vida y de la Muerte, the Tree of Life and Death, which in the Inquisition testimony the Latin scribes record as *vita quod mors arbor*. Was this a reference to the Tree of Knowledge in

374

Genesis? Was it meant to be taken literally or figuratively? What do you think the source is, Dr Kelly? What do you think we'll find up that tunnel? The source of all miracles?'

'Just one,' said Kelly. 'The planet's greatest miracle: life. And it's got nothing to do with God or religion.'

Torino smiled. 'We'll have to agree to disagree on who or what's behind it. The point is, we both want to discover what it is.' He turned to Sister Chantal. 'Sister, is whatever butchered the conquistadors in the Voynich still in the tunnel?'

'I've never been up there. No one has and lived. Except Father Orlando.'

'That's not strictly true. Is it, Dr Kelly? Marco saw you coming out of the tunnel when I arrived with the soldiers.'

Sister Chantal glared at Kelly. 'You went up it?'

Torino smiled. 'Dr Kelly told Marco he wouldn't believe what he'd seen up there. What did you see, Dr Kelly? Tell me, and after you sign a confidentiality agreement, I'll let you all leave here with the blessing of the Church.' He held out the crystal. 'I'll even let you take this with you. You can save your family, Dr Kelly. Isn't that what you came here for?'

'Whatever you saw, tell him nothing,' said Sister Chantal. 'He won't let you go, whatever legal forms he makes you sign. He can't risk anyone else knowing about this place. It raises too many questions.'

'Ignore her, Dr Kelly. I've already told you I don't

care about the garden or its creatures. Just *radix*, the source. We both want to uncover this mystery. Tell me what you know and save your family.'

Kelly sighed. 'I turned back when I heard your soldiers shooting so I didn't reach the end. I got close, though, and there's definitely something of great power up there.' To Torino's surprise, he suddenly dropped to his knees, only his open palms breaking his fall on the rocky floor. He raised his bound hands, clasped as if in prayer. 'I beg you, Father General. Let me save my wife. She's a believer. I've nothing against your religion. I don't care how you interpret this garden. I don't even care about the source any more. I only care about saving my wife.'

'Save her, then. Tell me all you know and you'll be out of here today. You could be back in the States within the week, if not sooner.' He held the crystal tantalizingly close to Kelly's bound hands. 'What did you see? Before I go up there with the soldiers I need to know if there was any sign of what killed the conquistadors. Did you see or learn anything that could help us?'

Kelly hesitated for only a second, staring at the crystal. 'I'll tell you,' he said. 'I'll tell you everything.'

63

'I can't believe you helped him, Ross,' hissed Sister Chantal, as Bazin led them back to the others. 'I warned you against going up the tunnel. I warned you against telling the Superior General what you'd seen. And you ignored me. How could you be so stupid?'

Ross said nothing.

Sister Chantal couldn't remember feeling such dejection. Over the long years she had experienced many black moments but she had always reminded herself of her vow to Father Orlando and told herself to be patient. When she had learnt of Lauren's critical condition, she had believed that the garden could cure her. But this time the enemy wasn't time, impatience or disappointment: it was the same implacable foe that had destroyed Father Orlando. To make it worse, her ally had proved himself weak and spineless. 'I can't believe you begged him on your knees. He was never going to let you save Lauren because he *can't* let you leave. Don't you understand that?'

When they reached the tarpaulin, Hackett and Zeb were lying at one end of the enclosure, gagged. Bazin pushed Ross and Sister Chantal to the other end, laid them on the ground and tied their ankles.

Sister Chantal waited for Bazin to leave. 'I warned you against going up the tunnel, Ross, because it *is* dangerous. Father Orlando told me so. He saw things.'

'I know,' whispered Ross.

'Then why did you tell Torino—'

'That it was safe? That I got close enough to touch whatever's up there and saw nothing dangerous? Because I don't trust the Superior General any more than you do.'

'You lied?'

'Of course. The only way we're going to get out of here with what we came for is on our own. And anything that distracts them up that tunnel can only help us.'

A slow smile creased her lips. 'Perhaps you're not as stupid as I feared.'

Ross looked back at Bazin who was standing by the stack of weapons, talking to two of the soldiers. After some discussion they selected a shotgun, two Heckler & Koch sub-machine guns and a flame-thrower, then walked back to the forbidden caves.

They're going up the tunnel, thought Ross.

As he watched them, he noticed the yellow parcels he had seen the soldiers unpacking earlier. Most were now distributed in strategic piles around the garden. He wondered what they were, and why they were there. He glanced at Zeb and Hackett lying at the other end of the enclosure. They were staring at him. He wanted to tell them what had happened but feared raising his voice and being overheard by the remaining guard. 'I still don't understand why Torino's so dismissive of the garden and so focused on the source,' he whispered to Sister Chantal. 'I thought the whole point from a religious angle was that this was the Garden of God.'

'He wants the miracles because the Church can exploit them. But the garden and its creatures raise too many doubts and questions about Genesis and evolution. Religion isn't like science. Science may thrive on doubt but religion demands unquestioning faith.'

'Whatever their faith, wouldn't most believers want to make up their own minds about the truth, however controversial?' said Ross. 'Like you told Torino, if you really believe in something nothing's going to challenge your faith, only your understanding of it. Science is constantly adapting its understanding of the natural world, based on new evidence.'

She shook her head. 'Torino and those who wield power in Rome would rather ignore evidence than modify their beliefs. Never forget, the pope is infallible, God's envoy on Earth. He *can't* be wrong.'

Bazin and the other men were almost at the caves. The smaller soldier was carrying the flame-thrower over his shoulder, the pack of fuel strapped to his back. Ross glanced at the stack of weapons and the second flame-thrower. At that moment something Zeb had said last night, about the pharmaceutical industry, entered his head, and a connection between that and the yellow parcels fired in his brain.

Shit.

He was now pretty sure what they were and why Torino had brought them here. 'We've got to get free,' he said.

'I know that.' Sister Chantal raised her bound wrists. 'But how?'

He opened his hands. In his right palm was a thin shard of crystal rock he had picked up off the cave floor while kneeling before Torino. 'It's small but sharp. I can't reach my plastic tie, but I could cut yours.'

She smiled as a shadow loomed over them. Bazin had returned with one of the soldiers. 'Gag them,' he said. Ross closed his hands but didn't struggle as Bazin placed an oily rag over his mouth and knotted it at the back of his head.

Bazin stepped away and pointed at them in turn, muttering under his breath, first at Hackett, then Zeb and Sister Chantal. Ross wondered why he was counting them. Then Bazin's finger skipped Ross, went back to Hackett and counted the other three again. Something hard and cold formed in Ross's stomach. Bazin wasn't counting them. He was selecting one.

His finger settled on Hackett, who glanced questioningly at Ross. 'Bring him, Weber,' he said to the soldier. As they cut Hackett's ankle ties and pulled him to his feet, Bazin turned to Ross. 'Just in case anything unpleasant's waiting for us up the tunnel the good doctor will lead the way. Father General wanted you to lead us, Ross, but since you saved my life I excluded you from the count. Consider my debt settled.' He smiled. 'Don't worry about him,' he said, over his shoulder. 'As you said, there should be no danger.'

Ross strained against his gag. It was one thing to let his heavily armed enemies walk into a trap. It was something else to allow an unarmed friend to do the same. But Bazin was oblivious of his stifled pleas as he led Hackett to the forbidden caves. When Ross craned his neck to keep them in view, he saw Zeb silently willing him to tell her their friend would be safe. That there was no danger.

Moments later, an eerie sound issued from the forbidden caves. Ross knew it was the nymphs singing, warning Torino and his men away from the tunnel. Then the sound changed. The nymphs were no longer singing. They were screaming.

64

Moments earlier

In the antechamber Feldwebel Fleischer handed Torino a steel helmet and helped him strap on a Kevlar vest. The Jesuit was so excited his hands trembled on the helmet buckle. He pointed to Hackett, who was gagged and had his wrists tied. All of the men were wearing sunglasses to protect their eyes against the dazzlingly bright light up the tunnel. 'He goes at the front, yes?'

'Yes,' said Bazin, 'then Weber with the flame-thrower. You and I follow, with Feldwebel Fleischer taking up the rear.'

Fleischer shook his head. 'These are my men and the Superior General is under *my* protection. I'll stay by his side. You take up the rear.'

Bazin eyeballed him, then shrugged. 'As you wish.'

Fleischer handed a two-way radio to the other soldier. 'Gerber, wait down here. If we need you I'll call.'

Torino frowned. 'Have you briefed him on what to do if we don't return? If *I* don't return?'

The soldier checked the radio. 'Everything's prepared, Father General. I know what to do.'

'Where's Petersen? Watching the prisoners?'

'Yes.'

'Good. Let's go.'

As they approached the tunnel, the singing started – a disquieting, sinister chant that emanated from the dark recesses of the cave. Then the nymphs emerged from the shadows and blocked the entrance. Torino counted ten. The soldiers stopped, unnerved by the startling creatures.

'Push them back,' said Torino. 'Get them out of the way.'

Bazin shouted and waved his shotgun at a nymph with blood-red flowers entwined in its hair-like fronds. It ignored him and continued to chant. Bazin stepped back and turned to Weber. 'Use the flame-thrower.'

Weber raised the nozzle, flicked the igniter and pressed the trigger. Fiery liquid jetted towards the nymphs. They screamed and fled back into the shadows. Their cries echoed through the caves and Torino smiled at how quickly they had retreated. Controlling the garden and its creatures wouldn't be difficult. He would soon fashion this place so that it brought only glory to Rome – and what glory it would be! He tapped Weber's shoulder.

Weber prodded Hackett with the hot nozzle of the flame-thrower. 'Go.'

They walked slowly up the path and with each step the light grew more dazzling, the glare intensified by the gilded crystal that encrusted the tunnel. Torino could only guess at what lay ahead but was convinced that it had nothing to do with Kelly's dry theories on creation and evolution. Father Orlando's *radix*, his Tree of Life and Death, would offer no proof of any scientific hypothesis, only proof of God's presence on earth, a physical manifestation of His divine majesty and power. Like Moses witnessing the burning bush, Torino was convinced that he, too, would soon glimpse the face of God.

Suddenly Weber stopped.

Peering past him, to the path ahead, Torino saw a waterfall. Beside it, the path widened into a small chamber, then rough steps led to the top of the waterfall where the path widened again, forming another chamber before continuing onwards.

'Why have we stopped?'

'He won't move,' said Weber, gesturing to Hackett.

'Make him,' said Torino. Hackett turned, sweat pouring down his face, eyes darting meaningfully to the top of the waterfall. 'Let him speak.'

Weber pulled off the gag.

'I saw something moving,' Hackett panted.

Torino narrowed his eyes. 'Where?'

'In those holes up there.'

Torino peered up to the chamber on the next level. He could see the holes and a network of tunnels but nothing else. 'Can anyone else see anything?'

'No.'

Torino heard a click as Weber undid the safety on the flame-thrower. The others raised their weapons. 'Go on.'

Hackett shook his head. 'No.'

Weber released a jet of flame. 'Go.'

Hackett jumped and shuffled forward, blinking against the sweat that poured down his face.

Hackett stared at the black holes, every muscle in his body alert and trembling. He was sure he'd seen something moving within those dark spaces, something from his nightmares. A stab of anger penetrated his numbing fear. It would be so unfair to die in this remote place just as he had found his lost city. It incensed him that he might never enjoy the glory of his discovery or benefit from its gold.

He shuffled up the path to the top of the waterfall and saw that, as well as the holes in the walls, countless fissures led to a maze of dark passages. Straining to see beyond the blinding light into the blackness, he walked faster, wanting instinctively to get beyond the holes. He broke into a jog, then began to run up the path.

'Slow down,' hissed Weber.

Hackett ignored him. The soldier's flames could make him move but they couldn't make him stop. It felt good to release the adrenalin rushing through his body, and for a moment he dared to believe that he had imagined the glimpsed shapes in the dark.

Then Weber screamed.

Hackett should have kept running. But, despite his terror, he was a doctor and turned instinctively to help. When he looked back, he froze, unable to process what he was seeing. The black holes seemed to be moving, telescoping out of the walls. It was only when he saw Weber collapse on the path screaming, blood pouring from perfectly circular wounds in his thigh and shoulder, that Hackett realized black, worm-like creatures were twisting out of the rock, circular rows of teeth protruding from their jaws, biting into Weber's flesh then recoiling into their lairs. He stared open-mouthed, registering the myriad holes that riddled the walls.

Was there one of those things in every hole?

'The flame-thrower. Use the flame-thrower.' Bazin's shout, from further down the tunnel, galvanized Hackett into action. He rushed to Weber and knelt behind his bleeding body. Shielded by the fuel tanks strapped to Weber's back, he took the flame-thrower nozzle from Weber's limp hand and pressed the igniter.

Fire suddenly enveloped the creatures and another, louder, scream echoed in the tunnel. Different from Weber's, inhuman, it seemed to come from deep within the rock. The sound of rapid machine-gun fire intensified the shrieks as Hackett kept pressing the flame-thrower igniter.

Suddenly, a worm-like creature thicker than Hackett's thigh spiralled through the flames and tore into Weber's protective vest, pushing the soldier on to Hackett, pinning him down but also protecting him. Other dark shapes rifled towards them, taking chunks out of Weber. Then something hit Hackett's left shoulder. Such was his shock that he felt no pain until he saw that a neat circular chunk had been taken out of his flesh, exposing muscle and bone. His shirt was soaked with blood – he had never seen so much. The pain came now, running through him like fire. He tried to move his left arm but the agony was excruciating. Using his other arm, he pulled Weber's body closer to him and, with detached horror, realized the soldier's right buttock had gone. He pushed himself flat against the sharp crystal path as one of the creatures smashed through Weber's elbow, breaking bones, trying to reach him. Weber was still alive but they kept coming, devouring him piece by piece.

'Help me,' the soldier screamed, above frantic gunfire, but Hackett could barely help himself. One of the twisting creatures came straight at Weber's face, directly in front of Hackett's own, its baleful red eyes staring right at him. Its tubular body was made up of dusty, interlocking armoured plates. As it struck, it opened its mouth wide, exposing circular rows of protruding teeth, breath reeking of decay and rotting flesh.

Weber tried to scream, but when the creature bit into his face and recoiled back to its lair it took his tongue with it. The next took his cheek and left eye. Hackett tried to curl up into the foetal position as one of the creatures ripped into his right calf muscle. The agony seared through him.

Then he felt rough hands dragging Weber off him and pulling them both away from the monsters. The attack had lasted just seconds but they had been the longest of Hackett's life. All he could think about as he crawled, bleeding, to safety was the last thing Weber must have seen before the creatures drilled into his face.

Moments earlier

Standing on the path beside the waterfall, Torino stared up at the vision of Hell unfolding before him. Bazin pushed past him, pumping and firing his shotgun, while Fleischer opened up with the Heckler & Koch. The heads of two rock worms exploded, and the flailing headless trunks recoiled into the wall leaving a trail of blood. Bazin rushed forward and tried to reach Weber but the flames held him back. The flame-thrower seemed barely to deter the frenzied rock worms, though. Through the inferno, Torino glimpsed Weber's body being consumed by the hellish creatures, while Hackett lay pinned beneath him, trying in vain to keep them at bay. Worse than what he could see, however, was what he could hear: an inhuman screaming that filled the acrid air and forced him to put his hands over his ears. He couldn't tell if the sound, which surrounded him, came from the rock worms, the nymphs below, or something further up the tunnel.

Shell-shocked, he watched Bazin and Fleischer drag Hackett and Weber past him. As he followed them away from the flames and the worms, he kept looking back, beyond the carnage, to the light beckoning from higher up the tunnel. The creatures were Satan's demons, placed there to test his resolve and prevent him from reaching God's light. They would not deter him. He would find a way.

Watching the stream redden with blood, he peered at Hackett's wounds and Weber's butchered body. Dr Kelly had lied to him that the tunnel was safe. He must have seen the conquistadors' nemeses, and known they were still there.

How much more had Kelly not told him? How much more did he know?

65

Sister Chantal chewed at her gag and shook her head again. Ross glanced over his shoulder at the soldier who had been watching them for the last hour. At this rate, they would have to wait till dark for him to cut Sister Chantal's tie with the shard of crystal he had taken from the cave. The good news was that the light was fading. The bad news was that, though darkness would give them cover, he would be working blind.

Suddenly Sister Chantal was nodding frantically. Ross glanced behind him. The soldier was holding his two-way radio, looking anxiously towards the forbidden caves. Then he put down the radio and rushed away.

Trying not to think about what was happening in the tunnel of blood, Ross reached across to Sister Chantal. She held up her hands to help him, but it wasn't easy with his own wrists tied. The crystal was so small and the plastic so sheer that he found it difficult to get any purchase on it. Eventually he managed to make a nick in the plastic and saw along the groove.

Manipulating the crystal was laborious, finger-aching work and it was impossible to tell whether he was making any progress. He became so absorbed in his task that only when Sister Chantal pulled her hands away did he look up. Torino, Bazin and the others were coming out of the forbidden caves. Two men were dragging Hackett and the soldier who had been carrying the flame-thrower. The latter's mutilated body was limp and covered with blood. At least Hackett was moving.

'Take them to the lake,' Bazin ordered. 'Immerse them in the water. Make them drink.' Hackett crawled into it and began to drink, oblivious of the red cloud blooming around him.

Then Ross saw the sergeant shake his head. 'Weber's gone. Nothing can help him now.'

Ross grimaced. It appeared that even the garden's miraculous powers had limits.

Torino and Bazin were striding over to him, Fleischer following. Torino's face was white and contorted with rage. 'Take off his gag, Marco.'

'How's Nigel?' was Ross's first question.

'He'll live,' said Torino, 'but he was badly injured, thanks to you. And Weber's dead. He was ripped apart by the creatures you failed to tell us about.'

'*You* killed a good man,' spat Fleischer.

Ross said nothing as he felt Zeb's and Sister Chantal's eyes on him. He hadn't purposely put

Hackett in harm's way. He hadn't forced him up the tunnel. Torino and Bazin had done that. And he certainly hadn't killed Weber. But as he watched the soldiers pulling Hackett out of the lake and laying him on the grass, guilt seared him.

'You saw the creatures when you went up the tunnel, didn't you, Dr Kelly?' Torino accused him. 'Yet you came down alive. What did you see? What did you learn?'

Ross remained silent, unable to clear the image of the rock worms devouring the nymph from his mind, imagining Hackett and Weber in its place.

'Tell me all you know,' insisted Torino. His voice was menacingly quiet. 'Who else do I have to push up that tunnel and feed to those creatures before you tell me everything?' He pointed at Sister Chantal. 'Her?' Then at Zeb. 'Her? How many more have to die? Marco, Feldwebel, take their gags off. Perhaps they can help to persuade him.'

'What the hell's he talking about, Ross?' said Zeb, when her gag came off.

'I saw the creatures when I went up the tunnel. They attacked and ate one of the dying nymphs. The others sacrificed it to them. They have a way of controlling the creatures.' He explained how the nymphs had stilled the creatures with their chanting.

As Torino studied him Ross could almost hear his mind working. 'You're suggesting I push the nymphs up the tunnel ahead of us? Let them still the rock worms and follow in their footsteps?'

'I'm not suggesting anything. I'm just telling you what I saw and heard.'

'We can easily round up a few and check it out,' said Bazin.

Two of the soldiers dragged Hackett back to the enclosure. His shoulder and leg were badly wounded, but the bleeding had slowed. His face was pale but he managed a weak smile when Zeb and Ross asked how he was. 'It's not as bad as it looks and I feel a lot better after being in the lake. I got off lightly compared to the other guy.'

Bazin and Fleischer moved to replace their gags, but Torino stopped them. 'No, let them speak. They've a lot to talk about.' He turned to Ross. 'I'm sure your friends will want to ask why you put one of them in peril.' At that moment, the sound of thunder echoed round the garden and rain fell, hitting the taut tarpaulin like stones on a drum. Torino had to shout to be heard above the noise. 'We'll take the nymphs up tomorrow, Dr Kelly. And this time you'll lead the way.'

Torino, Bazin and Fleischer hurried away to their tents, leaving Ross struggling to be heard above the thunderous rain, trying to explain to Hackett and Zeb all that he knew, and how he had inadvertently put Hackett at risk.

As soon as he'd finished, they bombarded him with questions, but now was not the time for talk. He raised his bound hands, revealing the crystal shard on his open palms, and Sister Chantal immediately proffered her bound wrists. In the dying light, during a lull in the pounding rain, Ross said, 'Zeb, Nigel, do you want to waste any more precious time asking questions or do you want to get out of here?'

They fell silent, and Ross went back to work.

66

It took more than an hour to cut through Sister Chantal's ties but once her hands were free she released Ross and helped him to free Hackett and Zeb.

The heavy rain was a blessing and a curse. It prevented anyone's seeing what they were doing but compromised visibility. 'What do we do now?' hissed Zeb, peering out into the dark. There was a glow further up the garden towards the caves where Torino and his men were quartered in tents.

'Our backpacks are piled up over there,' said Hackett, pointing away from the tents, towards the entrance to the garden, 'and they're still packed with the supplies we'll need to make our way back to the boat. I vote we find them and scarper. I doubt there'll be any guards out on a night like this.'

'But what about your wounds?' said Zeb.

He pulled up his trousers and showed his leg. The chunk out of his calf now looked more like a swollen bruise. 'I'm healing. It's incredible. My shoulder's the same.'

'You sure?'

'I'm sure.'

'You three go ahead, then,' said Ross. 'I'll join you later. There's something I need to do first.'

'What?'

He pointed to the forbidden caves. 'I'm not leaving here without the one thing I came for.'

'The crystal for Lauren?' said Zeb. 'I'll come with you.'

'We'll all go,' said Sister Chantal.

'No,' said Ross. 'I'll be better off on my own. One person might be able to do it unseen. Take my backpack with you and I'll meet you beyond the sulphur caves on the other side of the causeway. If you hear anything, or I'm not there within an hour, go on without me.'

Sister Chantal tried to protest but Ross shook his head. 'Let me do this, Sister. It's the only way you'll ever fulfil your vow and pass on your legacy to Lauren. This place will become her problem then, not yours. Now go.'

The rain had eased but was still as hard as any Ross had experienced. Beyond the protection of the tarpaulin the warm drops stung like airgun pellets. It was difficult to keep his eyes open, let alone see anything. Head down, he let the dull glow from the phosphorescent lake guide him to the caves. He steered clear of the tents: thankfully, the shapes silhouetted in the illuminated interiors told him that Torino and his men were inside, keeping dry. He passed several neat piles of the yellow parcels he had registered earlier. Close up, he could see they were stamped with the manufacturer's brand name, a yellow warning triangle and 'Thermate-TH3'. He reached the forbidden caves with relative ease, grateful to escape the rain. By the dull glow emanating from the tunnel he navigated his way to the stream, knelt beside it and reached into the rushing water.

As his hands closed over a sizeable shard of rock crystal, a sound made him look up. The nymphs were emerging from the shadows at the back of the antechamber. In the half-light they appeared threatening, until his friend with the red flowers in its frond-like hair began to chant the James Bond theme Ross had taught it on their first encounter. Ross smiled and responded. The nymph emitted a staccato burst of laughter-like chatter and approached closer. The others followed until they surrounded him. As he edged closer to the exit, the nymph with the red flowers reached for the crystal in his hand. Instinctively, Ross clasped it tighter. The creature made another chattering sound, went into the tunnel, selected a larger, even more iridescent shard from the stream and presented it to him. Ross put down his sample and took the gift. 'Thank you.'

The nymph copied his words, making Ross smile again. He glanced up the tunnel one last time, mesmerized by the light coming from the source – whatever it was. He considered how the lake water had failed to save Weber and wondered how its power compared with that of Father Orlando's *el origen*. What if the crystal in his hand failed to save Lauren? What if the injuries to her brain and spine needed something even more powerful? The question was academic, of course. Even if he could negotiate the rock worms there was no time to explore the tunnel. He must go now before the guards realized they were gone.

He turned to leave and a piercing sound silenced the nymphs. The high-pitched whine of an alarm.

Shit.

As the nymphs skittered nervously around him, he pushed past them and peered out of the antechamber into the rain. Figures were spilling from the tents and moving through the rain towards where the others had made their escape – or tried to. The soldiers must have installed a trip alarm by the entrance to the garden.

Shit.

Two figures stopped, turned and headed for the forbidden caves – towards Ross.

Shit. Shit. Shit.

He was trapped. Unless . . .

He pushed through the nymphs towards the dark recesses of the antechamber. There was another way out: the exit across the magma pool, via the broken bridge. It was dangerous and he would have no supplies in the jungle, but he had the crystal to sustain him. There was one other route, of course. He could try his luck up the tunnel of blood. He stopped, torn with indecision.

'Dr Kelly!'

He glanced over his shoulder. Torino stood in the entrance to the antechamber, waterproof dripping with rain, two-way radio in his hand. Bazin stood beside him, peering down the sights of a rifle.

The radio crackled and Torino held it to his ear. 'Excellent, Feldwebel. If they give you any more trouble shoot them.' He smiled. 'The others are being rounded up, Dr Kelly. The great escape is over.'

Bazin spoke next: 'My rifle is aimed at your heart. Drop the crystal, raise your hands and walk back here.'

'You're going to shoot me, Marco? How does your God justify killing an unarmed, innocent man who wants only to save his wife?'

'No one's innocent, Dr Kelly,' said Torino, 'and this place is bigger than your wife. I can't let you leave with the crystal. Not till I've decided what to do with the garden.'

As the nymphs swarmed round Ross, pushing him back into the shadowy recesses of the cave, he tried to keep Torino talking. 'But you've already decided what to do with the garden, Father General. I've seen the yellow parcels. I know what they are.' Ross saw Bazin glance uncertainly at Torino. 'But I don't care about your plans. If you want to rewrite history or evolution, if you want to change the truth to fit your beliefs, then go ahead. I only want to save my wife.' He pointed up the tunnel. 'Once you've done what you want to do and gained control of *el origen*, or the *radix* or whatever's up there, you needn't worry about me – or any of us.'

'That crystal in your hand is now the property of Rome,' Torino said. 'Only the Holy Mother Church can dispense miracles. Not you.' More nymphs spilled out of the shadows, shepherding Ross to the back of the caves. 'Enough of this, Marco. Shoot him.'

'Stop screwing about, Ross,' said Bazin. 'Drop the crystal, put your hands up and walk over here. Those things can't protect you.' There were at least thirty nymphs surrounding Ross now and they were forcing him into the shadows. 'Come on, Ross. I don't want to shoot you, but I *will*.'

Ross had a decision to make. To have any chance of escape he had to drop to a crouch, use the nymphs as cover and make a dash for the other exit. Or he had to give himself up and try to escape another time – if there was another time. Either way, he had to decide now.

In that split second, however, the decision was made for him. The nymphs surged with such force that he slipped on the damp rock floor. And as he fell Bazin fired. The shot echoed round the caves but the sound didn't concern Ross. His only concern was the bullet throwing him on to his back.

And the pain.

Lying there on the hard rock, each breath more agonizing than the last, he looked up at the nymphs and clutched his chest. He raised his hand and saw it was dripping with blood – *his* blood. Despite the intense pain, or because of it, his mind was eerily devoid of panic. With chilling clarity he knew he was dying. He thought of Lauren and their unborn child and a heavy sadness descended on him. He wasn't supposed to die. He was supposed to save them.

He reached out for the crystal shard he had dropped beside him and tried to raise it to his mouth. If he could bite it and ingest some of its power, he might stave off death. But his arms had no strength.

'We warned you, Ross,' he heard Torino call, from some distant place. 'We warned you.'

Yes, thought Ross, you warned me.

The nymphs crowded round him. The smell of stale sex and mustard seed was overpowering. Cool, clammy skin touched his arms. Small hands gripped him – he had no idea how many. He was Gulliver, but these Lilliputians weren't tying him down, they were reaching under him, lifting him, carrying him.

Where?

He was dimly aware of Bazin trying to reach him and being thwarted by the nymphs. Lying on his back, he looked towards his feet and saw light ahead: the tunnel. They were taking him up the tunnel of blood. As he entered it, the light was so bright that his dying mind saw the nymphs as angels bearing him aloft to Heaven. The thought amused him as he lay back, on the cusp of consciousness, staring up at the shimmering patterns and colours of the tunnel's crystal-encrusted ceiling. His vision was dimming and the pain was fading, replaced by a warm glow. Death wasn't so bad. Perhaps there was a God, Heaven too. Perhaps, in time, he would be reunited with Lauren and their child.

A familiar chant pierced his fractured thoughts, and he knew instantly where they were taking him: to his funeral. He'd read once that fallen Vikings were burnt on a funeral pyre, but as he listened to the nymphs' two-note incantation he knew his pyre would be different. He heard the waterfall and felt them carry him up the steps towards the dark chamber with its pock-marked walls infested with rock worms. He felt a cold shaft of fear.

He glimpsed the friendly nymph with the red flowers. Was it some kind of honour to be consumed by the worms?

He closed his eyes, grateful suddenly for the imminence of death, willing its dark embrace to claim him before the creatures did. He didn't want any more pain. He just wanted sleep. As his mind folded in on itself, he listened, waiting for the pacifying chants to stop and the worms to attack.

Moments earlier

The shot had been a reflex. Bazin had pulled the trigger as soon as Ross had made his sudden move. His experience told him it had been a death-shot but when he tried to move closer and confirm it, the nymphs hissed and bared their teeth. Sharp teeth. There were too many and he wished he had brought the flame-thrower with him. As he hung back with the Superior General, and watched them carry Ross up the tunnel, something nagged at him. It took him a moment to recognize it as guilt. He had barely known the people he had killed in the past, let alone befriended them. And not one had ever saved his life.

'I saw the wound in his chest,' said Torino. 'Is he dead?'

'As good as,' said Bazin. 'I shot him through the heart. Why are they taking him up there?'

Torino narrowed his eyes. 'Can't you guess?' They followed as far as the waterfall and could see shapes moving in the dark holes above. Then the nymphs started their chanting and carried Ross's motionless body to the place where the worms had attacked. Torino turned to Bazin. 'Remember what Kelly told us about the dying nymph being fed to those creatures?'

'I hope, for his sake, my shot *did* kill him.'

'It doesn't matter now,' said Torino. 'Either way he's dead.'

Four of the nymphs turned suddenly, bared their teeth and hissed at them. Other nymphs closed in. 'We've seen all we need to,' said Torino. 'Tomorrow we'll use the nymphs to get to the top. Let's go.'

They walked back down the tunnel, the sound of chanting in their ears.

67

The first thing Ross became aware of as he flickered awake was that the chanting had ceased. Then the pain kicked in again. And the fear. He didn't dare open his eyes – he didn't want the last thing he saw to be the rock worms.

Why the hell am I still alive?

He felt hands under him and realized he was still moving. He opened an eye. The light was even more dazzling than before. Above him, the crystalline ceiling of the tunnel sparkled with increased intensity. He turned his head and saw no sign of the dark chamber or the infested holes and passageways. Relief coursed through him. The nymphs had taken him further up the tunnel, beyond the rock worms.

He glanced at his feet and his relief turned to excitement. The tunnel was ending. He was rounding a corner and passing through a wide portal into a chamber of such brilliance that it made the tunnel appear gloomy by comparison. Had he any breath left he would have gasped. The whole place seemed to pulse as if its phosphorescent walls and ceiling were alive; he could see small glowing creatures in the lattice of crystal that encrusted the walls. It was warmer here too. He heard a rushing sound, looked up and saw water falling from the high ceiling through an opening concealed behind crystalline, chandelier-bright stalactites. It filled a small pool in the middle of the chamber, which fed the stream that ran down the tunnel into the garden, but before it reached the pool it hit an object so dazzling that the spray ricocheting off its surface fizzed and sparked like electricity. But it was the object itself, and what appeared to be growing from it, that commanded Ross's attention.

Even as he coughed up blood and felt his chest contract for the last time, tears stung his eyes. In all his years studying the natural wonders of the world he had never seen anything so beautiful. He felt a burst of gratitude. If he had to die, if he had to leave Lauren and never know their child, then at least he had seen this. As the darkness claimed him and his heart stopped beating, he smiled at the irony of dying now, here – in the presence of what had given birth to all life on this once barren planet.

The Sacred Heart Hospital, Bridgeport, Connecticut
As Ross Kelly lay dying, Lauren lay comatose in her hospital bed in Connecticut, watched over by her mother. The unborn child inside her womb now weighed more than one and a half pounds.

Although it looked normal on the scans, many of its vital organs, particularly its lungs, were still underdeveloped.

It would be difficult for a baby so premature to survive undamaged outside the womb but, amazingly, with the help of ventilators, monitors and medication, it could be delivered in a few weeks and live. It would need to spend time in hospital but the truth was that, although its current chances of survival were slim, they were now significantly better than those of either its mother or its father.

PART FOUR

The Source

68

By the next morning the rain had stopped and the sky was as clear and blue as it can be in the rainforest. Sitting with Hackett and Zeb, Sister Chantal couldn't help but contrast the frantic buzz of activity coming from Torino's men with their own quiet despair. Last night's escape attempt had been disastrous in its futility. In their hurry they hadn't seen the tripwire in the rain and the alarm had sounded before they could reach the passage to the sulphur caves. The soldiers had rounded them up in minutes.

When Torino and Bazin had told them Ross was dead she had seen her own shock and disbelief reflected in Zeb's and Hackett's eyes. Juarez's death had been terrible but no one had purposely killed him. Ross, however, had been shot. Not only had Bazin murdered him, but Torino — the Superior General of the Society of Jesus — had sanctioned it. It appeared there was nothing he would not do in the name of protecting his precious Church.

Hackett looked exhausted. All his dreams had been dashed. He would never return to his lost city and reveal its treasures to the world. Zeb seemed equally subdued. She had come on a grand adventure to save her friend and discover the mythical place described in the Voynich. But things hadn't turned out as she'd hoped. As for Sister Chantal's long-cherished dream of fulfilling her vow, it took all her self-control not to bow her head and weep. She glanced at the mound of stones where Father Orlando was buried. Was this how she would end her long vigil, fruitlessly, without passing on her burden?

'I hope Lauren never wakes up,' said Zeb. Her unkempt red hair no longer made her look feisty and individual, just young and vulnerable. 'She'd hate to think Ross died trying to save her. Nigel, I bet you wish you were back in your lost city and had never set foot in this "miraculous garden".' She spat the last two words.

He managed a rueful grin. 'Wouldn't have missed it for the world. My only regret is that I came to protect you and made a bit of a hash of it.'

She reached across with her bound hands to pat his arm. 'You didn't do so bad. You saved me from the snake when we passed that mound of bat shit.'

'I suppose.' He shrugged and gazed out across the garden to where two soldiers were cleaning their guns and refuelling the flame-throwers. Torino, Bazin and Fleischer stood in a huddle by the tents. 'The question is, what's going to happen to us now?'

Sister Chantal sighed. 'Whatever the Superior General has planned,' she said. 'We'll find out soon enough.'

Torino paced outside the tents. 'I want everything in place before we go up again. Are the devices ready?'

Feldwebel Fleischer nodded. 'Gerber has placed all the thermite and napalm to achieve the maximum effect you asked for.'

Bazin frowned. 'You're not really going to use them, are you, Father General?'

His half-brother was beginning to annoy Torino. He hoped Bazin wouldn't become a problem and interfere with his plans. 'Relax, Marco, it's just a contingency.' He rested a hand on Fleischer's shoulder. 'Feldwebel Fleischer understands. It's a scorched-earth policy to ensure no one can use this unusual garden and its creatures to harm the Church. Prevent its falling into enemy hands, so to speak.'

Bazin nodded, apparently satisfied.

Torino turned back to the sergeant. 'How do I activate them?'

Fleischer handed him a matt-black box, no bigger than a radio. On one featureless face was a green light diode and a flip switch, which covered a red button. 'Gerber has fitted the devices with wireless detonators. Flick the switch to arm the device and reveal the detonator button. You can press it as soon as the green light comes on.'

'How about getting up the tunnel?'

'We're going to round up two of the nymphs now, Father General.'

'If they don't co-operate, shoot them and get two more. They'll soon learn. And when we go up this time I don't just want to get past the worms. I want to destroy as many of them as possible.'

'They'll be easier to kill when they're still,' said Fleischer. 'Shotguns worked best last time. And we'll load the Heckler & Kochs with armour-piercing rounds.'

'Good,' said Torino. 'Come and tell me once you've got everything ready, Feldwebel.'

When Fleischer left to talk to his men, Torino pulled Bazin closer and lowered his voice. 'The new Vatican will be built around whatever's up that tunnel, and its miracles used for the good of the Church. To do the most good, however, we must keep it secret. No one must know about the source of these miracles, except the Holy Mother Church. This is holy work, Marco, and you are privileged to be part of it.'

Bazin indicated the three prisoners. 'What about them? How can we be sure they won't talk when we leave?'

Torino narrowed his eyes. 'No one will leave.'

'Is it necessary to kill them?'

It amused Torino that his half-brother, a remorseless assassin when he had killed for money, should worry now about killing for a righteous cause. 'No one will leave,' he said again.

'The soldiers?'

'They have a purpose for now. But once their job is done, only you and I will leave here. You understand? Only you and I can be trusted to protect the purity of this place. If you do this, Marco, if you fulfil this sacred task, your sins will be wiped out and the Holy Father himself will bless you for your work in claiming this shrine for the Holy Mother Church.' He paused. 'You still need redemption, don't you, Marco?'

Bazin nodded again. This time more slowly. 'Yes,' he said.

69

Two hours later

Sister Chantal entered the tunnel of blood shackled like a slave to Hackett, Zeb – and the two nymphs in front of them. Their hands were bound and a connecting rope looped round their necks. Behind them marched Petersen, Gerber and Bazin, with the rope secured round his waist. Fleischer and Torino took up the rear. Torino evidently hoped that the nymphs would pacify the creatures that had devoured Weber, Ross and the conquistadors. If they failed, she, Zeb and Hackett would act as human shields.

Sister Chantal had always suspected that Torino wouldn't let them leave the garden alive but she hadn't expected to die like this. When the Inquisition had handed Father Orlando to the secular authorities to be burnt at the stake it had been a case of *ecclesia abhorret a sanguine*, the Church shrinks from blood. This time, however, the Superior General would simply distance himself from her death – allow it to happen. This time there would be plenty of blood.

Her fear and anger that her long life of sacrifice should end so pointlessly was only tempered by the hope that the nymphs would perform their task and she might see what lay at the end of the tunnel.

The nymphs stopped abruptly by the waterfall.

'They're up there,' said Bazin, pushing her aside.

'Where?' said Zeb. She held Hackett's hand, squeezing it.

'Top of the waterfall,' Hackett said. 'Right side of the chamber. The holes in the wall.'

Sister Chantal peered up and thought she saw movement but couldn't be sure. She heard a click, then a jet of flame shot past her at the nymphs. As they ascended the steps by the waterfall they began to chant. The rope tautened and Sister Chantal followed. Torino and the soldiers waited until the nymphs walked past the dark chamber. As Sister Chantal followed, she glanced at the deep recesses in the rock to her right and saw countless red eyes staring balefully at her. Besides the holes the walls were riven with dark passageways that led to places she didn't even want to imagine.

'The chanting's working,' Bazin hissed behind her.

Torino and the others moved quickly, passing her and the nymphs, until they were beyond the holes – safe. Then, just as she thought she, too, would reach safety, she felt the rope slacken. Bazin had blocked the nymphs' path, leaving them standing directly in front of the hole-riddled chamber. Then he and the three soldiers approached the holes. One stood back with a flame-thrower, while the other three advanced, laden with guns, and opened fire. Immediately one weapon was spent they switched to another. The noise was deafening and the carnage devastating. For many moments the creatures remained motionless, as though their instinct to obey the barely audible chant of the nymphs was more powerful than their instinct to survive. By the time any reacted the holes were oozing with viscous, black-red blood, and the few that attacked were easily repelled. Through the gunfire she heard an inhuman scream well up from deep within the bowels of the caves, building in volume and intensity. The tunnel shook and trembled, dislodging shards of encrusted crystal. When the soldiers eventually ceased firing at the gaping, bleeding holes in the wall, she heard a loud whispering: the rustle of worms moving through the rock around her. Escaping.

Although the carnage sickened her, her legs trembled with relief. She was prepared for death but this was not how she wanted to end her life. Moreover, she wanted desperately to see the Source before she died. Torino and the others turned to continue the ascent and she moved to follow. But Bazin blocked the way, and for a chilling moment she thought he was going to leave them there. Then he took her arm and helped her up the path. As he did so, the Superior General turned to her and smiled, but she couldn't read his dark eyes.

* * *

As they rounded the final corner of the tunnel Torino saw a portal ahead, leading to a chamber of breathtaking brilliance. An overwhelming sense of anticipation, privilege and responsibility descended on him. He had always known the Church had singled him out for greatness, ever since the Jesuits had plucked him from the gutters of Naples, nurtured his talent and pushed him to become the best he could be. He had repaid their faith by eschewing all worldly pleasures, becoming the Society's youngest ever Superior General and the Holy Mother Church's most dedicated and committed servant. However, even his sense of destiny hadn't prepared him for this. He sensed he was about to glimpse the face of God, and the notion humbled him. God had chosen him not only to witness whatever lay ahead but also to be its guardian.

He turned to Bazin and the others. 'Wait here.'

Not waiting for their response, he walked into the chamber.

He took only four steps inside before he gasped and clasped his hands in prayer. The chamber was nothing less than a temple to God's miracle of life. The air itself fizzed with it. He could *feel* its power in his hair and fingertips. A pool in the centre glowed as if lit from beneath, and the crystal rock formations that encrusted the entire chamber were host to countless phosphorescent life forms, which added to the ambient radiance. But they were as nothing compared to the twelve-foot-high mass that loomed over the pool and dominated the chamber. In this temple to life this towering object, this *presence*, was its altar.

Torino knelt in worship, careful not to get too close to the multifaceted, crystalline monolith before him, which radiated intense heat and light. One facet had a gold metallic crust, another was pearlescent, a third a clear prism, with veins of silver and gold that reflected all the colours of the rainbow. Protruding from one facet was a huge, hydra-like growth, whose trunk rose to the crystalline ceiling and spread out into countless tubular branches or tentacles, which burrowed into the walls and across the chamber. They appeared to possess both plant and animal features: stems and leaves, flesh and pulsing veins. Yet the section of trunk nearest the monolith appeared metallic and crystalline, as though it had taken on the properties of the object from which it grew. The combined entity formed a unique hybrid of flora, fauna and mineral, fused so seamlessly that it was impossible to discern where one ended and another began. From one angle the hydra's iridescent roots were visible deep within the monolith's crystal heart, which shimmered and pulsed with life. Though the water falling from the ceiling formed a clear channel in its crust, exposing clear, crystalline rock, there was no apparent erosion in the crystal. The monolith appeared to be constantly renewing itself, forever changing and forever the same.

No doubt Dr Ross Kelly would have explained the phenomenon as the result of some alien rock falling from the heavens, and he might have been right. Torino, however, knew that God had sent it. He couldn't help but smile when he considered the small black meteorite that formed one of the cornerstones of the Kaaba, the cubic building within the Sacred Mosque at Mecca, believed by Muslims to have been built by Abraham. Some regarded the black stone as sacred, believing it had fallen from the sky during the time of Adam and Eve and that it had the power to cleanse worshippers of their sins by absorbing them into itself. They claimed that the stone was once pure and dazzling white and had turned black because of the sins it had taken into itself.

This beautiful stone, however, really *was* sacred. Its *demonstrable* miraculous powers would become the brilliant cornerstone of the Holy Mother Church, underpinning its power, eclipsing all other religions. He felt giddy at the prospect of what the future held and had to suppress a nervous impulse to laugh. Whatever the pope and Vasari had felt about his coming here, Torino knew that after seeing this the Holy Father would forgive – and give – him anything. He got to his feet, stepped closer and studied the hydra growing out of the fertile crystal. *Radix*, meaning 'root' as well as 'source', took on a fresh significance. This must be what Orlando Falcon had meant by *vita quod mors arbor*, the Tree of Life and Death.

But why death?

He walked round the chamber. As well as the entrance from the glowing tunnel and the opening in the ceiling, through which the water flowed on to the monolith, there was a darker exit, which appeared to lead down into a warren of black passageways. He thought of the rock worms and shuddered.

There was a sharp intake of breath behind him. Bazin was standing in the doorway to the chamber, his face illuminated by the monolith's rainbow hues. 'It's so beautiful.'

Torino smiled. 'Now who can doubt that God exists?' Suddenly he felt magnanimous. 'Let Sister Chantal and the others come in. Everyone should see this once before they die.'

70

When Sister Chantal saw the monolith she did exactly as Torino had done: she fell to her knees and prayed. After waiting centuries to see it she had no doubt in her mind that it was God's work – it was too beautiful and awe-inspiring to have been anything else. She noticed Torino watching her.

'Surely now you understand why the Holy Mother Church must claim it,' he said.

'No religion may claim it. It's far greater than any church. Whoever sees this glorious jewel of creation – whether Christian, Jew or Muslim – will see their God reflected in it, and that's how it should be.' It dawned on her then that religion was merely a language. How we spoke with God depended on which culture we were born into. Nothing more. Nothing less.

As Zeb Quinn stared wordlessly at the monolith she knew, with utter certainty, that the object before her had nothing to do with any abstract god but with

Gaia. When people talked about climate change, global warming, acid rain and every other ecological concern – it all boiled down to one thing: keeping Mother Earth alive, keeping her heart beating. This pulsing crystalline rock, with its tree-like growth, was nothing less than Gaia's beating heart, the engine of life that drove all that was good on Mother Earth.

She considered mankind's unique and contradictory position as the one species capable of both protecting and destroying Mother Earth. This pulsing rock epitomized humanity's stark choice: either to nurture the mother that had given it life, or to exploit her.

As a doctor, Nigel Hackett saw nothing remotely religious or spiritual in the monolith, but he was no less awestruck by it. The monolith's significance was so immense that he felt no need to overlay it with God or Gaia. To him, this was simply the point of origin for all life on the planet, the first genotype, containing the original building blocks and base genetic instructions that had led ultimately to humanity's current genetic programming: DNA. He could feel the radioactive charge in the air and wondered what level a Geiger counter would show. He knew that radioactivity had the power to affect DNA; it was infamous for causing cancers. So it wasn't a great leap to see how this incredible rock might positively affect the human genome – repair it, create it.

As he watched the water rushing over the monolith's surface, washing microscopic elements of its essence into the pool beneath it, then down the stream in the tunnel to the lake in the garden, he could only marvel at its power. If just this dilute contact with water was enough to create the miraculous garden and all its creatures, and engender the crystals that encrusted the tunnel to the antechamber, it was no surprise that it had once seeded a whole planet. And when he looked at the hydra-like growth he wondered how long it had been growing from the crystal – its branches or arms probably extended throughout the cave system. A sudden insight came to him then, heaping wonder upon wonder: the hydra might be the oldest living organism on the planet, as old as life itself, a multicellular creature that continued to evolve within its own lifetime and need never die.

Anger intruded on Hackett's awe. How could Torino use something as wonderful as this to bolster his superstitious belief in an invisible god? Far from proving God's existence, Hackett believed this amazing entity proved that nature was miraculous. However, as he absorbed its shimmering beauty, he said none of this. His words would be wasted on Torino. Instead he told himself to feel grateful that he had at least seen this wonder.

Torino turned to Bazin and the soldiers. 'We'll go back now and finalize plans for when we leave this place. And I need a rock hammer.' He indicated the monolith – the Source. 'I want a sample.'

'We didn't bring one,' said Fleischer.

'Dr Kelly was a geologist. Look in his backpack. He may have something.'

Bazin glanced at Hackett and the others. 'What about them?'

'You know what to do.'

71

Twenty minutes later
Fuck, fuck, fuck.

Zeb was amazed by how quickly the most intense sense of wonder could evaporate in the face of imminent danger. From being transfixed by the Source, she was now too busy panicking to give it a second thought. She still couldn't believe that Torino, Bazin and the soldiers had left them tethered to a rock near the blood-and-viscera-splattered worm holes, then continued down the tunnel with the nymphs.

'What if those things come back?' she had shouted after them. 'What if others come?' As she'd watched their backs disappear down the tunnel she had known the answer and, sure enough, ten minutes later, she could hear the rock around her whispering.

Fuck. Fuck. Fuck.

'Hurry, Nigel, hurry. They're coming back.' The place was like a charnel house from the earlier slaughter but Hackett seemed oblivious of the mess as he knelt between them, holding the rope in his bound hands, sawing it against the sharpest edge of the rock.

'Hurry, Nigel! Hurry!' Sister Chantal pressed.

'What a good idea,' Hackett said drily, through gritted teeth, fingers working furiously. 'That had never occurred to me.' He had already tried to untangle the knot but with bound hands it had been impossible. Zeb could see that some of the fraying rope strands had parted but plenty more were still intact.

'We're running out of time,' she said. 'They're coming.'

'I know,' said Hackett. 'I can hear them. What *exactly* do you suggest I do that I'm not doing now?'

'Bite it!' snapped Sister Chantal.

Hackett kept sawing the rope against the rock. More strands parted, but the whispering was harsher – and louder. Zeb's knees turned to jelly as she imagined the worms' rough carapaces rasping against the rock. All she could think about was whether it would be better to be devoured first, or watch Nigel and Sister Chantal torn to pieces before her. The noise increased and the surrounding rock shook.

Zeb had a sudden desire to fill these precious moments with human warmth before pain and death claimed her: to pull Nigel away from his futile task and kiss him on the lips, then hug Sister Chantal close. She wanted to tell them how important they had become to her – especially the Englishman.

'Almost there,' said Hackett, stubbornly refusing to give in.

She could smell the creatures now as they rushed through the warm, confined space: rancid and fetid. She glanced down at the rope. Hackett had made good progress but when he pulled at the remaining strands they held firm.

'Bugger,' he said, then continued to saw.

She spied movement in three of the deepest holes, all at head height. Mesmerized, she watched three pairs of red eyes racing towards her – one straight at her face. Such was her terror that she didn't even try to move out of the way – there was no point. All she could do was rasp, 'I can see them. They're here.'

For the first time, Hackett looked up from his task. Despite her shock, she marvelled at his expression when he saw the creatures. He didn't exhibit the terror she felt or the horror she saw on Sister Chantal's face. He looked annoyed, as if the worms weren't playing fair. Then he went back to his task.

'Break, you bastard. Break.'

Even if Hackett cut the rope now the creatures were too close. She saw Sister Chantal start to pray. Zeb wanted to look away, but couldn't. She felt compelled to see what was about to kill her.

'Done it,' said Hackett, pulling the rope apart. Zeb detected a note of satisfaction in his voice, even though it was too late and they were seconds from death. She felt his hand take hers and squeeze. 'It's okay,' he said. 'We're all in this together.' He spoke with such composure that he almost calmed her.

When the first worm rifled out of the hole she closed her eyes and braced herself. Her anticipation was so intense that she didn't hear the sound at first. It was only when the attack didn't materialize that she became aware of the chanting. She opened her eyes. The worms had retreated into their holes and were now motionless.

The nymphs have returned, she thought, and looked down the tunnel, expecting to see Torino and the soldiers coming back. Sister Chantal raised her bound hands and pointed frantically towards one of the dark passages by the holes. Zeb saw an indistinct figure chanting the calming incantation and beckoning to them. She registered the staring rock worms and shuddered at the prospect of seeking refuge in their black, infested warren. No one wanted to enter the dragons' lair.

Then she heard more chanting coming from the tunnel of blood. Torino was returning with his nymphs in harness. 'The others are coming back,' said Hackett. 'We can't let them find us.'

They had no choice now. Zeb and the others ran into the dark passage. In the gloom, the shadowy figure stopped chanting, reached out and cut their wrist ties. 'Come with me,' a voice said, and led them into the darkness. 'I know another way down.'

Zeb gasped. It was impossible. Bazin had shot him and the worms had devoured him. Torino had told them as much. And yet, as his strong hand gripped hers and pulled her deeper into the passage, Ross Kelly didn't sound dead. On the contrary, he sounded and felt very much alive.

72

As they descended the dark passageway, Sister Chantal heard more shooting behind them. But she didn't care. Ross was alive. All was not lost.

'Must be killing more of the worms,' Hackett hissed. 'The bastards probably think they've eaten us.' He reached out for Ross. 'Torino said they'd eaten *you*. I can't believe you're alive. What happened?'

'Yes,' said Zeb. 'I thought—'

Ross put his fingers to his lips and resumed chanting. Then he pointed into the gloom. On each side of the dark passageway there were even darker fissures and side passages. Red eyes watched as they passed and Sister Chantal could almost hear the creatures breathing. The others might be desperate to know what had happened to him, but she felt no need for questions. Somehow the Source had saved him and that was enough for her.

His miraculous resurrection was a sign from God that she could still fulfil her sacred oath. She clutched the crucifix Father Orlando had given her and smiled at the demons in the dark.

Do the dead dream? Do they have thoughts and feel emotion? mused Ross, as he continued to chant and led the others down the dark passages to the antechamber.

They must, he concluded, as his mind drifted back to the Source, to when he had died and looked down upon his body . . .

He feels no pain or grief as, from above, he watches the nymphs strip off his clothes and lower his naked body into the small pool beneath the monolith and the hydra. He floats in the mineral-rich water, like a bather in the Dead Sea, as the bullet wound on his chest and the larger exit wound on his back bloom rose-red in the milky water.

The nymphs, at least twenty, form a semicircle round the monolith, as though in worship. Some of its facets remind Ross of the metallic, phosphorous-rich Schreibersite meteor-stone he gave Lauren after his last trip to Uzbekistan – but every other aspect of it is unique, unlike anything he has seen in all his years of geology.

The nymphs begin a new chant, high and pure, which makes the monolith vibrate. Then a small section of its crust cracks and shears off to reveal clear crystal, which quickly clouds, like metal oxidizing. As the segment falls into the pool and breaks into perfectly regular shapes the nymphs step back. The water fizzes and bubbles like a witch's potion and, as Ross's head sinks below the surface, his perspective changes. He is no longer in the chamber looking down on himself: he is staring out at an endless horizon, unlimited by space or time. He had read once that a dying man's life flashes before him in his last moments, but in this instance the curtain of time draws back and the history of all life flashes before him. He sees everything – from the birth of the planet 4.5 billion years ago to the present – with godlike intuition.

He can see hundreds and thousands of meteorites raining down from the heavens, scarring and deforming the Earth's barren crust. Until one seminal meteorite with exactly the right amalgam of amino acids hits a section of crust containing the perfect complementary mix of chemicals, heat and water. The massive energy generated by this unique marriage of amino-acid-rich meteorite and receptive Mother Earth fuses the donor amino acids into peptides – only a step away from life-giving proteins – and creates a miraculous progeny: the monolith.

They say that water plus chemistry equals biology. In this instance, water catalyses the monolith's life-giving properties, seeding bacteria, germinating the hydra, and helping spread the spores of life across the globe. He sees the hydra begin as a single-cell bacterium then evolve to encompass all life forms – fauna, flora and mineral – in one organism, in one epic lifetime. He now understands why Father Orlando called it the Tree of Life and Death: it embodies every facet of existence.

He witnesses the moment, millions of years ago, when the Source and its garden are eventually cordoned off by lava and sealed in volcanic rock. By then, however, the genie has escaped from the bottle. The last outpost to benefit directly from – and need – the Source's miraculous power is the fountain in the doomed lost city. All other life on earth has long since learnt to adapt outside its orbit, upgrading its original genetic instructions to the more self-sufficient DNA. Only the garden and its inhabitants now depend on the Source's concentrated life force to survive.

Time rushes forward to Pizarro's conquest of Peru half a millennium ago. Ross sees the conquistadors and the Church lay claim and waste to the jungle and its inhabitants, exploiting what they can. Then he witnesses the loggers and the oil companies follow in their destructive footsteps. When Ross considers how he has served the oil companies, without thinking or caring about the consequences to the planet, over-whelming shame washes through him.

So this is what happens when you die, he thinks. There's no God or Devil, no Heaven or Hell, only a final reckoning with your conscience, when all lies are stripped away and you feel the collective pain of all those you've wronged and the collective joy of those you've helped.

Suddenly the nymph with red flowers in its hair appears before him, stroking its distended abdomen. It begins to speak in a disconcertingly familiar voice, list-ing Ross's actions, good and bad, as if it knows his innermost thoughts and motives. As it recounts his

*balance sheet of deeds, the nymph morphs into his wife.
Lauren stands before him, naked, beautiful, stroking
her pregnant belly.*

'Are we dead?' he asks.

*With a heartbreaking smile, she tells him that deeds
are everything and that he can still make amends for
any wrongdoing.*

'How? What do you want me to do?'

*'I love you, Ross, and I know you love me, but there's
something you must promise me you'll do.'*

*When she tells him he begins to cry. 'But I can't do
that.'*

*'You can, Ross, and you must. This is important.
Promise me.'*

*He tries to argue with her but it makes no differ-
ence. Deep down, after self-interest and self-delusion
have been stripped away, he knows he has no choice. 'I
promise,' he says.*

*Suddenly he's choking. He can't breathe. A wave of
panic rushes through him. He tries to open his eyes but
they sting as though bathed in acid. A reflex makes
him swallow. He retches and sits upright, gasping for
air. He opens his eyes again and the stinging is gone.
He is sitting in the pool in the middle of the chamber.
And he is alone.*

*He looks up at the looming hydra and crystalline
monolith, then down at the pool. There is a strong
mineral taste in his mouth. The water is less cloudy
than before, almost clear, and it is no longer bubbling.
He has no idea how long he has been lying there
but as he looks down at his chest he knows one thing*

with cold certainty: he is no longer dead. Or dying.

He feels his chest, unable to find any trace of where the bullet entered his body, pierced his heart and exited his back. Sister Chantal claims to have subsisted for centuries by visiting the garden's lake, and taking away crystals from the tunnel. These by-products of the Source have limits, though: Weber died, even though he was immersed in the lake. Ross, though, has supped directly from the source of life. It has brought him back from death. He is sure of it.

He stands up, as naked as the day he was born, and climbs out of the pool. Studying where the water flows into the chamber, his caving experience tells him it will lead eventually to the surface. His clothes lie beside the pool and he can see samples of healing crystals everywhere. Though inferior to the Source, they appear brighter than those in the tunnel, which Sister Chantal is confident can cure Lauren. He can easily take one, climb out and escape. Within weeks he will be at Lauren's side with the means to save her and their child. He can have everything he wants, everything he dreamed of when he embarked on this insane quest . . .

Nevertheless, as Ross emerged with the others from the dark passageway into the relative light of the caves behind the antechamber, he knew he had received the gift of life so that he could fulfil the vow he had made to Lauren when he had died – if that was what had happened to him. Even if it had been only his conscience speaking, he knew that his vow reflected Lauren's thoughts and desires. He stopped chanting and Zeb touched him as if to check he was real. 'What happened to you?' she whispered. He heard the awe in her voice. 'The Superior General told us Marco shot you through the heart.'

'He did.'

'He said you were dead,' she said.

'I was.'

'I don't understand,' said Hackett. 'They said the nymphs fed you to the worms.'

Ross pointed to the white shapes flitting in the shadows. 'They took me to the Source.'

Sister Chantal smiled. 'It brought you back.'

'Yes.' As Ross led them to the antechamber he explained all that had happened to him. 'When Torino entered the chamber I slipped out of the back exit into the dark passageways, which eventually led to you.'

There was a pause, then Hackett said, 'You could have escaped. You could have got out and saved your wife. Why didn't you?'

'Too much unfinished business here.'

'But you could have cured Lauren,' said Sister Chantal. She sounded angry. 'That was why I brought you here. So she could be the new Keeper.'

'The Keeper of what?' said Ross. 'By the time I got to Lauren's bedside, the Superior General would have killed all of you and gained control of the Source.' He turned in the gloom and put his face near the nun's. 'And he'd have destroyed the garden. Wiped it off the face of the Earth.'

'What?' said Sister Chantal, horrified. 'He wouldn't do that.'

'Why not? You yourself said it embarrassed the Church, raised too many questions. The point is, Lauren would never forgive me for letting that happen. I led Torino here. I'm responsible. I must stop him.'

'You sure he's going to destroy the garden?' said Zeb.

'Not just the garden. Every living thing, except the Source. Those yellow parcels the soldiers brought are incendiary devices – firebombs. I've seen stuff like that used to clear ground for oil exploration.'

Hackett frowned as they passed the ledge by the magma pool and the broken bridge. 'I can see how he might napalm the garden and kill everything in it. But how's he going to kill the nymphs and rock worms – and those?' He pointed at the tubular tentacles running along the walls.

'His soldiers just need to place a few incendiary devices throughout the tunnels. Thermite generates huge temperatures – over a thousand degrees – and in these confined spaces a fireball would destroy everything. Now they've thinned out the worms they could conceivably get close enough to do the same thing with them. The Source would be untouched but everything else would be purged.'

Sister Chantal shuddered. 'So what do we do?' she said.

He smiled at her. 'It's time to stop being the passive Keeper of the Garden and waiting for the cavalry to come. We *are* the cavalry. It's up to us to stop Torino abusing this place – particularly the Source.' He turned to Hackett and Zeb. 'What about you guys? I know it's not really your fight—'

'Bollocks,' said Hackett. 'Of course it's my bloody fight. I'm not letting some arrogant priest control what I saw up there. Count me in.'

'Me too,' said Zeb. 'You're not having all the fun, Ross, just because you finally jumped on the conservation bandwagon. I've *always* been on it.'

73

As they headed for the glow of the antechamber, a throng of nymphs appeared, silhouetted against the light. Ross heard an electronic crackle and a man's voice. He gestured for the others to be quiet and pushed them into a recess. Although they were together again, united behind a single purpose, he still wasn't sure how they could stop four trained, armed killers and a fanatical priest convinced he was on a mission from God. Peering out, past the nymphs, he saw a soldier talking into his short-wave radio. He was alone, laden with a flame-thrower and a bulging backpack. 'There are about ten of them,' the soldier was saying. 'Probably more in the tunnels behind them. Over.'

'Disperse them with the flame-thrower, Gerber, then place the charges,' said a crackly voice. 'Don't worry. So long as you have the flame-thrower, you're safe.'

'I can handle them,' said the soldier, curtly. 'Over.'

'Then handle it. Out.'

There was a click, then a roar of flame. The man laughed as the nymphs turned and ran. The one with the red flowers tore past Ross in a blind panic, heading for the dark tunnels. The soldier followed, throwing out bursts of flame. 'Run, you fuckers,' he shouted. 'Pest Control's here. You can run but you can't hide.'

Ross and the others pressed themselves deeper into the recess. As the soldier passed, Ross held his breath. He didn't allow himself to think about what he was going to do next. He just acted. He leapt on the soldier's backpack and pulled back with all his weight and strength. The other man was strong and for a few seconds he supported Ross's weight as well as the cumbersome backpack and the flame-thrower fuel canisters.

Then he grunted and fell on to his back.

Hackett leapt on him and wrestled the flame-thrower nozzle from his hands. Zeb grabbed for his radio and pulled it from his fingers. Even Sister Chantal held down one of his legs. Between them they peeled off the backpack and flame-thrower. The soldier struggled and cried out but when he saw Ross take his gun he froze. 'You're dead.'

Ross levelled the pistol at the man's head. 'Apparently not.'

'But the Superior General saw you die. He said the nymphs took you to the worms.'

'You can't trust everything he says. By the way, where is the Superior General, Gerber?

And where's Marco Bazin and the other soldiers?'

Gerber spat at him. 'You're all going to die.'

Zeb kicked him hard in the genitals. He doubled up and she cocked her leg ready to kick him again. He pointed to the tunnel.

'They're up there?'

A nod.

'All of them?'

Another nod.

Ross saw the nymphs closing in. There were more than before. Many more. His friend with the red flowers was in the vanguard. 'Can you defuse the incendiaries in the garden, Nigel?'

'If you tell me how.'

Ross took a yellow parcel from Gerber's backpack and pointed at two pegs sticking out of it. 'Just remove these detonators. It takes an incredibly high temperature to activate this mixture and without the detonators the stuff's pretty inert. But you'll need to remove them from every parcel in each stack. Only one needs to go off to generate the necessary heat to ignite the others.'

'I'll come with you,' said Zeb.

The nymphs were pressing closer and Ross felt something touch his arm. The nymph with the red flowers pulled at him and pointed away. Nymphs were shepherding the others away too. When he and Hackett grabbed Gerber the nymphs reacted angrily, exposing their razor-sharp teeth – the same powerful teeth Ross had seen chewing through crystal rock.

'I think they want us to leave him to their tender mercies,' said Zeb, as two nymphs pushed her and Sister Chantal away.

'We can't do that,' said Ross.

'I don't think we've got much choice, unless you want to start firing at them,' said Hackett. 'And considering they saved your life I wouldn't recommend it.' The nymphs reached for the terrified soldier and began to drag him away.

'Help me!' Gerber begged. 'I was only doing what the Superior General told me to.'

'Just obeying orders, eh?' said Hackett, gathering up Gerber's backpack and the flame-thrower. 'Where have I heard that before?'

Ross held on for a moment longer but the red-flower nymph and others kept pushing him until he had to release his grip. He weighed the pistol in his hand but knew he wouldn't use it against them. For a long while, he stared into the dark, listening to Gerber's screams echoing in the tunnels.

Hackett was the first to speak. His face was pale. 'Ross, what are you going to do while Zeb and I defuse the incendiaries?'

Ross pointed back to where they had come from. 'I'm going to stop the Superior General carving up the Source.'

'I'll come with you,' said Sister Chantal.

Ross was about to protest until he saw the look in her eyes. She had as great a stake in this as he did – if not greater. 'You sure?'

'I'm sure.'

As they wished each other good luck and prepared to go their separate ways, Zeb gripped Ross's hand and kissed his cheek. 'Lauren would be proud of you,' she said.

'I hope so,' he said.

As Hackett and Zeb set off for the garden, Ross and Sister Chantal retraced their steps into the dark recesses of the antechamber, grateful that Gerber's screams had finally stopped.

74

Torino was convinced he was about to touch the face of God. As he stood in the crystal chamber and reached for the Source his hands trembled. The fizzing static round the monolith was so strong that the air had acquired a palpable texture. He pushed harder and encountered more resistance until, six inches from its surface, his fingers seemed to meet an invisible barrier. The harder he pushed, the stronger the resistance. When he pulled his hand back and thrust it at the rock, it was deflected with such force that the air seemed to ripple outwards. The hydra shook and the ground trembled.

He studied the falling water. It made direct contact with the Source so why couldn't he? It was as if his body shared the same polarity as the magnetic rock. He tried again but this time he moved his hand slowly towards it. He still sensed resistance but the less he pushed the weaker it became until, finally, he felt the rock beneath his fingertips. He pulled his hand away: the smooth surface was hot and live with electricity. The feeling of power was overwhelming. His whole body shook and his fingertips were inflamed.

'Is everything okay, Father General?'

Fleischer and Petersen were waiting at the entrance with the two bound nymphs. 'Everything's fine, Feldwebel. Please hand me the rock hammer.'

'You need any help?'

'No.' Suddenly he felt self-conscious. 'Wait outside in the tunnel. I'll call if I need you.'

He waited till he was alone, then slowly pressed the sharp end of the hammer to the stone. The contact point sparked and again he noticed the disturbance beneath his feet. He raised the hammer and gently tapped the surface. The monolith pulsed, the hydra writhed like an angry serpent and a shock went up his arm. The two nymphs outside screamed at a pitch so high it hurt his ears.

'Shut them up!' he shouted to Fleischer.

He studied the surface of the monolith, found a raised slab of crust where the hydra grew out of the rock and angled the tip of the hammer against it. A few firm taps should chip it off. He took a deep breath, spread his legs for balance, then raised the hammer.

'I wouldn't do that if I were you.' The stern, familiar voice stopped him mid-blow.

He turned slowly to the far end of the cave, to the dark exit. Sister Chantal stood in the shadows watching him, but the voice that had raised the hairs on the back of his neck belonged to the ghost in front of her.

'You're dead,' Torino stuttered, throat dry. 'I saw the blood. I saw the bullet hit you.'

Kelly pointed to the hole in his bloodstained shirt directly over his heart. His eyes burnt with anger. 'It did hit me. I *was* dead.' He gestured at the Source. 'But that brought me back.' Torino didn't move as Kelly walked over to him, reached for his right hand and placed it on his chest. 'If you doubt me, feel my wound.' He turned to reveal an even bigger hole in the back of his shirt.

Torino dropped the hammer and put his finger through the holes in Kelly's shirt. There was no wound in his chest or back. Not even a scar. It was as if he had never been shot. Yet Torino had *seen* the high-velocity bullet pierce his chest and Bazin, the professional killer, had sworn it was a death-shot. 'I saw the nymphs take you—'

'They brought me here.' Kelly pointed to the pool at the foot of the monolith. 'They immersed my body in there and fed me from the Source.'

'You drank directly from it?' For all the miracles he had seen in the garden this was something infinitely more significant. Kelly hadn't merely been cured of some fracture or illness. He had been resurrected. Despite his shock, Kelly's appearance excited him: it confirmed the ultimate power of the Source. 'God is merciful, Dr Kelly. He gave you a second chance. You *must* appreciate His power now, and understand there's more to life than science.'

Kelly expressed a small, humourless laugh. '*You* must understand there's more to life than religion. This rock – the Source – is far more important than any church.'

Torino was appalled by the man's arrogance. 'More important than the Holy Mother Church?'

Kelly stepped forward. He held a pistol in his right hand. 'Of course it's more important. About four billion years ago the biggest miracle on Earth, perhaps in the entire universe, happened here. This monolith, the Source, was born of a unique life-sparking impact. Before that seminal moment, this planet was an unremarkable, charred rock bombarded by meteorites in a remote backwater of space. The seeds of life were sown on this exact spot. This is as close to sacred ground as it gets. But it's got nothing to do with religion or God. For most of the last four billion years, life evolved quite happily without religion or us. Then, in the last hundred thousand years or so, we arrived and our consciousness hungered to explain the things we couldn't understand, including our own existence. So we created religion. We created God.

'First, we worshipped the sun and the moon. Then we made our gods up. The Greeks and Romans had one for everything. Finally, a few thousand years ago, Abraham had a revelation: there was only *one* God. But even this single God seeded *three* distinct religions: Christianity, Judaism and Islam. Each divided again, with each subdivision claiming that they, and they alone, worshipped the one true God. If that doesn't sound man-made then I don't know what does.

'Father General, your Christ appeared on the timeline a mere two thousand years ago, less than a microsecond in the context of the history of life on this planet.' He pointed at the monolith. 'Yet you put your religion before something that's not only been here since the dawn of life, but was its genesis. Its powers are greater than any invisible god's. If anything's worth worshipping, this is it. So don't tamper with it or exploit it. Respect it. Protect it.'

Torino was incensed by the scientist's blinkered arrogance. 'How can *you* understand the power of faith and the need for religion?'

'I *do* understand. My religion was Big Oil. I had total faith in its power: without it there'd be no fuel, no plastics, computers, paints, golf balls – everything vital for the prosperity of modern civilization. My dogma was simple. Find more oil at any cost. Nothing was more important. I didn't care about the consequences – even though my wife continually challenged me. I didn't care that oil, which had taken millions of years to create, would be consumed within a few hundred years of man's discovering it. After all, man had total dominion over the world. Our God gave it to us to do with it as we wished. Isn't that what all religions claim?'

Torino was growing weary of this. 'You're a hypocrite. You talk about protecting the Source, Dr Kelly, yet you're happy to exploit it to save your wife.' He glanced at the tunnel and shouted, 'Feldwebel, I need your help.'

When Fleischer appeared and saw Kelly he did a double take and raised his sub-machine gun. Kelly, however, had already levelled his pistol at Torino's head. 'Perhaps I was a hypocrite,' he said evenly. 'But I have a proposal for you.'

75

Ross tried to ignore the black barrel of Fleischer's Heckler & Koch and keep his own gun steady. He had forced himself to remain calm while trying to reason with the man who had done so much harm to his wife and friends. However, he needed to summon all his reserves to voice what he needed to say next.

He kept thinking of when he had died, when everything had been stripped away and Lauren had appeared before him. 'Ross,' she had said, frowning in that intense way of hers, 'you must protect the garden and the Source, whatever the cost. Not *for* mankind but *from* mankind.' She had then told him exactly what he must do and made him promise to do it.

'So what's your proposal?' Torino asked.

'Before Marco shot me, you told me I couldn't take one of the crystals with me because this place was more important than saving my wife.'

'Yes.'

'Perhaps you were right. I'll accept that this place might be more important than what I love most in the world. But only if you're prepared to do the same.'

Torino said nothing.

Ross swallowed. 'I vow to leave this place, take nothing from it and never speak of it to anyone ever again – even though it means my wife and child will die.' He heard Sister Chantal exhale sharply behind him. 'And you must vow to do the same – even though it means you and the Church can never exploit its miracles.'

Torino laughed. 'You're seriously comparing your wife's life to the Holy Mother Church? You really think they have the same value?'

'No,' said Ross. 'Lauren's life is infinitely more valuable than any church. But I know you intend to destroy everything here except the Source, and I know Lauren would value this place above everything. If we leave this garden untouched, undiscovered, it need pose no threat to your precious doctrine.'

Torino frowned. 'You must understand something, Dr Kelly. Not only is it my legal right to shape this place so it brings glory only to the Church, it's my *duty*. This is God's gift to the world, and it can only be fully appreciated through the Holy Mother Church. Ever since Rome established the Institute of Miracles to show the hand of God in the world, the Holy Mother Church has been waiting for a gift like this. This sacred stone will allow us not only to validate miracles but *create* them. By controlling miracles we'll make the entire world believe in God. There'll be no reason not to. This will bring salvation to every single person — unite them under the one true God. Don't you understand, Dr Kelly? This sacred stone may have given life to this planet. It may have given birth to every one of God's children. But now it'll do something even more important. It will save their souls.'

Torino's blinkered need to twist everything to suit the Church reminded Ross of Pizarro's arrogant chaplain who had helped subdue the last Inca emperor in Cajamarca by asserting that his only hope of salvation was to surrender his empire, swear allegiance to Jesus Christ and acknowledge himself a subject of Charles V.

'Haven't you heard a word I've been saying?' he said. 'You're going to destroy the garden, and kill every living creature here, simply because it contradicts your church and your infallible pope. Don't you see how irrational that is? How ludicrous?'

'It's not ludicrous to protect faith. Purging this place is a small price to pay for saving the souls of all humanity. This garden — including its living creatures — is an unfortunate aberration that encourages meddling scientists like you to make irrelevant and confusing pronouncements on evolution and creation. It creates distracting white noise that can and must be removed. Nothing must be allowed to give succour to our enemies. Even if you don't agree with my mission, you must understand it.'

'All I understand is that your faith must be very weak if it can't handle the truth.'

'*My* faith isn't the issue. It's the faith of others I must protect.'

'When you say "others", you mean those who prefer to think for themselves and come to their own conclusions, based on evidence. Hell, if a person's faith is strong enough they're not going to let this put them off. They'll just interpret it differently. Sister Chantal's faith is intact because she doesn't believe in the rigid way that you do.' Ross could no longer control his anger. The man was beyond reason. 'But, of course, that's why you can't trust your flock to see this. Your goddamn doctrine isn't about nurturing faith. It's about *controlling* exactly how and what people believe.'

Torino's two-way radio crackled in his backpack and as he reached in to retrieve it Ross saw a black box: the detonator control for the incendiaries. The priest put the radio to his ear.

Bazin's voice: 'I can't reach Gerber. But I can see Hackett and Quinn in the garden. They've got Gerber's stuff and they're heading for the incendiaries. I think they're trying to sabotage your contingency plan.'

Torino's eyes never left Ross's. 'Stop them, Marco. Shoot them if you have to. I'll be down soon.' He clicked off the radio.

Ross kept his gun levelled at Torino's head. 'You've told Marco it's a contingency plan? He still doesn't know what you intend to do?'

Torino shrugged. 'We've talked enough.' He reached for the hammer and levelled it at the monolith.

'That's not a good idea,' said Ross. He remembered how the nymphs had kept their distance from the Source and used the pitch of their voices to break off a fragment. He dreaded to think what would happen if brute force was used on it. 'Don't do it.'

'Why?' Torino sneered. 'Are you going to shoot me? Do you honestly think God has led me here and entrusted me with this sacred rock only to let you kill me?' He turned to Fleischer. 'Shoot him *and* Sister Chantal if he tries to stop me.' Then, in a fluid movement, he brought the hammer down on the monolith, chipping off a slab of crust by the trunk of the hydra.

As it broke away from the Source, it set in train a series of events so fast they seemed to happen at once. A violent tremor rippled from the hydra's trunk, through its branches and throughout the chamber. The nymphs screamed. Ross leapt at Torino and pushed him to the floor. Fleischer fired at Ross – or where Ross had been standing – and missed. Ross rolled off Torino and shot Fleischer.

Suddenly everything slowed down. Ross watched Fleischer crumple, finger still on the trigger, the Heckler & Koch spraying bullets as his body fell twisting to the ground, pointing the gun at the monolith. When the first bullet hit the Source, all Hell broke loose.

A high-pitched scream rose from deep inside the

cave system, as if every creature within it had been wounded by the attack on the Source. Ross clutched his head in agony, blood pouring from his ears. The hydra's trunk rippled and its tentacles flexed, fracturing the latticework of crystal encrusting the walls, shaking the cavern. As the flailing tentacles broke free they prised off chunks of the crystal, exposing dark apertures in the rock walls and ceiling. The remaining soldier, Petersen, appeared in the entrance and pointed his gun at Ross. For a second, Ross thought he was going to shoot, but when the soldier saw the flailing hydra, he ran back to the tunnel, into a swarm of nymphs rushing up to protect the Source. Ross watched him fire into them, cutting them down like barley, then disappear into the tunnel.

The floor began to shake and when Ross looked back at the Source he saw why the soldier had run: red-eyed worms protruded from the dark recesses. It took him a second to register that they were part of the hydra, which he suddenly realized was one massive organism that extended throughout the whole cave system. Not only were the worms part of it, but so were the tubular growths that ran through the caves behind the antechamber. The pods that nurtured the nymphs and the worms that devoured them were merely different parts of the same entity: Father Orlando's Tree of Life and Death, embodying life in all its diverse forms. The colossal creature, whose roots lay deep in the Source, was probably as old as life.

A chunk of crystal fell beside Ross, then other rocks, which had been supported by the crystal lattice, tottered and fell. Amid the chaos, protected by the hydra, the monolith itself stood serene and inviolate – but for the fragment on the floor by Torino. As Torino reached for it, Ross threw himself at the priest, knocking him down, and picked it up. It glowed and shimmered in his hand as he looked towards the exit. Despite his vow to Lauren, the temptation to take it with him was overwhelming.

Torino struggled to his feet and lunged at him. 'Give it to me. It belongs to God and the Church.'

As Ross wrestled with him, trying to prise his hands off the stone, he heard his name: 'Ross!' Sister Chantal lay on the ground, clutching her belly. Ross glanced from the fragment in his hand to the exit, then back to Sister Chantal. It took him only a second to decide.

He surrendered the fragment to Torino and rushed to her. She had been shot in the stomach by one of Fleischer's stray bullets. Blood oozed through her clasped hands, and more trickled from the side of her mouth. Oblivious of the chaos and her pain she stared at the glowing monolith. 'It's so beautiful. It's so beautiful,' she kept saying.

Crouching, he lifted her and carried her through the falling debris to the healing pool. She began to struggle. 'No. Take me to the garden. Take me to Father Orlando's grave.'

He glanced back at the Source, searching for Torino. He had disappeared – with the fragment and Fleischer's gun. The path to the tunnel of blood was blocked with debris and rocks were falling in his path. A spear of crystal fell from the ceiling, missing him by inches. He had to get Sister Chantal out of there fast. He turned and left the way he had come, chanting to pacify the rock worms. As he negotiated the dark tunnels, cradling the dying nun in his arms, he kept thinking of Torino, holding the fragment in one hand, the detonator control in the other.

His only hope was that the priest wouldn't make it down the tunnel of blood alive.

76

Moments earlier

Torino had no intention of dying. God still had much for him to do. Immediately Ross had released the fragment, Torino had clutched it to his chest, thrown Fleischer's discarded machine-gun over his shoulder, picked his way through the falling rock and crystal, and run for the tunnel of blood.

Inside, he fought his way through hordes of panicked nymphs – many already dying or dead – squeezing himself against the walls. Above the shrieks he could hear the crack and tinkle of crystal, as its brittle structures broke away from the rock. He moved as fast as he could, trusting in God to protect him.

Halfway down the tunnel his backpack snagged on a projecting shard of crystal. As he tried to free himself, a worm uncoiled from an opening in the opposite wall and propelled itself towards him. He raised Fleischer's gun, pointed it and pulled the trigger. The weapon recoiled in his hand until the cartridge was empty, the storm of bullets shredding the creature, forcing it back into the wall. He dropped the gun, pulled hard and broke off the crystal snagging his backpack. Then he ran down the tunnel, holding the Source fragment close to him like a talisman – a shield against the pursuing demons.

Ahead, he saw Petersen crouching in a pool of blood. His machine-gun lay discarded beside him, surrounded by spent cartridges. The gory remains of slain rock worms formed a ring around him. His legs were badly mutilated but he was still alive. He held a pistol, waiting for his tormentors to return.

He saw Torino and tried to stand. 'Help me, Father General. Help me get down the tunnel.'

Torino stopped beside him. 'Is your pistol loaded?'

'I've got three bullets left.'

'Give it to me.'

Petersen's blood-caked face stared at him. Then he handed over the gun. 'Help me stand,' he said. 'If I lean on your shoulder I think I can walk.'

Torino turned away. Helping Petersen was futile, counter-productive. Not only would the soldier slow him down but Torino couldn't let him live and speak of the garden. This was God's will.

He could hear the worms returning.

'They're coming back, Father General!' Petersen screamed. 'In the name of God, help me!'

'In the name of God, I can't.'

'Then give me my gun. Or shoot me. Don't leave me like this.'

Torino didn't look back. Even when Petersen's pleas became screams, he only ran faster down the tunnel.

He had to get out.

He had to survive.

He had to complete God's work.

77

Covered with dust, Ross stumbled into the glare of the garden, holding Sister Chantal. Seconds later, the entrance to the forbidden caves collapsed behind him, damming the stream to the lake.

Not looking back, he carried her towards the mound of stones where she had buried Orlando Falcon's remains. He saw Bazin standing near the grave. The flame-thrower and the backpack of incendiaries that Ross and the others had taken from Gerber lay on the ground beside him. He held a pistol, pointing it at Zeb and Hackett. Zeb was arguing with him.

'Just tell me one thing,' she shouted. 'If this really is the Garden of God why do you hate it so much?'

'I don't hate it,' said Bazin. 'It's the most beautiful thing I've ever seen.'

'Then why destroy it?'

'I don't want to. I want to protect it for the Holy Mother Church.'

She pointed to the stack of yellow parcels a few

yards away. 'You don't protect something by putting incendiaries everywhere.'

'They're to stop the garden falling into the wrong hands. To stop people using it against the Church.'

'What people? Us? What threat are we?'

As Bazin began to answer, he saw Ross, blanched and fell silent.

Ross took no evasive action, just kept walking to the mound. He was exhausted. 'You've already killed me once, Marco. If you want to do it again, then shoot. Otherwise, leave me alone.'

'Ross, what happened?' said Zeb. 'We felt the tremors out here.'

'Torino chipped a chunk off the Source and unleashed Hell.'

'What about Sister Chantal?'

'Fleischer shot her.' Ross walked past the stunned Bazin, laid Sister Chantal on the mossy earth and cradled her head in his hands. Her breathing was ragged but she was still alive. 'Can I get you some water, Sister?'

'Not from this place. I'm dying and I don't want to be revived.' She looked beyond Ross into the middle distance and, despite her pain, a rapturous smile lit her face.

Sister Chantal could see him now, as clear as the day she had said goodbye to him in Rome. But now Father Orlando wasn't dressed in foul robes or limping from his torture at the hands of the Inquisition. He stood before her, handsome and ageless, resplendent in the black robes he had worn before the Church accused him of heresy.

'I knew you'd wait for me,' she said, oblivious of Ross and the others.

He smiled. 'I release you from your vow, Sister Chantal,' he said. 'You have done all I asked of you and more. Hand your burden to the new Keeper. Give him the cross.'

'He doesn't believe.'

'Give it to him. He may still find salvation in it.'

She focused on Ross again. 'Father Orlando is here. I can see him. I'm released from my vow. I can be with him again.' She reached for her crucifix and handed it to Ross. He tried to refuse but she insisted. 'Take the crucifix, Ross. Father Orlando gave it to me when I became the Keeper. One day, even you might find comfort in it.'

Ross frowned. 'I'm not the new Keeper and I've no use for a crucifix.'

She held out the cross. 'Take it. Release me.'

He hesitated a moment longer, then nodded reluctantly. 'I'll take it out of respect for you and because I know it symbolizes your burden,' he said. He took the cross from her and placed it round his neck.

Sister Chantal sighed and relaxed. She looked up at Zeb and Hackett and said goodbye. She saw sadness in their eyes but she felt none. She turned to Bazin. 'I forgive you, my son. You only did what the Superior General told you was right. Your mistake was to trust him and put the Church above your faith. Remember, the Church should always be your servant and guide, never your master.' She smiled at him. 'Like you, Marco, I believe this garden comes from God. If you truly want redemption, put your gun down and help Ross protect it. From everyone. Including the Church.'

She saw Father Orlando beckon and joy coursed through her. Finally she could rejoin him. She squeezed Ross's hand. 'I must leave you now,' she said. 'Father Orlando is calling me.' She smiled one last time then closed her eyes, welcoming the peace that greeted her.

Ross felt the life leave Sister Chantal and, for a moment, no one spoke. His sadness was tempered because she appeared so peaceful, as if enjoying well-deserved sleep. As he laid her down beside Father Orlando's grave he was acutely aware of the cross dangling from his neck. Fashioned from dull metal, it felt surprisingly heavy.

When he looked up he found himself staring into the barrel of Bazin's gun. 'So, what are you going to do?' he said. 'Help us protect this so-called Garden of God? Or help the Superior General destroy it?'

The gun trembled in Bazin's hand. He rarely gave a second thought to all the men he had killed. Killing Ross, however, had been different – not least because Ross had once saved his life. That fleeting guilt, however, was nothing compared to the confusion he felt now. Looking into Ross's eyes, knowing he had already killed him once, was more unnerving than anything he had ever experienced. He felt as if he was looking into the eyes of every man he had murdered. But what did it mean? *Was he being offered a second chance to redeem himself, or was this a test of his resolve?*

'I'm only doing what's right,' he said. 'I serve the Holy Mother Church, the true guardian of the Garden of God.'

Ross indicated the forbidden caves and the collapsed entrance. 'Do you know what happened in there? I told the Superior General I was prepared to leave this place with nothing and never speak of it again if he did the same. He refused.'

'Of course he refused. It's his duty to claim it for God and the Church.'

'He didn't just refuse. He took a hammer to the Source.' Ross paused. 'Tell me something, Marco. If the Source is intended only for *your* church, then why did it resist so violently when the Superior General tried to remove a sample? And if I'm such a threat why did it bring *me* back from the dead?'

Bazin glared at him, determined to keep indecision out of his eyes.

'The truth is, Marco, whatever you think of what I do or don't believe, I was prepared to sacrifice my wife to save the Garden of God. Torino, however, doesn't give a damn about it. He finds it embarrassing. He only wants the Source. He intends to destroy everything else – I saw the detonator control in his backpack. How can you let him destroy this magical garden, with all its creatures, just because it challenges Rome's doctrine? Why would any god approve of that?'

'The incendiaries are just a contingency.' He pushed the gun closer to Ross's face. 'The Superior General doesn't *want* to use them. Where is he, anyway?'

'I don't know. Perhaps he's dead.'

The two-way radio crackled in Bazin's hand. He put it to his ear and breathed a sigh of relief. It was the Superior General and he was very much alive.

78

Torino was breathing hard when he emerged from the tunnel of blood. The antechamber was darker than he had expected. So much crystal had fallen that the glow it threw into the chamber had significantly dimmed. It took him some seconds, however, to grasp the main reason for the low light: the entrance into the garden had been blocked with fallen rocks. The collapse had dammed the stream, raising the water level of the pools in the antechamber.

The nymphs were chanting loudly in the dark recesses behind him, but he ignored them. He felt safe with Petersen's pistol. He rushed to the entrance and pulled at the rocks but only managed to create a narrow, horizontal gap with a letterbox-shaped view of the garden. He angled his head, peered to the right and saw the lake. Then he peered to the left and smiled. Some distance away, gun in hand, Bazin stood over Kelly. Sister Chantal lay motionless between

467

them. Two other figures were partially visible: Zeb Quinn and Hackett.

He called out but couldn't make himself heard above the nymphs' din. He put the Source fragment and the pistol into his backpack next to the detonator box and pulled out his two-way radio. He pressed the transmit button and saw Bazin reach for his radio and put it to his ear.

'Marco, I'm trapped in the antechamber. The others are dead. Who's with you? I can only see you and Kelly fully.'

'I've got him, Zeb Quinn and Hackett here.'

'What about Sister Chantal?'

'She's dead.'

'Good. Shoot the others, then come and get me out.'

'Why kill them? They intend no harm to the garden.'

'Don't question me. If they leave here they'll tell everyone what they've seen. To do the most good, the Holy Mother Church must keep this place and its miracles secret.'

'And the garden? If I kill them we don't need to harm it.'

Torino clenched his jaw and bit back his impatience. 'This garden belongs to the Church, Marco. Rome will decide how it serves God best.' Of course the garden had to be destroyed. The pope had made it explicit that nothing here could be allowed to contradict his infallible doctrine. He had expressly stated that whatever Torino found could *only* bring glory to Rome, and that the Holy Father could have no personal knowledge of anything he might later have to deny. Therefore, before Torino presented this place to Rome, everything questionable had to be purged from it. There was no guarantee that his half-brother would understand this, though, and Torino needed his help to get out. He looked down at the detonator control. 'But, as I told you, the incendiaries were only ever a contingency. If you do as I say there shouldn't be any need to use them.'

'I understand.'

'Then do your duty. Earn your redemption.'

'I will.'

The radio went dead and Torino peered through the gap. Bazin was partially visible but the others were now out of view. He held his gun in his right hand while gesticulating angrily with the left. He appeared to be shouting.

Then Torino heard three shots in quick succession. He craned his neck but Bazin had walked out of sight. The next three shots were more spaced out, deliberate. Torino imagined him walking from body to body delivering the *coup de grâce*. Bazin reappeared, held the radio to his mouth and walked towards him.

Torino's set crackled.

'It's done,' said Bazin.

79

Torino heard but couldn't see Bazin pulling the rocks away from the far end of the collapsed entrance where the cliff face still provided support. He tried to help but most of the internal rocks seemed to support those on the outside. Alone, with his bare hands, Bazin worked with impressive speed. Within minutes he had cleared a narrow passage, and wriggled through. When his face appeared it was streaked with sweat and dirt. He stood up and dusted himself down.

'You okay, Father General?'

'Fine. But I need to get out of here.'

As Torino headed for the gap, Bazin placed a hand on his shoulder. 'Give me your pack. You won't squeeze out with that on your back.'

'I'll push it in front of me.'

Bazin looked pained. 'I want the detonator control.'

'Why?'

'You promised me that if I killed them you wouldn't need to destroy the garden.'

'I promised you nothing. I said it was a contingency.'

Bazin held out his hand. 'I've done everything you demanded of me since I came to you seeking absolution. Do this one thing for me, Leo.'

'Why, Marco? I owe you nothing. When you came to me you were a killer, a base assassin, the left hand of the Devil. I gave you purpose and showed you the path to redemption. I turned you into a crusader for God and the Holy Mother Church. I did *you* a favour.'

'I'm still a killer. I've killed for you.'

'Not for *me*. Everything I've asked you to do has been for the Church, for God, and for your own salvation.'

Bazin released a long, sad sigh. 'Ever since we were at the orphanage I've looked up to you, Leo. I didn't care that the Jesuits dismissed me as a thug. I took pride in how they nurtured you, my brother. I idolized you and wanted your approval. That was why I trusted you to help me and that was why I've done everything you asked of me. Now do this one thing for me. Give me the detonator box. Not as the Superior General, but as Leo, my brother.'

'I can't do that. I serve the Church, not you.'

'So you did lie to me. The incendiaries aren't just a contingency.'

'I didn't lie. I just didn't think you'd understand the truth. Enemies of the Church will twist what they find here. They'll talk about evolution and creation and undermine the scriptures, sowing doubt in the minds of the faithful. Only by destroying the garden and all its mutant life, then building a new Vatican over the ashes, will we harness the power of the Source and save the souls of mankind.'

'But this is the Garden of God. How can we destroy it?'

Torino groaned impatiently. 'I knew you'd be too stupid to understand, Marco.'

'Too stupid to understand? Or stupid enough to trust you?' He pulled a gun from his belt. 'Give me the detonator box, Leo.'

Torino glared at his brother. He had feared this might happen. He took the pack off his shoulders and reached in with both hands. 'As you wish.' While his left hand pulled out the detonator box, the right felt for Petersen's pistol, aimed it through the canvas and pulled the trigger three times.

Bazin's face showed more shock than pain when the bullets punched into him, knocking him to the floor. As he fell, he dropped his gun, which clattered across the hard rock into the shadows. Torino walked over to him and shook his head contemptuously. 'I offered you redemption, Marco, and you threw it away. For what? To save a worthless garden.' He held out the detonator and raised the safety catch, exposing the button and turning the light green. 'You haven't saved it. You've saved nothing.'

'You're wrong, Leo,' said Bazin. 'I have saved something.' A movement in the passage to the garden made Torino turn. Kelly was crawling into the antechamber. Now Torino saw why Bazin had been able to burrow so quickly through the fallen rocks. He hadn't been working alone. He had only pretended to shoot Kelly. The others were probably outside, too. Torino grabbed the gun from his pack, aimed it and pulled the trigger.

Click. No more bullets.

Kelly was almost inside now, rising to his feet. Torino threw the gun down with his backpack and clutched the detonator. His first priority must be to protect the Church. He glanced through the gap into the garden.

Then he pressed the detonator button.

The resultant firestorm sounded more like a hurricane than a bomb blast. It raced round the eye-shaped crater, gathering momentum, sucking up all the oxygen and incinerating everything in its path. When the fire reached the soldiers' stored ammunition, there were more explosions. From inside the cave it sounded as if a war had broken out. A plume of flame shot through the narrow passage Bazin had made in the fallen rocks, knocking Kelly to the floor. Torino's chest felt tight as oxygen was sucked out of the antechamber into the garden. There was a loud whoosh of displaced air, and black dust and smoke swirled through the opening.

Suddenly, it was over. What evolution had taken

billions of years to create had been destroyed in minutes.

'What have you done?' groaned Bazin from the floor.

Peering through the acrid, smoke-filled air, Torino saw that the garden was no more. In its place was a charcoal wasteland, surrounded by the bare granite walls of the crater. The stream had mostly evaporated and the lake was black with ash. Small fires still raged where there was anything left to burn but the destruction was total. Despite Torino's satisfaction, the desolation saddened him. Doing one's duty was never easy.

Kelly lay on his back on the rock floor, blood pouring from a gash on his forehead. One side of his clothes had been blackened where the plume of flame had scorched him. He appeared unconscious or dead.

Torino saw Bazin's pistol glinting in the shadows beyond his body and moved to claim it. He would return with more incendiaries and purge these caves of any remaining abominations: the hydra, the nymphs and the worms. Only the Source, which brought glory to Rome, would remain. The Holy Mother Church would build a new Vatican here. Leaving his backpack on the floor by the entrance, he stepped into the shadows to retrieve the gun.

80

Bazin groaned as Torino passed him. It was now painfully clear to him that his half-brother had not led him to salvation but to damnation. When he had been the Left Hand of the Devil, Bazin had sinned against man, but when he had killed for Leo, in the name of the Church, he had sinned directly against God. This pained him more than the bullets embedded in his gut.

After a lifetime of killing with impunity, it seemed odd to Bazin that his last act – sparing the lives of Ross, Zeb Quinn and Hackett – should be the one for which was punished. He was glad, though. As Ross was fond of saying, deeds were everything, and this one had been a rare act of self-less good in a life of selfish evil. As Bazin glanced at Ross's motionless body, however, he realized that this last attempt to save him, the others and the garden appeared to have been in vain.

As his lifeblood leaked on to the rock, he called to his half-brother, 'I know I sinned, Leo, but I came to you for absolution. I wanted to do the right thing. God may still forgive my sins but He'll *never* forgive yours. You've turned Eden into a wasteland in His name. Look around you, Leo. This isn't Heaven. This is Hell, and it's of your making.' Bazin knew he was close to death now, but he felt no fear. Not as he had in the clinic when he was ill.

Torino shook his head sorrowfully. 'You're dying, Marco. I tried to help you, I really did. But you turned against God and now you'll be damned for ever.'

Watching Torino bend to retrieve the gun, Bazin blinked at the shapes moving in the shadows behind him. As death closed in he turned again to Ross and something he saw made him smile. He called again to his brother. 'You should fear Hell more than I do, Leo.'

Torino laughed. 'I'm not going to Hell.'

Bazin summoned his final breath. 'No, Leo. Hell is coming for you.'

Marco's last breath sounded like a sigh of relief. Torino felt sad at his half-brother's passing – but only because he had thrown away his last chance of redemption. If he had kept the courage of his convictions and helped secure the Source for the Church, he would have saved millions of souls instead of sacrificing his own.

It was time to finish this. Torino retrieved the gun from the rock floor and turned to Kelly. He peered into the gloom. Kelly was no longer there.

Neither was Torino's discarded backpack, which contained the Source fragment. Panic surged through him. He whirled round and saw something moving in the half-light. He fired a shot into the dark.

'Kelly,' he shouted, 'there's nowhere to run. Give back the fragment.' Even as he spoke the words, Torino understood that the other man was trying to do exactly that: give it back. He was heading for the tunnel of blood. He had to keep to the shadows, though, to avoid being seen. Torino didn't. He ran directly for the tunnel.

Ross kept to the dark recesses until the last minute, but as soon as he broke cover and ran into the tunnel entrance he saw that he was too late. The tunnel was darker than it had been. Much of the luminous crystal had fallen from the walls and ceiling and lay in the stream or under fallen rock. But Torino was still visible. He stood five feet inside the entrance, smiling, his gun pointing directly at him.

'I have my brother's blood on my hands because of you, Dr Kelly. Now you see why I can't let scientists like you misinterpret this place with your poisonous theories. If you could use the garden to turn my brother against me, think of how your fellow scientists could have used it to turn the faithful against the Holy Mother Church.' He stepped closer and Ross clutched the backpack to him, feeling the warmth of the fragment within it. 'Give me the backpack, Dr Kelly.'

Ross looked up and froze.

'Have you nothing to say, Dr Kelly? No more arrogant attacks on the Church and my faith?' Torino seemed to want Ross to argue with him again, as if it might make shooting him easier, sweeter. He looked disappointed when Ross said nothing. 'Give me the backpack. I want the Source.'

'I know you do, but there's a problem,' Ross said. 'A big problem.'

'What's that?'

'I think they want it, too.'

Torino smiled. 'You mean those creatures behind you?' he said, pointing past Ross. 'I have a gun. Your friends don't frighten me.' Ross glanced over his shoulder. The ranks of silent nymphs blocking the tunnel behind him no longer seemed friendly. They were angry. 'Stop wasting time,' said Torino. 'Give me the backpack.'

Ross shook his head as calmly as he could. 'Actually, I wasn't talking about the ones behind me.' He pointed past Torino. 'I'm more worried about the ones behind *you*.'

'Do I look stupid?'

Ross didn't answer.

Torino glanced over his shoulder. And froze. The tunnel behind him was a seething mass of serpentine shapes. Some were tuberous, plant-like growths that ended in pods – like those depicted in the Voynich. Others were flailing rock worms that ended in grotesque, bullet-shaped heads, complete with red eyes and razor teeth. Torino raised his gun towards the creatures – or creature, as Ross now understood the hydra to be. 'I wouldn't fire at it if I were you, Father General,' he whispered. 'That's Father Orlando's Tree of Life and Death. That creature draws life from the monolith and delivers death to protect it. I'm guessing it's pretty pissed at what *you* did to the monolith and the garden. I suggest we give back the fragment.'

'The monolith is a gift from God,' Torino hissed. 'It belongs to the Holy Mother Church.'

'As I've been trying to tell you, I don't think God or the Church has much to do with this.'

Torino pushed the gun into Ross's face. 'Shut up and give me the fragment. It belongs to Rome, to the Church. Not these demons.'

Ross paused, then crouched, reached into the backpack and pulled out the fragment.

'Give it me!' demanded Torino.

Ross held out the fragment to him, then threw it past him so that it landed further up the path, in front of the swirling hydra.

For a second nothing moved.

Then Torino leapt on the fragment – as the branches of the hydra stretched out towards it.

Then the nymphs poured into the entrance, pushing Ross up the tunnel, towards the hydra's waiting arms.

81

Torino was so focused on the fragment that when he grasped it and pulled its luminous warmth to his chest, he felt a rush of almost orgasmic joy. Though God might have been testing him, he knew he would overcome whatever demons or evil stood in his way and secure the Source for the Holy Mother Church. Even as two serpentine tentacles wrapped themselves round his leg and neck, he didn't despair. That this demon was attacking him only reinforced the righteousness of his cause. As he struggled, other tentacles wrapped him in their embrace, dragging him up the tunnel.

He watched Kelly, surrounded by angry nymphs. For a second their eyes met and the horror in the scientist's eyes amused him. He almost felt sorry for him. Kelly still didn't understand that Torino had nothing to fear. He gripped the fragment tighter, confident that God would deliver him from this evil. He thought of the Jesuit motto: *ad majorem dei gloriam*, for the greater glory of God. As

Superior General of the Society of Jesus he was only doing his duty: claiming the Source for the greater glory of God.

As the sinewy tentacles tightened their grip and dragged him away from Kelly, Torino scrabbled on the floor, trying to find anything that would give him purchase. But the tentacles were too strong. The worms hovered around him but didn't strike, which reinforced his belief that God was protecting him. Even demons, whose purpose was to test the righteous, served and obeyed God.

After passing the scant remains of Petersen's corpse and numerous nymphs' bodies, Torino was delivered to the crystal cavern that housed the Source. Despite the devastation, the monolith and the hydra were seemingly untouched. A crowd of white nymphs stood motionless, watching, humming a two-note refrain like a perverse choir of angels.

Suddenly the tentacles released him. The hydra and the nymphs fell silent and still, as though waiting. Clutching the fragment to his chest, he scrabbled to his feet before the monolith and clasped his hands in prayer. 'In the name of the Holy Mother Church I claim this gift from God. I vow to deliver it from the demons that surround it and use its power to spread God's will throughout the world.'

One of the nymphs approached him and extended its hands, as if expecting something from him. He shook his head. 'This belongs to the Holy

Mother Church.' He pointed to the monolith. 'This all belongs to Rome.'

The nymph waited a moment longer, then stepped back into line with the others. One of the hydra's tentacles encircled Torino's right leg and another his left. Two more grasped his arms and began to pull them apart. He kept his hands clasped for as long as he could but the tentacles were too strong, forcing him to release his grip. As the fragment fell to the ground and the nymphs placed it by the monolith, he expected the tentacles to release him. But they didn't. They kept pulling his arms until they were stretched out on each side of him like a cross. Then they pulled apart his legs. Slowly and inexorably he felt his muscles, tendons and ligaments being stretched as if he were on the Inquisition's rack.

Now the pain came. Torino had never known such agony.

With it he experienced the first flicker of doubt: how could God let this happen to him? Surely the Lord must save him so he could finish his sacred mission.

The trunk of the hydra pulsed and throbbed as its tentacles slowly and relentlessly pulled him apart. Torino could feel his muscles tearing. Why was this happening to him? He had done nothing wrong. Everything he had ever done had been designed to bring glory to the Holy Mother Church. He heard his left elbow pop and his shoulder tendons tear. And he heard himself scream: 'Why, God, why?'

More serpentine tentacles hovered before him. However, unlike the appendages pulling him apart, these had bullet-shaped heads, razor teeth and baleful red eyes. The nymphs watched as the worms studied him: angels and demons united in their mission of torment. However, as terrifying as the worms were, Torino almost welcomed the release they offered. But how could he die now – here? He still had too much to do. Why had God forsaken him?

The first attack was so fast he barely saw the rock worm as it bored a perfectly circular hole in his stretched abdomen, then recoiled, dragging his entrails with it. Torino looked down at the intestines spilling over his belt and cried out in despair. The second worm bit into his left hip. Even as the third attacked, severing the fingers of his right hand, he still couldn't believe that the Lord wouldn't save him.

Only in the last seconds of his life, as the tentacles ripped his left arm from his torso, and the worms bored into his face, did his cries for salvation curdle into the screams of the damned.

Ross could hear Torino's screams from down the tunnel but he felt no satisfaction at his enemy's downfall. When the sound stopped, and the priest's blood flowed past him in the stream, he felt only fear – and shame. He had come here for no other reason than to save Lauren's life and, in this selfish quest, he had never once considered the garden's own need to survive. He had trespassed into the cradle of life, bringing death and destruction in his wake. Not only had he led Torino here but he'd failed to stop him and his men destroying the garden, killing nymphs and attacking the monolith.

As the angry nymphs and hydra closed in, he saw that he was as much an intruder as Torino, an unwelcome alien who had brought nothing but harm. The nymphs had saved him once – from his own kind – but now he was convinced they must punish him. As the tentacles came closer, he resisted the urge to turn and fight his way out. Instead he found himself reaching involuntarily for the heavy crucifix round his neck. The Latin cross, with its three-inch-long shaft and two-inch crossbeam, was crude in the palm of his hand. Etched into the soft metal at the centre were the initials AMDG, which Sister Chantal had explained denoted the motto of Father Orlando Falcon's Jesuit order: *ad majorem dei gloriam*, to the greater glory of God. He now understood that Father Orlando and Sister Chantal had lived and died by that dictum, putting their belief in their God above the doctrine of the Church. Whatever Ross himself believed, the purity of their faith humbled him now.

He felt something brush his skin. As he looked up, two tentacles touched his arm and dread coursed through him. Then the nymph with the red flowers in its hair appeared and reached for the cross. He took it off and surrendered it. As the nymph examined it others gathered round to touch it with a kind of reverence. He remembered how Sister Chantal had held it up to calm them when she had first entered the antechamber with him.

They gathered round it for some minutes, stroking it. Then the nymph with the red flowers returned it to him. Before he could replace it round his neck, the nymph pushed him hard in the stomach, forcing him to step back. It pushed him again and he took another step. The hydra's tentacles followed him, but when he glanced over his shoulder the nymphs behind him parted and formed an avenue. He continued shuffling backwards, holding the crucifix in one hand and Torino's backpack in the other, until he was out of the tunnel of blood. The nymph continued to push him through the antechamber until his back rested against the fallen rocks blocking the entrance to the garden. He knew he was no longer welcome and had to take his chances outside, however hot the garden might be. He backed into the narrow passage through which he and Bazin had crawled, keeping his eyes on the nymphs. The rocks on each side were hot but he dared not stop until he was in the garden, safe from the nymphs and the hydra.

As he left, he could see and hear rocks being moved, blocking the passageway, sealing the forbidden caves. The ground was hot underfoot and he coughed in the smoky air. He appeared to be in a vast incinerator, a grim funnel of granite in which all life had been extinguished. Nothing remained of the garden. The trees and plants were gone and a thick blanket of charcoal and soot covered the ground. Everything was black. Even the sky above was so thick with ash that it obscured most of the sunlight. The sooty lake betrayed no hint of its earlier phosphorescence.

The desolation shocked Ross, but he consoled himself that he had at least stopped Torino escaping with the fragment. If he hadn't, the Superior General would have returned with more firepower, destroyed the hydra and taken control of the Source, abusing its power to glorify his church. He looked down at the rocks sealing the forbidden caves and saw a tiny trickle of phosphorescent water leak out of the caves into what was left of the contaminated stream. He thought of how a forest regenerates itself after fire and reassured himself that, so long as the Source was safe, the garden would return. Life would find a way.

So long as the Source was safe.

Looking across the charred expanse, he thought of how Torino had tried to possess this place, and an idea came to him of how to protect it from future interlopers – whether the Church, oil companies or civilization itself.

Something crackled in the backpack and he heard Zeb's muffled voice. 'Ross, are you there?'

He retrieved the radio and put it to his lips. 'Zeb, I'm in the garden. Where are you? Is Nigel okay?'

'We're in the passage between the garden and the sulphur caves. It's a tad warm but it's safe,' said

Zeb. 'What about Marco and the Superior General?'

'Both dead.'

'The Source?'

'It's still there. So are the hydra and most of the nymphs. They're angry but okay.'

He looked across the expanse of the black lake to the far end of the garden as Zeb and Hackett emerged from the sulphur caves. He waved, then moved across the thick blanket of ash to join them. When he reached them they embraced him.

'Everything's gone,' Hackett kept saying. 'I can't believe it. *Everything* out here's gone.' His horror encouraged Ross. He was confident that eco-warrior Zeb would support his plan to protect this place, but he needed Hackett's full commitment, too. Though clearly affected by the garden and its destruction, the Englishman had joined their quest seeking glory and gold, and had found them.

'What would you be prepared to do to protect this place and stop this happening again, Nigel?' Ross said, watching him carefully.

The Englishman frowned. 'What do you have in mind?'

After they had listened to Ross's plan, Zeb nodded and squeezed Hackett's hand. 'Come on, Nigel. What do you say?'

For a long time he stared down at her hand in his. Then he looked up at Ross. 'Okay.'

Ross narrowed his eyes. 'You do realize what this means, Nigel? It'll protect both this place and the lost city, but – and it's a big but – you'll never be able to tell anyone about your mother metropolis. You'll never have your glory.'

Hackett absorbed the implications. 'If you can live with keeping your geological discovery secret, then I can keep quiet about my great archaeological find.' He smiled. 'We didn't discover them anyway. Father Orlando found this place and Sister Chantal the lost city. We're merely looking after them. Keeping them safe.'

'What about the gold?'

'It won't be easy,' said Hackett, 'but I've got contacts.'

'We need to get back to civilization and get started then,' said Zeb. She pointed to the sulphur caves. 'We salvaged our backpacks and supplies before the garden went up.'

Ross was glad they had something, even if it was only a few supplies for the journey home. He was leaving with less than he had brought with him. As he replaced Sister Chantal's crucifix round his neck he remembered their euphoria when they had first arrived, and the moment when Sister Chantal had placed the crystal in his hand and told him it would cure Lauren. He had been so full of hope then, but everything had changed. All he cared about now was getting back to his wife and saying goodbye before it was too late.

'Let's get out of here,' he said, leading Hackett and Zeb towards the sulphur caves. 'Let's go home.'

82

JFK Airport, New York, a month later

Sam Kelly checked the arrivals board and saw that the United Airlines flight from Lima had landed. Although he was looking forward to seeing his son he felt apprehensive. When Ross had called from Lima to say he was coming home, the emptiness in his voice had broken his heart. When he had asked Ross if he had found anything in the jungle, his son's non-committal answer had told him every-thing. It had been a wild-goose chase. The garden was a myth. There were no miracles.

Ross hadn't probed him about Lauren's condition, saying only, 'I assume there's been no improvement.'

Sam had purposely kept his response vague, volunteering little information on the phone, deciding to tell his son about the latest development face to face. However, he felt nervous now, waiting at the barrier, watching the passengers arrive through Customs. When he saw his son in the distance, lean, tanned and tired, the prospect of telling him the news weighed heavily on his heart.

Ross didn't notice his father at first because as he passed a news-stand he found himself staring into the face of Superior General Leonardo Torino. According to the Vatican, he had been missing for some weeks after embarking on a fact-finding mission into the jungles of South America. The Peruvian authorities were still working closely with Rome to trace his whereabouts, but hopes were now fading that the Superior General and his escort would ever be found. The pope was already mourning the loss of a fine priest and the Society of Jesus was considering a successor.

As Ross closed the newspaper, a smaller article caught his eye and almost made him smile. According to *Newsweek*, Scarlett Oil had discovered large reserves of what they termed 'ancient oil' in Uzbekistan. Larger oil companies – including Alascon, which had recently terminated a partnership with Scarlett that would have given them shared rights – were now queuing up with large cheques to license Scarlett's patented technology for finding and economically extracting it.

Ross saw his father and waved. Sam was smiling, but as Ross got closer he saw strain on his father's face. Something had changed. They hugged and Ross felt tension in his father's shoulders. 'Good to see you, son. Good to have you back safe.'

'It's good to be back, Dad. How're Lauren and the baby?'

His father reached for his luggage. 'Come, let me drive you home. We'll talk in the car.'

'I want to go straight to the hospital, Dad.'

His father paused. 'You're exhausted. Why don't you go home first? Get some rest.'

'I want to see her now, Dad. I *need* to see her. Something's happened, hasn't it?'

His father appeared to brace himself, confirming Ross's worst fears. 'There's been a development, Ross. There's a difficult decision to make.'

83

Though still in the Sacred Heart Hospital, Lauren had been moved from the spinal-injuries unit to an isolated high-dependency room at the far end of the maternity wing. She had it to herself, except for the battery of monitors and equipment that kept her alive. She was lying in the same position as she had been when Ross had left her. The one discernible difference was the now prominent bump in her belly.

Since Lauren was no longer regarded primarily as a neurological case, Dr Greenbloom had handed over her care to an obstetrician, Dr Anna Gunderson. This confirmed to Ross that Lauren was now officially a lost cause. She wasn't even Gunderson's priority patient. The baby was. Lauren was little more than an incubator.

One small mercy, thought Ross, as he sat in her room with his father and Dr Gunderson, was that Lauren's mother was visiting her sister in New England for two days. He wasn't ready for her questions about where he had been.

'As your father's told you, Lauren's condition is deteriorating fast.' The doctor spoke softly as if she didn't want Lauren to hear. 'We're now in a critical phase. Lauren is lost to us but we're entering the period where the baby *may* be viable outside the womb. We could deliver it now, but the chances of its surviving undamaged are slim. Every extra day the baby stays in the womb the greater its chances.'

The doctor cleared her throat. 'We've administered steroids to develop its lungs, and medication to stop your wife going into premature labour, but I don't know how many more days we can hold on. We monitor Lauren's condition constantly and any further deterioration will mean we have to get the baby out. It's on a knife edge. We want to keep her in for as long as we can but only so long as Lauren can support her.'

'Her?'

'It's a girl.' She reached into a manila file on the sideboard beside her and handed Ross a black-and-white scan. 'This is your daughter.'

The image struck Ross with surprising force. He had always been more concerned about losing Lauren than the abstract concept of their baby. Even the earlier scan he had seen, at sixteen weeks, hadn't altered that view. This grainy picture was different, though. The baby was suddenly real.

A little girl.

His daughter.

He walked over to the bed and stroked Lauren's belly. He felt movement, which scared him. He had something to lose again. And something to gain.

Raw hope was so much crueller than numb despair.

He turned back to the doctor. 'Every day my daughter stays in the womb, her chances increase?'

'Yes.'

'How much longer before she's safe?'

The doctor frowned. 'At least another three or four weeks.'

'How likely is it she'll get that?'

A pause. 'Extremely unlikely.'

'Given Lauren's current condition, how many more days do you think my daughter can stay in the womb?'

'Like I said, every day increases the odds on survival.'

'How many days?'

'It's hard to judge, Ross.'

'What's your best estimate?'

Another pause. 'Two, three. A week maximum.'

'So you want my permission to intervene and deliver the baby as soon as you think it's necessary?'

Gunderson nodded.

'Even though the chance of the baby's surviving undamaged is minimal?'

'Yes.'

Ross took a deep breath. 'Thank you for being so honest.'

Gunderson brushed a blonde hair from her face. 'Have you any more questions?'

'No, thanks. I've been away, and all I want now is some time alone with my wife. I'd like to stay with her tonight.'

84

Sitting in an uncomfortable chair, looking at Lauren and the scan, Ross obsessed about the opportunities he had had to save them. He remembered when he had held Lauren's cure. He recalled the Source bringing him back from the dead when he could have escaped with an abundance of healing crystals. But he had stayed to help the others and stop Torino controlling the Source because he had thought it was what Lauren would want him to do.

Gradually, as Ross listened to the lulling rhythm of the apparatus, his exhausted body overruled his racing mind. He slumped in the chair, exposing the heavy crucifix, and fell into a fitful sleep.

Hours later, he woke with a start, clutching the cross and sweating. In his dreams he'd relived his near-death epiphany and his vow to Lauren. Back then, in his heightened state, he had *known* Lauren was making him vow to protect the Source and sacrifice her. And in the surreal context of the garden it had seemed the painful but right thing to do. Even at the end, surveying the scorched Eden, ashamed of what man had done, he'd focused on a plan to protect the Source. In many ways he had done more to protect it and its creatures than he had to protect his own family.

At that time, and in that place, it had felt right. Now, in the sober gloom of a sterile hospital room, inches from his comatose wife, his vow to Lauren felt very different. Especially when he considered his daughter, growing in Lauren's belly. What difference would it have made if he'd taken some of the crystals for Lauren? How much damage would he have done to the Source or its ecosystem? He touched the crucifix and could almost hear Sister Chantal's voice: 'A vow is black and white. There's never a plausible excuse or justifiable reason to break it. You either keep a vow or break it. There's no middle ground. A vow is for ever.'

But what about your vow, Sister Chantal?

Sister Chantal had taken him to the garden for the express purpose of saving his wife. The Source was *meant* to save Lauren so she could become its protector, the Keeper, but instead Sister Chantal had placed that burden on *his* shoulders. *He* had become the Keeper. He studied the crude, ugly crucifix she had passed on to him, which Father Orlando had given her four and a half centuries ago, and rage built within him.

He considered all the pain it symbolized. Not just Christ's suffering but all the evil done in the name of religion. He thought of what Torino had done in the name of his church: harming Lauren, destroying the garden, abusing the Source. He thought of how Torino had used Bazin, offering redemption, but merely making him kill for a different master. Ross didn't see the cross bringing salvation to anyone – only suffering and damnation.

In his anger and despair he ripped it from his neck and threw it, with all his strength, across the room. The instant it hit the wall, narrowly missing the clock, he felt foolish and contrite.

The instruments by the bed began to beep.

Shit.

But the cross hadn't hit anything important. Had it?

Within seconds a nurse was rushing into the room.

Panicked but unable to help, Ross went to where the crucifix had fallen. The impact had dented it badly. He picked it up and, as he turned it in his hand, he noticed two things that dried his mouth: the welted seam at the back of the crucifix had buckled, revealing a hollow interior; and the second hand on the wall clock had stopped. Ross recalled Hackett dropping his watch into the pewter goblet, and how the shielding properties of its lead and tin had helped restart the mechanism. Then he remembered the reverence with which the nymphs had treated the cross. Had they sensed something?

With trembling fingers, Ross pulled back the

malleable metal seam to reveal a crystalline sliver in the hollow. No larger than a toothpick, it glowed and pulsed with a life of its own. His heart raced. Father Orlando must have concealed it there when he had discovered the Source. He must have learnt somehow that certain metals could contain its magnetic and radioactive properties. The sliver of crystal would also explain how Father Orlando had healed his burnt feet after his first session of torture all those centuries ago, only forgoing its benefits when he realized that the Inquisition didn't regard his cure as proof of the existence of the garden, but as proof of possession by the Devil.

When Father Orlando had given the cross to Sister Chantal and told her to seek salvation within it in times of crisis, she hadn't understood he'd meant it literally. She had remained ignorant of the cross's secret for four and a half centuries. She *can't* have known about it, Ross thought, or she would have used it on Lauren when she first visited her in hospital.

Unless . . .

The thought sliced through his excitement like an icy draught. Sister Chantal had told him that the crystals in the tunnel only worked if they were of a certain size. This sliver was undoubtedly from the Source, but it was very small. Was it large enough to cure Lauren?

Ross re-formed the crucifix, sealing the seam. The instruments immediately stopped beeping, and the clock resumed ticking.

'That's strange,' said the nurse behind him. He turned and she smiled apologetically. 'Sorry about that. I'm not sure what happened but everything's fine and your wife's in no danger. I'll alert the technical team.' When she'd left the room, he clutched the crucifix to his breast and shifted his focus to Lauren's feeding tube.

85

The next morning Ross awoke in panic. It was six eighteen and something had happened.

Something that wasn't good.

The alarms on Lauren's life support were bleeping more insistently than they had last night, and her vital signs oscillated erratically.

Dr Gunderson tried to appear calm, but her voice was shrill. 'Ross, we must prepare Lauren for surgery *now*. We can't wait another minute. We must get the child out immediately. It may already be too late.'

He wiped sleep from his eyes. 'What's happening? What's wrong?'

Gunderson and other doctors were wheeling Lauren out of the room and heading for the lift. 'OR nine,' shouted Gunderson. 'Hurry. Hurry.'

Ross followed. 'I want to come.'

'That's not a good idea. Wait here. We'll update you as soon as we know more.'

He stepped into the lift. 'I want to be there. It's a birth. I'm the father. I should be there.'

Gunderson's eyes were cold. 'It's not a birth. It's an operation. Chances are it'll be the opposite of a birth.'

Ross didn't flinch. 'If this is the last I'm going to see of my wife and child I want to be there.'

'I really don't think it's a good idea,' she sighed, 'but if you insist.'

'I do.' Ross couldn't understand what was happening. After finding the fragment in the crucifix he had taken it to the main washroom and steeped it in a beaker of water, then poured the solution into Lauren's feeding tube. He'd done it three times. The water should have catalysed the Source. It should have worked. But it hadn't. Not only had the Source not helped Lauren but it had exacerbated her condition.

What had Dr Gunderson said? Every day inside the womb would increase the baby's – his daughter's – chance of survival. So being delivered now, today, was the worst possible outcome.

In the operating room, Ross was given surgical greens and a face mask and told to stand away from the table. He watched them roll Lauren from her bed on to it. Suddenly, a nurse looked up. 'We might not need to do a Caesarean.'

Gunderson called from the scrubbing suite. 'Why?'

'Her waters have broken.'

A midwife, present more out of hope than necessity, stepped forward. She was an older woman and something about her eyes, visible above her mask, reminded Ross of Sister Chantal. Compassionate and wise, they seemed to have seen everything there was to see. She examined Lauren and smiled. Ross loved that smile. It spoke of confidence and possibility. 'Her waters *have* broken. She's going into labour.'

'You sure?' Gunderson said, approaching the table where her instruments had been laid out. She reached for a scalpel.

'It's happening,' said the midwife. 'She's almost nine centimetres dilated.' She didn't wait for a reaction from Gunderson. She attached sensors to the baby's head and checked the monitor. 'Heartbeat's stable.' She pointed at Gunderson's surgical instruments. 'You won't need those. The mother's having contractions.'

'She's in a coma,' said a nurse.

'Her body appears to be taking over,' said the midwife. 'I think she can do this.'

Gunderson hesitated, then put down the scalpel.

Ross watched in amazement as Lauren's body began to push and, for the next twelve minutes, the midwife coaxed the baby into the world. Eventually she gave a whoop of joy and the baby emerged. She picked her up and, as she handed her to the paediatrician, asked Gunderson, 'How many weeks is this baby?'

'Twenty-six.'

'That's incredible. I've delivered thousands of babies. She may be tiny but she looks full-term to me.'

As the paediatrician examined the baby at the far end of the room, Ross watched Lauren. Her face was so peaceful that he felt an overwhelming rush of love and sadness. When he heard the baby cry for the first time he felt like crying with it. He walked over and she cried again, louder. A nurse handed her to him, and as he held his daughter in his arms he wondered what he should call this miracle of life. Lauren and he had once agreed that if they had a son she would name him, and if they had a daughter he would.

'Ross!' Gunderson sounded pinched and breathless.

He looked back at the operating table. Everyone was white, staring at him, gauging his reaction. His heart sank. It had happened. He thought of the nymphs, how when one was born another died. Briefly, he couldn't bring himself to look at Lauren. Then he held his daughter, took strength from her and turned to his wife.

Lauren's eyes were open. And she was looking at him.

'She opened them when the baby cried,' said Gunderson, testing Lauren's legs. 'Her reflexes are fine, too.' Her voice cracked with emotion. 'This is impossible. It's a miracle.' She stroked Lauren's left sole and the foot moved away. 'She has feeling and she can move her legs.'

He moved closer and Lauren's eyes followed him. 'Where have I been?' she whispered weakly.

He knelt by the table, not trusting his legs to hold him. 'It doesn't matter now. You're back,' he said. He showed her the baby. 'And now here's someone I want you to meet. Our daughter, Chantal.'

86

Six months later

As the plane landed in Lima's Aeroporto
Internacional Jorge Chávez, Ross smiled at Zeb. So
much had changed since the first time they had
flown here with Sister Chantal.

It had been hard to leave Lauren and the baby at
home, but this time it was only for a couple of
nights and he was excited about joining up with
Hackett again – though not as excited as Zeb.

For the last six months, while he had been
engrossed with Lauren and Chantal, Zeb and
Hackett had been in Peru working tirelessly on the
project; however, they had returned to the States
from time to time to talk with the New York banks,
visit Lauren and admire Zeb's new goddaughter.
Last week, Zeb had joined Lauren at Yale's Beinecke
Library for the triumphant presentation of their
officially recognized translation of the Voynich
Cipher Manuscript. It was now accepted in
academic circles that the final section, written in a

totally invented synthetic language, would never be translated without the author's original notes. In their submission, neither Lauren nor Zeb revealed the author's name or suggested that the document was anything other than an allegory.

Hackett was waiting for them at the airport, tanned and fit: a different man from the pale asthmatic who had first approached them in Cajamarca. Zeb ran into his arms with such enthusiasm that it dispelled any doubts Ross might have had about how serious an item they had become.

Hackett shook Ross's hand, then embraced him. 'How are Lauren and the little one?'

'They're fine.' And they were fine, thought Ross. They really were. Lauren had made a full recovery and Chantal was a delight. Despite her size at birth she was now of average weight for her age and she was going to be tall. 'How are things this end?'

'Everything's prepared. Come. I'll show you.'

Hackett drove them to the anonymous offices he and Zeb had hired in Lima. Inside the main room, pinned to a corkboard behind the desk, there was a large map of the world. On it, a significant section of the Peruvian Amazon had been sectioned off with red pins linked with ribbon. Ross smiled. It stood slap-bang in the path of Alascon's proposed pipeline. The company would have to go round the area now or abandon the project. On the desk a pile of stationery bore the logo of a stepped pyramid, a ziggurat made of gold bricks. Hackett unlocked a drawer, took out a cheque and handed it to Ross.

He looked at it and whistled. Made out to the Peruvian government, it was for an enormous amount of money. 'I've never seen so many zeroes.' Both Hackett and Zeb had signed it, but there was space for a third signature. Hackett passed him a pen. 'It needs to be signed by all three trustees.'

Ross scribbled his name. 'What now?'

Hackett checked his watch. 'I'll drive you to the hotel so you can freshen up. We're meeting the Minister of the Interior at six to hand over the cheque, followed by a press conference. Though we're paying them shedloads of money, the government wants to gain some environmental Brownie points for enabling a large swathe of virgin jungle to be protected in perpetuity.'

Ross studied the cheque, then handed it back to Hackett. He thought of the gold in the lost city, and how it was finally doing what its ancient owners had originally intended when they had stacked it in the ziggurat: protecting their city and the source of the fountain that had once sustained it. 'How many tears of the sun did that cheque soak up?'

Hackett smiled and led him to the door. 'It barely dented the pyramid. There's loads left. And we found more gold there. My contacts can sell it, without alerting the authorities, but I don't know how we're going to spend it all.'

Glancing over his shoulder at the map, Ross considered the endangered areas of the world. 'I'm sure we'll think of a few things.'

The Vatican, the next day

Cardinal Prefect Guido Vasari hurried down the long, wide corridors of the Apostolic Palace to the Holy Father's office. Ignoring the guards, he pushed open the door and strode in. The pope looked up, pen hovering over a pile of unsigned documents. 'Cardinal Prefect, what is it?'

Vasari placed an open copy of *Time* on the desk. 'It's about the Superior General.'

'Have they found him?'

'No.'

'Then what? I thought this unfortunate matter was closed and that we'd put it down to over-zealousness on his part.'

'Look at the article.'

The pope skimmed it. 'So? The Voynich has been translated but there's no mention of the Church's involvement. No suggestion that the garden exists. What's the problem?'

'The person who translated it, the person in the picture holding the baby, is the geologist's wife, the one who was paralysed with a broken neck and comatose, the one who was *dying*, the one the geologist sought out the garden to save.'

'She recovered. It happens. You're not suggesting . . . ?'

Vasari threw a copy of the *International Herald Tribune*, open at page four, on to the desk. There was a picture of two men and a red-haired woman standing with the Peruvian Minister of the Interior. The pope began to read the article Vasari had ringed with blue ink.

'The man in the left of the photograph is the geologist, Dr Kelly,' said Vasari. 'He and his colleagues have done what the Superior General planned to do and bought a tract of virgin jungle. Their land is now protected in perpetuity and can only be entered with the trustees' permission.' He paused. 'I fear the Superior General's obsession with the Garden of God may have been justified.'

At first the pope didn't respond or react. Then his face changed and Vasari knew the Holy Father had seen what he had seen: the name of the trust that had bought the land. A name that – apart from the missing Superior General – only they were supposed to know.

It was the name of a man their predecessors had burnt at the stake four and a half centuries ago for claiming to have discovered a miraculous Garden of God in the Amazon jungle, a man whose Devil's book had become known as the Voynich Cipher Manuscript: Orlando Falcon.

Epilogue

The jungle surrounding the eye-shaped crater is a vibrant lush sea of green splashed with primary tints. The crater, however, is a patch of desert in the forest, a negative oasis devoid of life or colour – only grey and black.

As the sun penetrates its hidden depths, its rays reveal the desolation: white ash and black charcoal. It is said that the purging power of fire can revitalize life, encourage new, more vigorous growth. However, the ash is so thick on the ground it is hard to imagine anything ever growing there again. And the circular black lake in the centre, the pupil of the eye, looks stagnant, blind.

But all is not as it seems in the eye-shaped crater. Some parts of its soot-covered floor are blacker than others, particularly beside the fallen rocks blocking the caves at one end. Ironically, it is in these blackest sections, where a trickle of phosphorescent green water seeps out through the fallen rocks to darken the ash, that the first signs of life can be found.

Pushing up through the black ash is a small flower with unique leaves. It is unlike any other plant in the surrounding jungle, unlike any other plant in the world.

THE END

Acknowledgements

I plundered many books and periodicals to research the scientific and historical aspects of this novel, but I found the most inspirational source material in the pages of the Voynich Manuscript, which the Beinecke Rare Book and Manuscript Library has generously reproduced and presented on its website.

I want to thank Patrick Walsh and Jake Smith-Bosanquet, at the Conville & Walsh Literary Agency in London, and Nick Harris at the RWSH film agency in Los Angeles for their sterling efforts in selling this novel around the world.

I also thank Bill Scott-Kerr for his perceptive editing and continued encouragement, and Hazel Orme for the final polish.

My greatest thanks, however, are reserved for my wife, Jenny, who has always been my most ruthless critic and most ardent supporter, and for our daughter, Phoebe, who makes everything worthwhile.

The Messiah Code

Michael Cordy

AT THE MOMENT of his supreme triumph, a man of science dodges an assassin's bullet and loses everything that truly matters in his life. Now only a miracle can save Dr Tom Carter's dying daughter: the blood of salvation shed twenty centuries ago.

In the volatile heart of the Middle East, amid the devastating secrets of an ancient brotherhood awaiting a new messiah, Tom Carter must search for answers to the mysteries that have challenged humankind since the death and resurrection of the greatest Healer who ever walked the Earth. Because suddenly Carter's life, the life of his little girl, and the fate of the world hang in the balance . . .

After two thousand years, the wait is over . . .

'The quest for the Holy Grail meets
Raiders of the Lost Ark'
MAIL ON SUNDAY

'I was transfixed'
NEWSDAY

'Engrossing and intelligent'
SAN FRANCISCO CHRONICLE

'Taut and gripping'
THE TIMES

9780552154055